WILLIAM NICHOLSON

SEEKER

THE FIRST BOOK OF THE NOBLE WARRIORS TRILOGY

EGMONT

EGMONT

We bring stories to life

First published 2005
by Egmont UK Limited
239 Kensington High Street, London W8 6SA

Copyright © 2005 William Nicholson

The moral right of the author has been asserted

ISBN 1 4052 2295 6

3 5 7 9 10 8 6 3 2

A CIP catalogue record for this title is available from the British Library

Typeset by Avon DataSet Ltd, Bidford on Avon, Warwickshire
Printed and bound in Great Britain by the CPI Group

WILLIAM NICHOLSON

SEEKER

THE FIRST BOOK OF THE NOBLE WARRIORS TRILOGY

Contents

Part Two: THE SURROGATE

Part Three: RADIANCE

Part Four: SACRIFICE

PRELUDE

THE LEGEND OF THE NOBLE WARRIORS

After many wanderings, on the longest day of the year, the Brother came to the island where the world began, which was called Anacrea, because it was the place of first creation. He made a house there, and he lived quietly by himself.

In that winter, when the days were short and the nights were bitter, the Brother was woken from sleep by a crying in the darkness. He rose and lit a lantern and went to the door. 'Who's there?' he said. 'Why do you cry?' A voice answered, 'I am the Lost Child.' So the Brother opened the door and saw by the light of his lantern a little child shivering with cold. He brought the child into his house and put fuel on the fire. He wrapped the child in a blanket and made broth for the child to eat, and put the child to sleep in his own bed.

That night the Brother had a dream. In his dream the child spoke to him again, saying, 'I am the All and Only. I am the Reason and the Goal.' Then in his dream the child changed form, and became a gentle lady. 'I am the Loving Mother,' she said. 'I will comfort you.' Then the form changed again, and became a warrior in bloodstained armour. 'I am the Wounded Warrior,' he said. 'I will make you strong.' Then the form changed again, and became a blind man. 'I am the Wise Father,' he said. 'I will guide you, until the day of the coming of the Assassin, who must find me at last.'

The next day the Brother said to the child, 'Stay with me. I will build you a Garden where you can live in peace.'

So the child stayed.

Others came to live on the island, and they pledged themselves to protect the Lost Child, whom they knew to be the one true god.

One day there came a great warlord called Noman, who was feared by all. He wanted to see the child god for himself. He entered the Garden, and stayed there for a day and a night. When he came out he knelt humbly before the brothers and sisters, and offered them his warrior strength, so that they could protect the Lost Child.

Noman built a great fortress round the Garden, and called it the Nom. He learned the secret of true strength, and passed it on to the brothers and sisters, and they became powerful. They made Noman their leader, and called themselves Nomana. But Noman never forgot the warning revealed in the First Brother's dream.

'One day the Assassin will surely come. On that day, our god will die.'

Before he left them for the last time, Noman addressed the brothers and sisters.

'Do not seek power. Our power is not given us for

ourselves, but for others. Fight the cruelty and injustice of the world. This struggle will never end: but the little we can do, that we must do, so that others will know good men too can be strong.'

So began the missions of the Nomana, in which the brothers and sisters travelled far and wide, asking nothing for themselves, bringing justice to the oppressed and freedom to the enslaved. For this they were loved, and became known as the Noble Warriors.

PART ONE

ANACREA

My brothers:
We face a grave and imminent danger.
Those who fear us seek to destroy us.
We do not know when the attack will come,
or from what quarter, or what powers will be raised
against us. We know only that a new weapon is being
prepared for our destruction.
How are we to defend ourselves
against unknown danger?
With vigilance. With wisdom. With sacrifice.

CHAPTER ONE

SUNRISE

SEEKER woke earlier than usual, long before dawn, and lay in the darkness thinking about the day ahead. It was high summer, with less than a week to go before the longest day of the year. In school, it was the day of the monthly test. And it was his sixteenth birthday.

Unable to sleep, he rose and dressed quietly so as not to wake his parents, and went out into the silent street. By the light of the stars he made his way to the steps that zigzagged up the steep hillside, and began to climb. As he did so he watched the eastern sky, and saw there the first pale silver gleams on the horizon that heralded the coming dawn.

He had decided to watch the sun rise.

At the top of the steps the path flattened out and led into the stone-flagged Nom square. To his right rose the great dark mass of the Nom, the fortress-monastery that dominated the island. To his left, the avenue of old storm-blasted pine trees that led to the overlook. He knew these trees well, they were his friends. He came to this place often, to be alone, and to look out over the boundless ocean to the very furthest edges of the world.

There was a wooden railing at the far end of the avenue, to warn those who walked here to go no further.

Beyond the railing the land fell away, at first in a steep slope, and then in a sheer vertical cliff. Hundreds of feet below, past nesting falcons and the circling flight of gulls, the waves broke against dark rocks. This was the most southerly face of the island. From here, there was nothing but sea and sky.

Seeker stood by the railing and watched the light trickle into the sky, and shivered. The band of gold now glowing on the horizon seemed to promise change: a future in which everything would be different. With this dawn he was sixteen years old, a child no longer. His real life, the life for which he had been waiting so long, was about to begin.

The gold light was now turning red. All across the eastern sky the stars were fading into the light, and the feathery bands of cloud were rimmed with scarlet. Any moment now the sun itself would break the line of the horizon.

How can a new day begin like this, he thought, and nothing change?

Then there it was, a blazing crimson ball bursting the band of sea and sky, hurling beams of brilliance across the water. He looked away, dazzled, and saw the red light on the trunks of the pine trees, and on the high stone walls of the Nom. His own hand too, held up before him, was bathed in the rays of the rising sun, familiar but transformed. Moving slowly, he raised both his arms above his head, and pointed his forefingers skyward, and touched them together. This was the Nomana salute.

Those who wished to become Noble Warriors entered the Nom at the age of sixteen.

He heard a soft sound behind him, and turning, startled, saw a figure standing in the avenue. He flushed, and lowered his arms. Then he gave a respectful bow of his head, because the watcher was a Noma.

'You're up early.'

A woman. Her voice sounded warm and friendly.

'I wanted to see the dawn.'

Seeker was embarrassed that she had seen him making the salute to which he was not entitled; but she did not reprimand him. He bowed again, and headed down the avenue, now flooded by the brilliant light of the rising sun. As he passed the Noma, she said, 'It's not necessary to be unhappy.'

He stopped dead, and turned back to look at her. Like all the Nomana, she wore a badan over her head which shadowed her face. But he sensed that she was half-smiling as she met his gaze.

'I am unhappy.'

The Noma went on gazing at him with her gentle smile.

'Who are you?'

He gave his full name, the name his father had chosen for him, the name he hated.

'Seeker after Truth.'

'Ah, yes. The schoolteacher's son.'

His father was the headmaster of the island's only school. He was raising Seeker to be a teacher like him.

'Your life is your own,' said the Noma. 'If it's not the life you want, only you can change it.'

Seeker made his way slowly back to the steps, and down the steps home, his mind filled by the Noma's words. All his life he had done what his father had asked of him. He had always been top of his class, and was now top of the school. He knew his father was proud of him. But he did not want to live his father's life.

Seeker wanted to be a Noble Warrior.

CHAPTER TWO

THE HARVEST TIME APPROACHES

THE morning sun had just climbed over the mountains, and its bright rays, slanting down the western slopes, were washing the plains with golden light. The goats quietly grazing on the high pasture-land cast elongated shadows on the dew-damp grass. The lanky goatboy felt the warmth of the sun on his back, and raised his stick high above his head, and his shadow reached all the way down to the glittering bends of the river far below. A road ran alongside the river, and on it he could make out a convoy of bullock carts, tiny as a child's toys, but perfectly clear. There were three carts, each drawn by a pair of bullocks, crawling slowly westward. He could hear the clop of the hooves and the creak of the wheels in the clear air. Then a barge came into view alongside them, gliding down the river in the lazy breeze, its sails drooping, and he could hear the voices of the bargees calling out morning greetings to the carters. The goatboy moved his stick to make its distant shadow tickle the barge's sail. It was a game he played each morning, for these few minutes in which the angle of the light was just right. Soon the sun would be too high in the sky, and it would be too hot for games. Then he would find the shade of an umbrella pine, and like as not the goats would join him there.

'Come along, old lady. Shuffle along.'

One of his goats was lame in a hind leg, and lagged behind the others. She always looked round at him when he spoke, and seemed to understand his words. He passed the long summer days alone, and liked to hear a voice from time to time, even if it was only his own.

Then came another voice that the goats could not hear.

Goatboy!

He dropped his stick at once, and sank to his knees. He touched his forehead to the ground.

'Here I am, mistress.'

We have need of your eyes.

'Command me, mistress.'

He trembled as he knelt, hearing the beloved voice within his head, and already anticipating his reward.

Stand, and look steadily on the land below you.

The goatboy stood, still trembling, and gazed out over the plains. He felt the soft buzzing in his head that always came at such times. The first time it had frightened him: the voice, and the buzzing, and the sensation that something had entered him that he could not control. But he had learned there was nothing to fear. And when it was over, there would come the sweetness.

They are watching.

Through the goatboy's eyes they see the sunlight shimmering on the land. They see the bright river, with the barge disappearing round the slow bend. They see the bullock carts creeping down the dusty road. Deep underground, the silent walls tremble with pictures from far away.

They are old, all of them. So old that when they speak, their lips do not move, and the sound of their words barely shivers the damp air.

'There, there. The city by the lake.'

They gaze intently, greedily, on the distant glitter of golden roofs that hug the shore of the great lake. The city of Radiance.

'The people are ruled by priests. They will believe what they are told to believe.'

'There are many? We need many.'

'There are many. They will give us what we need.'

The voices follow each other after long silences. Time has no value here, in the darkness and quiet of the deep caves.

'Better for a few to live forever young than for all to die.'

'Forever young!'

The words are repeated by ancient throats, passing softly from mouth to mouth like a prayer.

'Forever young!'

It is their dream, their passion, the only hope that keeps them alive. It has been their life's work, and the life's work of those who went before them. Preserved here, deep underground, barely moving, safe from extremes of heat and cold, they live on, their mighty brains working more slowly now, but getting nearer, nearer. They can smell it now, these withered creatures whose nostrils have known no fresh sensation for decades; they can smell the coming of new life.

They call it the harvest.

Now their old eyes track slowly over the shimmering scene before them, following the broad river as it runs down to the sea. There where the river meets the sea there is an island: little more than a rock in the river's mouth. This is Anacrea, the home of the Nomana, who are also called the Noble Warriors.

'And what of the Nomana?'

Only the Nomana stand in their way. Only the Noble Warriors have the power to resist their will.

'The Nomana will be destroyed.'

'Ah!'

The soft exhalations breathe out approval.

'A weapon will be built at our command. This weapon will destroy the island of Anacrea. And when Anacrea is gone, the power of the Nomana will be at an end.'

'Ah!'

'Then the harvest will begin.'

'Soon,' came the answering murmurs. 'Soon, soon. Let it come soon.'

'It will be soon. The harvest time approaches.'

*

On the mountain pasture the goatboy felt the buzzing cease inside his head, and knew it was over.

'Am I deserving, mistress?' he asked.

You are deserving.

Then the sweetness came upon him. He slipped down to the ground and lay there, sprawling and abandoned, giving himself up to the hot soak of ecstasy.

CHAPTER THREE

A SMALL REBELLION

SEEKER sat at his desk in the classroom, looking out of the window at the whitewashed wall and the straight line of the ocean horizon beyond. He thought of what he was about to do, and he shivered.

It was the start of the school day, and he was alone in the classroom. From the open door behind him he could hear the shouts of his classmates as they chased each other between the plane trees, delaying their arrival at school to the last possible minute. A bird flashed past the window: under-wings black on white, hook of beak, black cheek and white throat, a peregrine falcon cruising for prey. He knew them all, had learned their names. He liked to know names.

From high above, the monastery bell sounded the hour with its slow deep bumps of sound, felt more than heard. There followed the brisk footfall of his teacher-father. The screek of the door handle as he entered. The rustle of papers in his hands. His father padded up and down the lines of desks, laying a test paper face down on each: flop, flop, flop. Then he took his place at the table in front of the class that was not yet there, and turned his attention to paperwork of his own, without a word or a glance to his son, the one other living, breathing creature in the room.

Seeker watched him in silence. His father was a tall man with a high smooth brow and a long smooth face. His usual expression was one of polite impatience. Those blue eyes had a way of gazing at you without blinking that seemed to say he knew already everything that you were going to say, and had his answer prepared before you started to speak.

The bell jangled for the start of the school day, and the cries fell silent outside as the students made their way to their classrooms. Seeker's father did not look up from his paperwork until the last chair had scraped into silence. Then he laid down his pen, and raised his blank blue eyes, and spoke in his mild, implacable voice.

'Your test paper is on your desk. Write your name on the top of each sheet of paper. Remember that a correct answer is not enough. Marks are also given for grammar, spelling, punctuation, legibility, and neatness. You may begin.'

There was a rustling all across the classroom as the test papers were turned over. Ten questions; an hour to answer them. Seeker wrote his name on the blank sheet before him: Seeker after Truth. Then he read the first question.

A man wishes to measure the height of a tree near your home, and he asks for your help. His method is to measure the tree's shadow when it is exactly equal to the tree's height. You know that sunrise is at 5.08am and sunset is at 6.40pm. At what time should you tell him to take his measurement?

Seeker stared at the paper for a long moment. He was an excellent problem solver, and could see at once how to answer the question.

He realised his hand was shaking too much to write. He put his left thumb to his mouth and bit hard, using the sudden pain to steady his nerves. Then he wrote quickly:

This is a bad man who cuts down trees which are all different to make planks which are all the same. I will not help him.

A long slow release of breath. It was done. No going back now. The rest was much easier.

The second question went:

Describe, with diagrams, the rainfall cycle.

Seeker wrote more carefully this time, to be sure of his misspellings.

Furst the rain fall down from the cluods and make pudles then the rain fall up from the pudles and make cluods.

He drew a little diagram with arrows, in which the arrows all pointed in random directions. His hand had stopped trembling.

The third question went:

Using your own words, describe the sacred mission of the Nomana, also known as the Noble Warriors.

Seeker wrote:

The Nomana do biff bad fellows noses bash-squish yip whoopadoo.

He was beginning to feel light-headed. He looked round furtively at his classmates, but they were all bent over their test papers. He looked at his father. He too was intent on his work. He dipped his pen in the ink-well and, holding it over his test paper, dropped blobs of ink on to the white spaces. Each blob splattered on impact, throwing out little legs like a spider. Beside the splattered blobs he wrote *Dady Spidder, Mumy Spidder,* and *Babey Spidder.*

After that, he answered no more questions. He spent the remainder of the session writing with his left hand, so that the handwriting would be as bad as possible. He wrote:

I have forgot evrything

My head is emty

I no nothing

I am a stupid

Each question was worth ten marks, so the highest possible mark for the test was one hundred. Seeker had never yet been given a mark lower than eighty. On this paper, with marks deducted for bad spelling and untidiness, he would be well into minus figures. In one single test he would crash from top to bottom of the class. And maybe then, at last, his father would listen to him.

When the session ended, he handed in his test paper just as he always did, but inside he felt strange and giddy, as if he had no body-weight and was floating a little off the ground. He couldn't imagine how his father would react to what he had done. All he knew was that everything would change.

'Results after the break,' said his father evenly, as he always did.

Leaving the classroom, Seeker overheard Precious Boon speaking to Fray.

'How did you do?'

'Useless as usual,' said Fray, taking her arm. 'Let's go and do stupid things in the shade.'

They strolled away with their arms linked, and Seeker followed behind, alone. It was a hot day, too hot to stand out in the sun. The others threw themselves down on the dusty earth in the shadow of the plane trees. On the terrace below, a class of smaller children were playing a chasing game round the ornamental pond in the paved forecourt, uttering sharp cries and calling out each other's names. Seeker leaned his back on the warm whitewashed wall, the same wall he could see from his classroom desk, and remembered how he too had run round and round the pond when he was little, back in the days when his brother had been in the school. So long as Blaze had been there, everything had been all right. Blaze was tall and sturdy, and he had taken care of his little brother from his first day in school to the day he left. But then Blaze had gone, to train to be a Noma.

Seeker looked up the terraced streets that furrowed the steep sides of the island, to the great castle-monastery of the Nom at the top. Blaze was there now, somewhere. Three years ago he had been accepted as a novice, and Seeker had not seen him since. He missed him very much. He thought about him every single day. It wasn't just that Blaze had protected him. Somehow, when Blaze had been there, his father had left Seeker alone. After all, Blaze was the eldest, the pride of his father's heart, the child he had pledged to the Nom the day he was born. Blaze had always been destined to be a Noble Warrior, and had been named accordingly: his full name was Blaze of Justice.

Seeker scanned the long granite wall of the monastery that seemed to hang suspended over the sheer cliffs of the island's ocean face. That part of the Nom was closed to all except members of the Community. Sometimes he waved at its high windows, thinking that Blaze might be looking out, and might see him waving, and so would remember him. When he did so, he could almost see him, looking down at him with his broad open features and his ready smile. He could almost hear his familiar voice saying, 'Time to go home, little brother.' He could almost feel that strong arm round his shoulders.

A falcon swooped overhead, perhaps the same peregrine he had watched from his desk before the test. The bird's flight brought his gaze round and down, to the windows of his classroom. There sat his father at the table, alone in the room, marking the test papers.

Results after the break.

His father believed that tests should be marked right away, while the memory of the questions was still fresh. He was a fast marker, and he was scrupulously fair. Seeker felt himself flush as he imagined his father reading his test paper. He would be angry, of course. Probably bewildered. Perhaps even hurt. But it had been done now.

The bell rang for the end of break. This time Seeker was one of the last into the classroom. He avoided meeting his father's eye as he went to his desk. He sat there, looking down, squeezing his left thumbnail under the fingernails of his right hand, one after another. The sharp sensation this produced was not quite pain and not quite pleasure, but it stopped the shivering.

His father paced slowly between the desks, handing back the test papers, calling out the mark achieved, adding a brief comment with each one.

'Precious Boon, fifty-eight. Careless calculation there, Precious. Always check your answer.'

'Yes, sir.'

'Rose, seventy-one. A great improvement, Rose. Third from top.'

'Thank you, sir.'

'Fray, thirty-eight. Only six questions answered, Fray. Does that satisfy you?'

'No, sir.'

'Nor me. Better next time, please.'

· Seeker felt his father's presence as he approached his desk. He saw his test paper fall on to the desk top, face down. He went still, not raising his eyes.

'Seeker,' said his father, his voice as even as ever. 'Ninety-six. Best in class.'

Seeker's head jerked up, his eyes reaching for his father's eyes. But his father was already striding on past. Behind him he heard Fray murmur something to Precious Boon, and he heard Precious laugh. With a sensation of sickness in his stomach, he turned over his paper. No marks had been given to any of his answers. Across the top of the first page his father had written: *See me after school.*

*

22

'Here is what I propose to do about this paper.'

His father held it out before him, and slowly and methodically tore it into small pieces.

'That was not the work of the best scholar in the school. That was not the work of my son. It would be quite unfair of me to mark it as if it represented a serious set of answers. Instead, I have averaged your last five test results, and given you a mark that reflects your true ability.'

Seeker hung his head and said nothing. What could he say? His father would never understand. He stood before him in the school's assembly hall, surrounded by the trophies and the honours boards of bygone years, and waited for his punishment to be handed down.

'Have I been fair to you?'

Seeker nodded.

'Then you must be fair to me. Why did you do this?'

Seeker shrugged. His tongue felt thick and heavy in his mouth. His mind was muddy.

'Well? I think I deserve an answer.'

'Don't know,' said Seeker.

'You don't know?' His father's voice sharpened. Now he was going to get angry. 'I'm afraid I don't believe you.'

Seeker said nothing. He hated standing before his father like this. It was no use, for either of them. He just wanted it to be over.

'Did you want to get a low mark?'

Seeker gave a very small nod.

'Why? To be more like the others?'

That was a surprise. Seeker hadn't expected his father to understand any part of his feelings.

He nodded again.

'I thought as much.'

His father lowered himself on to one of the hall benches, and gestured to Seeker to do the same.

'Now tell me truthfully. Are you being bullied?'

'No . . .'

'Do they say unkind things to you?'

'Not exactly.'

'What do they say?'

'That I'm cleverer than them.'

'Anything else?'

'No.'

'You are cleverer than them. You do realise that?'

'I don't want to be.'

'You want to be the same as them?'

Seeker didn't speak.

'Very well. I think I understand now.'

He stood up and pressed the palms of his hands together, and gazed into the far distance. This was what he always did before making a speech. Seeker hated it when he made speeches.

'I do not propose to punish you,' he said. 'What you have done is a deliberate act of disobedience. But I don't want obedience alone. I want understanding. You're not the same as the others in your class, Seeker. Any more than I was the same as the others in my class when I was in this school. You have a first-rate brain. Just as I have.'

He went over to the honours board and tapped it where his own name was painted in gold letters, as the top scholar of his year.

'One day your name will be written here, as my name is written. One day, or so I dare to hope, you will hold the position I occupy now. One day you will be the headmaster of this highly respected institution. That is why I will not allow the record to show that your test results ever failed to reach the highest levels. You and I, Seeker, do not fail. We have exceptional natural ability. We work hard. We are therefore the best. This desire you have, to be the same as the others, is a denial of your true self. You are not the same as the others. You are superior to them. That, I promise you, will bring its own reward.'

'I just want to be – '

'What's that you say? Open your mouth when you speak. I can't hear a word you're saying.'

Seeker knew he was mumbling. Whenever he tried to tell his father something important he mumbled.

'I want to be – I want to join – the Nom – '

'The Nom? What are you talking about? Do you mean you want to be a Noma, like Blaze?'

Seeker nodded.

'But you're not like Blaze. My dear boy, it's no use wanting to be something you're not. That's what dreamers do. Dreamers never get anywhere. And anyway, you would never be selected, even if you were to apply.'

Seeker wanted to say, How do you know? But there was no point.

'You have different talents.' Now his father was speaking more gently. 'Fine talents. Talents I'm proud to claim as my own. Blaze will fight for justice. But you will seek after truth. What could be a nobler mission in life than that?'

Your mission, not mine, thought Seeker. Your name for me, not mine. But still he said nothing.

'Today is your birthday. Your sixteenth birthday. A suitable day, I think, to reflect on your coming responsibilities as an adult. I'm glad we've had this little talk.'

There came a tap at the door. It was the school meek, a sweet old man called Gift.

'Visitor to see you, Headmaster.'

'Just coming.'

He turned back to Seeker, and extended a hand for his son to shake.

'So we'll put this little incident behind us, shall we? No need to tell your mother. It shall be as if it never happened.'

'Yes, father.'

His father dropped the torn scraps of paper into the wastepaper basket. They fluttered from his hand like falling blossom. Seeker's rebellion was at an end.

Outside, a silent Noma was waiting.

CHAPTER FOUR

THE OPEN DOOR

SLOWLY, miserably, Seeker climbed the two hundred and twelve steps from the school up to the summit of the island. At each turn in the steep flights of steps he paused and looked down the terraces to the little port at the bottom, and the surrounding sea; then he looked up to the high walls and domes of the great castle-monastery, at the heart of which lived the one god with the many names: the Wise Father, the Loving Mother, the Lost Child, the Quiet Watcher, the All and Only. Seeker felt sick in his heart, a sickness deeper than hunger, deeper than tiredness. It was as if all colour had gone out of the world, and all smell, and all taste, and the very air he breathed had turned stale. He felt as if he was already old, and his life had passed him by without surprise or joy. He had nothing to complain of, he was safe and healthy in a world where so many were in danger or in pain; but nor had he anything to make him rejoice. His life would unfold in the same familiar fashion, dull lonely day after dull lonely day, and one day he would see his name inscribed on the school's role of honour, as his father's was; and one day he would point to it, and tell the sad little boy who was his own son to work harder, to achieve the same distinction.

How could he bear it?

He reached the top of the steps, where there grew the avenue of old pines. He stopped again, to catch his breath, and looked out to sea. There was a fishing boat passing, far below, beating its slow way up the coast, trawling a long net. The little vessel seemed to him to be so brave, its sails spread to the wind, its net straining behind. A lonely life, the fisherman's, but at least the loneliness was part of the job. It was different at school. If you were lonely at school it was your own fault, and everyone knew it.

A peregrine came swooping up from the cliff, high into the air, cruising for prey. There were doves nesting in the pines, and the great falcons hunted them, especially at dusk, hovering silently above the trees, before dropping like bolts for the killer blow. Blaze had shown him once how to stand still and watch. You didn't have to hide, just to stay still. 'They only see you if you move.' Once, standing motionless by Blaze's side, he had seen a kill. The peregrine's dive was noiseless, breathtaking, irresistible. 'Now the eggs will go cold,' Blaze had told Seeker. Such a strange yoking of thrill and pity.

He and Blaze used to skim flat pebbles over the water, down by the harbour side where the barges and the river boats moored. Back then Seeker couldn't skim pebbles, not really, though when Blaze wasn't looking he would pretend, crying out, 'One! Two! Three! Three jumps!' Now he could do it, and suddenly, with a fierce ache, he wanted Blaze to be there to see. He wanted to go down to the harbour once more with him, and show him how well he could skim stones. He wanted to tell him how much he missed him, how he had thought of him every single day for the last three years, how life was hard for him but he could bear it, because he had no choice.

He felt his eyes sting, and blinked to hold back tears. Only one place to go now, only one refuge. He hurried down the avenue of trees towards the Nom, and the high arch of the Pilgrim Gate. This was the part of the monastery that was open to islanders, and, on certain days, to pilgrims. This was the way to the holy of holies, the place where the god lived. And it was here Seeker always came when he was sad, to whisper the truth, and to find peace.

Two Nomana stood by the gate, but Seeker was familiar to them, and they nodded him through. He entered the first hall, a wide and dusky atrium called the Shadow Court. This, and the two further halls into which it led, were designed to calm the spirit and prepare for the nearness of the All and Only. There was no one else here. On the far side, three sets of double doors stood open to the second hall, which was called the Night Court. This was a large, circular, windowless chamber, with a domed roof that was pierced with hundreds of tiny holes. The bright sunlight above pushed through these holes like stars, and fell in pencil-thin rays of light to cast a pattern of bright spots all across the floor. Again, there was no one here.

Beyond the Night Court, through a further set of double doors, was the Cloister Court, the innermost chamber of

29

the Nom apart from the Garden itself. Here, in striking contrast to the Night Court, was a cool, light, pillared space, luminous with the glow of the white marble out of which the floor and the columns were made. The ceiling high above was formed of pearl-stone, a translucent milky stone which turned bright sunlight into tranquil day. The gleaming pillars stood close together, rank upon rank, so that many people could be present, and yet remain unaware of each other's nearness. And at the far end, where the pillars ceased, and the ceiling lay open to the blazing sun, was the Garden.

Seeker stopped here for a moment and prayed the entrance prayer. His eyes reached between the forest of pillars to the gleam of the silver screen that surrounded the Garden. Beyond those delicate and beautiful panels of pierced silver, within that sunlit glade, dwelt the Always and Everywhere.

'Wise Father, you are the Clear Light, you are the Reason and the Goal. Guide me in the true way.'

Then he moved slowly forward through the white pillars towards the dazzle of light that was the Garden. As always there were Nomana here, standing quiet and still. He could see two, but without doubt there would be more. Sometime pilgrims became over-excited and tried to climb the silver screen, and had to be removed. And always there was the threat that was told in the legend, that had been present from the very first coming of the Lost Child, the threat of the Assassin. No one knew who or what the

Assassin was, a man, or a band of men, or a god; but all knew that one day the Assassin would find his way into the Garden at last, because the dream of the First Brother had told them so.

Seeker came close to the screen. The holes in the fine lace of silver were in the shapes of diamonds and stars. Through them he could see a bright riot of growth shaded by a canopy of leaves: wool-white blossom in nests of deep green, scarlet petals of weeds speckling the butter-yellow petals of flowers, golden creepers lying down to rest in blue grasses, a wild jungle untouched by any gardener for two hundred years. Here there were ancient rocks overgrown with moss, and a spring of clear water bubbling up into a pool where dragonflies danced in the sun. Here were places to walk and places to sit, and peaches hanging ripe on low branches, and plums rotting richly in the grass unpicked, and here was deep violet shade. Here too, sometimes, there flashed a shiver in the grass, and you could swear you saw someone slip by between the trees. For this was the actual living home of the being who had made the world, and who knew why all things must be as they were, even the bad things, even loneliness, even feeling old when you were still young.

Seeker heard a soft rustle nearby, and, turning, saw one of the Nom meeks quietly sweeping between the pillars. The sound was comforting, like the gentle strokes of his mother's hand over his brow when he couldn't sleep. He slipped to his knees before the gleaming screen and sought comfort, not from the Loving Mother, not from the Wise Father, but from the Lost Child.

'You too have been lost and alone,' he said, whispering softly but aloud. 'You know how I feel, without me telling you. Be my friend. Show me you hear me. I'm so tired of being alone.'

Now he slipped all the way down on to the cold white floor, and spread himself out prostrate, as the pilgrims did.

'Save me,' he said. 'The sadness goes on too long. Show me a way out of the sadness.'

After that he lay there in silence and felt the spirit grow calm within him, as it always did when he came to this holy place. His cheek pressed to the marble floor, he let himself drift into a half-sleep, soothed by the distant swishes of the meek's broom.

Then he heard a voice. The voice was clear and real, but it was right in the middle of his head. It was the voice of a child.

'Surely you know,' said the voice, 'that it's you who will save me.'

Surprised, Seeker rose to his knees and looked round. But even as he looked round he knew that the voice had been inaudible to others. There were the guardian Nomana, still as statues. There was the industrious meek. The voice had been a child's voice, and it had been inside him.

It came again.

'Surely you know,' it said, 'that where your way lies, the door is always open.'

With that, he heard the faint creak of an opening door. He looked round. Some way off, between the pillars, he saw a small side door standing ajar. The door was in the wall on the far side of the Cloister Court, the wall that bounded the Community quarters. Such doors were only ever opened to Nomana.

He rose to his feet and looked round. The watchful Nomana were either unaware of the open door or were not concerned. Seeker felt a sudden surge of intense excitement. The voice could only have come from the Lost Child. The door could only have opened for him. He hesitated no more. He padded quietly between the pillars to the door, and pushed it open, and entered the realm of the Nomana.

The room in which he now found himself was windowless, lit by glazed panes in the roof. All round the walls were racks, from which hung white garments. Seeker recognised them as the ceremonial clothes worn by the Nomana on the great festival days. They were identical to the Nomana's everyday clothes, but in place of the tough grey serge they were made of a light white cotton. The Nomana wore very few garments: a pair of loose britches, tied at the waist and the ankles; a simple vest; a calf-length tunic with short, loose sleeves, its skirt slit on either side from the waist down; and finally a broad scarf worn over the head like a hood. This last item, the badan, was unique to the Nomana. At each end of the long strip of material there was a net of threads holding a pebble. The two weighted ends of the badan were worn hanging down, one at the front and one at the back.

So this was a vesting room. Here the Nomana came to change into these clean, light garments that made them seem, when they processed into the square in their hundreds, on the day of the Congregation, like spirits from another world.

Seeker moved down the racks, not daring to touch the cool white fabric. He knew he had no right to be here. He also knew that this room was not his destination, because at the far end was another door, and it too was open.

Where your way lies, the door is always open.

He passed through this second door and found himself in a courtyard. In the middle of the courtyard was a wide circular bed of sand that had been raked into a pattern of overlapping fans. There were many doors leading out of the courtyard, but only one other was open. From this door there came a sound like the buzzing of bees, only deeper and harsher. Seeker walked slowly round the yard, keeping to the cobbles, and so came to the open door. Here the sound was much louder, almost painful. He winced, and put his hands to his ears. He stepped through the door.

He was in a wash-house. Pipes ran round the walls, and channels on the stone floor carried gurgling water to corner drains. Pipes also crossed the high ceiling, and from them projected smaller pipes, with taps on their ends. One tap was open, and gushing water: and dangling from this overhead pipe, tied by a strip of cloth which ran round his wrists, was a half-naked man. His arms were pulled high above his head, and his head hung down on his bare chest, and the water from the pipe ran in a ceaseless stream down his arms and over his drenched hair and down his body to trickle from his bare feet to the floor.

Round this dangling man were gathered a crowd of Nomana, men and women, filling the wash-house. Every one of them had their hands over their ears, as Seeker had, and every one of them had their eyes fixed on the dangling man. As they stared they made the deep buzzing, grating sound that seemed to chisel into the very brain.

Seeker saw, and was afraid. The look on the faces of the Nomana was so intent: that stare, and the relentless drill of sound, offered no pity to the soaked and dangling man. It was hard enough to endure the buzzing even from the doorway. To be its focus must have been unbearable. And indeed, every few moments the poor man twisted his head, as if to escape the torment, and groaned in his distress.

What was happening? Was this some terrible punishment? The dangling man was a Noma too, as Seeker could tell from his clothing. The cloth that bound his wrists was his badan. Perhaps this was some kind of test. Seeker had heard tales of rigorous training in the novitiate. But even as he thought this, he knew that it could not be so. This was more than a test. This was a form of torture.

The dangling man groaned again, and tried in vain to block his ears with his straining arms. The effort cost him pain. He let his head drop further. Then, struck by some unseen wave of torment, he raised his head and cried out loud in his agony. That was when Seeker saw his face. Even streaming with water, even twisted in pain, even three years older, Seeker recognised that face.

'Blaze!' he cried.

The dangling man's eyes jerked open. He looked directly at Seeker, in the doorway. He saw him: there was no doubt about that. But he did not know him. His eyes were empty. Something had been done to him, and now, at last, Seeker understood.

Blaze was being *cleansed*.

'Blaze!' he cried again, in terror and grief. 'Blaze! Don't let them do it!'

His beloved brother stared back at him, with that familiar broad face, that wide mouth; but the eyes had changed, and he did not know him. It was as if his brother was no longer there in his own body.

Seeker heard a voice screaming. The terrible buzzing sound stopped. The Nomana turned towards him. The scream was his own voice.

The Noma nearest to him said to him, 'Look at me.'

Seeker looked at him. He knew at once he shouldn't have done it, but it was too late. The Noma's gaze held him, and Seeker felt the strength slip away from his body, and he knew he was falling.

CHAPTER FIVE

AN OLD MAN'S TEARS

WHEN Seeker woke, he was lying on a hard bed in an unknown room. He gave no sign that he was awake, because he realised at once that he wasn't alone in the room, and he wanted first to work out how he came to be here. As his confusion of tangled thoughts slowly regained focus, he found that he was unharmed, and that he was not bound or restrained in any way. Judging from the stone vault of the ceiling above him, he was still somewhere in the Nom. He risked turning his head very slightly, and saw that there were two figures at the far end of the long room, both of them Nomana. They were talking in soft voices, presumably so as not to disturb him. One was a man's voice, the other a woman's. Seeker lay very still and listened, and tried to work out what had happened. They had been doing something bad to his brother. What had it been? Yes! Blaze had been cleansed! With the returning memory came a burst of anger that made his cheeks burn. Cleansing was almost a form of death in life. Cleansing was for criminals and murderers. A person who was cleansed by the Nomana lost all memory, and will, and desire. It was a return to infancy. How could they do this to Blaze?

He caught the odd word from the far end of the room,

whenever the man raised his voice. The woman's voice was too soft and low for him to hear. He caught the words 'secret weapon', and then 'great danger'. There was one word that recurred several times, which at first he didn't understand, but he made it out at last. It was 'Radiance'. They were talking about the great city of that name, the heart of the empire that dominated the land to the north.

Then the woman turned and saw that his eyes were open.

'He's awake.'

She came to his side. She had short, cropped grey hair and a kind face, deeply lined with age. Like all Nomana when within the Nom, she wore her badan down over her shoulders.

'How do you feel?' she said, and pressed her dry hand to his brow.

'All right,' said Seeker. 'Where am I?'

'You're in the Nom. In the sickroom.'

'Why?'

The man now stood over him, frowning down at him. Seeker recognised him. His name was Narrow Path, and he was said to be a brother of great holiness. He had a high, bald brow and a lean, bony face.

'That is for you to tell us,' he said.

'Later,' chided the woman. 'The boy's still in shock.'

'He looks perfectly healthy to me. Can you sit up?'

Seeker sat up.

As he did so the door opened, and a wheelchair rolled

in, carrying a shrunken old man, pushed by an old woman. The old woman was one of the Nom meeks. The old man was the most revered of all the Nomana, the Elder of the Community. He was fast asleep, and snoring. Narrow Path glanced towards the Elder, frowned a frown of irritation, and turned back to Seeker.

'Explain yourself,' he said. 'You have no right to be here.'

Seeker was ready to explain, as best as he could, but Narrow Path's sharp tone reawakened his sense of anger.

'You've no right to do that to my brother!'

'Brother? What brother?'

'Blaze. The one you were – you were – '

Tears sprang into his eyes. The kind-faced woman understood him.

'Oh, my dear!' she said. 'Blaze of Justice is your brother?'

Seeker nodded. Narrow Path seemed to find in this even more reason to frown.

'Has Blaze of Justice communicated with you?'

'No,' said Seeker.

'Then why did you come sneaking into the Nom?'

'I wasn't sneaking. I was – I was – '

He realised he had no sensible explanation. Narrow Path shook his shiny bald head, and looked yet more grave.

'You knew precisely where to come. You knew how to find your brother. Who told you?'

'I didn't know. No one told me.'

Narrow Path turned to the woman and spoke in a low voice.

'This is not good. Something here is not right at all.'

Seeker's distress burst out of him, even though he tried to keep silent.

'I'll tell you what's not right! What you were doing to Blaze! That's not right! You were cleansing him! I saw! You had no right to do that!'

He knew there were tears in his eyes, and his voice was shrill like a hurt child's, but he couldn't help it.

'No right?' exclaimed Narrow Path. 'Your brother is a traitor!'

'He is not!'

'Blaze of Justice has shown himself to be too weak to withstand temptation. He has placed the entire Community in grave danger. He is to be cast out. Of course he must be cleansed! Would you have us turn loose a weak and bitter man with all the powers of the Nomana at his command?'

Seeker was too stunned to reply. In his struggle to understand, he recalled the words he had heard as he lay on the bed.

'Is it because of the secret weapon in Radiance?'

Narrow Path gasped.

'You see!' he said to the woman. 'He's part of it!'

Now the woman too was looking grave.

'What do you know of a secret weapon?' she said.

'Nothing.'

Seeker's heart was sinking. He realised how bad it must look to them.

'What does it matter what he knows?' said Narrow Path. 'Already it's too much. He must be made safe too.'

'No!' cried Seeker, shrinking away.

'Don't scare the boy!' said the woman.

'You know it as well as I do. He can't be sent back until he's been made safe.'

'Please!' said Seeker. 'It was a voice. I did what the voice said.'

'Of course,' said Narrow Path with a shrug of incredulity. 'A voice told you. How convenient.'

There came a grunt from the wheelchair, and a series of snuffling noises, and the Elder woke up.

'A voice?' The words emerged without his mouth seeming to move, a sound creaky with extreme age. 'Did the boy say he heard a voice?'

He fixed Seeker with his small, bright eyes, like the eyes of a bird. His face was so deeply lined that it was hard to read his expression, but the eyes seemed to Seeker to be alert, and kind.

'It was a voice in the middle of my head.'

'In your head?' The Elder nodded, as if this made perfect sense to him. 'Have you heard such a voice before?'

'No, Elder.'

'Where were you when you heard this voice?'

'In the Cloister Court, Elder. Just in front of the Garden.'

The Elder nodded once more. Then he looked up at the other two Nomana, and said to them gently, 'Leave me alone with the boy.'

'Elder,' said Narrow Path, 'in the light of the present danger – '

The Elder raised one bony hand.

'I know all about the present danger, brother. Leave us, please.'

So the two Nomana left, and Seeker was alone with the Elder and his silent attendant meek.

'Now, boy,' said the Elder. 'When you heard this voice, did you also feel a sensation of sweetness?'

'No, Elder.'

'Or pain?'

'No, Elder.'

'Very good. So tell me what this voice in your head said to you.'

'The voice said – the voice said – '

Seeker found he was unable to finish his sentence. The Elder watched him with his bright little eyes, and seemed unsurprised.

'No matter what the voice said. Who do you suppose it was speaking to you?'

'I don't know, Elder.'

'But you can make a guess.'

'I think perhaps it was the Lost Child, Elder.'

The Elder closed his eyes and nodded his head.

'Why should the One who made all things speak to you, boy?'

'I don't know, Elder.'

And truly he did not know. It had never happened to

him before, or to anyone he had ever heard of. Even his mother, who was very devout, and spoke of the All and Only as you might speak of an old friend, never claimed to have heard an actual voice.

'But you believe,' said the Elder, with his eyes still closed, 'that whoever spoke to you wished you to enter the Nom.'

'I don't know, Elder.' As he said this, Seeker realised this was exactly what he did believe, even though it made no sense. So he added, 'Yes, Elder. I do think that.'

'Of course you do. And whoever spoke to you led you to your brother.'

'Yes, Elder.'

The old man mused a while in silence. Seeker's thoughts returned to Blaze, to that terrible blank expression on his soaked face, and the way that when he saw Seeker he didn't recognise him.

'They were wrong to do that,' he said in a low voice.

'The Nom is not wrong, boy. The Nom makes no mistakes. If you don't understand, it is because you lack knowledge, not because the Nom is wrong.'

'Blaze can't be a traitor! He just can't. He's nothing to do with this secret weapon, or Radiance, or anything like that.'

'What is done is done,' said the Elder mildly. 'The question now is what to do with you. It seems you know a little, and that is dangerous. You must either know enough to understand our situation, or you must know nothing at all.'

43

Seeker knew what that meant: it meant the buzzing noise in the wash-house, and the water flowing over his head, and all his memories and everything that made him what he was washing away down the drain.

'I think I had better trust you, Seeker after Truth.'

Seeker looked up, surprised.

'How do you know my name?'

'You are the brother of Blaze of Justice. The son of our valued schoolmaster. How old are you now, boy? Fourteen? Fifteen?'

'Sixteen, Elder. Today is my sixteenth birthday.'

'Sixteen already. Forgive me. You have a young face. So, Seeker, this is what you should know. The priest-king of Radiance has decided that Anacrea must be destroyed.'

'Destroyed! Why?'

'That we don't know. Something has changed. The empire of Radiance has never had reason to fear us before. We don't have the power to overthrow kings, or the will to rule empires.'

'But if you chose to do it, Elder,' said Seeker, burning with anger at the presumptuous threat, 'you could call the Noble Warriors to battle, and our enemies would crumble before them!'

'One battle, boy, and what then? You know how it is with our power. We can do great things, but we pay a great price. The strength we have at our command is driven by a life-force that is slow to gather, and quick to release. When we unleash that force in violence, the impact is overwhelming, but our strength is then gone. For long hours after, we're as weak as babies.'

Seeker heard this with consternation, and his proud anger turned to dismay.

'I didn't know,' he said.

'Yes, you knew.' The Elder's voice was gently reproving. 'You're familiar with the words of the Legend. The Legend tells us that our strength is the strength of a wounded warrior, and victory makes us weak.'

'I thought . . .'

'You thought that was just a story.'

'But Elder – the Nomana! No one can beat a Noble Warrior! The Nomana are trained – they have such powers – they can do anything!'

'Not anything, boy. But we can do something. And the little we can do, that we must do, so that others will know good men too can be strong.'

'Yes, Elder.'

'And we won't let our enemies destroy us if we can help it, will we?'

'No, Elder.'

'So this is all we know so far. A weapon is being built in Radiance, a weapon of such explosive power that it could sweep this entire island away like a mound of dust. We don't know what form this weapon takes, or where it's being made. But we do know that our enemies will be looking for ways to bring it on to the island. If they succeed – '

He raised both hands, and opened his bright little eyes wide, and smiled.

'Then it's all over.'

'And my brother has something to do with this?'

Even as he said it, it seemed absurd.

'Your brother is no longer a danger to us.'

Seeker hung his head, in confusion and grief.

'Can I trust you, Seeker after Truth?'

'Yes, Elder.'

'Then this is how you can help us in these dangerous times. Go home and comfort your parents. They already know Blaze is to be cast out. Say nothing of all you have seen and heard today in the Nom. Look at me, boy.'

Seeker looked. The Elder's eyes held his, and reached deep. Seeker looked back, unable to withdraw his own eyes from that penetrating gaze. Then he in his turn looked properly, looked to see how far he could reach. For a few moments he saw nothing. Then he gave a gasp, and shut his eyes tight. It was as if he had been looking into mist, and suddenly the mist had parted, and there beyond was an infinity of suffering.

When he opened his eyes he saw that the Elder was still gazing at him, but now his eyes were filled with tears. The Elder of the Community, the wisest of all the Noble Warriors, was weeping for him.

Seeker felt a tremor of fear.

'Speak to me, Elder. Please.'

'What am I to say? That there are hard years ahead for

you? You know that already. As for the rest, you must come to it in your own time.'

'Will it make me weep too?'

'I hope so. We weep for pity of those we must hurt, and our hearts break for those we love. But while we can still weep we're not entirely lost. Beware of old men who don't weep.'

Now Seeker's own eyes were filling with tears, even though he didn't understand what it was he must fear. He brushed the tears away with a clumsy fist.

'Go now, boy,' said the Elder. 'Say nothing.'

CHAPTER SIX

SUBMISSION, SUBMISSION

SEEKER left the Nom by the Pilgrim Gate. He made his way slowly across the stone-flagged square, and passed between the rows of pine trees to the steps. As he went he tried to make sense of all he had learned, and to decide who to believe. There was the voice that had spoken in his head, and there was the voice of the Elder. But stronger than either in his memory, there was the sight of his brother's face, and the sound of the groan he had uttered as he was cleansed. Seeker looked back at the high walls of the Nom, the castle-monastery that had stood all his life for what was good and strong, and for the first time he questioned its justice. If he must choose between his brother and the Nom, he chose Blaze. If the Nom said Blaze was a traitor, then the Nom must be lying; and if the Nom lied, then the Nom was bad. But at the same time, he loved the Nom, and the Noble Warriors, and had already begun to dream that he might be the one to save Anacrea from this new and terrible danger.

As he hopped down from step to step, it seemed to him that with each step his feelings changed.

I love Blaze. I hate the Nom.

Who hurts the Nom? Let me fight and kill them!

Who hurts my brother? Let me fight and kill them!
Surely you know that it's you who will save me.
The little we can do, that we must do . . .
But what is it I'm to do?

When he got home he found the street door to the house
was open, and the downstairs rooms were empty. At this
hour of the day his father was always to be found in his
little library, and his mother in her chair by the street
window, book in hand, pencil in her mouth, reading and
making notes. One of her many jobs was reading and
assessing new books, and, where suitable, adding their
titles to the list approved by the school.

But she was not in her reading chair.

Seeker climbed the stairs to the roof. Here on the flat
roof there was a little private terrace that looked out to sea.
His mother was sitting in one of the faded cane chairs,
beneath the bamboo awning. She was crying.

'Mama!'

Seeker threw himself into her arms. His mother never
cried. It almost hurt him more than seeing Blaze suffer. He
wanted to comfort her, but instead, unable to stop himself,
he began to cry too. The tears he had brushed from his eyes
when he stood before the Elder now flowed freely. His
mother held him tight, and kissed his face, and their tears
mingled on their cheeks.

'Darling boy,' she said. 'My darling boy. On your
birthday too. I don't know how to tell you.'

'I know already, Mama.'

'My poor Blaze.'

'It's a mistake! It must be!'

'Don't say that, darling. In some way we can't understand, this is the will of the All and Only.'

'It can't be! You know Blaze! They say he's a traitor to the Nom. Blaze would never betray the Nom!'

'They say that? Oh, my dear.'

She bowed her head so he wouldn't see how much she suffered. Seeker racked his brain for something he could say to her to give her hope. He knew she would never take refuge in anger against the Nom, as he had done. Her faith was too strong. So he said to her the only truth of which he was certain.

'I love Blaze and I'll never believe anything bad of him.'

'I love him too, darling. Even if – even if – '

Silence and tears. Seeker had no more consolation to offer. Her suffering was unendurable. He wanted to make everything right again, and burned with frustration that he couldn't, and felt once more the rising up of a confused anger. Who was doing this to them? Why? He would track down these unknown enemies and claw them and throttle them until they confessed it was all a lie, and Blaze was good and honourable and the best of all the Nomana, and his mother would smile again, and his father would –

'Father! Where is he?'

'He's at the school. He sent me a note.'

She had it still in her hand. Seeker read it. Not his

father's usual strong, clearly formed writing at all: this was a half-blinded scrawl.

Blaze to be cast out at Congregation. I know nothing more. Submission, submission. Trust in the All and Only.

Submission! His proud father, before whom the teachers as well as the students trembled – how could he submit? Seeker knew all too well that this catastrophe would pierce his father with a double agony, because he would lose both his first-born son, and his pride.

'I'll go to him.'

'Yes, my darling. Go to him. Comfort him.'

Seeker didn't know how to tell his mother that he too had failed his father, that very morning. Then he recalled the silent Noma who had been waiting outside the door as he had left. That must have been when the blow fell.

'Go to him,' said his mother again. 'Bring him home.'

Gift met him as he entered the school's outer gates. The old meek was trembling with distress.

'He's in the assembly hall,' he told Seeker. 'He won't speak to me, and he won't come out. What am I to do? I should have locked the school hours ago.'

'I'll talk to him,' said Seeker. 'He'll come home with me.'

He went to the hall door and knocked.

'Father. It's me.'

There was no answer.

He opened the door and went in. His father was there, standing by the honours boards, gazing up at the line of

51

gilded letters, painted there twenty years ago, that spelled out his own name.

He turned at the sound of approaching footsteps. Seeker saw with a shock how grief had aged his father. The smooth, stern face had crumpled.

'I remember it all so well,' he said, his voice low. 'The day the announcement was made, here in this same hall. How proud my mother was when they read out my name. I had hoped, of course. But you can never be sure. Not until you hear it. Your own name read out. And then you know you can be sure for all the rest of your life.'

He ran his fingers over the painted letters.

'It is something, to be first in your year,' he said. 'It is something.'

All this was so unlike his father that Seeker forgot Blaze for a moment, and looked on in dismay. As if divining his thoughts, his father shook his head, and gave a small smile.

'It's all right. I've not lost my wits. It's only that some-times it helps me to – to remember.'

'Yes, Father.'

'So have you heard?'

'Yes, Father.'

'Nothing could have hurt me more.'

His voice trembled as he spoke. Seeker ached to touch him, but his father was not one for caresses.

'It must be a mistake,' said Seeker.

'The Nom makes no mistakes.'

At this, his father bowed his head. Seeker thought of

the words on the note: *Submission, submission.* He wanted to say, Don't submit! Resist! Fight!

'Perhaps,' his father said, 'perhaps I was too proud of – of the boy.'

He couldn't even speak his name. This was how it would be from now on. It would be as if Blaze had never been born. And all this would happen in public, at the Congregation due to take place on midsummer's day. That was just four days away.

'Time to go home, Father.'

'Yes . . .'

He touched the painted letters of his name on the honours board once more, and looked at Seeker with an attempt at a smile.

'Your name here soon, eh?'

It was the half-smile that made Seeker turn his head away, with a sudden jerky movement. He didn't want to cry in front of his father.

'You're right.' His father misunderstood that quickly averted look. 'We mustn't tempt providence. But you're a good boy, Seeker. You've always been a good boy.'

Seeker said nothing. His father sighed, and composed himself.

'Ah, well,' he said. 'We at least know how to behave. We will attend the Congregation as if nothing has happened. We will conduct ourselves with dignity. You understand how important that is?'

'Yes, Father.'

'Everything will be done as it is always done.'

Then at last they left the school, and the old meek locked the gates behind them. Seeker said no more, and his father believed he had accepted, like him, that there was no choice but submission; but it was not so. The rebellion that had begun for Seeker in the classroom that morning was not over after all.

Surely you know, the voice had said, *that it's you who will save me.*

CHAPTER SEVEN

THE WILDMAN

THE hottest hour of the hottest day so far, no clouds to haze the sun, and the dazzle on the river was turning mud to gold. On either bank the eucalyptus trees trailed deep green leaves in the shallows, and the scavenger dogs lay still and panting in purple shade. This was the hour of the snake, when bronze-skinned vipers uncoiled on burning rocks, languid and vulnerable, careless of predators, drunk on heat. This was the hour of still water, when the turbulent gully fish sought the depths, and lay quiet as stones on the cool river bed. No sentient creature had business to do at such an hour.

Except the Wildman.

'Heya! Do you lo-o-ove me?'

More like a song than a cry, the syllables stretched beyond endurance, hurled bouncing and ricocheting from bank to bank, all down the easy turns of the great river.

'Do you lo-o-ove me?'

No answer came. No answer required. All the world loved the Wildman, for his dark eyes and his golden hair; for his youth, just eighteen years old, and for his beauty; and out of plain common-sense self-preservation. They called him the Wildman because he had been known to kill those who did not delight him, and it did not delight him to be unloved.

He stood on the prow of the *Lazy Lady*, his golden-skinned silver-braceleted arms reached out on either side, his face turned to the sun. His eyes were closed, and his voice soft as a lover's.

'Dance with me,' he told the sun, feeling his body soften in the noon burn. 'Dance in my loving arms.'

Now he was dancing, all alone on the prow, in the sun. His crew watched him and shook their heads and smiled. Crazy as a catfish but dangerous with it, more dangerous than a starving mealy dog, and who's complaining? The Wildman made them rich, and every day was show time. That was the truth of it. Run with the crazy golden boy and the lights shone bright and the days smelled sweet.

'Heya, bravas! Company ahead!'

The thatched roofs lay hidden in the trees, brown fronds among green, but the Wildman had sharp eyes. He saw the riverside village downstream, and he saw that it was deserted, it being siesta time, and he knew the people would be waking soon enough now. And they would be sleepy and afraid. And they would give him all he asked. This made the Wildman feel cheated and irritable.

'Chickens!' he growled to himself. 'Chuck-chuck-chickens! Here comes the Wildman!'

The Wildman liked opposition. He needed opposition. This was how he came by the surge of anger that flooded him, and fed him, and made him feared. When he lost control he entered an ecstatic state of violence which was both his joy and his power. The feelings were good and the effects were good, so no need to argue over what came first. The Wildman knew how to get results. He could smell the squirt of fear that came out of those who roused his anger. He loved to see the way their eyes went wide as they discovered, in shocked and helpless terror, that they were about to die.

But not in cold blood. Never in cold blood. There was neither honour nor satisfaction in that. He had learned the respect accorded to lethal violence, but only in combat and battle, only in love and hate. When the sweet juice flowed he cared nothing for his own preservation, and his fury knew no limits. At all other times he was a dove, a lamb, a honeychild.

A bell started to clang in the village temple.

'Heya, bravas!' the Wildman cried to his crew. 'Chuck-chuck-chickens!'

His men knew what to do. Down came the rippling brown sails, out struck the oars. Now swishing downstream under man-power, the *Lazy Lady* closed in on its prey. The leader of the spiker band, barely out of boyhood, stamped his bronzed bare feet in the prow and sang out to his crew.

'Heya, bravas! Do you love me?'

Oh, they loved him all right. They loved their Wildman.

As soon as the boat banged against the jetty the river pirates were leaping on to land, whooping and grinning, in a gush and clash of colours, shirts orange and crimson and emerald green, jewelled belts flashing and silver bracelets jangling in the sun, their unfriendly intent expressed by the long curving knives they juggled from hand to hand. The villagers streamed out of their houses, groggy with sleep and fear, and huddled round the temple at the heart of their homestead, and stared and prayed.

The spiker leader came prancing across the river bank, casting his black eyes over the cattle in the day barn and over the sacks in the granary, and looking for all the world as though he was the favourite son coming home.

'Heya, chickens!' he sang out. 'Do you lo-o-ove me?'

The village priest came shuffling forward, with sweat on his brow and lowered eyes. He mumbled some words which the spiker leader failed to catch.

'Whoa!' cried the Wildman, his spirits rising. 'Open wider, brava!' In demonstration, he gaped his own mouth wide, showing bright white teeth. 'Let me hear you.'

'We are protected,' said the priest, still speaking low, and with his eyes on the ground. 'Our god Shom protects us.'

'Protect? What's this protect? Chickens! Rat-piss! You don't love me no more, brava?'

The priest trembled. The spiker leader's voice changed its tone, turned soft and whispery.

'You don't love me?'

One of the village children carolled out through the sun-drugged air the secret that the priest had told them all.

'We got a spirit fence! You can't hurt us!'

The Wildman heard this. He looked up and down the path with a widening smile.

'Spirit fence? You got yourself a spirit fence?'

The priest raised one hand to dab at the sweat streaming down his face.

'Shom protects us,' he mumbled, praying silently to his village god that it might be so.

The spikers watched, grinning broadly. They knew the signs. When the Wildman talked sweet like that, throats got slit.

'Show me your spirit fence.'

The priest gestured up and down the path, his hands trembling.

'Cross the spirit fence,' he said, his voice also trembling, 'and you will die.'

The spiker leader looked surprised.

'Die? Like, dead?'

'Cross the spirit fence,' said the priest, 'and Shom will strike you dead.'

He caught a flicker of uncertainty on the spikers' faces, as they exchanged looks.

'Strike me dead?' said the spiker leader in an awed voice. 'Whoa! You hear, bravas? These chickens gonna strike me dead!'

He approached nearer to the path.

'Right here?'

'All along the path,' said the priest.

'Whoa!' The Wildman made as if to touch the spirit

59

fence, and pulled back his hand in mock fear. He did a little dance, stepping close to the imaginary barrier and bounding away again.

'Heya, bravas!' cried the Wildman to his men. 'Strike me dead!'

At this moment, a stranger stepped out of the trees that ran close by the river bank. He had the appearance of a poor man. He carried no pack, and no weapon. He stood looking down. He wore a long grey tunic, with a pale grey scarf over his head like a hood, and he was barefoot. He was tall, and had white hair, cut very short. There was something about him that was hard to grasp, as if the more the Wildman looked at him, the more his attention slipped away.

'Noble Warrior!' cried the priest. 'Help us!'

So this was one of the Nomana, one of the famous Noble Warriors. The Wildman had never met one face to face. He was disappointed. People said the Nomana had magic powers. But what did it come down to? A man alone, with no weapon. The Nomana had no army. They had no treasure. They ruled no country. Just a band of fools lost on a rock in the sea. Not much opposition there.

The stranger now looked up, to reveal pale blue eyes.

'Leave these people in peace,' he said.

'You want peace,' said the Wildman, 'you come and fight for it!'

He spun his curved knife in the air so that it turned on itself once, twice, three times, and the hilt thocked into his palm. The stranger made no move.

'Chuck-chuck-chickens!' he cried, turning away, and lofted the blade high over his head, ready now to sever these little people's foolish faith. Down he swung –

'Heya!'

His arm went limp. His fingers parted. The knife flew from his hand. To the priest, it seemed that the spirit fence had repulsed the blade. He cried aloud, 'Praise Shom!'

The Wildman snatched up his knife, smarting with shame, and hissed at the priest like a fighting cat.

'Blubber-piss! I'm gonna slit your neck!'

He saw the priest's terrified eyes reach past him. He saw how all the villagers were looking past him. Turning, he too fixed his dark eyes on the stranger, who was standing very still, his eyes cast down once more, in the shadow of the trees, melting into the stripes and dapples of light. Was it him? Had he somehow made him drop his blade?

'Heya, brava!' the Wildman whispered. 'You want to dance with me?'

His men grinned when they heard that. Oh, the Wildman knew how to dance.

The beautiful youth tossed back his golden hair and, reaching out his arms on either side, he jangled the silver bracelets on his wrists. Rising on tiptoe like a dancer, he stalked towards the stranger, his knife sweeping softly before him.

The stranger made no move as he approached. His face showed nothing. How could a living being communicate so little? Surely this was a hollow man, his sliced veins would hiss stale air, he would fold like a paper bag –

The Wildman smiled and struck, so fast the blade seemed not to move, so precisely that the fine-honed edge would draw blood but not kill, the blood of the tall white-haired stranger, who was –

Gone.

No effort in it: a sigh of motion, high into the air, down again, and there he was, elsewhere, motionless once more. Not a flutter of his tunic, not a flurry of his headscarf. From stillness to stillness, through a perfect parabola of motion that was already fading from the memory, that was forgotten, that was impossible and therefore could not have happened.

The Wildman released a howl of rage.

'Kill, bravas! Kill!'

The spikers closed in on the stranger with swinging knives, and the stranger made no move, but the knives never touched him. The falling blades skidded on empty air. The Wildman saw this and began to experience a new emotion that he could not name. He feared it and courted it, knew it to be dangerous, knew he would go towards this danger.

What sort of man was this?

He heard a deep humming in his ears, and there was a mist before his eyes. These signs he knew. He sought a death. No more games now. He slid out his throwing spike, slender as a reed, and fixed his dark eyes on the tall stranger, on his chest, on the drab grey fabric of his tunic, on the patch of fabric over his heart, on the warp and woof of interwoven threads, on the space between the threads. He released the coiled spring of his arm, and the spike screamed through the air, true as lightning from cloud to cloud.

The stranger raised one hand, opening the fingers as he did so. His hand closed. When it opened again, there was the spike, caught in flight, and now dropping harmless to the ground.

The stranger's eyes looked up, and the Wildman saw an emptiness there that he could not escape. The stranger's hand turned again. Two fingers, close together, extended towards him. The Wildman felt the weight of those far fingers on his head, on his shoulders, on his chest: a weight he was powerless to resist.

He sank to his knees.

For a fragment of a second, gazing up at the stranger, he saw a giant before him, a sky man, his head haloed by the sun: so near that he was close enough for him to reach out and touch, and so far that he filled the world. Then the moment passed, and the Wildman could hear the priest mumbling, 'Shom be praised!', and could smell the fear on his men's skin, and saw how they shrank from the stranger. But he cared nothing for that. He was breathing cool air. He was drinking cool water. He was flooded with a new sensation – no, he had entered the flood, which was so much greater than him, he had dropped into it as he was accustomed to dive into the slow-flowing channels of the river, down to the cold depths – and now in the heat of the day his body was bathed in coolness, and he was washed clean of all his anger and all his pride. He was experiencing awe.

There came a high, far-off sound, like the cry of a bird. The stranger raised both arms above his head, pointing the forefingers of each hand skyward, and touched the fingertips together. As he did so, the wide sleeves of his tunic fell back to expose his bare forearms. There he stood, for a few short moments, his bare feet planted apart on the ground, making an arrow of his body, as if in answer to the cry. This was a signal, but saying what? To whom?

Then out of the trees there came two more strangers, similarly hooded and barefoot. Had they been there all the time, content to let their companion fight his battle alone? Or had they just arrived, making no sound, drawing no attention to their coming?

The first stranger lowered his arms, and his eyes met the Wildman's.

'Leave these people in peace,' he said. 'Seek your own peace.'

The beautiful youth was silent with amazement. He understood nothing of what was happening to him, except that this stranger possessed a greater power than he had ever known, and that this power gave him a giant stillness that must be this thing called peace. For all his beauty and his laughter, the Wildman had never known peace.

'Where?' he said. 'Where is peace?'

The tall, white-haired stranger gazed at him with his pale blue eyes, and the youth saw that they were not empty after all. They were brimming, overflowing, as immense as the sea.

'You will find peace,' came the answer, 'when you live in the Garden.'

The strangers left as noiselessly as they had come. The Wildman watched them until they were lost in the dappled shadows of the trees. Then he raised one arm, and, his bracelets flashing in the sun, he signalled to his men to return to the boat.

The *Lazy Lady* slipped out once more into the river currents. The Wildman stood once more on the prow, but he did not dance. His men watched him, filled with unease. They saw how his gaze reached far ahead, to some unknown adventure where they could not follow him.

For the Wildman, everything had changed. He had met the Noble Warriors. He wanted their power. He wanted their peace.

CHAPTER EIGHT

MORNING STAR

THE night before her sixteenth birthday, Morning Star stayed with her father on the hillside, and together, long before dawn, they watched for the rising of her namesake, the true morning star. Her father's brindle sheepdog, Amik, lying curled up by his feet, snuffled softly in her sleep. Her one remaining puppy from a litter born eight weeks ago, a little bundle of white fur called Lamb, was asleep in Morning Star's lap. Round them the sheep lay still and quiet, each on a patch of earth made warm by their own bodies. The night was clear, the air cold. Then low on the dark horizon, the small sure light for which they waited appeared, and began its steady climb, which would in turn be overtaken by the greater light of the new day.

'There you are,' said her father in his slow voice. 'Come to tell me the night won't last for ever.'

'I wish it would.'

'No, you don't. You don't wish any such thing.'

The puppy woke at the sound of their voices, and stretched, and poked his head out from under the rug. Seeing his mother, he went to her and nuzzled eagerly for a teat. Amik growled and rolled away. The puppy was supposed to be weaned. Morning Star felt for her father's hand under the rug that covered them both. She was thinking: I can't tell him. How can I tell him? It will break his heart.

For as long as she could remember she had been waiting to be sixteen. Now she could join the Nomana, as her mother had done. But how would her father bear the loneliness without her?

Goaded out of sleep by the puppy, Amik suddenly jumped up and shook her shaggy brown-and-white coat, and trotted away over the wet grass. The puppy sat with his nose raised high, looking after her with a hurt expression on his fuzzy white face. The sheep began to wake. As the light of the unseen sun strengthened in the sky, the brightness of the morning star began to fade. They watched the dawn in silence, father and daughter, as they had done countless times in the sixteen years of her young life.

'There you go,' said her father at last.

The morning star was no longer visible in the dawn sky. Usually when they watched the new day together, after he said, 'There you go,' he would look at her and smile and say, 'Here you are,' because it was her name too. But today he said no more.

He was one of the hill people, who had long made their living grazing stock on the lower slopes of the mountains. They were a quiet-spoken breed. They rarely travelled far, and kept themselves to themselves. His name was Arkaty. His wife, Morning Star's mother, had been a lowlander from the coast, where they named people differently.

67

Her name was Mercy. They had named their child according to her custom, not his; and so she had become Morning Star.

Morning Star in her turn had named all of Amik's five puppies; and now they were all gone to neighbouring homes but Lamb, the smallest of them all. Lamb turned out to have a poor sense of direction, and was constantly getting himself left behind and lost, and so, in this land of working dogs, he had not been picked. Morning Star loved him all the more for this, and worried about what would become of him after she was gone.

Right now, abandoned by Amik, Lamb turned about and trotted back to Morning Star. He scrambled on to her lap, and set about licking her ear. She sat still, and felt each nuzzle of his soft probing tongue, and smelt his warm milky smell, and worried about him.

'What will happen to Lamb?' she said aloud.

Her father glanced at her, and then looked away.

'He'll be found a home.'

'Can't he stay?'

'That one'll never be a sheepdog. Any dog of mine must work for his keep.'

'So what's to happen to him?'

'Someone'll take a liking to the pup. You don't get many come out all white like that.'

The sun was rising now. They got up and folded the rug and packed their night-bag, and set off down the steep sloping pasture towards home. Arkaty whistled to Amik, who fell obediently into place at his heel, and Morning Star carried the puppy in her arms.

As they reached the village track they met Filka the goatboy, leading his goats out for the day. Filka greeted them, staring at Morning Star with his slow stare, and then came closer to examine the puppy.

'Still got one left, then?' he said.

'Just the one,' said Morning Star, cradling the puppy close. She didn't like Filka: he was too long and thin, and he gawped too much, and she didn't like the way he smiled. Once, many years ago, she had come upon him catching earwigs and burning them in a candle flame. She didn't like earwigs, but she hated the look on his silent, staring face as he had watched them burn.

'Dog or bitch?' he said.

'Dog.'

'I could use a good dog.'

'You can't have him,' she said at once, and covered the puppy's head with one hand.

If she'd been thinking, she would have come up with an excuse. She would have said he was no good at herding, that he couldn't even find his own way home. But in her eagerness to make Filka go away, she spoke the simple truth; and Filka didn't like it.

'Why not?' he said. 'An't I good enough?'

'We're keeping him.'

'No, you're not. You got a dog.'

'You can't have him,' said Morning Star.

'I've a right,' said Filka stubbornly, turning to Arkaty. 'An't that so?'

Arkaty caught Morning Star's imploring look.

'My girl's taken a liking to the puppy,' he said, speaking gently, hoping to mollify the goatboy.

'And so've I,' said Filka. 'She don't need a dog. I could use a dog. I can pay.'

He reached into his bag and drew out some coins.

'See! What do you say to that?'

He leered triumphantly at Morning Star, as if the coins presented an unanswerable argument.

'We don't want your money,' she said.

The leer gave way to a scowl.

'My money not good enough?'

'Come on, Papa.' She set off down the track. 'We have to be getting home.'

'You think I'm not good enough for you!' shouted Filka after her. His face had gone red. 'You don't know about me! You just don't know!'

Morning Star went on down the path without looking back. Her father gave the goatboy an awkward nod, designed to be an apology, and followed after her.

'Your mam ran away from you!' shouted Filka. 'Your mam never loved you, and she ran away!'

It was the worst thing he could think of to hurl at her departing back. She made no reply. He turned at last and walked on up the hillside after his goats, talking angrily to himself as he went.

But Morning Star had heard him, and sharp tears pricked at her eyes. She shook her head to banish them, and then bent down to kiss the puppy's wet nose.

'He'd no call to say that,' said her father, now by her side. 'And you know it's not true.'

'Yes, Papa. I know.'

They reached their house, which stood on the edge of the village with its back to the hill stream. The last embers of yesterday's fire were still glowing in the stove. Arkaty brought in wood from the pile under the back eaves, while Morning Star put the puppy in the basket under the table, and set about cooking breakfast. Who would cook the porridge for her father after she was gone? She had been seeing to the household duties since she was five years old.

As the oatmeal bubbled in the pan, her father laid out his writing implements on his work desk. Pens, ink, blotter, quire of paper, all ranged on the left side; and open on a sloping stand before the chair at which he sat, the day's text. Arkaty did two jobs: he was a shepherd and he was a book-copier. The money he earned from this second job he put away for her. So all those hours bent over his desk tracing the letters with his neat and careful pen were for her; and she was planning to abandon him.

She told herself she would raise the matter over breakfast. But Amik came into the house, and the puppy tried again to suckle her, and Amik kept shuffling about in the most comical way to make her teats inaccessible to the

71

puppy, so that they started to laugh and talked about the dogs instead.

'Even so,' said her father, 'we'll have to find a home for the pup somewhere.'

'I know. Just not Filka.'

'You know your mama loved you dearly. You've got the letter.'

'Yes, Papa. I've got the letter.'

Her mother had left them when Morning Star was just three years old, at the height of the summer rains. When she was old enough to understand, her father gave her a letter her mother had written for her, that he had been keeping. The letter said:

My only beloved child. I weep as I write this. In leaving you I am leaving my best self. But I am called to another life, by a voice I must obey. I give you into the hands of the one Loving Mother of us all. May she watch over you and bring you joy. Forgive me if you can. If not, have mercy on me. My heart is breaking. I kiss you as you sleep. Goodbye, heart of my heart. Every day at sunrise I will send you my love, till the day I die. Goodbye, beautiful child of my youth. Until we meet again.

She knew the letter by heart, every word of it. She had only the faintest memory of her mother, but in that memory her mother was very beautiful, and her nearness flooded the child with sweet protective love. Her mother's name, Mercy, merging with the words in her letter – 'Have mercy on me' – had always seemed to her to be beautiful, loving, and fragile.

Of course she had asked her father why her mother had left them. He replied, 'She left to serve the All and Only, who is greater than you or me.'

In time Morning Star had come to understand that her mother had joined a community of holy people called the Nomana.

'It's the highest calling of all,' said her father. 'Many offer themselves, but few are chosen. We should be very proud that your mother is among their number.'

Morning Star was more than proud. Secretly, she had vowed that as soon as she was old enough, she too would join the Nomana. She had two reasons for believing they would accept her. One was that her mother had been chosen before her. The other was that she could see the colours.

Morning Star had been able to see the colours all her life. When she had been younger she had tried to tell other people about them, but they never understood. Even her father didn't understand. They thought she was talking about feelings, using the names of colours, in the manner of people who say, 'I'm in a black mood.' But what she saw was real colours. She didn't see them all the time, and they were mostly very faint, but they were there, just like the red headscarves of the hill women. The colours came from people, they came out of people, like a soft coloured mist that clung round them. Over the years she had learned the colours had a meaning. Angry people were rimmed with red. Sad people, or sick people, gave off a colour like straw-yellow, or sometimes a dull blue. People who were cheating or telling lies glowed orange. Kind people had a red colour, but a different red from the angry red, a soft rose-red. There were hundreds of colours, all with their shades of feelings, more than she could ever say; but then, there was no need to say. All she had to do was see, and feel.

She knew this was a gift, but it was a gift that brought her no advantages. Her friends and neighbours in the remote hillside village where she lived knew nothing about it. This made her feel strange, as if she didn't quite belong.

After breakfast was cleared away, and her father was at work on his copying, and she still hadn't spoken, she sat on the floor by the stove and played with the puppy. She had a short length of knotted twine, which she pulled along the floor, and the puppy hunted it, and pounced on it, and shook it by the throat until it was dead. As she played, she let her thoughts run free. What she thought about was the puzzle of the mask.

Morning Star believed she was quite different on the inside from the way she looked on the outside: so much so that it was as if she went about wearing a mask. Her mother had called her beautiful in her letter, and her father often called her beautiful too, but she knew it was not so. She had a pale, oval-shaped face, with a little nose and a little mouth, and timid pale blue eyes. The masked Morning Star was docile and useful, and lived her life without being noticed. But inside, the real Morning Star was quite different: much more knowing, and sharp, and critical. It wasn't that she was clever, in the sense of being able to talk cleverly. But all she had to do was look at someone and she knew what it was they most wanted or most feared. A lot of what people said was lies, or at best a kind of noise designed to distract. What they actually did depended on what they wanted and what they feared.

Take the goatboy, Filka. When he had asked for the puppy, his colours had gone a browny red, one of the early stages of anger. She had seen the resentment in him, the readiness to take offence, the fear of rejection. It was all in his colours. He didn't want a dog, he wanted to be given the respect that he felt his neighbours denied him.

All this Morning Star understood, because she had taught herself to trust the colours and ignore the chatter. But no one apart from her father knew this about her. They thought she was silent because she was shy. They thought she was sweet but dull, like a bun.

'What do they know, little Lamb?' she said to the puppy.

The puppy, responding to the affection in her voice, pranced up on his little hind legs and tried to lick her face.

'Maybe you can see the colours,' she said to him, bending down. 'Maybe all animals can.'

Morning Star often wondered whether her mother could see the colours. Her father said no, she had never spoken to him about seeing colours. But he said it in a hesitating way. When she pressed, he told her that there had been times when her mother had been troubled, and had spoken of a darkness that came in the day. It was as if for her the shadow of night fell over the light of day, and she alone was lost in the darkness. Then the shadow would pass, like clouds blown by the wind, and she would smile again.

'When the darkness came over her, there was nothing I could do. I don't believe she even heard me.'

'Poor Mama. What was it that made her sad?'

'That I never did know. Perhaps she knew her home here wasn't where she was meant to be.'

'So she's happy now.'

'Oh, she'll be singing like a bird now. It was all she ever really wanted.'

Now it seemed to Morning Star it was all she wanted too. She had learned all that could be learned, from travellers who passed through the village. She knew that she must make the long journey to the holy island of Anacrea. She knew that she must present herself there on the day of the annual Congregation. She knew that this day was due in three days' time. Therefore she must begin the journey the morning after tomorrow.

Her father would expect her to leave home soon, to take up a job, or to marry. Most of the village girls married at sixteen. But even so, she dreaded the moment of telling him, and kept putting it off, all through the day.

Then at last the day was ending, and the sun was dropping in the sky, and her father was preparing to climb back up to the hill pastures to watch over the sheep.

'Maybe I'll come with you again, Papa,' she said.

This was not usual, for her to spend two nights running on the hillside. But her father just nodded and said, 'As you wish.'

She took the puppy with her, as before. And so they set off with rug and bag up the steeply sloping path.

Near the sheep fields, in the fading evening light, they came upon the goatboy again. He was standing by the track, still as a statue, staring into the far distance. He seemed unaware of their approach. Morning Star caught sight of an unfamiliar colour round him, a silvery glow that made her shiver. Puzzled, she kept her eyes on him as she went by. She was still watching him when suddenly he twisted his head round towards her and stared directly into her eyes.

'Stop!' he cried. 'Stand still, where you are!'

She stopped. His command sounded so urgent, so unlike him. His eyes were fixed on her, but in some strange way she felt he still didn't see her.

'*They* want to see you,' he said.

'Who? Who wants to see me?'

'You interest them.'

He stared at her, eyes popping, shining with that disturbing silvery glow.

'You're mad,' she said.

She felt the puppy wriggle in her arms, and she was about to move on, when he shuddered all up and down his body, and his expression changed. It was as if he was waking from a trance. He saw her bewildered look, and he leered at her.

'See?' he said. 'Didn't know about *them*, did you?'

'About who?'

'I got special friends.'

The puppy gave a sharp yap. Filka's eyes flicked down. Before she knew what he was doing he had reached out one hand, seized the puppy, and pranced away from her. It was so quick and unexpected that he was right over on the far side of the track before she could react.

'Give him back!' she cried.

'I got him now!' he replied, taunting her. He held the bleating puppy high in the air above his head.

She took a step towards him, but he danced back, away from her.

'You come after me, I'll smash him!' he cried. 'I'll smash his head on a stone!'

'No!' Morning Star came to a stop. 'Don't hurt him!'

The puppy was squealing and struggling in the goatboy's big-knuckled hand. Amik stood, ears pricked forward, growling softly. Morning Star, choking with fear and anger, turned to her father.

'Papa! He can't!'

'You let me be,' called Filka. 'You got a dog already. This dog's mine now.'

Arkaty tried to calm him down with his gentle voice.

'Come along now, Filka. This is no way to do things. We're all friends and neighbours.'

'I'm not good enough for you,' retorted Filka. 'Don't think I don't know. Funny-in-the-head Filka, you say.

But I got special friends.'

Arkaty made a move towards him.

'Let me be!' cried Filka. 'Or I kill the little dog!'

And he really did swing the puppy down towards an outcrop of rock; but he stopped short when Morning Star screamed. Arkaty lowered his hand.

'This is not kind,' he said reproachfully.

'Not kind!' jeered Filka. 'When was anyone ever kind to Filka? But I got special friends now. So you can all just let me be!'

With these words, he turned and ran off up the hillside, into the deepening twilight.

Morning Star burst into bitter sobs.

'He's so horrible! So horrible!'

Her father put his arm round her and comforted her as best as he could. She clung to him and sobbed and sobbed.

'I'll go and have a word with him tomorrow,' he said.

'He's hateful, hateful, hateful.'

'He's a cranky lad, I know. But he's good to his goats. He'll be kind to the little pup.'

'I never even said goodbye.'

There was nothing to be done for now. They climbed the path on into the sheep field, and there her father settled her down and pulled the rug over her and let her cry out all her tears. When at last she fell silent he kissed her wet cheeks and said to her, 'So who else do you need to say goodbye to, then?'

She looked up at him, blinking her tear-stained eyes.

'Are you going to tell me?' he said. 'Or is it to be mumbo-dumbo all the way, until you go?'

'Go where?'

'To your holy island.'

'You know!'

'How could I not know? You're my own child, aren't you?'

'Oh, Papa! How can I ever leave you? Say you don't want me to go, and I won't go.'

'Oh, so you won't go. And what then?'

'I'll stay here with you.'

'And what will you do here with me, all the rest of your life? Nothing, is what you'll do. No, my lambling, you go, and see what's to be seen, and come back one day, and tell me all about it.'

'How will you get along without me?'

'Am I new-born? Didn't I get along for almost thirty years before you showed yourself?'

'Won't you be lonely?'

'No doubt I shall. And maybe you'll be lonely too.'

'Yes. I will.'

She put her arms round him under the rug and hugged him close, and was filled with love for him.

'So you'll be off the morning after next, I think.'

'Oh, Papa. You know everything.'

'And it's a long way to your holy island, and a dangerous way to get there.'

'I'll not come to harm.'

'You'll not come to harm because you'll not go alone.'

'Not go alone? But you can't leave the flock.'

'And that is why I've arranged for you to have a companion on the road.'

In this way, to her astonishment, Morning Star learned that her father had been quietly preparing for this time. He had made arrangements to hire an escort to go with his daughter all the way to the holy island. So all the time she had been fearing to break it to him that she was leaving, he had been planning her departure.

'What sort of companion?'

'A man who knows how to chase away any spikers who want to cause trouble. The book factor is arranging it all. The book factor is bringing him.'

'Papa! How much are you having to pay for this?'

'That's of no importance. What else is my money for?'

'But I don't want a companion. Truly I don't.'

'Then take him for my sake. You're safe with me, and you'll be safe on the holy island, but between the one and the other there's bad men and mad men and all sorts else.'

She hugged him even tighter under the rug.

'I shouldn't leave you.'

'The sooner the better,' he said. 'I shall be able to do as I please for once in my life.'

But she could see the colours glowing round him, and there mingled with the rose-red of his love for her was the darker violet of heartache. She closed her eyes, not wanting to see; but even with her eyes closed, she felt his pain.

'You're too good to me.'

'And why shouldn't I be?' he said. 'Being good to my child is the same as being good to myself.'

CHAPTER NINE

PARTING WISDOM

THE book factor arrived punctually the next morning, bent low under the weight of his pack of books. He carried his pack in his own peculiar way, taking the full weight on a strap that went over his forehead. Thus laden, he would tilt himself forward and, balanced by the weight on his back, would proceed at a steady trot that looked as if he was forever running to stop himself falling on his face.

'Here I am again,' he declared, letting his pack sink to the ground. 'And glad of the rest, believe you me.'

With him was the biggest man Morning Star had ever seen in her life. The book factor watched Arkaty's face, and saw with satisfaction his expression of awe.

'Well, old friend. Have I done right by you?'

'Right enough.'

The big man held out a big hand and boomed out in a big voice.

'Barban at your service.'

'Trained as an axer,' said the factor with pride. 'Retired from active duty now.'

'You're most welcome, sir,' said Arkaty.

'And this must be the little lady.' Barban stooped down to place his face at the level of Morning Star's eyes, and showed her his strong white teeth. 'We'll get you to your destination, little lady, as safe as if you was still at home.'

'Thank you,' said Morning Star. To her dismay she realised that she disliked him intensely.

'You'll take a glass before you go?' said her father.

'I never say no to a glass,' said the big man, and laughed a booming laugh.

They went into the house, and Arkaty poured out four glasses of his most special wine. Morning Star knew the bottle had been saved to drink on her last day. Barban, who did not know this, drank down his glassful in a single swallow, as if to show what a big throat he had. Her father, wanting the moment to last, raised his glass to his daughter and gave her a sweet smile.

'To you, my star.'

She raised her glass to his, and they clinked.

'And to you, Papa.'

Barban put down his glass, tore open his jacket, and bared his naked torso at them.

'Hit me!' he cried. 'Go on, hit me! Any of you. Hit me anywhere you like.'

They looked at him in surprise. He was standing with his legs apart and his arms pulled back, inviting a blow to his bare chest or stomach. A gold medal hung round his neck, with an image of the sun on it.

'Hard as rock! Go on! Hit me!'

'I'm confident you're a suitable escort for my daughter,' said Arkaty.

'Try the goods before you buy,' said Barban. 'You're paying for the best. I want you to know it.'

'I'm not really accustomed to hitting people,' said Arkaty.

Barban turned to the book factor.

'You, sir. Take a swing at me. Do your very worst.'

'Well,' said the factor. 'If you think I should.'

He struck the big man lightly on the abdomen.

'No, no!' cried Barban. 'I didn't say tickle me. I said hit me.'

Morning Star found the whole display ludicrous. She put down her glass. The book factor hit Barban again, rather harder. The big man laughed.

'Still can't feel you!'

'Let me try,' said Morning Star.

She reached out her fingers, found a plump fold of flesh just above his hips, and pinched hard. Barban let out a shrill shriek of pain.

'Ow-ow-ow!' he screamed.

'I think he felt that,' said Morning Star, her eyes round with innocence.

'That was a pinch!' He glared at her, as he rubbed the hurting flesh. 'That wasn't a hit, it was a pinch.'

'I think you should apologise, my dear.'

'I'm sorry, Mr Barban.'

'Only girls pinch,' he said bitterly.

'That's all right, then,' she said. 'I'm quite sure we won't be attacked on the road by girls.'

The big man buttoned his jacket up again. He turned to Arkaty, no longer smiling.

'You have the money?'

'Yes. I have it here.'

He took a money-box and tipped its contents out into a small bag. Morning Star realised he was proposing to pay out the full fee there and then.

'Papa,' she said, 'I'm sure the usual practice is to pay half the fee now, and the other half when the job is done.'

'Is that so?' said her father. 'Is that the usual practice?'

'Usual when there's no trust,' said Barban. He threw an angry look at Morning Star. His colours had gone orange-red, the very worst combination.

'Perhaps you would rather not accept the job,' she said.

'Oh, no! You don't catch me like that! I've come a long way to be here. I'll do my part, and I expect to be paid for it.'

'So you shall,' said Arkaty.

'You don't seem to realise,' went on Barban, still crossly rubbing at the pinch-mark on his side, 'that you are hiring the very best in personal protection.' He pulled out the medal that hung round his neck. 'See that? That means axer! Yes, sir. I was one of the mighty axers of the empire of Radiance!'

'I'm afraid I don't know what that is,' said Morning Star.

'Axer!' exclaimed Barban indignantly. 'The name that strikes dread into the hearts of all men! Axer! Axer!'

Morning Star gazed back at him with no visible signs of dread in her heart.

'Papa,' she said, 'give Mr Barban half his fee, and give me the other half. I will pay it when we get to Anacrea.'

The big man gave an angry shrug.

'Do as you please. It's all one to me.'

'If our friend is happy to accept the arrangement,' said the book factor, 'it is perfectly usual. The fee is substantial.'

'The best costs more,' said Barban sullenly.

So it was settled. Morning Star watched as her father counted out the money, and was shocked by the amount. Two hundred shillings! Her father earned a shilling a week for his copying. How could this man be worth so much?

Arkaty put one hundred gold shillings into a little money pouch and gave it to his daughter. The rest he gave to the big man.

'You'll take good care of her, won't you?'

'So long as she takes good care of my money.'

'It's a dangerous world.'

Arkaty and the book factor then completed their own business; and so at last the time had come to part. Morning Star fetched her bag, which had been packed and ready for days. The book factor heaved on the broad strap of his load, and went out on to the path, beckoning the big man to follow him. Father and daughter were left for a last moment together.

'So it seems like you're on your way,' said her father.

'But I'll come back. I'll come back to tell you all about it.'

'As to coming back, let that fall as it may.'

'And maybe I'll bring Mama with me.'

'And again, maybe not.'

He gazed at her with his shrewd and gentle eyes.

'There's those that think we hill people a little foolish and backward in our ways,' he said. 'And I'm not saying it isn't so. But don't trouble yourself to tell them they're wrong. There's all sorts of uses to being thought foolish.'

'You're not foolish. You're the wisest person I know.'

'And how many people do you know?'

'So you must give me some wisdom, to carry with me.'

'So now you're wanting wisdom?'

He made a show of fashioning great thoughts. Then he spoke with gravity, and slowly, giving his advice.

'Never miss breakfast. Know more than you say. Leave rooms quietly.'

She kissed him, and he held her close for a moment or two, and both knew that all that needed to be said had been said. Even though they had their arms tight around each other, there opened up a gap between them. For Morning Star, this was the beginning of what she thought of as her real life. For her father, it was an ending.

So they separated. Her father reached into his pocket and took out a little roll of black cloth tied up with string.

'There's for you,' he said.

She untied it, and found inside a braid of pure white lamb's wool. She put it to her face, and felt its softness, and smelled its smell.

'A tickle of home,' he said. 'In case you forget.'

'I won't forget.'

She went outside. There was the book factor, his pack on his back, the strap over his brow. He now tipped himself forward, and had no option but to set off. Barban strode along by his side. Morning Star followed.

She looked back once, and saw her father still standing in the doorway, solid and silent as ever, watching her, with Amik by his side. She raised her hand to wave, but he did not wave back. He stood there, glowing rose-red with his love for her, and all around the rim of his aura was the tinge of deep violet, because his heart was breaking; but there was nothing she could do. So she lowered her hand, and walked on.

On the edge of the village, where the pathway forked, the book factor bade them farewell and turned north. Morning Star and her escort kept to the track that ran due west.

As they went along, they heard the bleating of goats; and there on the steep hillside above was Filka, leading his flock down the mountain. He had a bag over one shoulder, and poking out of the bag was the furry white head of the puppy. He increased his pace when he saw Morning Star, so that he would reach the track before she passed by.

At first Morning Star pretended she hadn't noticed him, because she didn't want to give him the satisfaction of knowing how much he distressed her. But he leered at her as she came closer, and put one hand on the puppy's head, as if to say, 'No, you can't have him back.' Then, getting no reaction, he held the puppy's head in his hand and turned it from side to side, so that Lamb too seemed to be saying to her, 'No, no, no.'

Morning Star felt herself tremble with the intensity of the anger rising within her. She gave a low whistle in the direction of the village. Then she walked directly up to Filka, taking care to make no threatening gestures, and spoke to him in a humble and pleading voice.

'You will be kind to him, won't you?' she said.

'So long as others is kind to me,' said Filka, grinning.

Behind her she heard the patter of a dog running from the village. She glanced to her right, and saw Barban waiting.

'Oh, I'll be kind to you,' she said.

All at once she stumbled, fell against him, and screamed out, as if he had struck her.

'Don't hurt me!' she cried. 'Don't hurt me!'

Barban acted with gratifying force and speed. He seized the goatboy and jerked him high in the air.

'You want trouble?'

'No – no – no – !' stuttered the terrified Filka.

'You touch her, I snap you in two!'

He threw him back down on to the ground. The goatboy fell with a thud, and lay there, whimpering. Morning Star pulled his bag free and lifted the puppy out, just as Amik came bounding up to her side.

'Go, little Lamb!'

She pushed the puppy at Amik.

'Home, Amik! Home!'

Obediently the sheepdog turned and headed back to the village. The little puppy trotted bleating after her.

'Home, Lamb! Home!'

Morning Star didn't take her eyes off the puppy until he was safe back in the village. It wasn't far. For a flicker of a moment, she thought she might change her mind, and follow Lamb home. Her father would never think the worse of her for it; he would just be happy to have her back. Those few simple houses, straggling along the hill stream beneath the mountains, were the only world she knew. But there was Barban, standing over the goatboy, scowling and prodding at him with the toe of one boot.

'Do I let him go?'

'Yes. Let him go.'

The village was the past; as was the goatboy, and even little Lamb. She knew she couldn't go back, any more than she could bring back yesterday. So she turned her eyes away to the west, and set off once more down the track.

CHAPTER TEN

THE AXER REPAID

'SO now you've seen an axer in action,' said Barban, 'I hope you're satisfied.'

'Yes,' said Morning Star. 'Thank you.'

This wasn't quite enough for the big man.

'I'm surprised you've not heard of axers,' he said. 'Axers are famous the length and breadth of the empire.'

'The empire of Radiance is far away,' said Morning Star. 'We hill people keep to ourselves.'

They were making steady progress along the ridge way, rising and falling with the undulation of the hills. Behind them in the hazy distance rose the mountains. Before them, the plains. By now Morning Star was further west than she had ever been in all her life. She tried not to look back, not to think of home; reaching forward with her eyes and her mind across those plains to the faraway forested banks of the Great River, and down the river all the way to the sea. She had seen rivers before, but she had never seen the sea. Hard to imagine looking out over a distance that has no markers, that goes on seemingly for ever. And hard to imagine the place to which she was travelling, the rocky island in the river mouth, where her mother was waiting for her.

Until we meet again.

'The empire of Radiance is never far away,' said Barban. 'If you were to go to the lake city, you'd see a thing or two you've not seen before. There's nothing like it in all the world. There's houses there with golden tiles! Roof tiles made of real gold!'

Morning Star said nothing to this. She wasn't interested in the empire of Radiance, or the city by the northern lake. But after an hour or so in which they had walked in silence, her escort had begun to talk, and ever since had kept up a ceaseless chatter.

'I expect you're thinking, Don't thieves come in the night and steal the gold from the roofs? But what would you say if I told you there are no thieves in Radiance?'

Morning Star said nothing at all. Barban didn't mind. It suited him to conduct both sides of the dialogue.

'You'd say, how can that be? And I would tell you, because no one breaks the law in Radiance. And you would say, surely, Barban, there are evil-doers everywhere. Why don't the evil-doers do their evil in Radiance? And I would answer you, because of the axers!'

This was always his conclusion: the fearsome glory of the mighty axers of Radiance.

'We axers trained every day,' he told her. 'We did rock-running – that's running races, carrying great rocks. And log-splitting. Not with our axes. Oh, no! With our fists!'

'Had you mislaid your axes?'

'Mislaid? No, not at all. That was the training. To

strike with the fist, but with the power of an axe!'

He struck the air before him.

'We axers could stun an ox with a single punch.'

'Poor ox! Why did you do that?'

'Training! All training! Do you have any idea how much armour an axer wears? Or how heavy it is?'

'None at all.'

'The chest guard alone would be heavier than you are. Thick iron plates, overlapping each other, stitched on to heavy canvas. Like wearing two smallish adults on your back. Imagine that!'

'Very peculiar,' said Morning Star.

'And the helmet. Put that on and you know about it! Solid iron, sits on your shoulder pads, heavy as a child.'

'So you go about wearing two smallish adults and a child?'

'Now you're getting the idea.'

'Very peculiar indeed.'

'That way, when you go out on a strike, no one can touch you. Great Sun, that's a sight to see! When you're an axer on strike with your team about you, you're a god come down to earth! One sweep of your chain and nothing's left standing. The little people scream and run, I can tell you! It's a sight to see, when an axer's on the march.'

He stomped down the track reliving the moment, sweeping the air before him with an imaginary chain.

'Get the height of the chain just so, you could slice the little people's heads off, plop! plop! plop!'

'You must have liked that,' said Morning Star.

'Best time of my life,' he replied. 'I was never happier.'

'So why did you leave?'

The smile fell from his face. The sweeping arm dropped back down by his side.

'Retirement,' he said.

'Oh, I see. You're old.'

'I am not *old*!' He spoke with sudden bitterness. 'Look at me! Do I look old? I'm stronger than ever! Watch this!'

He jumped down off the track and planted himself before a tree that grew in the ditch. Raising his right fist, he took aim at one of the lower branches.

'Ya-*ha*!' he cried.

His fist struck the branch close to the trunk, where it was as thick as his thigh. With a rending crash, the branch tore away from the tree, and fell to the ground.

'Does that look old? Does it?'

He glared at Morning Star. She looked down at his right hand. The knuckles were raw and bleeding.

'That must have hurt,' she said.

'Didn't feel a thing. Look at that! Look at it!' He dragged up the heavy branch and thrust it in her face. 'Could an old man have done that?'

'No.'

'Well, then. Maybe you'll agree now that I'm worth two hundred shillings.'

'That was my father's agreement. It has nothing to do with me.'

'Except you've got half my money.'

'Deliver me safe to Anacrea, and it's yours.'

They walked on. Barban discreetly nursed his bruised right hand. When they reached a stream, Morning Star said, 'You'd better wash that hand.'

He knelt and bathed the bruises, wincing as he did so.

'Of course,' he said, 'if I'd been an axer on a strike, I'd have been wearing armour-plated gloves.'

'So they don't let you keep your armour when you retire?'

'No,' he said. 'You get a medal.'

He pulled it out from where it hung round his neck: the sun in splendour, issuing rays to the world.

'That's the sun, isn't it?'

'That's the Radiant Power. The source of all life.'

'You believe that?'

'Of course. Look!'

He shaded his eyes and pointed up at the sun burning in the cloudless sky above.

'What could be more powerful than that?'

'The one who made it.'

'Who could make the sun? No, trust me. That's where it begins and where it ends. The Radiant Power rules the world, and the king and the priests of Radiance are its favoured sons. You know how I know that?'

'How?'

'Because nowhere is as powerful, or as rich, or as glorious, as the empire of Radiance!'

'I see.'

'So that's the proof of it. The strongest people have the strongest god. It stands to reason.'

'I see.'

They walked on in silence for a little while. Barban was feeling better now. It seemed to him that this odd moon-faced child was at last beginning to understand the realities of the greater world.

'Look who we have here,' he said.

Ahead of them, approaching them down the track, was a little family of spikers: a scrawny woman, a man with tired eyes, and a two-wheeled cart drawn by a half-starved bullock. Two small children rode in the cart, on top of what looked like the family's entire worldly goods.

'Road scum!' said Barban with disgust.

As they passed, he struck the bullock to make it pull off the track.

'Out of our way!'

'Stop that!' said Morning Star. 'Leave them alone! It's their road as much as ours.'

'They're spikers! Homeless gutter-filth!'

'Forgive my companion's rudeness,' said Morning Star to the spikers. 'He's an ignorant man.'

She led the bullock back on to the track, watched in a cowed silence by the spiker family. She didn't need to study their colours to know that they were frightened and hungry.

'Who are you calling ignorant?' growled Barban.

'You,' she said.

She felt in her money bag and gave the spiker woman a

gold shilling. The man bobbed his head in mute gratitude. The woman held the coin tight, and tears welled up in her eyes, but she had no words. Who knew how far they had come? Perhaps they even spoke some other language. The roads were full of sad little families like this, driven from their homes by war or plague or famine.

Barban couldn't believe his eyes.

'That's my money! You're giving away my money!'

'It's not your money.'

'You gave money to spikers!'

'It's my own money. I do as I please.'

Morning Star walked on, to force the big man to follow after her and so leave the spiker family in peace. One gold shilling was a substantial sum to such poor people. It would buy them food and lodging for the next week.

'You're no better than a fool!' said Barban.

'I'd rather be a fool than a brute.'

'Give me my money! Right now!'

'No.'

'Then I stop here!'

He came to a stop, and stood with his trunk-like arms folded across his chest, bristling with injured pride. Morning Star simply went on walking.

'You come back here!'

She did not even look round.

'You stupid, wicked girl!'

He came striding after her, and seized her with one great hand.

'Give me my money!'

She clutched the bag tight to her chest. He shook her violently.

'That's mine, and I'll have it!'

He squeezed her arm in his powerful grip. She winced with pain, but did not let go.

'Do I have to rip your arm off?'

'Yes! Go ahead! Rip my arm off!'

'I could crush you like an ant!'

'Go on! Crush me! Kill me!'

For a moment it seemed he would. Then he gave her a push that sent her staggering away down the track, and growled at her.

'Don't think I won't!'

Morning Star calmed her pounding heart and made her face smooth. She held her head high, to show he had not frightened her.

'You can go now,' she said. 'I don't want your protection any more.'

'I go where you go,' the axer replied, 'till I get my money.'

After that, they kept well apart from each other, and did not speak. Barban walked ahead, making no concession to the girl's shorter legs, and from time to time she was forced to break into a run to keep up. But she was too proud and too angry to ask him to slow down.

The big axer was a good hundred paces ahead of Morning Star when they came to the river. This was not yet the Great

River that flowed down to Anacrea, but it was too wide and too deep to cross on foot. A canoe was moored by the river bank, and there were two boatmen lounging beside it beneath a makeshift sun shelter. Even from this distance Morning Star could tell from their colours that something was not right about the boatmen. She saw Barban reach them, and speak to them. She saw them nod in response, and unhitch the canoe. The closer she came, the surer she was that the boatmen were not what they pretended to be.

Barban now turned towards her, waiting with open impatience for her to catch up. He reached out a hand and snapped his fingers.

'Money!' he said.

He meant money to pay the boatmen, as she well understood. But she stopped short.

'No,' she said. 'Something's wrong.'

The orange glow that hovered round the boatmen was now all too clear.

Barban lumbered towards her.

'Wrong?' he said. 'Why should anything be wrong?'

Morning Star backed away, but he was too quick for her. His hand shot out and seized her bag and ripped it from her, snapping its cord. He ran back to the riverside and jumped into the canoe. The boatman with the mooring rope followed him. The canoe shot out into mid-river.

Barban held up the bag in triumph.

'Nobody gives my money to spikers!' he called out to her. 'Nobody cheats an axer!'

Morning Star was speechless. She had been so focused on the boatmen that she had failed to guard against Barban.

'Show more respect next time!' he crowed from the canoe. 'Nobody insults an axer!'

The boatman with the paddle turned the canoe upstream, while the second boatman rummaged for a bundle in the bottom of the canoe. Morning Star was still bewildered. The boatmen's colours had been strong and clear, even before Barban had spoken to them. How could she have misread the situation so completely?

'Evil little witch!' shouted Barban. 'I hope the spikers get you!'

The second boatman gave a flip of his arm to unloose the bundle, and a net swooped upwards like a wave, and fell down over Barban even as he called out his taunts. The net was weighted all round its edges, and the man who threw it was skilled in his business. Before Barban knew what was happening the net had closed tight all round him, and dragged him down into the canoe bottom. There, both working together, making swift, well-practised movements, the boatmen covered him with a heavy blanket, and pinned him down with iron bars. Trussed, bundled and caged, the bewildered axer could be heard howling out his muffled rage as the canoe carried him away upriver.

Morning Star had no idea who the boatmen were, or why they wanted Barban; but her faith in her colours was restored. Barban had schemed to rob her, certainly; but the boatmen were cleverer schemers and robbers than he. Now already the canoe was gone from sight. Slowly the rapid beating of her heart became calmer, and she turned her thoughts to her own situation.

She had no regrets about the loss of her escort. Nor was she afraid to continue her journey alone. She had no fear of travelling spikers, and, as for robbers, she trusted to her acute senses to keep her out of trouble. But with Barban had gone all her money. All she had left was the clothes she was wearing, and the little twist of lamb's wool that had been her father's parting gift.

She took it out of her pocket now, and pressed it to her cheek.

'I'm sorry to lose your money, Papa,' she whispered. 'I know how hard you worked for it. But you've no cause to worry about me. I'll find my way to Anacrea, one way or another. And then I'll be with Mama again.'

PART TWO

THE SURROGATE

They are watching.

Day by day their bodies grow weaker.

Day by day their minds grow stronger.

Their will reaches out to the little people. Their will finds those who know how to obey.

For the old ones, this is a matter of life and death.

Their life. Everyone else's death.

CHAPTER ELEVEN

HATE TRAINING

'UH! Uh! Who do we hate?'

Bam-bam! Ba-ba-ba-bam!

'Nomana! Nomana!'

Ba-ba-bam! Ba-ba-bam!

Radiant Vision, son of Radiant Harvest, inheritor of the imperial throne, priest-king and ruler of the empire of Radiance, and most favoured son of the Great Power above, stood with his legs apart, beating with his fists on a drum, his face red and sweating with effort, and yelled at the top of his voice.

'Uh! Uh! Who will we kill?'

Bam-bam! Ba-ba-ba-bam!

'Nomana! Nomana!'

Ba-ba-bam! Ba-ba-bam!

Only one other person was in the room with the king, and that was his personal secretary, Soren Similin. He was a strikingly ugly young man. With his long narrow nose, his bulging eyes, and his prominent ears, his face looked as if it had been put together out of spare parts, none of which matched. But when he spoke, as he did now, it was in an unexpectedly sweet and musical voice.

'Jab out their eyes, Radiance.'

The king took his cue, hammering on the drum.

'Uh! Uh! Jab out their eyes!'

Bam-bam! Ba-ba-ba-bam!

'Nomana die! Nomana die!'

Ba-ba-ba-bam! Ba-ba-ba-bam!

This hate training was the secretary's own idea, introduced by him shortly after his arrival at the court of Radiance. Similin was an outlander, raised in the poor north, with none of the rights and privileges of the citizens of the empire. His rapid rise to favour with the king had astonished all at court. The High Priest in particular had done his best to warn the king against putting too much trust in the ugly young man.

'We know nothing about him, Radiance. We have no idea what has brought him here, or what it is he wants.'

'Yes, we do,' retorted the king. 'He wants the Nomana destroyed. It's no secret.'

'But why, Radiance?'

'They refuse to worship the Radiant Power. They think they're superior to everyone else. But I mean to teach them who's superior!'

The High Priest frowned and shook his head.

'We have found it best to leave the Nomana alone, Radiance. They do have powers – '

'Tricks!' shouted the king. 'Tricks! I'll show them tricks!'

So the High Priest and the rest of the court were obliged to look on as the seed planted by the ugly young outlander blossomed into an obsession with the king. Whatever doubts and questions they had about this, they had to admit that the hate training did wonders for the king's morale. He emerged from each session glowing and invigorated.

'Uh! Uh! Rip out their hearts!'

Bam-bam! Ba-ba-ba-bam!

'Nomana die! Suffer and die!'

Ba-ba-ba-bam! Ba-ba-ba-bam!

Within three weeks of Soren Similin's arrival in Radiance, the priest-king declared it was his imperial will that Anacrea be destroyed.

On the day that this new policy was made public, Soren Similin returned to his modest quarters and dropped to his knees. He touched his forehead to the ground, and murmured aloud, 'Have I done well, mistress?'

You have done well, came the reply that only he could hear.

'All that I do, I do for you.'

You are the cup into which we pour our wine.

'I brim with your fullness.'

The harvest time approaches. The little people will kneel before you and call you their lord.

'My power will be your power, mistress. I am your surrogate. You command me as the heart commands the hand.'

Your obedience is pleasing to us, said the soft sweet voice.

'Am I deserving, mistress?'

You are deserving.

Then the sweetness came upon him. Swooning in bliss, he received his reward.

The time of the evening offering was now approaching. The sun was descending over the Great Basin Lake. In the royal temple of Radiance the priests and the court officials were assembling to perform their ritual duties. The keeper of the Corona was dressing the sunflower heads in the great fan-shaped structure that would sit on the king's shoulders. The royal wives were entering, one by one, each shepherding her single child. The procession of three crimson-robed priests, tinkling their little silver bells, was on its way to the holding tank to collect the evening's tribute. And six levels below in the temple square, the broad plaza that ran down to the shores of the lake, the people of Radiance were gathering to gossip and spend their money on the trinkets for sale from the wandering vendors.

The High Priest, arrayed in his golden robe, waited impatiently for the hate session to end. He could hear the king's great bellows of rage coming through the closed doors. Unaware that he was doing so, the High Priest curled his lips and murmured, 'Dangerous nonsense!' and, 'Ugly, ugly!'

A blood-curdling yell from beyond the doors signalled the climax of the session. The doors opened and the king came hobbling out. He was overweight, and his knee-joints gave him pain; but for all that, he was beaming.

'We'll see them squirm yet,' he said, rubbing his hands.

'We've a surprise in store for them! Eh, Similin?'

'Yes, Radiance,' said the secretary, following a few paces behind with lowered gaze.

'Let it be soon!' said the king.

'Not long now, Radiance,' murmured the secretary.

The king nodded at his wives, who all dimpled and dipped as he passed, and, reaching out his arms on either side, he prepared to be dressed in his ceremonial garments. The High Priest spoke low to the secretary.

'What is this surprise?'

'I am no more than the king's humble servant,' said Soren Similin.

'Something to do with the Nomana, I suppose.'

'Forgive me, holiness. The king commands my silence.'

The tinkle of silver bells sounded again as the crimson-robed priests passed by, now leading the evening's tribute: a man dressed in white, his eyes blank, his steps uncertain. The priests held him by the arms on each side, to help him on his way. The High Priest saw, and shook his head. The tribute had been doped again. Gone were the glory days when the tributes were prisoners captured in war, who went to their deaths with their heads held high, screaming defiance at the world.

As for the king's secretary, and his pious silence, the High Priest reckoned he could guess the secret easily enough. The only surprise the king could be so eager for these days was news of the destruction of the Nomana. How this frog-like young man could give the king hope of such a thing was another matter. The Nomana were not so easy to destroy.

The Keeper of the Cape now presented the heavy gold-embroidered garment to the Handler of the Cape, who placed it on the king's back. Then the Keeper of the Corona gave the heavy object to the Handler of the Corona, who lowered it on to the king's shoulders. The stiff fan-like structure rose up behind the king's head, giving him a magnificent halo of fresh-picked sunflower heads, all golden petals and honey-coloured seeds.

The High Priest checked that the tribute was now in place, and he gave a sign to the temple choir. The choristers were lined up at the back of the broad open terrace outside, where the king would shortly present himself to his people. The choir now began to sing, their faces to the setting sun as it sank towards the waters of the Great Basin Lake.

'O Radiance! O Radiance!

Our lord, our life, our light!

Receive from us! Receive from us!

Our tribute for this night!'

Down in the packed square below, the people stopped chattering and turned their attention to the temple rock. This massive granite shaft towered five hundred feet above the lake, and leaned a little outwards over the water, towards the west. All up its eastern side the great temple had been built, terrace after terrace, rising to the highest level, which was just below the summit of the rock. There on the summit stood the three red-robed priests, holding

112

the tribute between them. Soon now, when the setting sun touched the water, the offering would be made. Then night would fall. But the people of Radiance need have no fear: so long as the offering was made, the sun would rise again. The Radiant Power would shine on them, and bring them riches and victories. Had it not been so for a hundred years? Was Radiance not the greatest power in the land?

The royal party now emerged on to the high terrace, to cheers from the people below. The king waved to the crowd, and then took up his ritual position, facing the setting sun, and spread his arms. This caused the gold cape to open out like the wings of a celestial bird, glowing gold and scarlet in the river of light cast by the sun over the surface of the lake.

The choir sang ecstatically.

'O Radiance! O Radiance!

This life we humbly give!

Return to us! Return to us!

Through you alone we live!'

The sun touched the water. The priests on the top of the high rock shuffled the tribute closer to the edge. The evening was warm and still, with barely a breath of wind.

The king's secretary stood at the back of the crowd of priests and officials, near the king's bodyguard, who was one of the massive armoured axers. The bodyguard had seen it all hundreds of times, and he was openly yawning. Similin was paying very little attention himself. His mind was wrestling with a particularly complex problem.

Soren Similin liked problems. He had a subtle and powerful brain, and he was confident that he would find a solution. The harder the problem, the more satisfaction he got from solving it, because it raised him all the higher above the little people. But for his brain, he would still be one of them. His father, and his father's father before him, had been poor village weavers. As a child, Soren Similin had watched as the merchants came to buy, and had seen the way his father sat with lowered eyes, and the merchants cheated him, and his father had said nothing. That was when he had known that his father was one of the little people.

Then everything had changed. He had been chosen.

When the voice had first sounded in his head, he had not been surprised.

You are cleverer than those round you, the voice had said. *You deserve more. Help us, and you will get all you could ever desire.*

He never knew who it was who instructed him; just that they were superior to himself and to everyone he had ever met. Their only limitation, it seemed, was the weakness of their bodies.

With our bodies we can do little, he was told. *With our intelligence, we can do much. Soon now all this will change, and we will become perfect.*

Until that day, they worked to achieve their goal through surrogates. Similin had no idea how many surrogates there were apart from himself, nor what the goal was towards which he worked. All he knew was that he obeyed them, and he was rewarded: not only with the sweet bliss he had learned to crave, but with worldly success. His unseen mistress had guided each step of his journey, and smoothed away all obstacles in his path. Now here he was, at the heart of the court of Radiance, on the point of accomplishing his greatest mission. He would solve the last outstanding problem, and so would please the one he sought above all others to please, and she would raise him to power.

Now the crowd in the square below fell silent, and the voice of a solo singer rang out over the golden roofs of the city.

'Receive our tribu-u-ute!'

The red-robed priests led the drooping man in white to the towering rock's edge. Here they released their hold on his arms. The tribute must never be pushed. He must be seen to go of his own volition to his death.

As the sun sank into the lake, the tribute crumpled to his knees. From this position, slowly, unstoppably, he toppled over the edge, and turned over and over as he fell.

The solo singer sang.

'Return to us!'

The tribute fell down and down, black against the red sky. His arms flailed out, but he made no cry. The timing was perfect. Just as the last of the setting sun dropped below the horizon, the tribute struck the water with a smacking hiss. Then came the sound of a more muffled impact, as he smashed on to the rocks just below the water's surface. A low sigh, like a passing breeze, rose from the crowd. Another day was ended. Another tribute paid. The dawn was secured, the sun would rise again. Life would go on.

The people started to leave.

As the royal children filed out with their mothers, one of them said, in a plaintive whine, 'I didn't see the blood! I never see the blood!'

Soren Similin, standing beside the broad open stairway that led down the levels, heard this complaint, and was struck by a sudden brilliant idea. Of course! he thought to himself. All this time the solution had been staring him in the face.

The king called out to the Handler of the Corona.

'Get this damn thing off me! It tickles my neck.'

The Handler of the Corona, a wealthy oil merchant proud to perform this ceremonial task, hurried forward with hands outstretched.

'Coming, Radiance!'

As he unbuckled the corona, he murmured in the king's ear, 'It will be my name day soon, Radiance. I have the honour of supplying the tribute for that day.'

'I hope he'll be an improvement on the riff-raff they drag out these days,' said the king. 'They think I don't know they're drugged, but I can always tell.'

'I believe you'll be proud of my offering,' said the oil merchant.

'Let's hope so. I've had enough droopy tributes.'

'My name is Cheerful Giver, Radiance,' said the merchant, not sure that the king knew who he was.

'Good, good.'

Waving a hand vaguely behind him as he went, the king hobbled off to his private quarters one level below. His secretary waited for him to go, his mind filled by the idea that had just come to him. It was a simple and elegant solution, and, as such, profoundly satisfying. And if it worked, he would soon be able to deliver the first of the mighty shocks that would raise him to glory.

CHAPTER TWELVE

THE SECRET WEAPON

THE great temple of Radiance was built on six levels, rising from the big public sanctuary at the bottom, through royal and priestly offices and quarters, to the grand terrace at the top. The temple was a complete world in itself. There were kitchens here, and storerooms packed with provisions; armouries where smiths worked before blazing furnaces; wash yards and laundry yards, slaughter yards for meat and dairy yards for milk and cheese. There was a tailor and a barber, and a hat-maker for the king's wives. And up at the highest level, hidden away at the back but conveniently placed for the evening offerings, there was a prison house. Here hundreds of prisoners were held in stone-lined pits known as tanks. Murderers, petty thieves, and homeless spikers were huddled together indiscriminately beneath the heavy iron grids, waiting their turn to be sedated and led out to the high temple rock. There they paid for their crime or folly or plain bad luck by being sent tumbling to their death, before the indifferent gaze of the people of Radiance.

When Soren Similin left the royal terrace that evening, it was to the tanks that he directed his steps. Beyond the tanks was a bleak stone-walled yard, built as an exercise area for the prisoners. These lost creatures in their last weeks of life had neither the need nor the desire for exercise; so very little difficulty had been made when the king's secretary had asked to be given the use of the yard. This had been five months ago. Since then teams of carpenters and glaziers and metal workers had transformed it into a glass-roofed laboratory, and teams of scientists had built within it a remarkable device; all in complete secrecy.

The only access to the laboratory was through the long room that contained the tanks. This alone made the secret project secure, and beyond the reach of idle curiosity. The guards on duty by the tanks knew better than to question the secretary and his team, as they came and went. It was the king's business, and in Radiance, the king's word was law.

An iron walkway ran over the top of the grids, raised a few feet above the bars to prevent the prisoners reaching up at passing ankles. Not that there was any danger. The prisoners had no way of escape, and knew they would not be leaving the tanks except to fall to their death; so they spent their days in a listless half-sleep, all hope lost.

The guards on duty saluted Similin as he hurried by. On the far side of the walkway there was a locked door, to which the secretary had a key. Beyond that door was a second door, which was locked on the inside, and had a spy-hole in the middle. This door was only ever opened to members of the team.

As Soren Similin entered the laboratory itself, he was

accosted by Professor Evor Ortus, a small, bald, middle-aged man, whose lined and stubbly face showed that he had allowed himself very little sleep for the past week.

'I've had a new idea!' he cried. 'See what you think of this.'

The lab was festooned with apparatus. Ranged all round the walls, rack upon rack, were hundreds of short glass tubes, angled to receive the light that streamed by day through the glazed roof. From the tubes ran traceries of fine copper pipes that fed into a tall copper cylinder, from which issued jets of steam. This cylinder in turn fed a sequence of ever-smaller glass vessels, the last and smallest of which looked for all the world like a bottle of plain water.

The professor drew Soren Similin past the table to a stand in one corner, where other members of the team were gathered round. There, draped over a clothes hanger, was a strange baggy garment, dripping moisture on to the floor. It was a sleeveless jacket, sewn in sections like a quilt, and each section was sagging under the weight of its contents.

'It came to me in the night,' said the professor. 'Of course, it's only a demonstration model. The actual jacket would have to be fully waterproof.'

Soren Similin studied the dripping garment. He knew at once that it was useless, but he also knew he must tread very carefully. The professor was an outlander like himself, but of far higher status. He had gained great distinction in the academies of Radiance, and was now its most eminent scientist; but he was also a proud man who took offence easily. Professor Ortus believed himself to be not only the leader of the team, but the sole creator of the remarkable device that had taken shape in the former exercise yard. This suited Soren Similin very well. He sought no glory; he wanted no credit for scientific invention. He was happy to remain unnoticed, in the background.

'Fascinating!' he exclaimed. 'What a fertile mind you have, professor.'

'The demonstration model is filled with plain water only, of course. It holds exactly four litres. More than sufficient for the task.'

'The perfect quantity,' said Soren Similin. 'And, I would guess, no heavier to wear than a thick winter coat. Has anyone tried it on?'

He asked as if it were a matter of no more than idle curiosity. Ortus signalled to one of his juniors.

'Put it on. Stand where we can see you.'

The junior stood in the light of the main lamps, and the professor studied the effect, frowning. Similin looked down. He knew he need say no more. Not only did the bulging jacket attract immediate attention; it caused even the idlest observer to wonder what was stuffed inside it.

'Ah,' said Ortus, his excitement fading.

'You think it might give rise to suspicion?' said Similin in his soft voice.

'It might.'

'I'm afraid you may be right. Never mind. We keep thinking.'

'Keep thinking!' In his disappointment, the scientist allowed his frustration to show. 'I've been thinking day and night! I've prayed to the Radiant Power above for illumination, but it's got me nowhere. I tell you, it's impossible!'

'Nothing is impossible,' said the secretary, 'to a mind as brilliant as yours.'

'Where has brilliance got me?'

'Now, please, professor! I won't hear that! Who has done all this? Who has found a way to take the radiant power of the sun and store it in liquid form?'

He gestured at the apparatus that surrounded them, from the simple bottle of water, up past the pipes and the tubes, to the glazed roof above, through which the moon was now shining.

'True,' said Ortus, recovering his spirits a little. 'It is, I admit, a historic breakthrough. Some might call it a triumph of pure scientific discovery. Not that anyone knows about it yet.'

'Patience, professor. The world will learn of your historic breakthrough when it is perfected. We have one last difficulty to overcome.'

'One last impossibility!' cried the scientist in exasperation.

Soren Similin believed he had the answer. But it suited him to lead the proud scientist to suppose he was making this final discovery for himself.

'I have only the mind of a common man, professor,' he

122

murmured. 'I have none of your brilliance and originality. But I can listen and repeat. Perhaps if I were to remind us all of the elements of the problem, your keen intellect will cast some new illumination on our dilemma.'

'I've been over it and over it,' said the scientist with a sigh.

'Then for my own benefit, perhaps. To make sure I understand the situation, before I make my next report to the king.'

'To the king. Yes, of course. Very well.'

'First, the achievements.' The secretary ticked off the list on his fingers. 'You and your team have found a way to store the energy of the sun in plain water, in sealed containers.'

'I have named it "charged water",' said Ortus with some pride.

'An apt name, professor. This "charged water" can be made to release its energy in the form of an explosion. A large enough quantity, we believe, could achieve our objective, which is to destroy the island of Anacrea.'

'Four litres or more.'

'Just so. And here is the brilliance of your discovery. The "charged water" is harmless so long as it remains sealed. Once exposed to the air, the explosion is triggered. This means the weapon can be carried safely on to the island, and triggered at the time of the carrier's choice.'

'Yes, yes, yes!' cried Ortus. 'But that's where it all falls down! The island is closed to outsiders. It is watched and defended. How is the weapon to be carried on to the island? In the night, unable to sleep, I thought of the water-filled jacket. But look at it! It's laughable!'

'Allow me, professor,' said Soren Similin in his most soothing voice. 'Allow me, in my slow and plodding way, to list the obstacles that are still in our path.'

Once more he ticked them off on his fingers.

'These so-called Noble Warriors do have certain limited powers, which have enabled them to repel direct attack, even by imperial axers. So our new strategy is to smuggle a massive bomb on to the island. Anacrea is a closed island, as you say, except of course to those who live there. Once a year only, for one day, it is opened to pilgrims. However, all pilgrims are searched. They are not permitted to carry bags. The holy places are watched over at all times by the Nomana. How then can our carrier convey our bomb – four litres of charged water, in a sealed container – into the heart of the Nom?'

'That's the question! We all know the question. But who can come up with an answer?'

The scientist threw a hopeless glance round his attendant team. Similin reworded the problem, as if to aid their deliberation.

'Where could a carrier hide four litres of charged liquid so perfectly that the Nomana would never find it?'

'Where indeed? He can't drink it. The stomach can't hold four litres.'

'If only,' murmured the secretary, 'the body had hollow passages capable of storing liquid in all its parts. In the arms – in the legs – in the – '

'By the Sun!' cried Ortus. 'I've got it!'

'Got what, professor?'

'Blood!'

'Blood, professor?'

'Blood! Blood!' cried the scientist, his excitement mounting. 'Why didn't I think of that before? The body is a sealed container within which flows more than four litres of liquid, in the form of – blood!'

'Remarkable!' said the secretary. 'It takes a genius to see something so simple.'

'We'd have to modify the apparatus, of course.' Ortus was now talking aloud to himself. 'A system to pass the blood through the charging vessels. I see no insuperable problem there.'

'So the blood would be charged, as you have charged the water?'

'Yes, yes. Let me think. Yes, it can be done! Sun be praised! What can match the heady joys of pure science! Method, persistence, a dash of genius, and – success! But of course, we must run a test, to be sure.'

'You propose, in short, to make a human bomb.'

'A human bomb? Yes, if you like. First we must run a test. We'll need a test subject, of course.'

Soren Similin was satisfied. He had achieved his objective. Now he could slip into the background.

The scientist was energised by his breakthrough, and eager to get to work. He started to bark orders at his team.

'You – find a way to put a return flow on the assembly.

I want a pumped circuit. You – make me a good strong chair. You can cut wood, can't you? You – figure out the inlets and outlets. Not as simple as it looks. No air contact, remember! This is still a sealed system.'

Soren Similin headed for the door.

'When do you expect to be ready for the test, professor?'

'Soon! Very soon! Tomorrow. End of the day. We don't need sleep, do we, boys?'

The members of the team grinned and shook their heads. The excitement had infected them all.

'You just bring us a subject. We'll do the rest.'

'Very good, professor.'

'Oh, and make sure he's a strong one.' Professor Ortus was back in control, demonstrating by his commanding tone of voice that the king's secretary was no more than a minor member of his team. 'He'll need to be fit and healthy and strong to take the load we're going to put on him.'

'I'll do my best,' said Soren Similin.

CHAPTER THIRTEEN

A SCIENTIFIC SUCCESS

ON the far side of the city, in the warren of alleys that lay between the meat market and the lake shore, there were cheap rooms to sleep in, and cheap bars to drink in, and it was here that the transient population of unskilled workers, petty criminals and drunks were to be found. Here the elegance and opulence of the imperial city gave way to stinking tenements, where the occupants defecated openly in the gutters. So it was here that Soren Similin went the next day, in search of what he needed.

He could have commanded one of the prisoners held in the tanks to be handed over to him: his authority from the king certainly extended that far. But the wretches in the tanks were mostly spikers who had been caught seeking work in the city without permits, and had been half-starved even before their arrest. Also the secretary did not want the priests who picked out the daily tribute from the tanks to start sniffing round him, asking questions. So he had decided to buy what he needed, on the black market.

Soren Similin made it his business to be well informed. He knew that a trade existed, to supply tributes to the leading families of Radiance, so that they could present an offering on their name day. Back in the past, all tributes had been prisoners captured alive in battle, and the offering of a tribute had been a sign of prowess. But the days of such wars were long gone. Radiance was too rich and too powerful to require its prominent citizens to wield a sword themselves. So when a wealthy magnate wished to impress the king by offering a tribute, he had to go and buy one.

The king's secretary made his way to the infamous hostel known as the Ham Bone, and there sat himself down at a table in the crowded courtyard, and called for beer. When the drink came he held the bar-boy's hand and said, 'I'm here to do business.'

The bar-boy nodded and left. The secretary drank his beer and waited patiently. After a while two unremarkable men sidled up and sat on the bench facing him.

'We're told you want to do business, captain.'

Similin nodded.

'And what would be your desire?'

In such a place, in such company, Soren Similin did not trouble to pretend humility. He spoke briskly, and to the point.

'Male. Strong. Prime condition.'

The two men looked at each other, and mimed astonishment.

'You hear that, Sol?'

'I do hear.'

'Wouldn't you call that a coincidence?'

'Like the captain had read our minds.'

'We brought just such a one in, only yesterday. Male,

128

you say. Strong, you say. Prime condition, you say.' He leaned across the table and exhaled his brandy-smelling breath at Similin. 'What do you say to an axer?'

'An axer!'

'Retired, of course. But not long retired. A great big bull of a man!'

'How much?'

'For a perfect specimen like that? Five thousand shillings.'

Soren Similin stood up, as if to go.

'I'll give you five hundred.'

The two traders got up from the bench together, shaking their heads and sighing.

'We wouldn't want to waste your time, captain.'

The secretary spoke with menacing softness.

'That was not a request.'

He drew out his royal medallion. The traders' faces went white. The king's power was absolute, even in this sordid corner of the city.

'You should have said, captain. Always happy to oblige a servant of the king.'

'Where is this man?'

'Right now? Right now, I'd say he's resting after his travels. Wouldn't you say, Sol?'

'Fast asleep, captain.'

'You mean he's drugged.'

'You'd have done the same, captain. He would keep wriggling and roaring.'

'I'll send a cart for him. Be sure to have him ready.'

*

It took four young men from Professor Ortus's team to carry the doped axer into the laboratory. They complained loudly all the way.

'That's enough!' chided Ortus. 'True science is hard work. Great Sun! He's magnificent!'

Barban lay on a stretcher, his wrists and ankles bound, his mouth gagged. He was awake, but too drugged to do more than roll his eyes. It took the combined efforts of everyone in the team to heave him off the stretcher and into the chair. Once there, they cut his bonds, and strapped his arms and legs tightly to the chair, which was itself bolted securely to the floor.

Soren Similin looked on, noting the additions that had been made to the apparatus. In the twenty-four hours that had passed since he had left them, the team had made impressive progress. Above the chair, itself a piece of new work, there hung an iron and rubber harness, from which dangled thin rubber pipes, and straps, and clips, and needles.

'I would never have believed it was possible,' he said. 'You truly are miracle workers.'

Ortus didn't reply. He was examining the big man in the chair. Barban sat lolling forward, unable to control his posture. The scientist passed one hand back and forth in front of the axer's eyes. There was no reaction.

'He's very heavily drugged,' he said.

'Is that a problem?'

130

'In this condition, he's incapable of obeying even the simplest instructions.'

'Does that mean you can't carry out the test?'

'Oh, the test won't be a problem. We have him entirely under our control. But when it comes to the real thing, we're going to need a carrier with his wits about him.'

'Then that is what we will find,' said Soren Similin.

That and more, he thought to himself. He had known from the very first moment he had solved the final problem that the carrier would have to be a volunteer – and a very special kind of volunteer. He said none of this aloud.

'But for now, professor, you can proceed?'

'Certainly. I'm extremely curious to know if my theories will be proved correct in practice.'

'I'm sure they will, professor,' purred the secretary. 'You've not been wrong yet.'

The harness was lowered on to Barban's slumped shoulders, and there strapped in place. The fine needles were inserted into the axer's neck and arms, and connected to the dangling rubber tubes. Professor Ortus himself then checked every connection, to be sure the seal was unbroken. Then he gave a brisk nod, and the charging process began.

The machine made a soft roaring sound. The pipes and tubes began to quiver and throb. The drugged axer stiffened, but gave no sign of resistance. He seemed not to be in any pain.

Ortus watched intently.

131

'The subject's blood is now passing through the charged gases,' he reported.

One of the juniors began to feel uneasy. Something about the experiment troubled him.

'Professor,' he said. 'I think there may be some aspect we haven't checked.'

Ortus frowned. This was no time to discover mistakes in the experimental process. On the other hand, he always stressed to his team that science was built on evidence, and evidence was the product of close and unremitting attention to detail.

'Yes, yes. What is it?'

The junior wasn't sure himself. He struggled to express his niggling doubt.

'The test subject,' he said. 'I mean, does he – can we – is he – ?'

'Is he in perfect condition?' snapped the professor. 'No, not at all. But we can allow for that.'

'What I meant, professor, was – well – is it all right?'

'Is what all right?'

'I mean – from his point of view.'

'His point of view? That is not our concern.'

He turned to check the state of the big axer strapped in the chair. To Similin he said, 'Now, you see. The charged blood is re-entering his body.'

Then, to settle the mind of his troubled junior, 'If we don't do this, others will. Do we want this great power in the hands of others? Think what destruction that could unleash! It could mean the end of the world as we know it! Whatever you or I do, science marches on. We have a duty to follow the flame of knowledge wherever it leads. To carry the torch – to make what sacrifices must be made – to serve, and protect, and enlighten – '

The axer uttered a long gurgling groan. His mouth opened and shut, and his legs shook. The team of scientists crowded round.

'He's not going to be able to take much more.'

Barban started to vibrate violently. His eyes protruded from his head. His tongue lolled out.

'All right. That'll do.'

The team shut down the pumps, and unharnessed the axer. They wore thick soft gloves, and handled him with care.

'How long was that?'

'Twelve minutes, professor.'

'Not as long as I had hoped.'

'Will it be sufficient, professor?' asked the secretary.

'We are about to find that out.'

The test site was in an abandoned quarry on the far side of the belt of sunflower fields. Here, surrounded by craggy stone cliffs, was a broad rock-strewn area into which Ortus and the team carried the shivering axer, lighting their way with lanterns. In the centre an iron post had been hammered into the ground. To this they tethered their test subject: not that he showed any signs of trying to run away.

He slumped to the ground and lay there, shuddering. A dozen or so other iron posts across the quarry had cows tethered to them. The cows lowed anxiously, as members of the team went from post to post lighting the torches fixed on their tops.

'Cows?' said Soren Similin.

'Part of the test.'

When everything was in place, Ortus, the secretary, and the rest of the team, retreated to a base located behind a shield of rock. The professor then turned to the junior who had expressed doubts back in the laboratory.

'You,' he said, handing him a small, sharp knife. 'Show us you're a true scientist.'

The junior took the knife.

'Yes, professor.' He spoke too loudly, eager to affirm his commitment to his profession. 'Now, professor?'

'Now.'

The junior set off at once across the quarry to the tethered axer.

'Is he in any danger?' asked Similin.

Ortus shrugged.

'The trigger time is unknown, of course. One shallow cut, anywhere on the body. Just enough to cause bleeding. The charged blood reacts when exposed to the air, setting off a chain reaction. The stored energy is released, in a force-wave. But how quickly? And how powerfully? We have no idea.'

'The flame of knowledge sometimes burns the hand that holds it,' said Similin with a smile.

The junior with the knife made his cut, and came racing back to the shelter of the rock. He had barely dropped to the ground when there came a sound like a deep, dull thud. This was followed by a shiver in the air, a distorting ripple. Then a shriek of high wind. The force-wave ripped outwards from the centre, blasting the loose fragments of rock across the quarry floor, and into the surrounding cliffs. The tethered cattle were carbonised where they stood. The blast slammed into the rock cliffs and caused the very ground to shudder beneath the crouching team. Then, like distant thunder, the blast expended itself, rolling away across the fields and the lake.

Cautiously the team members rose from their sheltering place, and, relighting their lanterns, which had been doused by the blast, they went back into the quarry. The entire quarry floor had been swept clean, as if by a giant broom. In the centre, the iron post had melted into a simmering mound. Barban was gone. Not one trace of him remained.

'Stupendous!' said Soren Similin.

'And that,' said Evor Ortus, swelling with pride, 'is a fraction of the power we can release.'

'What a weapon! Professor, I salute you!'

Ortus could no longer contain himself.

'My friends, what we have all just witnessed is beyond question a major scientific success. You should all be very proud. As for me, I'm not ashamed to say that this is my finest hour. My discovery will change the world!'

The team, all as excited as their leader, pumped each

other's hands in their delight. The doubting junior, who had so nearly been swept away in the blast himself, set up a cheer of triumph.

'Science is marching on!' he cried.

Soren Similin watched, and was well pleased. Such a weapon could never be detected by the Nomana, because what was there to see? The carrier could walk naked into the Nom, and need do no more than scratch one finger to detonate an explosion that would wipe the holy island off the face of the earth. Then the king in his gratitude would raise his secretary to a position of power; and Soren Similin would be able to proceed to the final stage of his long-unfolding plan.

'We must present ourselves to the king,' said Ortus, eager now for his rightful praise. 'We must tell the king of our success.'

'We must indeed,' said the secretary. 'But would it not be wiser to wait until we're ready to act?'

'We are ready! The test was a triumph!'

'There is still the matter of the carrier.'

'Pooh! That's easy. Take a spiker out of the public tanks.'

'Professor, our carrier must go alone and unaided on to the island. I think you'll agree with me, once you give the matter some thought, that a common spiker won't do at all. We need a very special kind of carrier. We need a volunteer.'

'A volunteer?' The scientist frowned as he took in this notion. 'It's true, a volunteer would be desirable.'

'And we need, you would agree, a person who has

access to the holy island. One who lives there, perhaps. Or a pilgrim.'

'Yes. I can see that would be an advantage.'

'One who is brave enough to penetrate to the shrine at the heart of the Nom.'

'Yes . . .'

'And one who hates the Nomana so much that he or she would gladly die to destroy their power.'

The professor's face had been falling more and more with each requirement. Now all his excitement evaporated.

'But how can such a person ever be found?'

'Where there's power,' said Soren Similin, 'there's hatred.'

'It seems to me to be beyond all possibility. Why should anyone who lives on Anacrea, or anyone who goes there to worship as a pilgrim, have any desire to destroy the island – let alone themselves?'

'That is now my humble task. To find such a person. To convince them of their mission. You have your genius, professor. You have shown it in the making of this weapon. My abilities are more modest; but I do possess a certain plodding persistence in the pursuit of simple goals. You have defined what is needed. I will now seek out our perfect carrier. In this way, between us, we will achieve our final victory.'

At the time that Soren Similin spoke these words, the scientist could not but agree. He told himself that with the ugly young man's help his full glory was now close at hand. But as soon as Similin had left him, he began to harbour suspicions. The more he told himself that he was about to reap the just reward for his life's work, the less certain he grew. He kept hearing in his mind the secretary's soft voice saying, 'Between us we will achieve our final victory.' *Between us?* The ugly young man had done nothing. But Similin was in high favour with the king. And now he had taken upon himself the final stage of the operation, the finding of a carrier.

So Ortus brooded, and became ever more angry, until he succeeded in convincing himself that he was about to become the victim of a great injustice. He broached the subject with his oldest friend, a fellow scientist. His friend was sympathetic.

'If I were you, I wouldn't stand for it.'

'But what can I do?'

'Whatever it is that this other fellow is doing to steal your thunder, you do it first.'

'Me! How?'

'How would I know? You keep it all so hush-hush I haven't the least idea what it's all about. But I suppose you know. This final stage that will get all the applause – can't you do it yourself?'

Ortus became very quiet after that. He began to turn his thoughts in a more practical direction. Maybe there was a way. Maybe if he put out the word, discreetly of course, and let it be known what he was looking for – maybe he could give the ugly young man a surprise after all.

Soren Similin, meanwhile, proceeded with his plan,

unaware that he had left behind him an angry and suspicious partner. This was an unusual mistake for Similin to make. He always took great care to stroke the vanity of those he sought to use. He had made the mistake out of impetuosity. As soon as he had seen with his own eyes that the human bomb was a reality, his busy mind had leaped forward to the next stage in the long-conceived plan. He knew he must seek his perfect carrier on Anacrea itself. He also knew that the island would be open to pilgrims, for one day only, on midsummer's day. And midsummer's day was only two days away. The journey downriver would take a full day. He had no time to lose.

That evening he asked the king's permission to leave Radiance, allowing himself to hint that the day he had so long promised might now be approaching.

'You want to go to Anacrea yourself?'

'Yes, Radiance. In this final stage, I must see the shrine for myself, and make my plans accordingly.'

'Final stage! Let it be so! I pray daily to the Radiant Power above to guide you and give you strength.'

'Your prayers are heard, Radiance. I am guided. I am strong.'

'The Nomana will be destroyed soon now?'

'Soon now, Radiance.'

That night, alone, the surrogate fell once more to his knees.

'Have I done well, mistress? Am I deserving?'

You are deserving.

So came the sweetness, and his busy mind was still. His eyes closed, he moved his head gently from side to side, like one turning his cheeks to the warmth of the sun, and was bathed in a stream of bliss.

CHAPTER FOURTEEN

PILGRIMS

AS soon as light dawned on midsummer's day, pilgrims began to cross the water to the holy island of Anacrea. Some had camped out the previous night on the seashore, eager to pass as many hours as possible of this, the year's longest day, in the presence of the All and Only. Then as the morning wore on, the pilgrim barges began to arrive, each one crowded with men, women and children, all of them simply dressed, all of them devoted to the god of the Noble Warriors.

The Nom had no empire. The Nom owned no estates. The Nomana never preached their faith in public. These hundreds who had chosen to follow their example did so because they had been moved by the simplicity of the Nomana's lives, or awed by the Noble Warriors in action. So pilgrims came from far and wide, from the mountains of the east and the forests of the west, and from the broad fertile plains in between. Some had come every year of their lives. Some came for the first time, filled with excited curiosity. And some stepped on to the holy island bright with the hope that they would be accepted into the Community themselves, and would not be leaving Anacrea with the rest of the pilgrims that night.

Morning Star never forgot her first sight of the holy island. The river had grown steadily wider as it approached the sea, following a looping path between densely forested granite-walled banks. This was quite unlike her own home country of grassy foothills, where the trees clustered in the sheltered valleys. Here the land was broken by towering crags that burst up out of the endless forest like the humps of some giant petrified beast. She saw little evidence of life along the river's banks; the forest was too dense, the stone cliffs too steep.

Then seagulls began to appear in the sky, calling their mournful call, and she smelled salt on the wind. The chain of barges rounded a bend, and there it was, no more than half a mile away, in the wide mouth of the river where it met the sea: the high hump of Anacrea. Approached this way, from the north, in the mid-afternoon on mid-summer's day, the sunlight fell on the rock formations, and on the walls and towers of the great castle-monastery at the top, and caught the silver tiles on the dome that was its highest point. It was a beautiful sight, but also one that made her smile, because the castle seemed to sit above the town like a mother hen on her chicks, gathering the pink-roofed houses beneath her grey and silver wings. The terraced streets tumbled steeply down the island's craggy sides, transforming what must have once been a forbidding rock into a pyramid of domesticity.

On the east shore of the island, where the river met the

sea, lay a little port with a protective sea wall. Other river boats were already moored here, and other pilgrims were disembarking. On a high rock that looked down on the port there stood a solitary robed figure: a watching Noma.

'Look! There's one of them!'

The pilgrims round her called to each other, pointing to the lone figure, all eager to set eyes on the famous Nomana. On the quayside, where the pilgrims who had just landed were being divided into groups and searched, there were other Nomana, easy to spot because of the space that formed around them. They stood motionless, vigilant, ready to strike if it became necessary, but until then content to be still.

Morning Star too looked on the Noble Warriors with awe. She loved the simple clothing they wore, and the plain grey badans that shaded their faces. She loved their containment and their silence. She loved the soft white glow that she alone could see round them, the colour of tranquillity. At last her goal was before her.

Her journey had taken the best part of two days. After the capture of her escort she had made her way alone, with no protection and no money. Neither had proved necessary. Other travellers on the way had let her join their company, and had shared their food with her; and when at last she had reached the Great River, other pilgrims had gladly clubbed together to pay her passage on one of the barges heading for the holy island. It was enough to name her destination to find herself among friends.

When the barges reached the dock, the pilgrims disembarked in orderly lines. Morning Star stepped on to the paved quayside with a shiver of awe, a little overwhelmed that after all these years of waiting she was at last on the holy island. She looked up at the windows of the castle-monastery high above and wondered if her mother were there.

Stewards were waiting on the quayside to meet each boat, and to search the pilgrims for weapons and instruct them on how to behave. Morning Star and the rest of her group, which numbered over a hundred, were ushered into an open-sided shed, where benches were lined up in the shade. Here one of the stewards made them what was evidently a standard speech.

'In the name of the All and Only,' he pronounced, 'the Community of the Nom welcomes you to the holy island of Anacrea. Please respect this sacred ground. We ask you to follow the signed pilgrim paths, and to go barefoot, as we do. No weapons are permitted on Anacrea. No alcohol may be consumed here. No animals are slaughtered and eaten here. A simple meal will be provided for you, after the Congregation. No charge will be made for this. We do not use money on the holy island.'

Every word he spoke, even though it was delivered in the singsong voice of one who repeats by rote, gladdened Morning Star's heart. All this was as she had expected, was as it should be. This life that she would soon begin would be different in every way from her old life.

'The Nom can only be reached on foot,' continued the steward. 'There are four hundred and twelve steps before you reach the Pilgrim Gate. Please use this long climb to empty your heart of all bitterness, and anger, and greed, and fear. With each step you take, shake the dirt from your feet, and come into the presence of the All and Only with a light and loving heart.'

There followed a general shuffling about, as those with shoes or sandals removed them; and then, escorted by stewards and watched over by the silent Nomana, the pilgrims made their way up the steps. Morning Star followed the others in perfect silence, but for the pad-pad-pad of bare feet, and the calling of seagulls high overhead. She was climbing towards her long-lost mother. She was climbing towards the Loving Mother of All, who waited for her in the Garden. She was climbing towards her new life.

The fast boat carrying Soren Similin downriver came in sight of the riverside store where the boatman was accustomed to break his journey.

'Do we stop for a little refreshment?' the boatman called to his passenger.

'We do not,' said Similin.

'You wouldn't be wanting to go all the way to the ocean without a single stop,' said the boatman.

'I would,' said Similin.

'We've at least four more hours to go, noble sir. More if the wind drops.'

'Then put up more sail, if you please, and make more speed.'

So the boatman swept on past the riverside store, saluting the old shopkeeper to show his regrets as he went by. His regrets were all for himself.

The old shopkeeper returned the boatman's salute with a slight stirring of one hand. He was dozing on his wide porch, with his peaked military cap low over his tired eyes. Above his head swung the wooden sign that read GENERAL STORE, to which he owed his name. No doubt countless years ago his father had given him some other name, but for as long as anyone living could remember, the old man had worn his soldier's cap and had saluted passing boats from his porch, and had been known as General Store.

Small though his hand's salute had been, it set off an answering motion in his stomach, which developed into a churning sensation. He knew then that soon now he must leave the comfort of his chair to empty his bowels. This urgent summons had become too frequent in recent months. No known remedy had made any difference. It had begun to obsess him.

'Boy!' he called. 'Take me to the po!'

His assistant emerged from the store. One of his chief duties had now become leading his ageing employer by the hand along the river path to the privy. But as he came out on to the porch, he saw a sleek sailing ship making its way

146

down the east fork of the river towards the store's landing stage, and he knew at once that it was bringing trouble.

'General!'

The General had already been informed by his own senses of the coming trouble. Exactly which senses he could hardly have said. He no longer heard very clearly, his eyes were misted with age, and he hadn't smelled a new smell in ten years. Perhaps it was a change in the movement of the air, an agitation driven towards his riverside post by the approach of the sailing ship. Barges were good. River boats were good. Sailing ships were not good.

'General!' cried the boy. 'Spikers!'

The old man cursed to himself, and spat over the rails into the brown water, and creaked to his feet. He peered through gummy lids at the boat even now tying up at his landing stage, and recognised the *Lazy Lady*. There was nothing to be done. The master of the *Lazy Lady* was mad, and not to be bargained with.

'Heya, General! Do you love me?'

'No, I don't love you, you crazy spiker,' grumbled General Store. 'If you've come to slit my throat, do it now, and welcome.'

He felt his bowels churn ominously.

'Whoa! I don't slit the necks of my friends.'

'So now I'm your friend, am I? So you rob your friends of the little they have, and leave them to starve, do you?'

The Wildman put one braceleted arm round the old man's shoulders, and hugged him affectionately.

'Share and share alike, brava! My boys must be fed, just like your boys.'

The Wildman's crew were all ashore now, lounging on the store's cane chairs, and passing round bottles of the store's brandy. The assistant cowered in a corner, watching them, but doing nothing to stop them. General Store saw all this with disgust.

'One day you'll meet justice, Wildman. And after they hang you I'll follow you to your burying place, and I'll piss on your grave.'

'You won't forget me, old friend, I know that. But I'm not here for provisions.' He saw his men now passing round cigars, and thought it likely they had not paid for them. 'Not much in the way of provisions, at least. Maybe a little refreshment for me and my boys. No, General, we're just passing through, on our way downriver to the sea.'

'What do you want with the sea?'

The Wildman drew up a chair close to the old man, because he knew the General was deaf.

'I don't want the sea, General. I want the hoodies.'

'Ha! The hoodies!'

The General snorted with amusement.

'You ever met any hoodies, General?'

'I should say I have! The only thing that keeps this wicked world from sinking back into the slime it crawled out of is the hoodies!'

'So you'll know they've got power. And that's why I want them.'

The old man snorted again. That was funny, the Wildman wanting to find the hoodies. So let him: anything to put a stop to shopping trips where nothing was paid for. Anything to leave the General free to visit the little house by the river bank.

Out on the river a barge was gliding by, laden with pilgrims. The spiker had chosen the right day to go looking for hoodies. General Store saluted, out of habit, and the passing boatman saluted back.

'Pilgrims,' he said. 'They're going to see the hoodies too.'

The Wildman's keen eyes followed the pilgrim barge out of sight.

'I hear they've got their own god on their island.'

'That's what they say.'

'What kind of god would that be, General?'

'There's gods all over. But there's those that say he's the only god. The one that made the world, and rules over all men, including no-good cut-throat spikers.'

'Seems like it's only fitting that I should pay him a call, then,' said the Wildman softly.

He stood up, and shouted to his men to get back on board ship.

'One more question, General. Everybody wants something. These hoodies – what is it they want?'

'Ask them.'

'I'm asking you.'

'Asking don't mean getting.'

The Wildman's dark eyes flashed with anger. He drew

his spike and touched its needle-sharp point to the folds of skin beneath the General's chin.

'For me it do,' he said. 'What I want, I get. Or necks get slit.'

The old man sighed. He had once spoken with a hoodie, who had told him something of his hopes and dreams, in words that made little sense. If the crazy spiker wanted to know, let him know, and much good may it do him.

'They want to live in the Garden,' he said. He liked the sound of it, so he said it again. 'They want to live in the Garden.'

The Wildman withdrew his spike. Softly he repeated the words of the white-haired stranger he had encountered in the riverside village. The sound of that quiet voice had never left him, from that moment to this.

'You will find peace,' he said, 'when you live in the Garden.'

'Peace?' growled the old man. 'What do you want with peace?'

'How would I know?' said the Wildman. 'But don't it just sound sweet?'

Then he swung round and saluted the old man, grinning all over his beautiful face, and sprang up on to the porch railing to call to his men.

'Heya, bravas! One last dance with the Wildman! Downriver it is!'

General Store watched the *Lazy Lady* safely out of sight. His stomach heaved and groaned. He held out one hand.

'Take me to the po, boy.'

By the time Morning Star reached the top of the steps, and
had passed between the ancient pines to the wide square
before the walls of the Nom, the many pilgrims who had
arrived earlier were already taking their places. Tiered
benches had been erected round three sides of the square,
under the shade of faded green canopies, facing the Pilgrim
Gate on the fourth side. Morning Star continued to the
entrance to the Nom itself, meeting other pilgrims on their
way out. The sun was descending in the sky, but there was
still an hour or more before sunset, and the start of the
Congregation. She was in no hurry. She wanted to take in
every detail.

She stood before the Pilgrim Gate, looking up at the
high stone walls of the Nom. Now that she was close, she
could see what an enormous building it was. No one knew
how many Nomana there were in the Community, but it
was said there were over a thousand. This great monastery,
their entire world during their training years in the
novitiate, was a small town in its own right. But unlike
every other town in the world, at the very centre there was
– her heart was beating fast, she could hardly frame the
words for the wonder of it – this gate before which she
stood led to the actual physical spot where –

All she could do was pray. Her lips moved as she spoke
her prayer aloud, but very softly.

'Loving Mother, make me worthy of your love. Wise

151

Father, teach me to know you. My All and Only, let me lose myself in you.'

The Pilgrim Gate was a high, undecorated arch. Everything on Anacrea seemed to her to be simple and beautiful, as if to show that all that was needed for beauty was to do the thing right. This arch rose up in a gentle curve that perfectly supported the immense weight above, and gave the impression of being no larger and no smaller than it needed to be. It was, however, very large.

There were watchful stewards everywhere, and many Nomana. The Nomana stood quietly, their badans over their heads, ready to be called on if needed.

Morning Star followed the stream of pilgrims through the gate and into the Shadow Court. She understood at once the function of this big, dark space. Light entered only from the archway, throwing her shadow far before her, but once well inside, all was twilight. Her beating heart slowed, as did her breathing. She passed slowly over the granite floor, beneath the plain-stone vaulted ceiling, and did her best to empty herself of the clutter of the day. She meant to do as she had been told, and come into the presence of the One who had created all things with a light and loving heart.

She moved on through the open doors into the Night Court. Here she stood still for a while in the darkness, seeing how the speckles of light from the pierced dome fell on the watchful stewards, and on the pilgrims, and on the walls and floor alike, causing the people to disappear.

She held out her hand before her, and the pinpricks of light on her hand joined the pinpricks of light on either side, and the shape of her hand was no longer apparent. She knew this was how it was meant to be. No one had told her, but she knew it even so. Those who came into the presence of the All and Only were to come stripped and empty, and with no expectations. It was impossible, of course. But as much as possible was to be left behind, here in the stippled darkness.

On through further doors, into whiteness: the forest of glowing columns that was the Cloister Court. She did not enter alone, and others were here before her, a great mass of pilgrims, but they moved slowly, and they passed in and out of sight between the pillars, and so for each and every one of them it was as if they were almost alone. The shining air' was full of soft murmuring sounds, as the pilgrims approached the bright presence on a wave of prayer.

So beautiful, thought Morning Star. So simple, and so beautiful. The ranks of columns were themselves arrayed like pilgrims, advancing towards the light. She looked up and saw the soft glow of the pearl-stone ceiling, the creamy veins and fissures of the translucent stone: then she looked ahead, through the guardian pillars, and saw the coming brightness, and felt weak with the wonder of it.

'Loving Mother, take me in your arms. Loving Mother, rock me in your arms. Loving Mother, grant me peace.'

She prayed as she went forward, sliding her bare feet over the smooth white marble, not wanting to intrude on the soft sigh of sound that was the pilgrims' prayer. She could feel her breathing growing calmer, as a new tranquil strength began to flow into her. Ahead, she caught a dazzle, a flash of silver. She was getting closer.

Now on either side she found herself passing other pilgrims lying prostrated on the floor. Overwhelmed by the nearness of the All and Only, they had come to a stop among the white columns, to abase themselves and call for mercy, to weep and to pray. They gave off a pale blue shimmer, which was the colour of devotion and prayer. Morning Star was as awed as they were, but she felt no fear. Had not her mother come here before her? Was she not coming home at last?

Now not so far ahead she could make out the dark and light of the pierced silver screen. She was not yet close enough to see through the rings of star-shaped holes into the sacred space beyond, but she knew that there, bathed in the last rays of the setting sun, lay the Garden.

All at once her heart began to beat painfully fast. She stopped and leaned against one of the pillars and closed her eyes. She felt weak, so weak she could no longer stand. She slipped to her knees. There, in a kneeling position, she opened her eyes and gazed on the soft dazzle of the silver screen, and once more she prayed.

'Loving Mother, I have nothing special to give you. I'm not beautiful and I'm not clever. But I'm hard-working and I'm willing, and all that I have is yours.'

Then, as she gazed, the forms and the colours before her

began to sway and dance. The bright pricks of silver light expanded, and round them rippled fringes of violet, and out from the violet burst strands of brilliant crimson, and from each crimson strand bloomed petals of gold. The colours flowed out from the Garden and clamoured round her, entirely beyond her control, splashing like spilled paint one over the next, endlessly renewing themselves. Afraid, overwhelmed, she reached up her hands as if to push the colours away, but at once she lost all sense of where she was, and found herself swimming, or falling, through star-bursts of crimson and gold. For the first time in her life her colours had escaped their bounds, and all creation was a sea of colour, and every wave was sorrow and loss and longing and joy, crashing over her head until she knew she must surely drown.

She closed her eyes and bowed her head, and little by little the giddying flood receded. She did not dare after that to go any closer to the silver screen. She rose and went stumbling out into the cool dark of the Night Court, and there drew long, calming breaths.

She was shocked by her own loss of control.

Am I really so weak? Am I so helpless?

For all the brilliance of the colours that had over-whelmed her, it had not been a vision of glory. She had tumbled into chaos, into formlessness, into a world where nothing had sense or meaning any more. No good, no bad, no up, no down: all cracked, all shattered, all spinning, all falling. A descent into madness.

155

But is the madness in me, or outside me?

Slowly the pounding eased in her chest, and the sweat dried on her brow. She felt strong enough now to move back out into the Shadow Court. There, through the high arched frame of the Pilgrim Gate, she saw the canopied benches filling up with pilgrims, as the time of the Congregation drew near. She saw the silent Nomana on guard, and was reminded that her mother was close now, and perhaps was even looking out for her. Her mother would surely guess that she would offer herself to the Nomana today, now that she was sixteen years old.

Strengthened by this thought, Morning Star went out into the square, and took her place among the pilgrims.

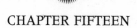

CHAPTER FIFTEEN

THE CASTING OUT

FOR Seeker, the days before the Congregation were unbearable: both tense with anxiety and achingly empty, at the same time. Nothing more was said at home about the impending disgrace. Nothing much was said at all. Meals passed in silence. His father retreated more and more into school business, his mother into her books. They were all waiting for the blow to fall, braced to endure the stares and whispers of the neighbours. They were also preparing themselves for the heartbreak of seeing Blaze one last time, before he left their lives for ever. A casting out was very rare, and when it took place it was before the assembled Congregation, as a warning to all.

Seeker kept himself to himself as much as possible. He was struggling with a confusion of feelings. He tried to recall the voice that had spoken to him in the Nom, but with every hour that had passed since, the doubts had grown. Where had the voice come from? Surely not from the god who made all things. Was it not much more likely that he had imagined it? And as for his certainty that Blaze could not have broken his vows – what did he know of what the last three years had done to him? What did he really know about his brother at all? He had loved him and he had admired him, but they had both been three years younger then. Perhaps he had changed. After all, why would the Nom tell a deliberate lie?

None of it made any sense. The more he turned it over in his mind, the less certain he became about anything. So in the end he too, like his father and mother, bowed his head and waited in silence for the nightmare to end.

The fast boat carrying Soren Similin moored at the island's dock just half an hour before sunset. Similin dismissed the boatman, and joined the last of the pilgrims in time to hear the weary steward run through his speech of welcome for the last time. As he spoke the words, 'Empty your hearts of all bitterness, and anger, and greed, and fear,' the secretary made his ungainly features suitably smooth, as if he too wanted nothing more than to surrender to this overweening god. As he climbed the four hundred and twelve steps to the Nom he kept a reverent silence like the others. And when his turn came to shuffle through the marble pillars to the silver screen, he too prostrated himself as if in awed prayer. But he was not praying. He was thinking how easy it would be to obliterate the entire edifice of superstition in which he lay, once the right carrier had been found.

By the time the setting sun was touching the long ocean horizon, and the great bell of the Nom had begun to toll, Soren Similin had taken his place among the mass of other pilgrims on the canopied ground that faced the Pilgrim

Gate. The pilgrims and the islanders and the meeks who served the Nom were all in their respective sectors, their watching faces illuminated by lines of flaming torches. There were five thousand and more, all told, crowded on to the banked benches. The Congregation was about to begin.

Now the sonorous boom of the bell fell silent, and the waiting people heard a new sound: a soft chant, floating out from within the building. The members of the Community were coming. All rose to their feet. Seeker, standing between his parents, felt for his mother's hand, and held it tight. Morning Star, lower down among the pilgrims, fixed her eyes on the high arched gate, and her mouth went dry with nervous anticipation. The chant came louder now: a song without words, made of deep harmonies, the song that was always sung at the start of the annual Congregation, the one called the Chant of the Nomana.

Out through the arch they came, walking slowly, their badans hooded over their heads, pair after pair after pair. In the light of the dying sunset, and in the flicker of the torches' flames, their pure white ceremonial clothing took on a warm reddish glow. The Nomana came out of the Nom singing, to present themselves to the people they served.

Seeker looked for his brother, and trembled for the coming disgrace. In this light, and with the head-coverings shadowing the faces, it was impossible to tell one from another. More and more flowed out through the Pilgrim Gate, venerable sages, famous fighters, and youngsters who had only just won their badans. The chant grew stronger and stronger. Seeker gripped his mother's hand, and took long breaths, and allowed himself, at least until the singing stopped, to feel his habitual awe at the power that was gathering before him. These men and women who had nothing, who all dressed alike to the point of anonymity, were the saviours of the world. If there was justice, it was because the Nomana administered it. If there was liberty, it was because the Nomana enforced it. These men and women, who carried no weapons and wore no armour, were the Noble Warriors of the true way, and none could stand against them.

Now the tail of the long procession was in view, and the last of the Nomana were taking their places. They stood chanting in their lines, ten deep, and filled the fourth side of the Congregation ground, beneath the towering walls of the Nom.

The ranks parted, and there, in his wheeled chair, pushed by his faithful old meek, was the Elder of the Community. The chair was wheeled out into the central open space, and there the attendant meek drew back the Elder's badan so that his deeply lined face could be seen.

The Elder raised one withered hand. The chant ended, and silence fell over the great gathering. Then one among the ranks of the Nomana stepped forward, a young woman. She walked softly, her eyes downcast, to stand beside the Elder in the middle of the open space. Here she paused a moment, then looked up, and began to sing, unaccompanied. Her voice was strong and beautiful, every word pure and clear to the listening multitude beneath the torch-lit sky.

> 'Mother who made us
> Father who guides us
> Child who needs us
> Light of our days and peace of our nights
> Our reason and our goal
> We wake in your shadow
> We walk in your footsteps
> We sleep in your arms . . .
> Always and everywhere
> Today and for ever
> Lead us to the Garden
> To rest in the Garden
> To live in the Garden
> With you . . .'

As the last note died away, the singer lowered her head once more, and returned to the silent lines of the Nomana. The Elder cleared his throat with a dry clicking sound.

'In the name of the All and Only,' he said, 'we, your servants, stand ready to be called to account.'

His creaky voice spoke the words that were required by the Rule, as laid down by their founder, Noman. For all their power, the Nomana were not a law unto themselves. Those who had grievances against them were entitled to come to the Congregation and speak out. But no one ever did. There was one there that day who might have spoken, had the time been right. But Soren Similin kept his silence, knowing that the day was not yet come; and that when it came, his intervention would be louder than speech.

The Elder waited for a decent interval. Seeker's eyes roamed round, and he saw the watchmen high on the walls of the Nom, and knew that even though the Pilgrim Gate had been closed, the entire Community remained on high alert.

The Elder then nodded to the Prior. The Prior unfolded a paper and read out, as he did each year, the numbers enrolled in the Community. In the course of the last year, thirty-five members had retired. Twelve novices had made their final vows. New applicants were invited to present themselves for selection this evening. But first, sadly, one existing member of the Community would be leaving.

A low murmur passed through the listening crowd. A Noma leaving? That was unusual.

'I call on this Congregation,' the Prior said gravely, 'to enforce the judgement of the Community, according to the Rule of the Nomana.'

An electric silence fell. A casting out! Seeker felt his mother's hand tremble in his. Out from the ranks stepped a lone Noma. Seeker's heart almost stopped beating. That big shambling gait, that open face. Only now he did not smile. He stared unseeingly before him.

Oh, my brother! What have they done to you?

Soren Similin watched with a sudden sharp attention.

Seeker turned to look up at his mother, and saw her eyes were shining with unshed tears. He looked up at

162

his father, and saw his face set hard, expressionless, not moving so much as an eyelid.

'Blaze of Justice,' said the Prior, 'you have been judged guilty of transgressing the Rule of our Community.'

There followed a pause, in which it seemed the entire gathering held its breath. Blaze stared blankly before him, as if unaware of the gravity of the moment.

'It is the will of this Community, in punishment of your most grave transgression, that you be cast out.'

A sigh rose up from the shocked crowd of pilgrims and islanders. Cast out! All eyes looked to the evil-doer. They could see it on that bland expressionless face. He had been cleansed. He would barely even remember his own name. The Prior reached up one hand and unwound the badan from his head. As he did so he recited the terrible words of the verdict.

'All we have given you now returns to us. Take nothing with you as you go.'

Seeker saw the tears roll down his mother's cheeks. *Brother!* He cried in his heart. *Speak out! Tell them this is wrong!*

'You are now like a child born again. You are innocent again, and therefore forgiven.'

Seeker felt his father shudder, and then go still again. Blaze himself stood motionless, looking so young, so vulnerable, without his badan. Seeker watched him with tears in his eyes.

Blaze! What have they done to you? Why? Tell me they're wrong!

163

'You were once our brother, and for that there will always be a welcome for you here. But the time has come for you to make a new life in a new place. Go now, and may the One who understands all things have mercy on you.'

Silent to the last, Blaze did as he was told. He set off across the paved ground towards the steps, not turning once to bid farewell to his family. Seeker made a move to run after him, but his father's hand closed over his arm in a grip so hard it hurt. He looked up at his father's face, wanting to see there pain, or at least pity, but all he saw was iron self-control.

'Father – it's Blaze. Your son!'

'I have only one son now.'

As his father spoke these words, Seeker felt the mist lift around him. What duty did he owe this father who could cast out his own son? The Noma had said to him on the morning of his birthday, 'Your life is your own. If it's not the life you want, only you can change it.'

If ever he was to change his life, today was the day.

Only if he entered the Nom would he understand the wrong that had been done to Blaze. Only if he became a Noble Warrior would he have the power to put it right.

The buried longing now exploded within him. What had always been impossible now suddenly seemed possible. The desire sprang into life with such intensity that he could barely speak. It was the wrong moment, the moment of Blaze's disgrace. It was the wrong desire, not his father's plan for him at all. But it was too strong in him to remain undeclared.

'Father,' he said, stammering. 'Father – I ask your permission – I would like to join – I ask to take Blaze's place.'

'You?' His father turned and looked down at him in cold surprise. 'I thought we understood that was out of the question.'

'Yes, father, I know. But now that – now that – '

There were no words. To be a warrior for the All and Only – to ask for nothing and to possess nothing – to protect the Lost Child and obey the Wise Father – to forge mind and body into an instrument of the true way – it was all he had ever wanted in life. Not to be a teacher: that was his father's dream for him, not his own dream. What had his father known of his nature when he named him? How could he read the heart of a new-born baby? But of course, it wasn't the baby's heart he had read, it was his own.

'Let me try! Please!'

'The Nomana would never accept you,' said his father, gripping his arm harder still. 'Yours is a different path in life. Don't torment yourself with what can never be.'

His steady, unfeeling gaze turned away across the crowded square, to watch Blaze pass out of sight.

Morning Star too was watching the departure of the exile. She didn't fully understand what was happening, but she could see from his colours, the blue and violet glimmer round him as he went, that he was enduring great pain. She kept expecting someone to reach out to him, or call to

165

him, with some word of farewell that would break the cruel silence. But no voice was heard.

After Blaze was gone, and as the business of the Congregation resumed, a second figure slipped away, unnoticed, and took the path to the steps. Soren Similin had seen enough. He believed he had his man.

CHAPTER SIXTEEN

SELECTION

'SEARCH your hearts,' said the Novice Master. 'Ask yourself why you wish to join our Community.'

His grave eyes ranged over the lines of young men and women before him. Most were just sixteen years old, and for them, as for Morning Star, this was the moment for which they had been preparing themselves for as long as they could remember.

'In the secrecy of your heart, answer that question with perfect truth.'

His eyes moved steadily from one to the next, holding each pair of young eyes for a moment, commanding their attention.

'If you want glory, this is not the life for you.'

Morning Star looked into her own heart and answered truthfully that she did not want glory.

'If you want dominion over others, this is not the life for you.'

No, she thought. I don't want dominion over others.

'If you want to win special favour with the All and Only, this is not the life for you.'

Is that what I want? Morning Star felt a sudden shiver of doubt. She did want to be close to the Loving Mother. Was that wrong? Did that mean she was weak? Would she be rejected because she wanted it? Her mind shrank from the prospect. It was unthinkable. How could she go back to her old life, and go on living in the old way, with nothing to hope for?

So what is it I hope for?

'But if, rather than seeking any benefit for yourself, you want to give your life in the service of others – '

Yes! she thought. That's what I want! To serve. To be of use. Not to allow my youth and whatever talents I have to trickle away like spilled water, and be wasted.

' – then it may be that you can follow the way of the Nomana. But that way is hard.'

Let it be hard! responded Morning Star joyously in her heart. The harder the better.

'It's lonely.'

Have I not been lonely all my life?

'It offers no material rewards.'

There's nothing I want but to serve the Loving Mother.

'On the day you enter the Nom as a novice, your old life ends and a new life begins. Ask yourself, is that truly what you want?'

Yes! Yes! Let a new life begin for me!

'Those of you who are so decided, go forward now in a humble spirit of acceptance.'

They heard the sounds of the bolts being drawn back on the Pilgrim Gate.

'Whatever happens is the will of the All and Only, and is for the best.'

Seeker was not among the applicants who had come forward for selection, but his place was nearby, and he could hear every word the Novice Master said. His father had let go of his arm, and now stood stiff and erect by his right side; his mother on his left. Seeker stood quietly, doing as he had been told. He watched as the Pilgrim Gate swung open to receive the applicants.

Surely you know that where your way lies, the door is always open.

Not the voice, only the memory of the voice. Seeker stared at the Pilgrim Gate. The world is full of open doors, he told himself. Why am I so sure that this one has opened for me?

The applicants were filing through the archway in a slow-moving line, guided by the attendant meeks. Morning Star moved with them, shivering with longing and doubt. Her moment of madness in the Nom earlier had shaken her confidence. Perhaps there was a fault in her, a weakness that made her unworthy. If she was not selected, she would go – she would go – somewhere – anywhere – but not back, never back. This new life was too long awaited. To go back would be a return to childhood, and much as she loved her father, she could never be a child again. She had no choice. She must go on.

But would she be selected? The other applicants all seemed so much more confident. She knew she looked like a simple-minded girl. Most times she could never think what to say. She had a face no one remembered. Why should they select her? They couldn't see inside her. They had no way of knowing what she was really like. But then, she thought, I'll tell them my mother is one of them. I'll tell them I can see the colours. Then they'll look at me differently. They'll say, there must be more to her than meets the eye. They'll see beyond the mask.

The last of the applicants had just passed through the Pilgrim Gate when she heard the thud of running feet, and a boy ran full-tilt into her, almost knocking her to the ground. His colours startled her: he was fizzing like a firework, fierce reds, greens, and gold. Red and green just meant a crass youth, but gold was rare. So rare she wasn't even sure what it meant.

'Sorry!' he said, panting, looking fearfully behind him.

Before Morning Star could ask him what he was doing, a man appeared in the archway behind them, and, pointing his finger at the runaway boy, called to him in a commanding voice.

'Come back at once!'

The boy got behind Morning Star, as if he was expecting the man to throw something at him.

'I won't!'

'You little fool! They'll never take you!'

The man glared at the boy for a long moment. The boy didn't move. Then the man turned and stalked away. The boy drew a long, shuddering breath. The colours blazing round him were so strong that Morning Star was almost frightened. He looked and felt younger than her, but his face was so alert, the expressions so fast-moving, that even without the colours she was able to pick up the anger in him, and know that it was stronger than the fear. His dark eyes caught hers for a fraction of a second, and she could see that he was on the point of saying something, but then he didn't. One look at her bun-like face and her peasant headscarf, and no doubt he assumed she wouldn't understand. This disappointed and annoyed her. For this reason, she found the courage to speak first.

'Who was that man?'

'My father.'

The boy shuffled along beside her in the line, eyes on the ground.

'Comforting to know he has faith in you.'

That made him look at her.

'But he doesn't.'

Goaded by his audible surprise, she became wicked.

'Whatever happens is the will of the All and Only. We go forward in a humble spirit of acceptance.'

That left the boy speechless. He could tell that her tone was mocking, but who was she mocking?

The line of applicants was now directed across the Shadow Court to a door on the right hand side. The door was marked COMMUNITY ONLY.

The room they entered was a long, high-ceilinged hall, lit by lamps hanging from the centre, with benches running along either side. On the benches sat some thirty or forty members of the Community, all wearing their badans down over their shoulders, as was the custom when inside the Nom. Morning Star's eyes searched the silent faces, looking for her mother. There were many women there among the Nomana, but none was looking towards the applicants. Wherever her mother was, she would surely be watching out for her.

At the far end of the hall, at a table set at right angles to the lines of benches, sat the two selectors. A novitiate meek, hovering by the door, indicated to the applicants that they were to wait, standing, until summoned. Then they were to make their way down the hall, between the two lines of Nomana, and give their names to the selectors. The Novice Master, who was one of the selectors, would then point to the left or to the right. The door to the left led into the novitiate. The door to the right would take them back into the Shadow Court. They were to go at once and in silence in the direction indicated. They were not to challenge the selectors' decision, which was final.

'Aren't we to speak at all?'

'You may ask one question, if you wish. But one question only.'

'One question! Is that all?'

The novitiate meek then tapped the first applicant on the arm, and he set off down the hallway to the selectors' table. Morning Star, watching, saw how the Nomana studied him as he passed, and then turned their silent faces one by one towards the selectors. She guessed at once that it was this wordless judgement that was the true process of selection. By the time the applicant reached the table, the decision had been made.

The exchange that took place at the table was too low for the others to hear, and shockingly brief. The Novice Master pointed to the right, and the applicant was rejected. Morning Star, watching this, was seized again with a shivering fear. How could she make them accept her? How could her entire future turn on a short walk under the eyes of strangers?

Seeker, standing beside her, was also waiting his turn with mounting nervousness. The Novice Master knew his father well, and would certainly recognise him when he stood before him. Would he know that he was there without his father's permission? Did it matter? He was of age. On the other hand, the Novice Master would know he was the brother of the disgraced Blaze. Could that be held against him?

Around him the other applicants were discussing in anxious whispers the best sort of question to ask. Seeker, like Morning Star, suspected this had nothing to do with the selection process. He didn't know where the true test lay, but in his instinctive faithfulness to the ideals of the Nomana, he took it for granted that they would get it right. His part was simply to present himself before the selectors, and trust to the wisdom of a process that was beyond his understanding. If he was rejected – well, he would trust that this too was right for him. But he dreaded rejection. Rejection would mean going home, to his father.

Who among them would be accepted? He glanced

round, and saw Fray looking at him, his eyebrows lifted in an expression of amused surprise. He looked away, and met the eyes of the girl he had run into, the one who had said such odd things. As their eyes met, she pulled a funny little face. It was a smile, but its meaning was, Isn't this unbearable? He shook his head, confused. Her smile implied she knew him already, but this was not so.

There came a loud bang from behind them. The rear door had been thrown open. A strong young voice called out, breaking the silence.

'Heya, hoodies! Do you lo-o-ove me?'

All heads turned, astonished. There stood a handsome youth in brightly coloured clothes, with silver bangles all down his arms. Seeker, staring with the rest, knew that he had never seen anyone like him in all his life. Not just the gaudy dress and the long golden hair: it was the swagger, and the smile, and the bold cry. The Wildman was everything the Nomana were not.

The novitiate meek hurried forward.

'No, no, no!' he said.

'Yes, yes, yes!' said the Wildman, sweeping the meek aside with one golden-skinned arm. He strode down the hallway, nodding and smiling to the Nomana on either side as he went.

'Heya, hoodies!' he greeted them. 'I want to be like you!'

When he reached the selectors' table he put one hand into his pocket and threw a scatter of gold shillings on to the papers before them.

'I pay my way,' he said with pride. 'I want your power. I want your peace.'

The Novice Master looked from the gold to the smiling youth standing before him. He spoke gently.

'What is your name?'

'They call me the Wildman.'

'We have no use for gold here, Wildman.'

The second selector, a thin, bony woman, started to pick up the gold shillings, one by one, to return them. The Wildman stopped smiling.

'You won't take my gift?'

'No.'

'Blubber-piss hoodie!'

His right hand shot out, reaching for the Novice Master's neck. The Wildman had a powerful grip, and the Novice Master had a thin neck. The Wildman had squeezed the life out of better necks than this. But somehow he misjudged the distance. His fingers closed on air.

He tried again, stabbing forward with his right hand, snatching for the throat. The owl-like eyes of the Novice Master stared back at him, never moving. But once again, the Wildman found he had not reached far enough.

The woman selector leaned forward and held out his gold shillings. On the back of the hand that held the coins he could see the tendons working her fingers like wires.

'It's not your time yet,' she said.

He took the coins. She then raised the hand that had held them, and, with the palm turned outward, gave the air a little push, towards him. The Wildman stumbled back-wards, as if he had been struck a soft but irresistible blow. Then he felt a jerking sensation in his legs. Quite unable to stop himself, he began to stalk towards the door that led out into the Shadow Court. Left foot, right foot, away his feet went, and the rest of him had no choice but to be carried away too. The situation was ridiculous. It was humiliating. It was exactly as if he was being marched away, except that it was he himself who was doing the marching.

'Blubber-piss hoodies!' he yelled as he went, shaking his gold shillings. 'You'll pay for this!'

The meek by the exit opened the door, and out went the Wildman, and peace returned to the selection process.

One after another the waiting applicants made the short walk down the hall, and most were rejected. Seeing this, and not knowing how to avoid the same fate, the spirits of those who remained sank lower and lower. When Seeker's turn came at last he was so sure he too would be rejected that he approached the table in a spirit of proud defiance.

'My name is Seeker after Truth.'

The Novice Master gazed quietly back at him, and said nothing. Seeker looked into those big blank eyes, and saw there that the decision had indeed been made. He was not accepted. There was no need to ask a question. He had been given his answer.

'It's not fair,' he said. He knew it was the wrong thing to say, but he couldn't help himself. And anyway, they knew what he was feeling. He could see it in their eyes. So why pretend?

'Just like you weren't fair to Blaze.'

The Novice Master gave a slight bow of his head, that might have been an admission of unfairness, and then he raised his right hand and turned it the smallest distance, towards the door. Seeker knew he was on the point of tears. He argued no more. All he had left was his pride. Keeping his head high, he crossed the floor, and the meek opened the door for him to pass through, and closed it after him.

As soon as he was outside, the hot tears came. They were tears of shame, tears of bitterness. He felt as truly cast out as Blaze had been. They had rejected him *without a word*! It had been enough to look at him to know he was not fit to join the Nomana.

But I am fit! I heard the voice! Why can't they at least give me a chance? It's not fair!

This was the worst of it. He burned with injustice. His father would say, 'I told you so. Do you believe me now?' But Seeker did not believe him, or the Novice Master. He believed the spirit in himself, and the voice that had spoken to him. He knew he was born to be a Noma. How could they not see it? He would prove them wrong. He would –

What could he do? Where could he go? Not home. Not to the schoolroom tomorrow. Not back to his father's plan for his life.

Then it came to him: the simple, the obvious, the

impossible, the only way to go. It was madness, but at least it offered hope.

Unaware that the tears were streaming down his cheeks, oblivious to the curious or sympathetic looks he received from departing pilgrims, he made his way down the steps, his new goal glimmering before him like a distant guiding light.

'My name is Morning Star.'

The two selectors looked up at her in silence. She felt her cheeks burning. Was this the time to ask her question? Should she wait for them to speak first?

Then the Novice Master was looking down. She saw his hand begin to move. Was it over? Was it decided? Surely that hand could not be beginning a move to the right?

'Please,' she said. 'I have a question.'

The Novice Master's hand became still. He looked up again. Morning Star had prepared several questions. What she actually said was not one of them.

'Where's my mother?'

She caught a flicker of surprise in the Novice Master's bulbous eyes. Of course: her question on its own would make no sense. Somehow she had assumed they would know.

'My mother joined the Nomana twelve years ago.'

'Your mother is a member of the Community?'

'Yes.'

'What is her name?'

'Mercy.'

The Novice Master reached for a book in front of him. He spoke to his colleague.

'Do you know the name?'

The second selector shook her head.

'We have no one in the Community of that name.'

The Novice Master ran his eyes down a list in the book.

'No,' he said. 'Your mother is not a member of the Community.'

Morning Star, already made intensely nervous by the process of selection, found herself unable to understand what they were saying.

'But she is! That's why she left us! To serve the All and Only.'

'It may be what she intended to do,' said the Novice Master. 'But it seems she was not accepted.'

Morning Star could see from their colours that they were telling the truth. But how?

'That's impossible! She must be here! If she's not here, where is she?'

'I'm sorry. I don't know.'

He lifted his hand, and turned it to the right. In a daze, Morning Star went to the outer door, and into the Shadow Court.

The shock of learning her mother was not a Noma was for the moment greater than the shock of her own rejection. She stood motionless in the dark and echoing court. Through the open doors of the high arch she could see the last pilgrims leaving the stands and making their way home.

The Congregation was over. She too must leave.

All these years she had believed her mother was one of the superior beings called the Nomana. That was why her mother had left her husband and child. That was the only reason that made sense. They had been proud of her for it. Morning Star had grown up wanting to follow in her path. And now – she wasn't here. What path had she taken? Where had she gone? Why hadn't she come home?

As this thought took hold of her, the full horror came rushing in, to fill up her heart and mind, making her feel sick and weak. It was just as Filka had said. Her mother had not come home to her because she didn't love her. What else could she believe? That she was dead?

Yes! Let her be dead! Then she could still believe in her love! Better dead than alive and not caring enough to seek out her child again!

One of the meeks coughed softly behind her, and indicated that she should move on down the steps, along with the last of the pilgrims. Morning Star had no resistance left in her. She obeyed, no longer caring where she went.

I'm a wicked girl, she thought. I want my own mother to be dead. No wonder the Nomana rejected me. Why did I ever think I was worthy of so high an honour? I'm ugly and dull and bad and even my own mother didn't want to come back to me.

Misery swept over her in a wave that was too strong to be contained. As the great sobs came rolling out of her, ashamed of her grief, she stumbled off the steps and along one of the island's terraced streets, and found a dark corner by a wall where she would not be seen. Here she crouched down and clasped her arms round her knees and cried and cried until she could cry no more. She fumbled in her bag and took out the plait of wool her father had given her, and pressed it to one damp cheek.

'Oh, Papa,' she whispered. 'How can I ever tell you?'

She spoke softly, but aloud. Her words were heard.

'Who's there?' said a voice.

There was someone on the other side of the wall. It wasn't a high wall, just a marker at the end of one property and the start of another. She uncurled herself and turned to look. There, rising up from a huddled crouch much like her own, was the boy who had run into her. His colours had turned to blue and violet, though here too there was the faint sparkle of gold she had caught before. A distant street lamp sent a glimmer of common light, by which she could see that his face was stained with tears. She remembered now: he too had been rejected.

He was staring at her with exactly the same expression of loss that she felt in herself. It was like looking in a mirror. Instinctively, as if to touch her own reflection, she put up one hand. He did the same. Their hands met, palm to palm. The flicker of gold light coming from him grew stronger. It fascinated her, this sparkle. It was like – what was it like? There was no name for it. It was like sun dust. She moved her hand, to feel the air close to his cheek, not touching his skin, reaching for the colours. He jerked back, as if fearful she would hurt him.

There came a long mournful hoot from the quay. The last boat was about to depart.

'You're crying,' he said.

'I thought my mother was here. But they sent her away.'

'Like my brother.'

'Your brother?'

'He was the one who was cast out.'

'He was your brother?'

'Yes.'

'Why didn't you go to him? You didn't even say goodbye.'

'No.'

'What has he done that's so unforgivable?'

'I don't know.'

She could see from his colours that he was ashamed, but she couldn't stop herself saying what she thought.

'If I'd been here when my mother was sent away, I'd have gone after her.'

'I wish I had.' The boy had fresh tears in his eyes. 'I wish I'd told him I don't believe it. I wish I'd said goodbye.'

'You still can. He can't have gone far.'

'There's something else I have to do. Something more important.'

'Doesn't look much like you're doing it.'

He stared at her and said nothing, but she could see the colours round him changing, as clearly as if he was speaking aloud. The blue was turning to purple, and then to red. He reached into a pocket and pulled out a pencil and paper. He wrote down some words.

'Wait here,' he said.

He ran off down the street. She saw him push the note under a closed house door. Then he was back.

'Let's go.'

Together they ran down the steps. They went as fast as they could, but long before they reached the bottom they could see the last barge moving away up the river. They kept on descending, but they didn't hurry any more. A night wind had risen, bringing with it the first patter of fat drops of rain.

The note Seeker had left for his parents to read the next morning was lying on the mat just inside the door. It read:

Gone to find Blaze. Don't worry about me. Seeker.

He said nothing about the other part of his plan. He knew they would never have understood.

CHAPTER SEVENTEEN

THE COMPACT

THE last ferry had gone, and all the other boats in the little port were tight-moored for the night; all but one. As Seeker and Morning Star reached the bottom of the steps, they saw one slender sailing boat on the point of departure. The crew had just cast off, and the bow was beginning its swing out into deep water. Here was a chance, the only chance, to leave the island that night. The rain was falling harder with every passing minute. Neither of them wanted to remain in the place of their humiliation. So without a word to each other, they both set off at a run across the flags of the quay, and jumped over the widening gap on to the boat's aft deck.

The crew were all gathered in a noisy cluster on the foredeck, on the far side of the raised cabin housing, so the arrival of the two extra passengers went unnoticed. Voices were raised in anger, and the boat was being left to drift where it willed. Some great commotion was taking place. Seeker and Morning Star huddled in the lee of the cabin, which gave some shelter from the rain, and through the slats of the cabin windows they witnessed what seemed to be a mutiny.

'Look!' said Morning Star. 'It's him!'

At the centre of the shouting crowd was the beautiful

184

youth who had burst in on the selectors, and who had been dismissed as they had been dismissed. Here, on the deck of his own boat, knife in one hand and spike in the other, careless of the falling rain, he was back fighting the kind of battle he knew how to fight.

'You don't love me no more?' he was shouting, slicing the air before his crew in an ecstasy of rage, forcing them away from him, back to the very rails. 'You don't love me no more?'

'Boss! Listen to me!'

'I've done listening! I've done too much listening! Now I'm gonna slit your chicken necks!'

'All we said was don't mess with hoodies – '

'Don't mess with me, chickens! You want to see the mess I can make?'

His sweeping blade stabbed and sliced, drawing a shriek of pain.

'You don't love me! Get off my boat! Jump!'

He swung again.

'And you jump! And you! I don't want any of you!'

He was crazier than they had ever seen him, yelling like a drunk, but he wasn't drunk, his eyes were as sharp as his spike, and he wanted blood.

'I said jump!'

The one he had slashed was the first to jump, eyes wide with terror, blood and rain soaking his left arm. After that they all jumped, fleeing the swinging blade and the stabbing spike. One after another they crashed into the dark hissing water, and struggled their way to the far bank.

There was no one at the tiller, and the Wildman didn't care. Let the currents take him where they wanted. His crew, now hauling themselves out on to the river bank, expected him to turn and pick them up again, but the *Lazy Lady* scudded on, heading for the open sea.

'I don't need any of you!' yelled the Wildman, alone on the foredeck, gleaming in the rain. He felt strong again. He had renewed himself. He was rid of the men who had witnessed his humiliation.

Then, with a punch like a fist, the storm wind swept out of the east, hurling the rain before it, and the boat bucked, and began to speed over the water.

Seeker stood up, holding hard to the cabin roof.

'We'll be swept out to sea!'

The Wildman turned and stared.

'You get off my boat!'

'You need help to sail her,' shouted Seeker, 'or you'll be swept out to sea.'

The gusting wind smacked the mainsail and threw the *Lazy Lady* on to her beam, whipping her out into the bay. The boy was right. The wind was driving hard, and it was coming off the land.

'You reef a sail?'

'No.'

'Take the tiller!'

The Wildman reached for the halyards and began to reef

the mainsail. The *Lazy Lady* was now running fast before the wind, through streaming rain. The jib sail must be tightened. Then suddenly there was a girl before him he had never seen in his life. No time for questions.

'Take that!' he shouted, throwing her a rope. 'Pull!'

Seeker had hold of the tiller.

'Take her round!' shouted the Wildman. 'Slow and strong!'

Seeker put his weight on the tiller and pushed, not knowing which way to go. The main sail was dropping, and with it the boat's speed. The Wildman saw the jib slacken, and yelled to Morning Star.

'Pull! Harder!'

They needed the last of their speed to make the jibe. Now he had the mainsail stowed, he ran back to take the tiller himself.

'Help the girl with the jib!'

Seeker and Morning Star between them kept the jib sail tight, and the Wildman worked the tiller, steering them in wide tacks against wind and rain back towards the coast. Slowly, skilfully, he brought the *Lazy Lady* into a small tree-lined inlet, where, in the lee of the land, the pounding ceased at last, and the boat righted itself, and they slipped quietly into shallow water.

The rain was still hammering down, the heavy drenching rain of summer storms. The Wildman let the boat's bottom grind into the sand of the river bed. They would be safe here till morning. Then he turned on the two strangers.

'You can go now.'

187

'Go where?' said Seeker.

'I don't care.'

'Thank you,' said Morning Star. 'We'll gladly take shelter in your cabin.'

'I never said – '

'You're very kind. You must have a wide circle of friends.'

The Wildman stared at her through the rain. Morning Star was already on her way down the ladder to the cabin. Seeker followed her.

'Fool girly!' exclaimed the Wildman, slashing angrily at nothing with his spike.

In the cabin, Morning Star squeezed the rainwater from her soaked clothing, and set about looking for something to eat.

'I don't know about you,' she said, 'but I'm hungry.'

'I'm starving,' said Seeker.

The Wildman came stamping down the steps into the cabin.

'You get off my boat!' he said.

Morning Star had found the provisions store.

'Cheese,' she said, putting it on the table. 'Shortbread.'

'You leaving?' said the Wildman. 'Or do you want your necks slit?'

'I'm not leaving,' said Morning Star. 'So if you really must cut my throat, you'd better get on with it.'

The Wildman stared at her, baffled. Both Morning Star and Seeker had started to eat, and were paying him no attention. This gave the Wildman a problem. He was quite capable of killing them both if sufficiently enraged, but he was not sufficiently enraged. They were disobeying him, but they weren't taunting or provoking him. Somehow it was not possible to lean across the table and cut their throats as they sat there eating his shortbread.

'That's my shortbread!'

'I bet you stole it off someone else,' said Morning Star.

'So I did! That's why it's mine now.'

'Have some. It's good.'

It was good shortbread. The Wildman realised he too was hungry.

'I'm not saying I won't slit your necks later,' he said.

'That's quite understood.'

So he too sat down at the table with them and ate. Everyone knows how hunger makes for bad temper, and how satisfying that hunger brings about, surprisingly quickly, a change of mood. So it was with the three who had fled from the holy island in the storm. They ate all the shortbread and all the cheese, and then felt inclined to be friendly.

The rain was still hammering down on the cabin roof.

'You might as well stay till the storm passes,' said the Wildman. 'Help me pull her off the river bed.'

'Can you sail her by yourself?' said Seeker, knowing he couldn't.

'Don't much matter.' The Wildman gave a shrug. 'It's not like I'm going anywhere.'

'You wanted to join the Nomana, didn't you?'

The Wildman blushed a deep red. Morning Star didn't

need to read his colours to know that this was the anger of humiliation.

'Who says so?'

'We saw you. We both tried to join too. We were both rejected too.'

'Rejected?'

'So you see,' said Morning Star, 'we're all the same, really, and you don't need to slit our throats.'

'Rejected!' said the Wildman again, with mounting bitterness. 'What's wrong with me? Why don't they want me?'

'Everything's wrong with you,' said Morning Star. 'You're violent and cruel and selfish and ignorant.'

'I'm not ignorant!'

'Yes, you are. What do you know about the Nomana?'

'I know they got power! And I know what they've got in their Garden.'

'What have they got in their Garden?'

'Peace.'

'What sort of peace?'

'How would I know?'

'You don't know much, then.'

'We can't talk,' said Seeker. 'They rejected us too.'

'That's right!' The Wildman glared at Morning Star. 'Fool girly!'

'I expect I am a fool,' said Morning Star, feeling the sadness return. 'I wanted so much to join the Community.'

'Me too,' said Seeker. 'It's all I've ever wanted.'

'They don't want me, just like they didn't want my mother.'

'Or my brother,' said Seeker.

The Wildman found he was not following.

'What mother? What brother?'

Seeker explained about Blaze, and how he had been cast out. The Wildman was more impressed by the fact that he had been accepted in the first place.

'Your brother's a hoodie?'

'He was.'

'They trained him in the powers?'

'Yes.'

'So he can train me!'

'I don't think so. Not any more.'

But the Wildman was wonderfully indifferent to the needs of others. It never once occurred to him that Seeker might be suffering at his brother's disgrace. Morning Star saw this and marvelled. He was a sort of human freak: a person with no heart and no conscience.

'How simple life must look to you,' she said.

'Simple? What's simple?'

'You see something you want. You demand it.'

The Wildman was baffled.

'What's wrong with that?'

'It doesn't matter. It's a long story.'

'I don't need you, girly. You get off my boat.' He turned to Seeker. 'Maybe your hoodie brother can tell me what I have to do so the hoodies want me.'

191

'I don't know where he's gone,' said Seeker. 'And he couldn't tell you anything anyway. He's been cleansed.'

The memory of Blaze's blank face made him frown and look away. He didn't want to cry in front of the bandit.

'But you're going to look for him,' said Morning Star. 'That's what you said.'

'What do you mean, cleansed?' said the Wildman.

'They've taken away his powers. And his memory too.'

'Whoa!' exclaimed the Wildman, impressed. 'Those hoodies!'

'You are going to look for him, aren't you?' said Morning Star, watching Seeker closely. She could tell from his colours that something strange was going on inside him. All round him glowed the soft lavender colour that went with dreaming and longing, and flickering within it there showed again those unfamiliar flashes of gold.

'Yes,' said Seeker slowly. 'Only there's something I have to do first.'

Morning Star read his mind. It wasn't hard. She could see from his colours that he was filled with longing, and she knew from his own mouth that he wanted more than anything to be accepted into the Community.

'You know another way to become a Noma.'

He looked up, startled.

'How do you know that?'

'I just do.'

'Another way to be a hoodie?' cried the Wildman. 'What other way?'

192

'I can't tell you.'

'You tell me, brava, or I slit your neck.'

'Do you always cut the throats of people who don't do what you want?' said Morning Star.

'Not always. Sometimes.'

'And after you've cut their throats, do they do what you want?'

'She always talk like this?'

'I don't know,' said Seeker, 'I only just met her.'

'Tell us this other way,' Morning Star persisted. 'Maybe I can help you.'

'You?' sneered the Wildman. 'What use is a fool girly to anyone?'

'More use than a fool spiker,' retorted Morning Star.

'Maybe you're right,' said Seeker.

He'd had a moment to think, and had reached the conclusion that his plan might have a better chance of success if he had help. Also, he found he wanted company.

So he decided to tell them.

'Not all the Nomana enter the Community the way we tried, by applying and being selected. Some get invited.'

'Invited!'

'Some of the most famous Nomana were invited. Because they'd done something praiseworthy, or of great value to the Community. Something the Nomana themselves couldn't do.'

'Something the Nomana couldn't do?' Morning Star was dismayed. 'We don't have the powers they have. How can there be anything we can do that they can't?'

Seeker had thought about this, and believed he knew how it could be done; but for the moment he wanted to keep his idea to himself. It was enough for now to tell them the objective.

'There's a secret weapon,' he said. 'It's going to destroy the whole island of Anacrea.'

'Whoa!' exclaimed the Wildman, impressed.

'It's somewhere in the city of Radiance. Only, no one knows exactly what it is, or exactly where it is.'

'Radiance!' Morning Star spoke the name with a shudder. 'That's a bad place.'

For once the Wildman agreed with her.

'Don't mess with Radiance,' he said. 'They're crazy there. They throw people off high rocks.'

Seeker paid no attention to this.

'If we could find this weapon,' he said, 'and destroy it before it destroys Anacrea, then I think the Nomana would give us everything we want.'

'The powers of the hoodies? The peace they've got in the Garden?'

'Everything.'

'Heya!' The Wildman's eyes shone at the prospect.

'How can we?' said Morning Star. 'We're nobodies.'

'Maybe,' said Seeker, 'that's why we can do what the Nomana can't do. We're just ordinary people. We won't attract any attention. We could go to Radiance, and no one would ask any questions. And once we're there, we can

194

start looking around.'

'Heya!' exclaimed the Wildman again. 'We find this weapon, and heya! ha!' He stabbed the air with his spike. 'That's when you'll be glad to have the Wildman by your side!'

'I think I will,' said Seeker.

'But we don't need the girly. She's no use.'

'You're wrong,' said Seeker. 'She knows things.'

'She don't know anything worth the knowing.'

'I know what you're thinking,' said Morning Star.

'So what am I thinking?'

She studied his colours carefully. Mostly the shimmer round him was the bright yellow of self-absorption, as she would expect. People who glowed yellow like that simply couldn't see anything or anyone else. But there were traces of other colours too: flickers of red, waiting to flame up as rage, and flickers of violet, that came from heartache; and round it all, an unexpected fringe of that soft lavender blue she had seen in Seeker, the colour of longing and hope. She interpreted instinctively, not waiting to attempt an analysis.

'You're thinking that everyone in the world is against you. You're so tired of that. You're thinking you've got yourself into more trouble over the hoodies than they're worth. But you can't let go of a kind of longing when you think of them.'

The Wildman jumped as if she had attacked him.

'Whoa!' he cried. 'How do you know all that?'

'I just do.'

'You get out of my head. Nobody messes with the Wildman!'

'See?' said Seeker. 'She knows things.'

'And I'll tell you something else I know,' said Morning Star. 'The hoodies don't use their powers for themselves. They use them in the service of others.'

'What do they do that for?'

'That's their vow. That's why people want to join them. So they can help people, and not let there be so much suffering in the world, and change things, and make things better.'

'Then they've not done too well so far, have they?' retorted the Wildman. 'I don't see things getting any better.'

'Maybe they don't do much, but at least they do something.'

Seeker quoted the words from the Legend.

'The little we can do, that we must do, so that others know good men too can be strong.'

'And until you understand that,' said Morning Star, 'you'll never be one of them.'

'Well, I don't care about that.'

He spoke defiantly, but Morning Star was watching his colours, and she saw a growing tinge of green. Green was the colour of uncertainty. If he was beginning to know that he didn't know, then there was hope for him.

The Wildman turned to Seeker.

'You and me,' he said. 'Outside.'

The rain was passing. Seeker followed the Wildman out

on to the glistening deck.

'There's things you can't say in front of girls,' he said.

'She has a sharp tongue.'

'I don't care about sharp. But girls are never the same thing. One day sweet, next day sour. One minute laughing, next minute crying. I like people to be the same thing all the time. When a man stands his ground, he's there and nowhere else. Do you follow me?'

'Yes. I think so.'

'So here's what I need to know. If we do this thing we're talking about – find the weapon – save the hoodies – what if they take you and not me?'

His voice suddenly sounded smaller. Seeker understood then what it was the Wildman feared. The bandit knew very well that he didn't understand the Nomana. He was afraid of being rejected a second time.

'I can't promise what they'll do,' Seeker said. 'But I can promise what I'll do.'

'What will you do?'

'If you come with us, and if together we do what we plan to do, then I'll say to them that they must take us all three, or none at all.'

'You'd say that?'

His eyes searched Seeker's face, hunting for any sign that this was a trick.

'Yes. I would. I will.'

'You wouldn't rat me?'

'Why should I?'

'Because that's what people do.'

'Well, it's not what I do.'

Still the Wildman gazed at him, with a look that was torn between doubt and longing.

'I've never trusted anyone in all my life. That's why I'm alive today. So if I come with you, and we do this thing, and you rat me, I'll kill you.'

Seeker saw it clearly now: the Wildman was proposing a compact of faith. Young though he was, Seeker knew that this was a grave commitment. And yet, for all his hard life and bold words, Seeker felt how much, how achingly, the Wildman longed to trust in someone other than himself. Out of his lifelong loneliness he had picked on Seeker, and was reaching out to him. Literally so: his hand was extended towards him.

Seeker knew almost nothing about him, but he responded instinctively, and without hesitation. He took the Wildman's hand, and felt the fierce power of his grip. The Wildman spoke to him, his dark eyes burning.

'Say: I stand with you.'

'I stand with you.'

'From today to the end of the world.'

'From today to the end of the world.'

The Wildman released his hand.

'No need to tell the girly,' he said.

PART THREE

RADIANCE

My brothers:

We have placed all our trust in one young heart.

Watch over him. He faces dangers beyond his years. He
may be called upon to make the final sacrifice.

May the All and Only give him courage, and light his way
with the Clear Light.

CHAPTER EIGHTEEN

CHEERFUL GIVER

CHEERFUL Giver had been in a rage all day. What made him doubly furious was that he had warned his wife, he had begged her, he had threatened her, but she had paid no attention whatsoever. He might as well have been talking to a puddle of water. He had told her repeatedly to leave the tribute alone, not to sit with him or talk to him, but she had done both, she had spent hours with him, she was always finding time to slip into his room for a few more encouraging words. The inevitable had happened. She had forgotten to lock the door after her. And now the tribute was gone.

'I'm sure I locked the door,' said his wife plaintively. 'I do lock the door every time. But if I didn't, and he got out, then I call it most ungrateful. After all I've done for him.'

It was this sort of remark that drove Cheerful Giver wild.

'Ungrateful! He was a spiker! A homeless, ignorant beggar! How can street sweepings like that be grateful?'

'If he was so worthless, why did you pay a thousand shillings for him?'

'Because I must offer a tribute on my name day! Great Sun! Have you lost your wits? Do you want our family to be disgraced?'

His wife began to cry, as usual. Her name was Blessing. At times like these he found himself wishing she would give her blessing to someone, anyone, else.

'I don't know why you have to be so unkind to me,' she whimpered. 'I was only doing my best. You know how everyone admires a willing tribute. And I thought I was doing so well with him. He'd really begun to appreciate the great honour of being a tribute. And now all you can do is shout at me.'

What could Cheerful Giver do? He had no choice. That very afternoon he had let it be known, discreetly, that he was in the market for another high-quality tribute. The money would have to be found. Meanwhile, the day was ending, and he had his duties to perform.

It had been a hot, hot summer's day. At last, as the sun sank towards the still waters of the lake, the air was cooling to a bearable temperature. All across the city the people were making their way towards the temple square for the evening offering. Blessing, who possessed a fine contralto voice, would already be at the temple, taking her place in the choir.

Cheerful Giver, herding his two young sons before him, took a route that ran between the city proper and the floating gardens. The boys liked to race up and down the walkways of the floating gardens, bouncing on the roped timbers to make them rock. By this time of day the migrant workers had retreated to their camps along the lake shore, where they could be glimpsed huddled together in weary clusters, watched over by officers of the street patrol.

The lake looked tranquil in the evening light. The range of mountains to the east glowed in the golden rays of the setting sun. What a beautiful city I live in, thought Cheerful Giver, feeling the frustrations of the day slip away. He liked to take this road to the temple for just this reason. A busy and successful man of affairs like himself had much on his mind. But at the end of the day he could afford to relax a little.

Then he saw Small Dream waiting for him at the turn in the road ahead. Small Dream was a fellow merchant and, in Cheerful Giver's secret opinion, a two-faced crawler who would do anything to gain royal favour. On his name day he had offered as tribute a beautiful young virgin, who was said to be neither beautiful, nor young, nor a virgin. The rumour was that he had paid two thousand shillings for her.

'I hear you lost your tribute,' said Small Dream with an odious smile of pretended sympathy. 'That's too bad.'

'One of them,' said Cheerful Giver, concealing a yawn. 'I really do believe this has been the hottest day of the year so far.'

'You have more than one tribute?'

'Oh, yes. Don't you?'

'How many more?'

'We have two. Mercifully, it was the old man that got out. We still have the virgin.'

This was a lie, and Small Dream knew it was a lie, but

Cheerful Giver carried it off with such assurance that all Small Dream could do was shake his head.

'I wish you good fortune in your business, then.'

This was his way of making it quite clear he knew Cheerful Giver would be having to put his hand deep into his pocket.

'With prices like these it's not easy for any of us.'

'Boys!' called Cheerful Giver sharply. 'Stop that!'

The boys were running up and down the walkways between the floating gardens, chasing scavenger cats. Cheerful Giver watched them run, as the light of the setting sun threw long shadows over the rows of ripening squashes and tomatoes. He reflected bitterly on how rich Small Dream must be, to be comfortable pretending he was poor.

'Boys! Do as I say!'

'Aw, Dad! We got one in a corner.'

'Well, just the one, then. We'll be late.'

Up on the highest level of the temple, the king was in the middle of his hate training session. The beating of the drum and the rhythmic howls of rage could be heard through the closed doors, as the court officials gathered for the evening offering. The High Priest himself had not yet arrived. He was detained on one of the lower levels by a visitor who brought him information of considerable interest.

'You say the king knows nothing of this?'

'He knows in general terms, Holiness. But the details, no.'

Sitting in a low chair in the High Priest's private office,

writing with nervousness and resentment, was the small but eminent scientist Professor Evor Ortus.

'So our ill-favoured young secretary hopes to present the king with a surprise victory?'

'For which he will take all the credit, Holiness. The credit that rightfully belongs to the Radiant Power above, and to me.'

'Of course it does. This so-called secretary is no scientist, whatever else he may or may not be. How could he have the effrontery to pretend he could create such a weapon?'

'He's a clever young man, Holiness.'

'But he's not the only clever man, is he, professor? You and I know a thing or two, I think.'

'So you'll help me, Holiness?'

'For the greater glory of the Radiant Power we both serve, professor, yes, I will help you. You say you want a volunteer. Tell me what sort of volunteer you're looking for.'

'One who can enter Anacrea without arousing suspicion. And one who has a passionate hatred for the Nomana.'

The High Priest looked grave.

'Not easy.'

'That hideous young man says where there's power, there's hatred.'

'And you say he's gone in search of just such a person himself?'

'Yes, Holiness. He could return any day.'

From high above the High Priest caught the tinkling

sound of the priests on their way to collect the day's tribute. He rose from his chair.

'We will see what we can do.'

Professor Ortus rose too.

'Say nothing of this to anyone else, professor. That way, perhaps it will be you and I who will be presenting the king with a surprise victory.'

Cheerful Giver hustled his boys across the crowded temple square, afraid that on top of everything else he might be late for his duties. The boys kept stopping to look out for the first appearance of the tribute on the rock high above.

'Will he be a screamer, Dad?'

'I've no idea. Come along. Hurry up.'

'Can I have a toffee apple, Dad?'

'No, you can't.'

Toffee apple sellers cruised the square, along with sellers of shelled nuts and corn fritters and bread sticks. Under the arches of the colonnades that ran round three sides of the square clustered stalls that sold wine, and brandy from the bag at a penny a suck, and roasted chicken legs, and fish baked in salt, and all the latest songs. Anything that could be bought and sold for ready money was to be had at the evening offering.

The boys ran off to bang at the wooden hatches that walled the kennels. There were air-vents in the hatch doors, and the noses of the temple dogs could be seen snuffling and dribbling, pushing through the holes. The boys kicked and poked at the dogs, daring each other to touch the wet noses. The dogs emitted low, rumbling growls, and, when hit, sharp yelps. They were big wolf-hounds, kept in a permanent state of semi-starvation, and therefore extremely dangerous. Their handlers, all men with broad chests and muscular leather-clad arms, leaned against the kennel doors and watched the boys at play with bored expressions.

'Don't hurt the dogs, boys!' called Cheerful Giver as he headed on up the stairway. 'Wait for me here.'

'They hurt the dogs,' said the head dog handler, 'they're dog meat.'

Cheerful Giver climbed the broad stairs to the royal terrace as briskly as he could, and arrived panting to find that the king had not yet finished his hate training. The corona was ready on its stand, with its keeper beside it, tweaking at its petals.

The High Priest, entering at almost the same time, turned his plump features towards him and raised his trimmed eyebrows. Cheerful Giver muttered the obligatory salutation.

'Guide me with your wisdom, Holiness. Protect me with your power.'

'I'm sorry to hear you've mislaid your tribute.'

'Only an old spiker, Holiness. We have a much finer tribute ready for my name day.'

Silently he cursed his wife and her foolish carelessness. But he had no intention of letting the High Priest know he was still in trouble.

The king himself joined them at last, just as the priests were passing by with the day's tribute. The tribute's white robe failed to disguise the fact that he was a wheezing and enfeebled old man. The king, energised by his hate session, frowned with displeasure.

'Surely we can do better,' he complained to the assembled officials. 'Is this how we honour the Radiant Power above? With beggars who can hardly crawl?'

The High Priest, who was ultimately responsible for the provision of the tributes, came hurrying forward.

'It shall be attended to, Radiance.'

'Look at him! This is too bad! And don't think I don't know what's going on.'

'Yes, Radiance.'

The king was referring to the rumour that the priests sold the finer specimens from the tanks, and pocketed the proceeds. The High Priest knew the best way to handle the king on such occasions. Offer no argument, and trust to the passing of time. The king had a very short memory.

However, to the High Priest's irritation, Cheerful Giver had also heard the king, and he returned to the topic as he placed the corona on the king's shoulders.

'It will be my name day in four days' time, Radiance. I can promise you a fine tribute then.'

'Good, good,' said the king. 'Sun's on its way down. Let's get on with it.'

Cheerful Giver retired, his ceremonial duty done. In his mind he was now more determined than ever to spare no expense. He would buy the finest tribute of all, and his name day would set a new standard, to which all others could only aspire.

The High Priest looked round the crowd of officials to locate the ugly little secretary, and then remembered that he had left the city on secret business. He frowned, and then nodded to himself. He had been right not to trust the outlander. He had found out only just in time.

The sun sank below the horizon. The tribute fell in silence. The offering was made, and the sun would rise next morning.

The royal party dispersed. When Cheerful Giver rejoined his sons down in the square, he found they had not been impressed by the evening's tribute.

'That was rubbish, Dad.'

'When's there going to be another screamer, Dad? The screamers are the best.'

'No, they're not! The fat ones are the best! The really, really fat ones that bounce!'

'I'm hungry, Dad.'

Cheerful Giver put an arm round each of his boys, and they set off for home. They were fine boys, he reflected; tall for their age, and good-looking too.

'You wait till my name day, boys. Your old dad may make you proud yet.'

CHAPTER NINETEEN

BLAZE

SOREN Similin left the holy island on the same barge as Blaze. In the darkness of the crowded deck, among the huddle of pilgrims, there was nothing to mark him out, and he was able to watch Blaze without himself being watched. When the rain came, and all the others took shelter under hastily rigged tarpaulins, Blaze remained uncovered, alone. He seemed to feel nothing and see nothing. Instinctively, the other pilgrims avoided him. That suited the secretary very well. He would befriend the friendless young man. He would teach that poor cleansed mind to hate the Community he had once served, and which had cast him out.

As he watched, he saw Blaze raise one hand to his face, and cup it over his mouth. Was it to warm his hand with his breath? Then Blaze turned a little to one side, responding to the rocking of the barge, and Similin was able to see why. He was sucking his thumb.

When the night storm swept down the river, the bargees tethered the barge to the bank, and the pilgrims squeezed together beneath the tarpaulins and slept as best they could. By the time the wind had died down and the rain had ceased, light was breaking in the east, and the barge continued on its way upriver into the dawn.

The sun had just risen over the horizon when they reached the riverside general store. The bargees had an arrangement with the General, the store's owner. In return for making their passengers stop at the store for an hour or so, the bargees were given a free meal. This morning, however, the old man was unimpressed.

'What's that you're bringing me? More lice-infested pilgrims! Pilgrims never have any money! Bring me travellers with money!'

'Shut your mouth, you old chiseller. Fry up some eggs.'

'This whole crowd isn't worth the price of a single egg!'

The pilgrims disembarked. Blaze followed the rest into the store. The waterfront porch, where General Store spent most of his day rocking in his chair, was no wider than a small house; but the store that ran back from the porch was deep. There were three long aisles, flanked by shelves crammed with all manner of trading goods, and these aisles ran back and back into deeper and deeper shadows. Light entered the store through slanting windows in the roof, windows that had gathered layers of dust and grime and rotted leaves over the years, so that the illumination that filtered through was feeble and intermittent. This gave the interior of the long shed a stippled look, with certain items picked out by shafts of light at random – here a clump of candles glued to each other by the heat, there a waterproof hat, shiny and never worn – while the rest of the goods were cushioned in soft shadow. Hammers and nails, black-iron kettles, scouring powder, spices, knife sharpeners, rubber over-boots, elastic suspenders, candied fruit, river maps, pencils, scented hair cream: the old man had it all in his store.

The long central shelves were open on both sides, so that as the customers made their way down the aisles they could glimpse, between stacks of tin plates, or past the ruby twinkle of glass-bead necklaces, the customers in the neighbouring aisle. In this way Soren Similin followed Blaze, keeping him in sight without himself being seen.

Blaze had been stripped of his badan, but he still wore the plain grey tunic of a Noma. Similin watched him as he stood before a rack of workman's clothing, and knew as exactly as if he had spoken what was passing through his mind. Blaze wanted to shed what was left of his past; but he had no money with which to buy new clothes. Similin decided the time had come to make a connection.

'Forgive me,' he said, coming up to Blaze's side. 'I was at the Congregation last night. I saw what happened.'

Blaze turned his broad face and blank eyes on to this stranger who addressed him.

'I don't know you.'

'The Community gave no reason for their decision. I can't condemn a man for an unknown crime.'

'What crime?'

Blaze spoke flatly, neither offended nor seeking a response. Soren Similin persisted, knowing that every word he spoke would be fresh to this new-born mind, and would become part of the new character that was now forming.

214

'You have been unjustly treated,' he said, speaking slowly and carefully. 'I would like to help you.'

'Help me?'

Similin held out a few coins.

'Here,' he said. 'For you.'

Blaze took the coins without a word of thanks. Similin withdrew. When, a little later, Blaze came out of the store, he no longer wore the grey clothing of the Nomana. He wore the faded blue work clothes of a field labourer. With what was left of the money, he bought himself breakfast. Similin noted with a private smile that he ordered bacon. The Nomana never ate meat.

The pilgrims from the barge were not the only people in the store. There were also a number of young spiker men, barefoot and dressed in ragged clothing tied with string. They loitered on the riverside deck, plainly penniless, and while not openly begging, they stared at the sausages and potatoes sizzling on the range with hungry eyes.

The bargees returned at last to their barge and clanged the dangling iron pipe that served for a bell, and the pilgrims trooped back on board. Blaze stopped by the chair where old General Store sat whistling and grunting in his almost permanent state of half-sleep.

'I'm looking for work,' he said.

'Work?' said the General. 'Are you a spiker?'

'What's a spiker?'

'Spikers are idle cheating thieves!' He squinted at Blaze from beneath gummy lids. 'You don't look like a spiker. What sort of work do you want?'

'Anything.'

'Anything for money, eh? The money's all upriver, in the lake cities. But they're a vicious crowd. Too many priests. You could try the plantations. There's always work to be had on the plantations. Corn harvest's just begun.'

'Where are the plantations?'

'Follow the road. Don't waste your time going to the plantation houses. The masters and mistresses with their fine linen and fancy manners don't have anything to do with the field workers. You want to go to the gangmasters. They see to all that.'

'Where are the gangmasters?'

The old man pulled out a much-worn map of the region, and showed him how the road inland met another road a few miles away, and formed a crossroads. Here the gangmasters came each morning to hire labour for the plantations nearby.

Blaze thanked him, in his blank voice.

'Oh, don't thank me. It's work, sure enough, and you'll be paid, sure enough, but it's no life. Those gangmasters know to a grain of corn how much to give you so you keep working, and not a morsel more. But it's work, if that's your desire.'

Blaze set off on foot up the track. Soren Similin watched him out of sight, and then beckoned to three of the spikers. They went aside with him into the trees, where they wouldn't be overheard, and there Similin showed them the

216

money he was carrying, and made them a proposal. In doing this, he took a risk. The spikers could choose to attack him then and there in the trees, and not go to the further trouble of carrying out his plan. But they were stupid, as he plainly saw, and once one idea for getting easy money was planted in their heads, there was no room for any other.

He then sent the spikers away through the trees, while he himself set off down the track after Blaze. The morning was now well advanced, and the sun was hot, but the young man strode along as fast as he could. Shortly he saw Blaze moving more slowly in front of him. And within a few minutes, he was passing him.

He nodded a greeting as he passed, and Blaze nodded back, but Similin did not attempt to get into conversation. Instead, he strode on round the bend in the track. There, as agreed, the spikers were waiting for him.

They played their part with more energy than was strictly necessary. One seized Similin from behind, and got an armlock round his neck, and bent him backwards. Another hit him several times in the stomach. The third searched for his purse.

'Help! Thieves!' yelled Similin.

Blaze came round the corner, which was a good fifty paces from the fracas, and saw that the man who had helped him was being robbed. He stared in surprise. He looked as if he had never seen one man attack another before.

'What are you doing?' he said.

The spikers, following their instructions, backed away,

taking Similin's purse with them. Blaze started towards them.

'What are you doing?' he said again.

He made no threatening gestures. But the spikers had done what had been asked of them, and gained their reward, and so now they vanished back into the trees. Soren Similin struggled to his feet.

'Are you hurt?' said Blaze.

'I'm all right. I can never thank you enough.'

'Thank me? What for?'

'You saved my life!'

'Did I?'

'Had you not come to my rescue, they would have cut my throat and left me for dead. You're a brave man, sir. Let me shake your hand.'

Blaze let him shake his hand, still clearly puzzled about what it was he had done.

'May I walk with you, since we take the same road?'

'Yes. Of course.'

They walked on down the track together, talking as they went. Soren Similin was skilful and patient, like a fisherman playing a fish on a line. There would be time enough to reach his true goal. For now what he needed was to make Blaze accept him as his one true friend and travelling companion.

'May I know the name of the brave man who saved my life?'

'Who's that?'

'You.'

'Me?'

'I would like to know your name.'

'My name? Yes.' Blaze's smooth brow furrowed as he puzzled over this question. After some searching, he found the required information. 'Blaze,' he said. 'Blaze of Justice.'

'Blaze of Justice! You certainly live up to your name.'

'Do I?'

'Your bravery was an act of justice. I can see that you're a man who means to put right the wrongs of the world.'

'Do you think so?'

'I most certainly do. Why, I wouldn't be surprised to discover you're the kind of man who'd even give his life in a just cause.'

'Give my life . . .' Blaze seemed to find that interesting. He said it again, as if feeling the shape of the idea. 'Give my life . . .'

'But for now, you're looking for work.'

'Yes, I am. You see, I have nothing.'

'I too am looking for work.'

Blaze's expressionless face slowly lit up in a pleased smile.

'Well, then,' he said. 'Why don't we look for work together?'

'Now there's an excellent idea,' said Soren Similin, smiling in return.

CHAPTER TWENTY

SPIKERTOWN

JUST to the south of the empire of Radiance, along the banks of the Great River, lay the sprawl of shanties and makeshift shelters known as Spikertown. Twilight was gathering as the *Lazy Lady* tacked slowly upriver to the mooring in the reeds that the Wildman called home. A crowd of ragged children formed to watch them tie up, and from a nearby bar came the lilting groan of a squeezebox, and the sound of drunken male voices singing. Lamps glowed up and down the narrow winding alleys, and smoke rising from hundreds of cook-fires trailed in the wind across the darkening sky.

Seeker and Morning Star had never heard of Spikertown, and were astonished at its size.

'I didn't know there were so many spikers.'

'There's more than you'll find in Spikertown,' said the Wildman. 'There's spikers all over. Wherever people have to leave their homes, you get more spikers on the move.'

'Is that all spikers are? People with no homes?'

'No homes. No land. No laws. No nothing.'

'I thought spikers were thieves and robbers.'

'You'd be a thief and a robber if you were hungry enough.'

The Wildman proposed that his new companions

remain on the boat while he went ashore to get provisions for an evening meal. He said this was for their safety, but the truth was he was ashamed to be seen with them. He was well known in Spikertown, and knew he would find it hard to explain what had become of his crew, and why he was travelling instead with these much younger companions.

The market stalls were mostly closed, but he found one where the slabs of moist corn pudding had not yet been put away. He bought three sizeable squares, and a ham sausage. Then he stopped at the fat man's bar for a glass of his fiery ginger wine. The wind was rattling the awnings, and jiggering the candle-flames in their jars, and three burly miners from the hills were singing a mournful song.

'Down down down she goes
Bubble bubble bubble
Love gets you nothing but
Trouble trouble trouble . . .'

The Wildman downed his drink in three gulps, took up his bundle, and turned to leave. Immediately outside the bar, in the narrow alleyway between the shanties, stood a strikingly handsome young woman. Her hands were on her hips, and she was waiting for him.

'Look who just blew in!' she said.

'Heya, Caressa,' said the Wildman.

'Coming to call on me, were you?'

'Not today, Princess.'

The young woman tossed back her tumble of dark hair

and smiled an angry smile with her full red lips. She was eighteen years old, the daughter of one of the bandit lords of Spikertown, and accustomed to getting what she wanted.

'Don't leave it too long, boy. Shab came for me the other day. Asking to marry me.'

'Nice for you.'

'No, it's not nice for me. He got a smack in the face.'

'See here, Princess – '

'No, you see here. You know you'll have me in the end, so you'll have me now, or you'll be sorry.'

'How will I be sorry?'

'I'll have my father's boys nail you to a door.'

'Whoa! Not nice, Princess.'

'Who said I was nice?'

'So I marry you, or I get nailed to a door?'

'That's the way it is.'

The Wildman seemed to ponder this choice. Then, 'Which door, exactly?'

'You louse!' She hit him across one cheek. 'You dung-rat!' She hit him again.

'Don't hit me, girl!'

She hit him again.

'I do as I please, boy!'

So he hit her back, a whack across her face with his open palm. At that she flew on him, pulling at his hair, pummelling his body, kneeing his groin, sending his bundle of provisions flying. He fought her off, pushing her to the ground, but she sprang up again, and locked her arms

222

round him, pinning his arms against his body.

'You squirt of pus!' she said, panting. 'You'll have me whether you want to or not!'

'I won't!'

'You can't do better. They all want me. You know they do.'

'I don't want anybody,' he said. 'Not yet a while.'

He pushed the girl off him at last. She stood there glowering at him with her handsome eyes.

'You're mine or you're nobody's,' she said. 'If you go with any other girl, I'll kill you both.'

'You won't have to do that, Princess. I'm going away.'

'You'll come back.'

'Maybe not for years.'

'I'll come looking for you.'

'No, you won't. You'll forget all about me. I'll come back one day and you won't even know who I am.'

'How's that?' she said. 'You planning on turning into somebody else?'

'Maybe I am,' he said.

'You're just fine the way you are.'

'Used to be I thought so too. Not any more.'

There was something in his voice when he said this that quietened her down.

'What is it you want, Wildman?'

'That's what I have to go find out.'

'Some other girl?'

'No. Not a girl.'

'If it was a girl, would it be me?'

'Yes,' he said. 'If it was a girl, it would be you.'

She could ask no more, and she knew it.

'That's all right, then,' she said. 'I'll wait for you.'

'Might be for ever.'

'Oh, no.' She sounded scornful. 'Boys always want girls in the end. It just takes them longer to find it out.'

She left him there, and he picked up his bundle and continued on his way back to the boat.

There he laid out the ham sausage and the corn pudding, and he and Seeker and Morning Star ate their supper and made plans.

'How far is it to Radiance?'

'Two days' walk.'

'You ever been there, Wildman?'

'Not me, no.'

Their plan was to enter the city as migrant workers, and then start their search for the secret weapon.

'That should be easy,' said Morning Star, 'considering we know nothing at all.'

'We could ask the River Prophet,' said the Wildman.

'Who's that?'

'She's like a fortune teller. But she's got real knowledge. All the knowledge there is to be had.'

'Is she a spiker too?'

'Oh, yes, she's a spiker. We've all sorts in Spikertown.'

When they had eaten, they settled down in blankets on the cabin floor to sleep. Morning Star found herself wondering about the Wildman's own past.

'So where did you come from, Wildman? Before you were a spiker.'

'Been a spiker all my life,' he replied.

'You must have had parents.'

'Not that I ever knew.'

'So who looked after you when you were little?'

'There was a whole crowd of us looked after each other. There was a kid called Snakey. He was good to me. He watched out for me. That's as far back as I can remember, lying down to sleep where I could see Snakey and thinking, I'll be safe tonight.'

'How old were you then?'

'Four. Five.'

'And how old was Snakey?'

'Eight or nine.'

Morning Star fell silent, thinking of how her own father had always been there, within close reach, every night of her life. It was not something she'd ever thought of as a kindness on his part; but now, listening to the Wildman, she found a new cause to love her father. She wondered what it was like for him now, alone in their little house, and knew it must be hard. So she felt in her pocket for her little braid of lamb's wool, and pressed it to her cheek, and said silently, *I love you, Papa.*

Seeker asked, 'What do you think happened to your parents, Wildman?'

'Never did know,' said the Wildman. 'Never did care.'

225

'Maybe they died.'

'Or maybe they just went off.'

He spoke lightly, as if it was a matter of indifference to him; but Morning Star could see the faint violet glow that hovered round his head, and knew he was hurt more than he chose to say.

Those who sought information in Spikertown, and those who sought guidance, and all the rest who just wanted their fortune told, walked the river path to consult the old lady who called herself the River Prophet. For the sake of convenience, her home and her place of work were combined, the one on top of the other, and both stood on a flat-bottomed barge that was moored by a bend in the river on the edge of town. The lower part of the structure was a miniature temple, built of wood and painted white. The temple had a handsome four-pillared portico on its front, the pillars necessarily close together, with a triangular pediment above. Inside the portico was a pair of white-painted wooden doors, and beyond the doors the temple itself, just big enough to hold the River Prophet's throne and a space before it for her petitioners to kneel at her feet.

On top of the temple, like a shaggy low-brimmed hat, sat a thatched cottage. This comical arrangement made the craft taller than it was long, and entirely unsailable. But the River Prophet had no plans to sail away. This was where she conducted her business, and it suited her very well.

A bell hung from one of the white pillars, and by it there was a sign that read: FOR PROPHET RING BELL. Here, early the next morning, came the Wildman and Seeker and Morning Star. There was a second sign by the bell that read: THE PROPHET IS OUT.

'She never goes out,' said the Wildman, frowning.

He rang the bell, long and loud.

'Go away!' shouted a shrill voice from the upper room. 'It's my day off.'

'We got fresh knowledge,' the Wildman called out. 'About the hoodies.'

This was met with silence.

'You wait,' said the Wildman. 'She can't resist fresh knowledge.'

He was right. The shutters on the upper window now opened, and the Prophet herself looked out: a round wrinkly face framed by a mass of frizzy white hair.

'Oh, it's you,' she said. 'Well? What have you got?'

'If we give you fresh knowledge, you got to answer our questions,' said the Wildman.

'Answers cost money,' said the old woman. 'I can't eat knowledge, can I? And the chances are I know it already.'

'This knowledge happened the day before yesterday. At the gathering of the hoodies.'

'The hoodies?' The Prophet stopped sounding irritable. 'Go on.'

'You'll answer our questions?'

'If you pay.'

So the Wildman told about the casting out of Blaze. The Prophet listened, and then nodded, to show she was satisfied.

'I'll come down.'

A few moments later, the temple doors opened to reveal a little girl. She was about nine years old and had curly orange hair and a face that was a mass of freckles.

'Kneel to the River Prophet,' she said in a high sing-song voice. Then, spoiling the effect, 'Usually the faithful bring me sweeties.'

The Prophet was already shuffling towards her gold-painted throne.

'Kneel, kneel,' she said. 'If you don't show respect, I'm nobody special. If I'm nobody special, I can't help you. Work it out for yourself.'

They knelt.

'Why haven't they got any sweeties?' asked the orange-haired child.

'Shut up about sweeties,' said the Prophet. 'So why was this Noma cast out?'

'We don't know.'

'Had they cleansed him?'

'Yes.' This was Seeker, blinking sudden tears from his eyes. 'He was my brother.'

'You're from Anacrea?'

'Yes.'

'Is your brother dead?'

'No.'

228

'Then I take it he still is your brother.'

Seeker bit his lip. He was already speaking of Blaze as if he was in the past.

'Tell me about your brother.'

The River Prophet was a kind of drain for information. Every little detail that trickled down the gutters of the days ended up in this vast tank of memory. While the freckled child twisted and whined for attention, Seeker told all he could think to tell about Blaze: how he had always been the favourite of their father; how he had been good and decent and strong; how he had wanted nothing in life but to become a Noma, and serve the All and Only.

'So you've no idea at all what this brother of yours might have done to get himself cast out?'

'No idea at all.'

'Humph.' The Prophet frowned with puzzlement. 'Very odd.'

'I wanna do wee-wee,' said the child.

'We've given you fresh knowledge,' said the Wildman. 'Now you've got to answer our questions.'

The Prophet shot the Wildman a sharp look.

'Answers cost money.'

The Wildman produced a gold shilling.

'Get on with it, then. Today's my day off.'

'We've heard about a secret weapon being built in Radiance. We want to know what it is, and where we can find it.'

'Secret weapon, eh?'

'I wanna do wee-wee!'

'Be quiet.'

The Prophet closed her eyes.

'Leave me,' she said. 'I'll call you back when I'm ready.'

All this time the three visitors had been on their knees. Now they got up and went back out into the portico, and the doors closed after them.

'There's something not right about her,' said Morning Star.

'You wait and see,' said the Wildman.

After about five minutes the doors opened again, and there was the River Prophet hunched on her throne, with the orange-haired child curled up at her feet, sucking on the loose end of one sleeve and looking sullen. The visitors forgot to kneel.

'Well?' said the Prophet. 'Don't I get any respect?'

They knelt.

'Not that I have much in the way of answers for you. This secret weapon must be very secret. I don't know where it is. I can only tell you it's an explosive weapon, and it's been tested, and it's very powerful.'

'Who tested it?' asked the Wildman.

'I don't know.'

Morning Star gazed at her. She had been growing more and more puzzled since their first sight of the Prophet. The puzzle sprang from her colours; or rather, her lack of colours. All that she could detect was a very faint tinge of green, which was not at all the colour she would expect

230

from one who was wise, and crammed with knowledge. Now, as she spoke to them, there were flickers of orange round her white-haired head.

'Make them go away,' whined the freckled child. 'I'm tired.'

Morning Star turned her attention to the child. Seeker was putting a second question.

'Can you tell me where my brother Blaze has gone?'

'No, no more questions. You've had your lot. You didn't give me much fresh knowledge, and it's my day off. Now go away and leave me in peace.'

'It's the girl!' cried Morning Star. All round the child was a deep blue gleam, a blue so dense it was almost indigo. Morning Star had seen this colour only very rarely before, and always on people of great age. It was the colour of knowledge. 'The answers come from the girl!'

'Nonsense!' said the Prophet.

'She knows nothing!' insisted Morning Star. 'The girl's the one with the knowledge!'

'It's a lie!' said the Prophet.

'How does she know?' said the child.

The Prophet took hold of the child and cradled her protectively in her arms.

'You can't have her!' she said, her voice cracking with emotion. 'Go away! Leave us alone! I won't let you take her! You'll have to kill me first!'

'We don't want to take her,' said Seeker, watching in surprise.

'You've brought that killer here! You mean to kill me and take my little girl!'

She was becoming frantic. Her little girl seemed quite untroubled.

'Tell her we won't take the girl, Wildman.'

'We don't want her. We want knowledge.'

Little by little, they calmed the old woman down. Then she bowed her white-haired head in shame.

'It's just a way to make a living,' she said sorrowfully. 'Don't blame an old woman for wanting to live.'

'So you have no knowledge after all?'

'Not me, no. Not a jot. But my little girl, she knows everything. Tell her what you like, she never forgets, do you, my flower? They said she was a Funny, but she's not a Funny. She's just different. Aren't you, my flower?'

'When will they go away?'

'Soon, my love. Soon.'

There was something oddly disconnected about the girl. Here was her protector almost in tears, confessing her fraud, and the child seemed not to be aware of it.

'So she gives true answers?'

'Oh, yes. True as can be. People come to us from all over, and they tell us what they know, and my flower remembers it all. Then when someone comes and asks a question, as you have done, she casts the question like a hook into her memory, and pulls out whatever catches the hook.'

'So it was the girl who said the weapon had been tested?'

232

'Of course.'

They looked at the child, who was back chewing on her sleeve and paying them no attention. It seemed impossible.

'How does she know?'

'There was a story about some cattle burned alive in the fields outside Radiance. Another about a freak wave on the lake that sank a fishing boat. She puts all the little pieces together without even knowing she's doing it, or what she's come up with when she's done.'

The child lay and sucked her sleeve and ignored them all.

'Is she your granddaughter?'

'Not exactly.'

'So what is she?'

'Well – you might say I found her. But we get on very happily together, don't we, my flower?'

'I like it when you give me sweeties,' she offered.

The old woman looked at them with pleading eyes.

'She couldn't do it without me. It's our living, being a prophet. Please don't tell anyone.'

'Not if you answer our questions,' said Seeker. 'I mean, not if she answers our questions.'

'What else do you want to know?'

'Where my brother's gone.'

'The Noma who was cast out? That's too new. She won't know that.'

Morning Star then spoke. Her voice trembled a little.

'Ask her where my mother is. She left twelve years ago.'

The Prophet frowned. 'You'll have to give her more to go on than that.'

'My mother's name is Mercy. She left us twelve years ago this midsummer to join the Community on Anacrea. They sent her away. She never came home.'

'Anything else about her?'

'I was very little. I don't remember. My father always told me she was very beautiful. And that it was a rainy summer when she left. The rainiest for years.'

'Well, we can try.'

'Shall I tell the child?'

'You've told her. She hears everything, and forgets nothing.' She stroked the little girl's head. 'Take a look, my flower.'

The strange child pulled a face, to show she was unwilling to make the effort.

'With them watching?'

'Yes, my love.'

So she sat herself up, cross-legged on the floor, and closed her eyes. She started to mutter and moan, and then the moan became a half-recognisable mumble of words and phrases with no connecting meaning.

'Anacrea . . . Pretty lady . . . Rain! So much rain! . . . Death in the family . . . Cry, cry, cry . . . The road to the mother bear . . . Someone needs to take care . . . Have you seen the new governess? . . . Naughty children! Do as you're told! . . . No better than a servant . . . White curtains blowing in the wind . . . Some have all the luck, not that she knows it . . . And the pretty little governess, crying behind closed doors . . . Well, well, well . . .'

Slowly the murmuring voice faded into silence. Morning Star looked up at the old woman, her eyes glistening with tears, though she hardly knew why.

'Does it mean anything?'

'A little,' she said. 'I think your mother is working as a governess to a rich family. She's been very unhappy.'

'Oh, Mama!' said Morning Star, unable to hold back a sob. 'Where can I find her?'

'The road to the mother bear. White curtains blowing in the wind.'

'I don't understand.'

'I'm sorry. Nor do I.'

CHAPTER TWENTY-ONE

SEEKER'S PLAN

AS they made their way back down the river path, Seeker and the Wildman spoke of their coming journey, but Morning Star remained silent. She was still distressed by the news of her mother. It had been enough to reawaken the pain of her memory, but not enough to be of any use.

After a while the Wildman noticed her silence.

'What's the matter with her?'

'She wants to find her mother.'

'We're not going chasing after any mothers,' said the Wildman. 'We're going to find this weapon, and we're going to join the Nomana, and we're going to get all their powers. And we don't need any mothers.'

'Are you stupid?' said Seeker. 'Or just nasty?'

The Wildman went very still.

'Nobody talks to me like that.'

'Can't you see she's upset?'

'You calling me stupid?'

'Stupid. And blind. And deaf.'

The Wildman shot out one golden arm and gripped Seeker by the throat.

'You don't love me no more?' he hissed, his eyes shining very brightly.

Seeker was choking too much to answer.

Morning Star drew back one arm and smacked the Wildman as hard as she could across the side of his face. He staggered back, releasing his grip on Seeker.

'You're stupid and nasty and blind and deaf!' she shouted at him. 'And we don't love you!'

Then she turned to Seeker, who was massaging his throat.

'Has he hurt you?'

'Not too bad.'

'What about me?' cried the Wildman. 'You hurt me!'

'Good.'

'You want me to slit your necks?'

'Go right ahead.'

She glowered at him fiercely.

'Come on, spiker! Bandit! Wild man! Let's see this famous neck-slitting! Start with me!'

She stretched out her neck, inviting him to attack her.

'No,' he said, now sounding peevish. 'I won't. Slit your own neck.'

'All right. So are you coming with us, or do you want to go on alone?'

The Wildman shrugged.

'Don't mind,' he said.

Morning Star turned to Seeker.

'Do we still want him?'

'Yes. We want him.'

'Why? He's no better than a dumb animal.'

Seeker rubbed his neck and thought about that.

'Even so,' he said. 'I rather like him.'

They were talking about him as if he wasn't there. The Wildman wasn't sure what he felt about that. It ought to have been humiliating to be 'rather liked', but it was a new sensation, and not an unpleasant one.

'You can come with us if you want,' said Morning Star, 'but you're to stop being stupid and nasty.'

'I'll do as I please,' said the Wildman, his pride flaring up again. 'If it pleases me to be stupid and nasty, then that's how I'll be.'

Before either of them could respond, out of the trees burst a spitting ball of rage. Morning Star just had time to register the flying hair, the wild eyes, the fire-red aura, before she felt the impact of a frenzied attack.

'Cow! Scum-face! Get off him!'

It was Caressa, beating, tearing, kicking and spitting her fury. The Wildman grabbed her by one arm and pulled her off.

'I'm going to kill her!'

He shook her violently.

'Whoa!' he said. 'Whoa! Mistake, Princess!'

'I'm going to kill her!'

'No, you're not. Nobody's going to kill anybody.'

The girl glowered at Morning Star.

'She's just a baby,' she said.

'So leave her alone.'

'Who is she?'

'She's a friend of mine.'

He let her go. Caressa smoothed her hair and clothing, and stared at Morning Star now with open contempt.

'How can you want a plop-face like that?'

'I don't want her. She's a friend.'

'She's a girl, isn't she? Boys don't have girls for friends.'

'We're helping each other.'

'How's she any help to anyone? She looks like a boiled pudding.'

Morning Star had now got over the shock of the attack, and did not appreciate what she was hearing.

'Hey, Sweetie-pie,' she said. 'Go on being so nice about me and I might have to thank you.'

'What?' Caressa wasn't sure she'd understood. She was older and taller than Morning Star, and could not imagine that the younger girl would dare to stand up to her. 'I wasn't being nice to you. And don't call me Sweetie-pie.'

'But you have such sweet lips,' said Morning Star. 'And such big eyes. And such a lot of hair.'

'Shut your mouth! Wildman, if she don't stop this I'm gonna smack her right in her plop-face!'

'Go home, Princess. We're leaving town.'

'With her?'

'Like I said, we're helping each other.'

The girl turned on Morning Star and hissed at her.

'You touch him, you die.'

'Really?' said Morning Star. And reaching out one arm, she laid her left hand on the Wildman's shoulder.

Caressa flew straight at her, but this time Morning Star

was ready. Her right hand swung hard and sure, catching the bigger girl right across the side of her face, sending her crashing to the dirt.

'Whoa!' exclaimed the Wildman. 'You smack hard!'

'That's enough,' said Seeker. 'Come on.'

He took Morning Star by the arm and half-led, half-dragged her away down the river path.

'This isn't about you,' he said.

'I don't like being told what to do.'

'So we see.'

The Wildman stayed by Caressa, and spoke to her in a voice too low for them to hear. In a while she got up from the dirt and put her arms round him, and they spoke some more. Then she turned and went back into town. He came up the river path to rejoin them.

'How did you make her go away?'

'I told her you'd smacked me too. We agreed you were a vicious little witch.'

'Thanks.'

'And plain and flat-chested.'

'Enough,' said Morning Star.

'I only said it to make her go away,' said the Wildman. Then he burst into laughter. 'Whoa! You smack hard!'

They reached the river crossing. This was a raft attached to a rope which stretched from bank to bank.

'Other side of the river,' said the Wildman, 'that's the empire. But it's still two days' walk to Radiance.'

'Is it dangerous?' said Seeker.

'Not so long as we don't break any of their laws.'

'How about bandits?'

'There's bandits. But then, I'm a bandit too.'

He spun his sharp spike in the air and caught it again, grinning as he did so.

'So let's go.'

'And what do we do when we get to Radiance?' said Morning Star.

'We look for the weapon,' said Seeker.

'And then? You said you had an idea, for when we get to Radiance.'

'It's just an idea. It may not work.'

'You can still tell us.'

Seeker hesitated.

'We're doing this thing together, aren't we?' she said.

'Maybe not this part.'

'You're saying you don't need us?'

'No, but . . .'

Morning Star could tell from his colours that Seeker was both excited and afraid.

'You're going to do something dangerous.'

'How do you know that?' said Seeker, surprised.

'I just do. So you might as well tell us.'

Seeker sighed, and told.

'Suppose,' he said, 'you'd built a weapon that could destroy the Nom. Your problem would be getting it close enough. Everyone knows the Nomana keep watch, day and night. So really what you'd need is someone who could come and go to the island, someone who lives there, to take the weapon for you. And so that's when I thought' – he gave an apologetic smile, as if he knew he was saying something foolish – 'that it might as well be me.'

Morning Star stared at him, shocked into silence.

The Wildman had failed to follow the plan altogether.

'Why?' he said. 'You don't want to destroy the Nom.'

'No, I don't,' said Seeker. 'But I could make them think I do. I could go about the city of Radiance saying I hate the Nomana, and want to destroy all Anacrea.'

'Why would they believe you want to destroy your own home?'

'Because of what they did to my brother.'

'Whoa!' The Wildman saw it now. He was impressed. 'Heya, Seeker!'

'It's true too, isn't it?' said Morning Star. 'You are angry about your brother being cast out.' She could see it even now in his colours.

'There's been a mistake,' said Seeker. 'Blaze would never do anything so terrible that he deserved casting out.'

'So why didn't he speak up at the Congregation?'

'Because he's been cleansed. He remembers nothing. He doesn't even know who he is any more.'

Morning Star saw it all now: the simplicity of the plan, and the courage.

'It's a good plan.'

'Thank you.'

'It's a great plan!' exclaimed the Wildman, understanding

it more the more he thought about it. 'You go round saying you hate the Nomana. They find you. They take you to the weapon. You destroy it. It's brilliant!'

'And very dangerous,' said Morning Star. 'You do realise what Seeker's doing?'

'What's he doing?' The Wildman stared back suspiciously.

'He's risking his life.'

'Risking his life? Heya! That's nothing! I've risked my life for a crust of bread. I've risked my life for no reason at all, except to tell the story later and laugh.'

'He's not like you.'

The Wildman put his arm round Seeker, like a taller, stronger older brother. Like the brother Seeker had once had.

'You afraid, brava?'

'Yes.'

'Don't be afraid. Anyone gives you trouble has to deal with me. I stand with you.'

'To the end of the world.'

'What about me?' said Morning Star.

'You too,' said Seeker. 'Right, Wildman? We stand together, all three.'

'If that's how it's got to be,' said the Wildman gracelessly. 'She's the one who smacked my face and called me a dumb animal. I don't see what she wants with me.'

'You add colour,' said Morning Star.

CHAPTER TWENTY-TWO

HAPPY WORKERS

BLAZE and his new travelling companion Soren Similin reached the crossroads in the late afternoon, and spent the night in one of the roadside shacks that served as inns. Here a bunk and a bowl of stew were to be had for three pence each; and with it, the rank smell of many more hungry and unwashed travellers, all come in search of work. The gangmaster, it appeared, took on new labour each morning.

Soren Similin slept badly on the hard planks, and woke long before dawn. There was nowhere to wash, and no breakfast, and his bones ached; but for all that, he felt a sense of satisfaction. By suffering discomfort alongside Blaze he was strengthening the bond between them. At the same time he was earning the reward that was to come. In his mind, as he lay in the stinking darkness, he heard himself tell the story of these days with a kind of pride. 'I too have slept in my clothes,' he murmured to himself. 'I too have gone hungry, and known what it is to be the lowest of the low.'

When the others began to rise, pulling on their boots and banging doors, he woke Blaze.

'Time to get up. The gangmaster will be here soon.'

Blaze woke in confusion, not knowing where he was.

'Who are you?'

'I'm your friend. We're going to find work together.'

The gangmaster's bullock-cart rolled up at last, and out jumped three men with short knotted ropes in their hands. They wore tight sleeveless vests, which showed the contours of their powerful chests. They set up a trestle table in front of the inn, and out from the best of the rooms came a stocky man with short cropped hair and little squinting eyes. He had an account book in his hands, which he laid open on the table in the flickering light of a lamp. Similin guided Blaze into the line of men who formed up before him, and one by one the gangmaster signed them in. As he did so, never troubling to look up, he spoke aloud in a low droning voice, in a manner that seemed to indicate he was speaking to himself.

'Daylight hours, lunch provided at agreed cost, company terms apply. Put your name there, payment at the end of the week, two shillings per man per week less agreed costs. Breach of company terms results in dismissal, those dismissed forfeit one week's pay. Work is daylight hours, lunch provided at agreed cost, company terms apply . . .'

And so it went round again. Similin and Blaze signed the book in their turn, and were directed to the bullock-wagon. Within a surprisingly short space of time the wagon was full. The three muscular men then climbed on board, still yawning. Finally the gangmaster himself took his place, on the only seat, at the front of the wagon.

'Men!' he said, loud and clear. 'Be thankful! You now have work.'

The men stood, pressed shoulder to shoulder, and said nothing. He had not asked a question. No reply seemed called for.

'I said, Be thankful! Associates! Show them!'

This was addressed to the three muscular men. Without a flicker of a smile, they replied in unison.

'Thank you, Pelican!'

'That's my name. Pelican! So what do you say?'

The men looked back uncertainly. Some murmured faintly, 'Thank you.'

'Associates!'

The muscular men cracked their knotted ropes against the wagon's side, making the men jump.

'Thank you, Pelican!' they chorused.

The wagon set off at a steady jolting pace down the road.

'You're all very lucky men!' shouted Pelican. 'Work means pay! Be happy about that! The owner of the plantation likes to have happy workers. So you will be happy workers! Is that understood?'

'Yes, Pelican,' they replied.

'How do they know you're happy workers? They hear you singing in the fields. Happy workers sing. My associates here will now sing you the Happy Workers song. Listen and learn.'

The three associates then raised their heads, and as before, without a hint of a smile, they bellowed out the song.

246

'O-ho! O-ho! A-harvesting we go!
The sky is blue and the corn is high
The sun shines down and the hours fly by
Who can be as happy as I?
A-harvesting we go!'

As the bullocks hauled the laden wagon down the long white road, now between tall trees, the dawn began at last to break. Similin and Blaze and the rest of the new recruits sang the song as best they could. The gangmaster was not much impressed.

'Now listen to me! All I'm asking is that you sound happy. You don't have to be happy. I want happy workers singing in happy fields. That way, the owner's happy. If the owner's happy, I'm happy. If I'm happy, you're happy. But if any one of you spoils the party by not sounding happy, you're out. There and then. So let's hear the song again.'

They sang again. He was still not satisfied.

'What's the matter with you? That's not the sound of happy workers. That's the sound of a bunch of miserable bastards who wish they'd never been born. If that's how you feel, go back home. I don't want you.'

'Please, sir. We've had no breakfast.'

'Happy workers don't need breakfast. You'll be fed at noon.'

The track now approached a pair of handsome stone gateposts, on the top of each of which stood the figure of a crouching bear, carved in stone. The wagon rumbled through, and on to a long, winding drive. On either side, the fields were full of ripe corn, the dusty grey leaves clicking in the early morning breeze.

'Welcome to the Mother Bear plantation,' said the gangmaster.

The bullock-wagon came to a stop at last by the side of a long store barn, which was already part full of corn. A line of two-wheeled handcarts stood against the barn wall. The sun now rose above the mountains, and shot bright streams of light over the standing corn.

'Everybody out.'

Similin and Blaze lined up with the rest. The gangmaster stalked up and down before them, booming out instructions.

'Four simple rules. Pick ripe cobs only. Don't stop. Don't talk. Be happy.'

Soren Similin realised that he must now endure the rigours of a long day of hard work. He consoled himself with the thought that the shared labour would bond him closer to the cast-out Noma. And in the hours of rest he would have time to work on Blaze, and transform him into the perfect instrument for his plan.

To start with, the day was pleasantly cool, and the physical labour not beyond his strength. But quite quickly he felt his arms begin to ache and his hands to sting. The work fell into a rhythmic pattern. Move to the next plant, reach up, clasp the coarse-leaved cob, snap it off with a downward twist, toss it into the cart, reach up again. A simple sequence of motions, but by the end of the first hour he was sweating, and had blood on his hands. Who would have thought corn-cobs could be so hard on the skin? He looked around him. Blaze seemed untroubled, working steadily down his row. The other men were sweating but not bleeding. Similin knew it was because his hands were softer than theirs, because he was not a labourer like them. This made him superior to them. But for now, it meant he was suffering more.

He glanced up at the rising sun, and wondered if he would be able to last the day. The only respite his weary hands got was when his handcart was full, and he was able to wheel it over to the barn. Trundling the empty cart back was blissfully free from effort. But then the picking must begin again. By the time a second hour had passed, he began to be afraid he would not make it to lunch. Already the heat was unbearable.

Three rows away a worker stumbled and fell, made faint by the heat and lack of food. The associates were on him in seconds, hauling him out. He recovered, and insisted that he was able to resume work, but the gangmaster wouldn't listen.

'Break the rules, you're out. No exceptions.'

'What about the work I've done?'

'Payment at the end of the week.'

'But I won't be here at the end of the week.'

'Company terms apply.'

The man had no choice but to set off on the long walk back to the high road, with nothing for his pains. Soren Similin looked round and saw that Blaze was watching the sad departing figure. But like all the rest of them, he went on picking corn as he watched.

A third hour passed. Similin began to be afraid that he too would faint in the field. He hurt all over, his arm shook as he reached it up, his mouth was dry, the skin on his scalp prickled in the heat, and the blood from his hands was crusted all down his arms. Then he heard the associates call out, 'Sing!' Slowly, from one end of the rows to the other, the workers began to sing. The associates stepped into the rows to lead them in the song, calling out the words for those who had forgotten.

'O-ho! O-ho! A-harvesting we go!

The sky is blue and the corn is high

The sun shines down and the hours fly by – '

There came the clop-clop-clop of bullocks, and into view rolled a high-sprung wagonette with a sun canopy over the top. In the wagonette sat a lady dressed in white, wearing a wide-brimmed sun hat, with two children by her side, also dressed in white. In the jump-seat behind, not protected from the sun, sat a governess dressed in grey. As the wagonette passed by, the lady and the children waved to the singing workers in the field, and the workers waved back, without stopping either singing or picking.

'Who can be as happy as I?

A-harvesting we go!'

The lady had very pale skin, and was very beautiful. The children caught the song and stood up in the wagonette and swung their arms about, pretending to pick corn, and sang too. The governess reached out her arms to catch them, fearing they would fall off.

'O-ho! O-ho! A-harvesting we go!'

So the wagonette rolled on, out of sight. As soon as it was also out of hearing, the associates strode down the rows and seized one of the workers, and dragged him out by the arms.

'I sang!' he screamed. 'I sang!'

'You didn't wave,' said the gangmaster.

'You never said to wave!'

'I said, Be happy. When the owner's children wave, the happy workers wave back.'

'You never said!'

'You're out.'

'It's not fair!'

The gangmaster had already turned away. Now he swung back, a look of fury on his face.

'Not fair? Did you say, *Not fair*?'

'I just meant – '

'I give you work. I tell you the rules. At the end of the week, I pay you. That's fair. If you want *Not fair* I can show you that too.'

He signed to his associates. One of them held the unfortunate worker from behind, while the other struck him hard in the belly, and then again in the face. The worker fell groaning to the ground. The associates then took turns kicking him, vicious swinging kicks that made him scream. The other workers watched, but they kept on working. In a little while the kicking stopped, and the man lay curled up on the ground, weeping and dribbling blood.

'That's *Not fair*,' said the gangmaster. 'Just so you know, for next time. Now get out.'

After that, Soren Similin decided he could keep going after all. But he also decided that one day of being a happy worker was the most he could manage. He looked at Blaze. Blaze was watching the departing worker, as he limped slowly away down the track. In Blaze's dull eyes he saw a hurt, puzzled look.

'I can guess how you feel,' he said.

'Can you?' said Blaze. 'How do I feel?'

'It makes you angry. It makes you burn with anger. That's why your name is Blaze of Justice.'

'You're right. It does make me angry.'

'Of course it does. You're the kind of man who can't stand by and see injustice done. You're the kind of man who wants to do something about it.'

'You're right. That's the kind of man I am.'

Really, thought Similin, it was almost too easy. Like training a puppy. Blaze's mind was an empty sheet of paper on which he could write what he chose. Soon now he would start to write: *There is no greater injustice than a false god.* But he knew he must not be in a hurry. He must form his instrument well, before putting it to work.

'You know what I think?' announced Blaze, unprompted.

'What do you think?'

'I think the workers here aren't happy at all.'

CHAPTER TWENTY-THREE

TRIBUTE TRADERS

WHERE the track joined the high road north to Radiance, the Wildman called a stop.

'Best to wait for the next convoy,' he said. 'There'll be tribute traders watching the road.'

'What are tribute traders?' asked Seeker.

'People stealers.'

Morning Star flinched, remembering Barban.

'Do they use nets?'

'That's them.' The Wildman spat in disgust. 'Nets and blankets. Tangling and smothering. That's not man's work.'

'Nets and blankets!'

'They want you alive. A dead tribute's no use. Can't sacrifice you if you're already dead.'

'Sacrifice!'

'That's what they do in Radiance. Throw people off a high rock. Every day. To make the sun rise again.'

'But that's just stupid.'

The Wildman shrugged.

'Gods make people stupid.'

Seeker frowned and said, 'All gods aren't the same.'

'Even so,' said Morning Star, not wanting an argument about gods, 'let's not get caught by the tribute traders.'

'So we wait for a convoy.'

It wasn't very long before the next large group of travellers came up the road. The group had formed some miles to the south, and consisted of thirty or so travellers and five bullock carts. The bullocks went no faster than a man, and on the rise they slowed down to a crawl. The three companions joined them, and so fell into the steady pattern of the convoy. They walked in the cool of the morning, rested in the middle of the day, and then walked on into the dusk.

Twice each day they stopped for food. Small roadside markets had grown up at just those points along the road where a traveller might begin to feel the need of a rest. Here, in the shade of spreading canopies, stalls sold pancakes and mugs of sweet tea, the poor man's lunch, for two or three pence.

This led to a difficulty. Seeker and Morning Star were willing to pay, but had no money. The Wildman had money, but was not willing to pay.

'I never pay,' he declared with pride. 'What I want, I take.'

Thrusting out his sharp-pointed spike, he said to the man behind the pancake stall,

'Start your frying, brava!'

'Put that away!' exclaimed Morning Star. 'What do you think you're doing?'

'I'm hungry. I want food.'

'So pay for it.'

'Why?'

'Because stealing's wrong.'

The Wildman shrugged and put away his spike.

'I have to pay for you too?'

'If you want to.'

The Wildman found he didn't want to eat his pancake alone, so he paid for their lunch too. They ate in silence, too hungry to think of anything else. But as the convoy set off once more, the Wildman returned to their disagreement with a new vigour.

'I don't see what's wrong with taking what I want.'

'It belongs to someone else,' said Seeker.

'So let him try to stop me.'

'What if he's weaker than you, and can't stop you?'

'Then too bad for him.'

'If you were a Noma, you'd want the weak to have as much as the strong.'

The Wildman laughed at that idea.

'How can the weak have as much as the strong? The strong would take whatever the weak have. Then you'd be back where we are now.'

'Unless the strong chose not to.'

'No one chooses to be weak,' said the Wildman, feeling like a grown man explaining the way of the world to children. 'You're strong, or you die.'

'So why do the Nomana go round helping people who are weak?'

'Don't ask me. Maybe it makes them feel big.'

'No,' said Seeker. 'They do it because they believe we're

all joined up with each other. Other people's unhappiness makes them unhappy. Other people's happiness makes them happy.'

'What, everybody?

'Yes,' said Seeker. 'Everybody in the whole world.'

The Wildman shook his head at that, but he said no more.

When darkness fell, exhausted by long hours on the road, the band of travellers called a stop for the night. They built and lit a bonfire to provide light, and the various sub-groups picked out sleeping places and trod down the tall dry grasses to make their beds. Before settling down to sleep, both Seeker and Morning Star sat still for a while with their eyes closed. Their lips moved in silent prayer. The Wildman saw this with surprise.

'You praying?'

They didn't answer him until they were done. Then Seeker said, 'Yes. I was praying.'

'But there's no one to see.'

'What do you mean?'

'You don't have to put on an act here. There's no hoodies watching.'

'It's not an act.'

'Not an act?' He looked from one to the other. 'You pray to your god even when no one's watching?'

'Yes,' said Seeker.

'Yes,' said Morning Star.

'But gods are for dummies!'

256

'Not the real god. Not the All and Only.'

'Whoa!' The Wildman waved his hands before him, as if to brush away such foolishness. 'I knew you wanted to be hoodies. But I didn't know you believed! Not really *believed*!'

'If you want to join the Nomana, you'll have to believe too.'

'Can't I be the hoodie without the god?'

'I don't think so.'

'Then I'll just have to pretend.'

'That's stupid,' said Morning Star. 'Why join the Nomana if you don't believe what they believe?'

'I want the power,' said the Wildman stubbornly. 'And I want the peace.'

A little later, as the three of them laid themselves down on the trampled grass, and looked up at the night sky, now speckled with stars, the Wildman said, not very graciously, 'So tell me about your dummy god.'

'What do you want to know?'

'I don't know. Anything. Why you believe.'

Morning Star said simply, 'I believe because my mother and father believed, and taught me to believe.'

'Same for me,' said Seeker. 'My life wouldn't make sense without the All and Only.'

'Why not?' said the Wildman. 'My life makes sense.'

'I can't see how. It seems to me your life is just taking as much as you can for yourself and then having to fight to keep it.'

'So what's your life?'

'I feel like my life hasn't begun yet,' said Seeker. 'But I can tell you what I want it to be. I want to be one of the Noble Warriors. Sometimes I have such a strong feeling that the world is hurting so much, and all the hurting happens in the darkness. I feel that if I can make there be light, instead of darkness, I can end the hurting of the world. Or make it less. And I want that light too. I want to come closer to it, so close that it dazzles me and floods me, so close that I'm not even me any more. That's when I'll hold the Lost Child in my arms, and the Wise Father will hold me in his arms, and keep me safe for ever. That's when I'll live in the Garden.'

He fell silent. The Wildman didn't understand him at all, but he was awed by the intensity of Seeker's feelings. This was not the kind of god-worship he had met before.

'Whoa!' he said. 'Dazzle me and flood me! That would be something!'

Morning Star too was moved by what she heard. She lay on her back looking up at the stars, and knew she felt the same. But she was afraid. She had not forgotten what had happened when she had come close to that dazzling silver screen. She was afraid of that explosion of colours. She was afraid of the madness.

'There's mysteries in the Nom,' she said. 'Who knows what happens when you go into the mysteries?'

'Into the mysteries,' said Seeker. 'And through the mysteries. And out to the other side, where there's clear light.'

She turned her head so that she could see him, lying on

the grass nearby. There, all round him, faint as before but easier to see in the darkness, was that flicker of gold, those dancing particles of shining dust. As she watched him she felt a flow of tender protective love towards him, as if he were infinitely precious and infinitely vulnerable.

I must look after you, Seeker. You're the best of us.

Such a strange thought. As soon as it had come, she smiled to herself, thinking: ridiculous! Who am I to protect him? And yet – and yet – she felt older than Seeker, far older. Perhaps it was all those long, lonely days she had passed in the hill country.

'That was good, Seeker,' she said softly.

'I don't get it,' said the Wildman.

'Nobody gets it,' said Morning Star. 'It gets you.'

They lay there, the three of them in the warm night, each unable to sleep, though for different reasons. Morning Star thought of her father, who would be so alone without her; and of little Lamb, who still needed to be found a home.

Seeker thought of the sunlit land where everything would one day be clear. He understood that this land was not some far-off place, but was the same world that lay all round him; only now, it was as if the land was veiled. It was as if he stood before an open window, where a white curtain billowed and swelled in the breeze. The curtain glowed with bright sunlight, and was beautiful in its way, but all its beauty came from the wind and the sun beyond. He longed to tear away the bright fabric, and see for ever.

As for the Wildman, he was feeling that the ground on

which he walked was cracking, and the simple certainties by which he had lived so far were no longer enough, and this excited him.

'Dazzle me and flood me!' he murmured to himself. 'Those hoodies! They're the real wildmen.'

Then the weariness of the day overtook them, and one by one, even as they thought their busy minds would never be still, they dropped into sleep.

The next day they headed on north, up the long road that wound now between fields of tall maize. They were in plantation country, and here and there they saw gangs of field workers picking the ripe cobs, sweating in the hot sun. In the early afternoon of the second day they passed a track that ran away to the west, through corn fields. They had no reason to pay it any attention, and soon it was behind them. Had they turned off the road and down that track they would have come to two tall gateposts that marked the entrance to a rich family plantation, gateposts capped with stone carvings in the form of crouching bears.

As they walked, they talked a little about the one subject that linked them all, which was the Nomana. Morning Star had been puzzling over Seeker's brother Blaze, who had been cast out. She remembered watching him as he had crossed the square all on his own, and left the Congregation. Something was nagging at her memory.

'When Blaze was cleansed, they took away his powers?'

'And everything else too.'

'Like what?'

'Like his past. Like his feelings. Like who he is.'

'So it wouldn't hurt him. I mean, if it took away his feelings, there'd be no pain.'

'There's worse things than no pain,' said Seeker.

Morning Star said no more. But there was something here that didn't fit, if only she could track it down.

The road crested the gentle rise up which they had been climbing, and now descended, just as gently, between more fields of standing corn, to the broad river a mile or so ahead. Absorbed by their talking, the three had moved away from the main convoy, which had stayed close to the slower bullock-carts, toiling up the hill. Now, as they began the easier downward slope, they moved out of sight of the other travellers altogether.

Morning Star pointed this out.

'Maybe we should wait for the others.'

'We can wait by the river,' said the Wildman. 'We can have a swim.'

The prospect of a dip in cool water was too much to resist. They strode on down the road, making ever faster progress. In this way, by the time they reached the river bank, the convoy was a mile or so back down the road.

There was a ferry crossing here, but the ferry was moored on the far bank. There was no sign of the ferryman.

'Lazy dog!' said the Wildman. 'He'll be sleeping in the shade of the willow trees.'

A copse of willows grew on the far bank, trailing their

long branches over the water. The river lay brown and gleaming in the afternoon sun, a broad expanse of water that seemed not to be moving at all.

'We should watch out,' said Morning Star, remembering the river crossing she had come to with Barban.

'I'll wake him up,' said the Wildman.

He threw down his bag and his blade and his spike, and, running to the river's edge, made a swift arching dive into the water. By the time he surfaced, he was in mid-river. With a few more strokes he was at the far bank, and pulling himself out, dripping, on to the ferry.

He shouted for the ferryman, but there was no answer. He loosed the mooring ropes and, taking hold of the heavy tiller beam, gestured downstream to indicate to the others where he was heading. So he pushed off into deep water.

'Let's hope he knows what he's doing,' said Seeker.

The ferry seemed far too big to be handled by one person. But the Wildman had seen the ferryman work the big raft across the river many times. He plied the tiller with skill, and the ferry began to cross the broad river. The golden-haired bandit, refreshed by his plunge into the water, stood tall, gleaming and handsome in the sun. He saw that his companions were impressed, and he was pleased.

'Heya, bravas!' he called to them. 'Do you lo-o-ove me?'

As he spoke, out from under the willows shot a long thin canoe, holding two men. Morning Star knew at once that she had seen them before. The canoe moved fast, driven by paddles that struck with practised force. It reached the big clumsy raft as it was passing the mid-river point, and the two men jumped on to the ferry, leaving the canoe to ride free alongside. Each man carried a net in one hand and a club in the other.

'Tribute traders!' cried Morning Star.

Seeker picked up the Wildman's blade where he had thrown it down. Morning Star picked up his spike.

The Wildman was alone on the raft, and unarmed. He could jump into the river, but the canoe would move faster than he could swim, and he had no wish to be netted in the water. He let go of the tiller and prepared to fight.

The tribute traders were in no hurry. They wanted him alive and unharmed. They advanced carefully towards the Wildman, backing him into one corner. The raft drifted downstream on the current, the empty canoe by its side. Seeker and Morning Star, running along the river bank, shouted at him to jump, to swim. In answer, the Wildman flexed his powerful hands, and taunted his attackers.

'Heya, chickens! Come and get me! Let me rip your throats out!'

He was dancing from foot to foot, charging himself up with rage for the fight. But the tribute traders had no intention of fighting him. They unfurled their nets.

Seeker padded along the river bank, the Wildman's long curving blade in his hand, watching the gap close between raft and shore. He could feel his heart thumping, and knew he was terrified, and knew he had to do something to help.

'I'm going to jump!' he said, to make it so that he had no choice. 'I'm going to jump!'

Morning Star ran alongside him, holding the Wildman's spike, also calculating how soon the raft would be in reach. Her thoughts had become as sharp and pointed as the spike. It was quite clear to her that she would attack. The only question was how.

The tribute trader nearest to the Wildman now made his move, sweeping the air with his weighted net, curling it over his prey. The Wildman reached up with his right hand, and, seizing the net, jerked it hard, throwing the tribute trader on to his knees. But even as he did so, the second man cast his net, and it fell over him, its multitude of tiny weights clattering on the deck. The net tightened with great rapidity, causing the mesh to close all round the Wildman, and for the first time in his life he found he could not move.

'Aieee!' he screamed.

Seeker jumped. He landed on the raft, fell, righted himself, and was at the Wildman's side with his blade. The tribute trader who had caught the Wildman lunged at him with his club, but as he did so Morning Star landed on the raft too, more gracefully than Seeker, and drove at him from behind with the spike. Taken by surprise, he sprang back, and fell overboard.

Seeker began slicing at the net that held the Wildman. Morning Star turned on the other tribute trader, who was now moving in, his net gathered once more in his hand.

'Only a girl,' said the tribute trader, making a swing at Morning Star with his club. She lunged with her spike. The spike struck the swinging club, and drove deep into the wood. The trader pulled, and ripped the spike out of her hands. At the same time, with his other hand, he cast his net, and Morning Star was caught.

'Help me! He's got me!'

Seeker heard her cry just as he cut away enough of the net to release the Wildman's arms. But already, the tribute trader in the water had scrambled into the canoe, and his companion was dragging Morning Star off the raft. Once they had her in the canoe, they bundled her under a heavy blanket, and seized the paddles. Before Seeker could reach them, the canoe was knifing away up river, and round the bend, out of sight. Morning Star was beyond help.

Seeker and the Wildman stood still, looking after her, still panting from the struggle. For a few moments, appalled by what had happened, they neither met each other's eyes nor spoke. The ferry banged at last against the river bank, and lurched to a stop.

'What did she do that for?' burst out the Wildman at last. 'Now the trib traders have got her! She should have kept away from them!' He seemed more angry with Morning Star than with her captors. 'Now they'll throw her off the rock! What did she have to do that for?'

Seeker spoke more quietly.

'We'll find her.'

'How? *How?* You tell me how! She should have watched

out for herself! If she'd looked after herself, she wouldn't be trussed up like a chicken now!'

'She did it for you, Wildman.'

'I never asked! Did I ask her to help me? Did I?'

'No.'

'So what did she have to do that for?'

The rest of the convoy now arrived, and were told of the attack. There was much shaking of heads at the news.

'She's as good as dead,' they said. 'No tribute ever came out of Radiance alive.'

In a silence that was very like mourning, the people and the bullock-wagons got on to the ferry, and the ferry carried them over to the far bank. From here they continued on their way to the city. The canoe was long gone. Seeker was filled with bitter thoughts. He went over the struggle on the raft again and again in his mind, looking to see what he could have done to save Morning Star, but it had all happened too quickly. The Wildman was right. She should never have taken the risk. But she had done so for the same reason he had done so, an instinctive act of assistance to a friend in trouble.

Only, the Wildman was hardly a friend. He shared none of their beliefs. They weren't kin. They didn't think alike on anything. Their only point of contact was their admiration for the Nomana, and their hope that they might one day become Nomana themselves. A common goal was hardly the basis for friendship. So why had they both risked their life for him?

He glanced at him, striding along, golden hair blowing in the wind. The Wildman caught the glance.

'I'll find her,' he said.

'Yes,' said Seeker.

'I'll set her free.'

'Yes,' said Seeker.

The dream of joining the Nomana would have to wait. Morning Star must be saved.

The Wildman said no more, but he was seething with a confusion of thoughts. He wanted to say to Seeker: she did what she did without asking me, let her take the consequences, I don't care if she lives or dies. But he did care. It was as if, by coming to his rescue, she had put a collar and chain on him, and now he had no choice but to be dragged towards her, wherever she was.

'What did she have to go and do that for?' he repeated angrily to himself as he strode up the road towards Radiance. 'Did I ever ask her to help me?'

CHAPTER TWENTY-FOUR

THE MOTHER BEAR

WORK in the cornfields began again at dawn. The gang-master and his three burly associates settled down to eat a substantial breakfast in full view of the hungry workers.

'Work hard,' said the gangmaster between mouthfuls, 'make money, and you too can eat when you please.'

By mid-morning two more workers had fainted in the corn rows, and been sent home with nothing.

'More injustice,' said Soren Similin. 'At this rate, by the end of the week there'll be nobody left to pay.'

Blaze let his eyes linger on the men who walked away, and the anger in them grew deeper and stronger all the time.

'My name is Blaze of Justice,' he said softly to himself. 'I can't stand by and see injustice done.'

He was repeating back the words Similin had planted in him.

'Sing!' cried the gangmaster.

The workers began to sing. The plantation owner's wagonette was approaching down the track, this time carrying only the lady of the house. The workers sang and smiled, and when she waved they all waved back.

'O-ho! O-ho! A-harvesting we go!

The sky is blue and the corn is high
The sun shines down and the hours fly by . . .'

Only Blaze did not sing, or smile, or wave.

'Blaze!' whispered Similin. 'They're watching you.'

Blaze seemed not to hear him. His eyes were fixed on the lady in white, who sat smiling and waving in the carriage. As it came close, he stepped out of the corn rows directly into its path, forcing it to stop.

'No!' cried Similin. 'Come back!'

But Blaze never even heard him. He had learned his lesson all too well. He was burning for justice.

'Lady,' he said. 'Your workers are not happy.'

The lady stared at him, her smile fading.

'Your workers are cheated and beaten and starved,' he said.

The lady turned round, as if for help.

'What's that he says?'

The gangmaster came running, beckoning to his associates.

'A troublemaker, madam,' he cried. 'Out of the road, you!'

'Now they'll beat me,' said Blaze, 'and send me away with no pay. But I can't stand by and see injustice done.'

'Can this be so?' said the lady.

She looked round at the other workers, all of whom had stopped work, and were watching her every move. There was something in their cowed faces that told her it was true. The associates hesitated, unsure what to do.

269

Soren Similin also watched Blaze, as caught by surprise as the rest.

'We'll deal with this, madam,' said the gangmaster, putting one hand on Blaze's arm. 'I'm sorry you've been troubled.'

Blaze made no move. His steady gaze remained fixed on the lady. She looked back at him, and saw how the gangmaster tugged at him, and how he remained still and firm. It was his stillness that convinced her.

'Come with me,' she said, patting the empty seat beside her. 'Tell me all about it.'

Obediently, Blaze climbed up on the seat beside her.

'Back to the house!' said the lady to the driver.

'Madam!' protested the gangmaster. 'This man's a liar and a troublemaker!'

But the lady had already told the driver to drive on, and the wagonette was rolling away down the track.

The gangmaster turned to the staring workers and spoke with thwarted fury.

'Any of you want to join him? You're free to go! Go now! I can get a hundred more for every one of you! There's always men ready to do honest work for honest pay. So if you don't like work, go now. I don't want you!'

Nobody went. Similin returned to the rows of corn and resumed picking cobs, along with the others. He worked away, his hands moving automatically, his mind on this unplanned and aggravating turn of events. He had done his work too well. Now he must find a way to rejoin

Blaze, and carry out his interrupted plan.

The solution came shortly. A house servant arrived to tell the gangmaster he was wanted at the plantation house. Similin at once put himself forward.

'Sir,' he said. 'I know the man who went away with the lady. I know why he spoke as he did.'

'You do?' The gangmaster glared at him suspiciously.

'He's filled with anger, sir. That's what makes him tell such lies.'

'Lies is the word for it.' The gangmaster turned to the house servant. 'You hear that? All lies!'

'Would you like me to tell the lady of the house?' said Similin.

'I can take care of my own concerns,' growled the gangmaster. Then, as if it were an afterthought, 'Come along, then, if you want to come.'

So Similin followed the gangmaster and the house servant down the track to the house. As he went, he thought through his plan. Blaze would make some confused half-understood accusations. Similin would be called on to deny them. Instead, he would speak up for Blaze. Both he and Blaze would be dismissed, he was sure of that. Then they could get away from this miserable place, and Similin could disclose to him there was a far greater battle ahead, in which the source of injustice could be destroyed once and for all.

The plantation house was set in a grove of trees, and not visible from the fields. As they passed between the trees, and the house came into view, Soren Similin forgot his schemes for a few moments, and was lost in admiration. It was the most beautiful house he had ever seen. The building was long and low, made of timber and clapboard, and painted a soft chalky white. Its shallow-pitched roofs were shingled with beech tiles that had faded to grey in the sun. All along its front face there stretched a deep veranda, over which climbed a green-leafed vine, the long deck broken by supporting posts into a series of bays. Within each bay, in cool shade, were open doors and open windows, where white muslin curtains swayed and bellied in the breeze. Everything about the house was simple, generous and refreshing. The secretary had seen the royal temple in Radiance, and knew it was far more magnificent, but this was a house you would want to live in.

He followed the gangmaster and the house servant on to the veranda and through a door at one end, which was evidently the servants' entrance. They passed down an internal corridor into a room the width of the house, with windows on either side, where two children were sitting at their lessons, with their governess. Like the exterior of the house, all the interior walls were made of timber boards, painted chalk white. The floor was a pale grey, the colour of the ash-wood from which it was made. The curtains that filtered the sunlight were a fine white gauze. The two children, a boy and a girl, wore white. Only the governess wore grey, but her face was bright and young. She looked up as the three men passed by, and threw a questioning look at them, but did not speak.

They passed on, crossing the main hall. Ahead was another wide light room, from which voices came.

'Never fear, my dear,' boomed a man's voice. 'We'll get to the bottom of this. There'll be no injustice on my land.'

They entered the room. The master of the plantation stood by one window, his arms folded over his chest, his bald head nodding to emphasise his words.

'We all work together, and the Mother Bear feeds us all.'

He was a large man, in his sixties, with a rich, creamy voice and a face now mottled by the years. Before him sat his wife, the lady of the house. And beside her stood Blaze.

'Aha! Here is my overseer! Come in, Pelican, come in!'

Blaze never even looked round. If he was surprised that Similin had come too, he didn't show it. The lady of the house looked up, her beautiful face shaded by sadness. Her skin was very pale, and she seemed almost fragile; an impression that was enhanced by the finelywoven material of her white dress. In the white room, where even the daylight was turned white by the curtains, she was lost in the light, and slipped away into nothing.

The master addressed his overseer.

'Now you listen to me!' he boomed. 'I won't have trouble on the plantation. What's this about cheating and beating?'

'It's lies, sir,' said the gangmaster. 'Your workers are happy in their work. And those who aren't happy, sir, why, they're free to leave.'

The lady turned to Blaze.

273

'Speak,' she said.

'The workers are not happy,' said Blaze, speaking as if by rote. 'They're starving.'

'Starving?' barked the master. 'Aren't they fed?'

'Two good meals a day, sir,' said the gangmaster.

'I really don't see the problem.' The master addressed his lady. 'You have only to walk through the fields at harvest time to see that the men are happy. It gladdens my heart to hear them sing as they work.'

'Your workers are not happy,' said Blaze, doggedly repeating his simple refrain. 'They work too hard for too little pay. They only sing because if they don't sing they're dismissed with no pay.'

'My men are paid the proper wage for the work. I insist on it.'

'And how is that decided?' asked the lady.

The master turned to his overseer for an answer.

'Pelican! Explain.'

'Well, madam, that sorts itself out in the natural way of things. If we were to pay too little, we wouldn't get the men to do the work. And then again, if we were to pay too much, the plantation would be ruined, and there would be no work for anybody. So in the natural way of things, we fall into the middle way.'

'Exactly!' said the master. 'The middle way.'

'This is no more than a trick, sir, to win the lady's sympathy, in the hope of getting more money for less work. We get his sort from time to time. They're lazy, sir, and envious, and do their best to stir up dissatisfaction among the men. The only solution is to let them go.'

'I believe you're right.' He turned to Blaze. 'If you're not happy here, my good man, you'd better go elsewhere. We're a happy team at the Mother Bear. If I've learned one thing in my life, it's that happiness promotes prosperity.'

'And, sir,' said the gangmaster, drawing Similin forward, 'if you have any remaining uncertainty – '

'No, no. I've heard enough. Away you go, all of you.'

The gangmaster gestured to Blaze.

'Come along. You've had your say.'

He led Similin and Blaze out of the room. As they went, the master could be heard saying to his lady, 'Well, my dear, I hope you realise now. Affairs of business are best left to men, who have minds adapted for such complex matters.'

As they passed through the hall, there was the pretty governess, now on her own. She jumped up and took a step towards them, but as she did so the house servant appeared, and she shrank back again.

Once they were back on the road to the corn fields, the gangmaster said to Blaze, with great satisfaction, 'So you've had your say. You've done your best to ruin me. And you've failed.'

Blaze said nothing.

'This fellow here' – the gangmaster nodded at Similin – 'was ready to call you a liar to your face. But I was pretty sure I could handle the situation. I understand these ladies and gentlemen pretty well. What you didn't reckon with is

275

that they have good hearts, the best hearts in the world, but when it comes to the details, they don't want to know. They pay me to look after the details. And do you know what? That's where the money is. In the details.'

He was extremely pleased with himself. Soren Similin, on the other hand, found himself in entirely the wrong position. Now Blaze would assume he had followed him to betray him.

'He's not a liar,' he said. 'Every word was true.'

'Oh?' The gangmaster was very surprised. 'So you're in league with him, are you? Is this some kind of plot?'

'I wanted to back him up,' said Similin.

'You'll get your chance to back him up,' said the gangmaster. 'You can back each other up. Because I mean to teach you what happens to troublemakers.'

They had rejoined the work group in the corn fields. Pelican now beckoned to his associates to come forward.

'Hold on to these two,' he said. 'And call all the men out to hear me. I've something to say.'

The burly associates seized Blaze and Similin. Blaze offered no resistance. The secretary found his arms were pinned behind his back, and he was unable to resist, even had he chosen to do so. The workers trooped in from the long rows of corn, curious to know what had happened, and grateful for a break from the hard labour.

'You see this man?" cried Pelican, pointing to Blaze. 'He went to the master to say he wasn't happy in his work. He said I cheated him. And you know what the master said? He said, if he's not happy, let him go. And I will. And this one here' – he pointed to Similin – 'he's not happy either. So I'll let him go too. Is there anyone else who's not happy?'

No one said a word.

'Do I take it that means you are happy?'

There came a mumbling nodding response.

'I can't hear you.'

'Yes,' said the men. 'Yes. Yes.'

'Very good.'

He clenched his fist, and nodded to the man who held Blaze, and called out to the crowd of workers.

'When a man calls me a cheat, I say – '

He struck hard with his fist, straight into Blaze's stomach. Blaze gasped and bent over, but the associates holding him jerked him upright again. Similin knew he would be next. He closed his eyes and braced himself for the coming pain. But Pelican wasn't yet done with Blaze. His fist was jabbing forward again, this time at Blaze's face. The blow brought bright blood streaming from Blaze's nose.

Blaze groaned aloud. Then he howled. Then he roared. And suddenly, like a giant awakening, he flexed his upper arms, and shook himself free. At once, roaring ever louder as he did so, he turned on the two associates and, using his right forearm like a club, smashed them to the ground. The men were more powerfully built than Blaze, but Blaze was driven by an uncontrolled rage that was like a madness, and they fell before him. The gangmaster had barely taken in what was happening when Blaze seized him by the shoulders and hurled him to the ground with such force that he rolled away in the dirt. Blaze chased after him, roaring.

'You bad man! You bad, bad man!'

As the gangmaster cowered on the ground, Blaze pummelled him with his fists, knocking him from one side to the other. The men holding Similin released their grip, to go to their master's aid. But the workers, astonished and excited, now began to shout too.

'Kill him!' they cried. 'Trample him! Crush him!'

The associates backed away.

'Kill them all!' cried the workers.

The associates turned and ran.

Blaze was roaring more quietly now. The terrified gang-master made no attempt to oppose him. The blows came more slowly, and then they stopped. Shaking with the violence of the tempest that had possessed him, bewildered, like one emerging from a trance, Blaze walked away and stood by himself, the blood still flowing from his nose.

The workers closed in on the gangmaster.

'Take his money! Make him pay! Make the cheating dog pay what he owes!'

They pulled at the gangmaster's clothing, and half-stripped him, and found his money bag. Shortly the coins came flying out, and the workers all fell to scrabbling in the dirt. The gangmaster, finding himself left alone, struggled to his feet, and limped away down the road.

Soren Similin went to Blaze, and wiped the blood from

his face. He saw his way forward now: his way to turn Blaze's explosion of anger to his advantage.

'You're a hero,' he said.

'A hero?'

'You fought against injustice.'

'Did I?'

'The gangmaster cheated us. He beat us. He was a bad man.'

Blaze remembered now.

'That's right! He's a bad man! Should I kill him?'

'He's gone now.'

There came a loud crash. The plantation workers had broken into the gangmaster's store shed. There they found his liquor supply.

'We do all the work!' cried one. 'The master gets all the profit!'

'The master!' cried the others, not quite knowing why.

'Let him share!'

They handed round the bottles of brandy.

'Share! Share!'

So shouting, drinking and singing, the workers streamed away down the track towards the plantation house. They sang the Happy Workers song as they went.

'They're happy now,' said Blaze.

'Because of you. You're the Noble Warrior.'

'The noble warrior?'

Blaze frowned, as if he had heard these words before, but couldn't remember where.

'You were a Noma once.'

'A Noma?'

'But they cast you out. They rejected you. They said you were bad.'

Blaze's frown deepened.

'I'm bad?'

'That's what the Nomana said.'

'But I'm not bad. I'm Blaze of Justice.'

'That's right. So the Nomana must be wrong.'

'The Nomana are wrong.' He spoke with emphasis. It made him angry to be called bad. Similin took note.

'The Nomana say you're bad. But you're not bad.'

'The Nomana are bad.'

'The Nomana are strong,' said Similin. 'Just like the gangmaster was strong.'

'I beat him. He was bad.'

'You did. You beat that bad gangmaster. Now it's the Nomana who are bad.'

'I'll beat them too.'

'They're very strong.'

'I don't care. I'll beat them.'

'Would you like to beat them all?'

'Yes. I'll beat them all. I'm Blaze of Justice.'

'But what if you get hurt?'

'I don't care.'

'What if they kill you?'

'I don't care.'

'You're willing to give your life in a just cause.'

'Give my life?' Blaze's face cleared. He had heard this before, so it must be true. 'Yes, I'd give my life.'

'You're a Noble Warrior.'

'A noble warrior . . .' Still it puzzled him; but he liked it. 'I am. I'll give my life. Because I'm a noble warrior.'

Soren Similin showed no outward sign, but inwardly he rejoiced. He had brought this poor deluded boy to the necessary place. So much for cleansing.

There came a sudden clatter of iron wheels behind them, and the rapid clop of hooves. It was the wagonette from the plantation house, driven by the master himself, at top speed. With him, white-faced and silent, were the two children, and the governess. The master cried out as he raced by.

'Robbers! Looters! They'll pay for this! I'll hang them all!'

Blaze stared after the wagonette as it disappeared in a cloud of dust.

'Not our problem,' said Similin.

But Blaze's gazing eyes were squinting with concern. 'Where's the lady?'

'What lady?'

'The lady who was kind to me. She must still be in the house.'

'They won't hurt her.'

'But he said there were robbers.'

Blaze rose to his feet and stood hesitating for a moment, his brow furrowed. Then without a further word he turned and set off at a loping run down the track to the plantation house.

The secretary cursed in silent frustration. He had come so close. All he needed now was to get Blaze to Radiance. So, with a sigh, he too set off down the track, to retrieve his perfect carrier.

As he came in sight of the house, he found the former plantation workers leaving it, in high spirits, carrying items looted from the house.

'You're too late!' they called to him. 'All the good stuff's gone!'

Similin made his way slowly up the steps. All the doors were open. Many of the windows had been smashed. Shards of glass glittered on the grey timber floors. Chairs and tables lay overturned. The delicate white curtains had been torn and tangled and ripped from their poles. The masses of fine fabric lay where they had fallen, like heaps of wind-blown snow. The workers had torn them down because they were a tangible part of the elegance with which the owners had lived; they had torn them as they might tear a lady's dress, to render her as ragged as they were themselves.

Soren Similin moved on through the house, from room to room, and so found Blaze at last, in what had once been the children's schoolroom. Here amid the sad chaos of the looting sat the mistress of the house, on an upright wooden school chair, with Blaze bending over her, speaking to her softly. Her cheeks were streaked with tears, and she was shaking her head.

Blaze looked up as Similin entered.

'They left her behind,' he said.

'No,' said the lady. 'It was my choice. They're better off without me.'

'You're good,' said Blaze. 'We'll look after you.'

Soren Similin's heart sank as he heard this. But he thought it best to support Blaze in his act of kindness.

'Do you know where your husband has gone?'

'He has a house in the city.'

'The city? Radiance?'

'Yes.'

That was a stroke of luck. With rather more enthusiasm, Similin said to Blaze, 'We'd better escort the lady to Radiance.'

'Yes,' said Blaze. 'She's good.'

Similin turned back to the lady.

'We have no carriage, I'm afraid. But if you feel able to make the journey on foot, we would be happy to accompany you.'

'On foot? Of course. Why not? I can walk.'

She stood up, as if to demonstrate; but then remained there, motionless, looking round at the wreckage of the schoolroom. The table had been broken in half. The school books lay scattered over the floor. A child's rocking-cow had been pulled from its rockers, for no purpose other than to make it useless.

'I'm so sorry,' said Blaze.

She turned to him, surprised.

'Why should you be sorry? You didn't do this.'

283

'The workers weren't happy. I beat the bad men. But now – '

He gestured at the destruction.

'Do you think I blame them?' Suddenly she became animated. 'Do you think I don't know? All this' – she waved one hand down the passage, towards the other rooms – 'all this for one family! For me! Of course I didn't deserve it. Of course it should all be taken away from me. Of course I should be punished. And now I have been punished. I have nothing and no one. I am an unnecessary creature. The sooner my life is over the better.'

The tears were gone now. Her beautiful eyes were bright as she spoke, and her gentle voice was urgent, demanding assent. Blaze was hypnotised.

'No,' he said. 'Each one of us has work to do, that only they can do.'

'Who told you that?' She shot the question at him accusingly, as if he had stolen it. 'That's the way the Nomana talk.'

Blaze blinked, and looked confused.

'He was a Noma once,' said Soren Similin.

'You were a Noma – once?'

She laughed. It was the kind of laughter that has more hurt in it than happiness.

'And did they cleanse you?' She looked into his puzzled eyes. 'They did, didn't they?'

'I don't know,' said Blaze slowly. 'All I know is, they cast me out.'

'Oh, you poor boy. And you call me good.'

'You are good.'

'I'm just another exile, like you.'

She set off down the passage, suddenly become active. Blaze and Similin followed.

She walked ahead of them, making her way down the steps and on to the path between the trees. She still wore the long elegant white dress of a lady of leisure, and soft kid-leather pumps that were not at all suitable for the baked earth and grit of the road. But none of this deterred her. She walked as if in a dream, down the track between the tall standing corn that would now never be picked.

Soren Similin followed, frowning with irritation. He was so close to his goal, and now this foolish, irrelevant woman was distracting Blaze from his destiny. However, she did have her uses. She had provided a timely pretext for doing what he wanted, which was to go to Radiance.

'We have to look after her,' said Blaze.

'She's a fine lady,' said the secretary. 'She's not used to walking. How long do you think she'll keep this up? An hour at the most. Then she'll collapse.'

'She's beautiful,' said Blaze. 'She's good. We have to look after her.'

Just what I need, thought Similin. Now the big booby's gone and fallen in love.

CHAPTER TWENTY-FIVE

EASE AND SOLACE

THE canoe that carried Morning Star reached the city of Radiance as night was falling, slipping from the river itself into one of the narrow waterways that led into the maze of city streets. Morning Star was no longer covered by the heavy blanket, but she made no sound, because her captors had tied a thick cloth gag over her mouth. She did not move, because her wrists were strapped tight to her waist belt, and a second rope tethered her belt to the canoe bench on which she sat. But she was able to sit upright, and she was able to see, so she looked about her all the way, and memorised everything she could. She saw the fine streets where the priests passed with their servants and their glittering gold robes. She saw the patrol officers on every street corner. She saw the plump, pampered citizens, and the starved yellow cats.

The two tribute traders who had captured her were called by the comical names of Ease and Solace. But Morning Star wasn't laughing. Clearly they knew their business, and were expecting to sell her that very night. All the way to the city they were alternately congratulating themselves and bickering over how best to proceed.

'She's a beauty! We shall break the record with her!'

'How much money has our man got, Ease? How high will he go?'

'They say he supplies all the oil for the temple, and the royal household too. He's got enough.'

'Oh, we shall squeeze him, shan't we, Ease?'

'And don't you go softening!'

'When did I ever soften? When it comes to striking a bargain, I'm as unyielding as flint! Why else am I known as the man of flint?'

'You're not known as the man of flint. You're known as Sol the Doll.'

'Sol the Doll! I never heard that before in my life!'

'So don't you go softening on me. This one will make our fortune, if we play it right.'

'Sol the Doll? Who calls me Sol the Doll?'

'I mean to make the oil-seller pay five thousand shillings.'

'Five thousand shillings! Oh, Ease! How magnificent! Oh, you dreamer of mighty dreams! Five thousand shillings!'

'You'll see. Just don't go softening on me.'

Morning Star sat still, and watched, and listened. She was extremely frightened, but the fear had the effect of making her concentrate. All her senses were focused on finding a means of escape. Her bonds were welltied. She was quite unable to call for help. The little backwater up which they were paddling was overlooked by the windows of lamp-lit houses, but if anyone was watching as they went by, they showed no sign that they saw anything out of the ordinary. No doubt bound and gagged prisoners were paddled past their windows every night. No, her chance would come later, she knew: when she was at last untied, and sold. It was such a strange idea that she should be sold like a loaf of bread. She understood very well the purpose for which she was to be sold, but it was hard for her to imagine what it meant to be a tribute, so she chose not to think about it. Then, just as the canoe was pulling up to a flight of dark steps, and her tether was being loosed, she looked up and saw a distant towering rock. It was far off, and black against the starlit sky, and from this distance seemed to be not so very high. But her heart went cold at the sight.

The tribute traders pushed her up the steps and through a doorway into a building that smelled of stale beer and frying pig-fat. They led her down an unlit passage into an unlit room, and there they sat her on a wooden chair and tethered her once more, this time giving her no freedom of movement. The chair, as she soon discovered, was bolted to the floor. Only when she was securely in place did they light an oil lamp, and hang it from a hook in the ceiling. Then they left, and she heard a key turn in the lock of the door after them.

At no point had they spoken to her directly, or looked into her eyes. She understood that for them she had become a thing, a package, a promise of wealth. She had watched their colours, searching for any sign of compassion or humanity, a flicker of the softer tones of pink or blue, but all she could see was the crude orange glow of greed. No hope of pity there. They had carried out this same transaction too many times before.

Her thoughts then turned to the one who was to buy her. Surely, if only her gag was removed, she could touch his heart? Surely she could make him feel that she was a living creature like himself? And once he truly felt that, he would not be able to send her to her death.

Cheerful Giver changed his clothes as soon as he received the message. He put on his most humble dress, in the hope of convincing the traders that he was not a wealthy man. He crossed the city on foot, without an accompanying servant. However, because he hoped to return with a vital purchase, he instructed one of his men to come after him with his wife's bullock-carriage.

So he made his way across the deserted marketplace and down one of the narrow stinking streets beyond, to the hostel called the Ham Bone. Here the traders were waiting to meet him. He felt his heart beating fast. His name day was only three days off, and it was now a matter of urgency that he obtain a tribute. But he tried to make himself calm, and to appear indifferent.

This plan disintegrated as soon as the traders told him the price they wanted.

'Ten thousand shillings!'

'For you, sir, being as you're the owner of all the oil fields between the river and the lake, and the supplier of oil to both temple and palace, why, what is ten thousand shillings to you?'

'Ten thousand shillings! Do you take me for a madman?'

'She's a youngster, good sir. An authentic and guaranteed virgin, healthy and plump, and pleasant to the eye.'

'And quiet,' said his companion. 'Obedient as a puppy.'

Cheerful Giver looked from one to the other and felt nauseated. Why did he have to deal with these smirking parasites? It offended his dignity almost as much as it hurt his wallet.

'My top price is two thousand,' he said. 'But I must see her first.'

'Most unfortunate, good sir. It seems our little arrangement is not to be. What time are we to see the next gentleman, Sol?'

'I believe he said he could be here within the hour, Ease.'

Cheerful Giver knew this was almost certainly a fiction. But what could he do?

'I must see her first,' he repeated.

'What do you think, Sol? Should we let the dog see the rabbit?'

'How do we know the gentleman is serious?' said Solace.

'That's the question,' said Ease. And they both turned their mock-humble eyes on the oil merchant.

'Very well. Three thousand.'

This was three times the most he had ever paid before. If the tribute really was a healthy young virgin, it was almost worth it.

'Three thousand gets you on to the racecourse,' said Ease. 'Ten thousand gets you the rabbit.'

Cheerful Giver found this vulgar racecourse metaphor almost more than he could bear. He himself was not in the habit of going to the dog races.

'I never buy unseen.' He tried to sound as if the whole affair was a matter of indifference to him.

'And we never shows till we sees the money.'

This retort seemed to strike them as neat. They smirked at each other. Cheerful Giver remained stony-faced and silent.

'Tell you what, good sir!' Ease spoke as if inspired. 'Give us your assurance that you're open to discussion where the price is concerned, and you shall see the rabbit.'

'Open to discussion,' agreed Solace. 'Well put.'

Cheerful Giver hesitated for a long, long moment in the vain hope that this would strengthen his position.

'Very well,' he said at last. 'But I haven't raised my offer by a single shilling.'

'Understood, good sir. Open to discussion is all we ask.'

With a bitter sigh, Cheerful Giver followed the two traders into a back room of the hostel.

Here, firmly strapped to a chair, was a small female figure with the red headscarf of the hill people. She was gagged, so only the upper half of her face was visible. She sat quietly, and turned her eyes towards them as she heard them enter. The tribute traders locked the door behind them. Cheerful Giver examined the girl closely, without actually meeting her eyes. He took care to show no sign to the traders, but he was very pleased with what he saw. She was clearly not a spiker. Her skin had none of the sores and abrasions associated with semi-starvation. Her hair, which was just visible peeking out from beneath her headscarf, was rich and fine. The city of Radiance, to his knowledge, would not have seen so perfect a tribute in years.

'She's too small,' he said, turning away. 'Almost dwarfish.'

'Oh, no, good sir! Remember, you see her sitting down. When she stands – not small, never small. What would you say, Sol?'

'Finely formed,' said Solace. 'Well proportioned.'

'You always were the one for words,' said Ease admiringly.

'Three thousand it is, then,' said Cheerful Giver. 'And that's three times more than I've ever paid before.'

'And if three, why not ten?' said Ease. 'Now that the strings are loosened, as you might say.'

'Three thousand shillings!' said Cheerful Giver, rapping with his knuckles on the wooden wall, in the way he did when bidding for oil fields. 'My final offer. Take it or leave it.'

So he paid five thousand shillings, and the girl was his. By some mysterious sixth sense the tribute traders had divined the exact sum he had brought with him, and they made him pay it all. His only consolation was that no one would ever know how much he had paid. The price was so stupendous it would turn him into the laughing stock of the city if it got out. But he would never tell, and the tribute traders swore they would keep the secret.

'Better for business that way, good sir. No one ever

292

knows for sure what's been paid and what hasn't. After all, who's to say you didn't pay ten thousand?'

Cheerful Giver had to be content with that.

The bullock-carriage was waiting outside the hostel, and he and the tribute rode home in it, unseen by all. The carriage was driven into the courtyard of his large house, and the outer gates closed, and the servants dismissed, before he took the tribute out. He carried her himself, in his own arms, down into the windowless cellar room in which, until recently, the escaped spiker had been kept. His wife followed.

'Oh, husband!' she exclaimed. 'She's beautiful! How clever you are! Oh, she's perfect! You're a good, good man!'

'And a poor, poor man now, thanks to you.'

'Can we take off the bindings?'

'Let me get her securely on the leash first. I'm taking no more chances with you and open doors.'

'I never left the door open. I'm not as stupid as you think. It was that key. It doesn't turn all the way.'

'Not if you don't turn it all the way, it doesn't.'

He screwed an iron wrist-band tight on to the tribute's left wrist. A light but extremely strong chain was forged to the wrist-band at one end, and to a ring sunk in the cellar wall at the other. Throughout this process the tribute stood still, and offered no resistance.

'Now,' said Cheerful Giver, addressing the tribute directly for the first time, though still not meeting her eyes, 'I'm going to remove your gag. But if you scream, or cause me any trouble at all, it goes back on again. Nod to show you understand.'

The tribute nodded.

Cheerful Giver unbound the gag. The tribute licked at her dry lips and wriggled her jaw. Then she spoke to Blessing.

'Thank you, my lady,' she said.

'Oh!' cried Blessing. 'She's so beautiful!'

Cheerful Giver studied his expensive purchase with a critical frown. He had to admit he had done well. There was an air of innocence about her that would be especially well appreciated on the day.

'What's your name, little one?' said Blessing.

'Morning Star,' said the tribute.

'I'm so sorry you had to have your mouth all bound up. We'll get you something to eat and drink. I'm sure you'd like that. My dear' – to her husband – 'see to it, will you?'

'She stays on the leash,' said Cheerful Giver, and left the cellar.

Blessing stepped forward, and a little nervously she reached out one hand.

'You're such a darling! I just want to pet you and pet you!'

'Who are you?' said the tribute in her dear little voice. 'Where am I?'

'You're in the house of a highly respected family. My husband is Handler of the Royal Corona. I myself am the lead soloist in the temple choir. I think you have reason to be proud.'

'What will you do with me?'

'Little one,' said Blessing solemnly, 'you are to perform a pure and wonderful service. May I hold your hand?'

Morning Star let Blessing take her hand. Blessing gazed on her with wide ecstatic eyes, and stroked her hand as she spoke.

'You are to bring new life! You are to save the whole world from the black grasp of night! Because of the pure and wonderful service you will perform, the crops will grow, and men and beasts will have food to eat. Because of you, there will be life!'

'I think,' said Morning Star hesitantly, 'you mean me to die.'

'To give your life for all!' cried Blessing, as fervently as if it was she herself who was to make the sacrifice. 'To be received into the bosom of the Radiant Power! To plunge into the very heart of life!'

Morning Star watched the dumpy round-faced woman before her, with her big round eyes rolled upwards to the cellar ceiling, and her palms too now uplifted, as if in communion with her god, and rapidly ran through the courses of action open to her. She had already examined the wrist-band, discreetly, and knew she could not release herself without help. Seeker and the Wildman would come looking for her, no doubt, but she could see no way they could find her. That meant she must save herself.

She had been able to make a thorough assessment of the master of the household during his negotiations for her purchase. His colours had shown him to be vain and vindictive. His wife was another matter. She glowed with a pale turquoise shimmer that Morning Star had encountered before, and that gave her some small hope: her colours showed her to be a brainless believer. With a little work, she could be got to believe almost anything. Therefore Morning Star decided, as a first step, to make her her friend.

'You don't know me,' she said in a small and humble voice, 'and yet I feel the love streaming out of you towards me. You must have so much love in you.'

'Child!' cried Blessing. 'You understand me so well!'

'I feel – I feel that you want only what is good and fine for me.'

'I do! Oh, I do!'

'I suppose,' said Morning Star, all wonderingly, 'I suppose everyone's life must come to an end one day. And you offer me an ending that has a purpose.'

Blessing gazed at her in awe. All her life she had dreamed of such a moment. Could it really be happening?

Her husband re-entered the cellar carrying a tray of food and drink. He had decided not to let the servants into the cellar at all.

'My dear!' cried his wife, running to his side. 'My dear, good, generous husband! I believe – truly, I believe – that at long last – after so many years – we have a willing tribute!'

PART FOUR
SACRIFICE

They are watching.

The old ones grow restless now. Their plans are unfolding
too slowly. They are angry.

They are hungry for eternal youth.

They dream of the harvest.

CHAPTER TWENTY-SIX

THE WILDMAN'S BITE

THE city of Radiance was officially a closed city, its perimeter patrolled by border police. Residents had identity papers which permitted them to come and go. Visitors had to seek permission to enter the city. Radiance had grown rapidly in recent years, and its residents had become ever more wealthy, with the result that a large number of workers were needed to do the low-paid jobs that the citizens of Radiance scorned to do for themselves. These migrant workers were issued with temporary papers, which had to be countersigned by a reputable employer every day. Those who could not find work, or who were dismissed from their place of work, and so failed to get their papers signed, were obliged to leave the city that same day. Those picked up by the street patrols with unsigned papers were sent to the public tanks.

Seeker and the Wildman crossed the city boundary after dark. Here they were accosted by two border policemen. They declared themselves willing to work, and were issued with temporary papers.

'Go down by the lake shore,' advised the first border policeman. 'Go to the floating gardens. There's always work to be had there. Keep your papers with you at all times.

301

And stay away from the market area. That's where the tribute traders do their business.'

'And here's some more advice for free,' said the second policeman. 'Always give way to priests, and don't brawl. You don't want to land in the tanks. There's only one way out of there.'

He nodded ahead towards the high crag that was the temple rock. No more needed to be said.

As they headed on their way into the city, the Wildman spoke low to Seeker.

'There'll be brawling all right. When we find those blubber-piss traders, there'll be brawling all right.'

'We have to be very careful,' said Seeker. 'We can only help her so long as we're free.'

The Wildman groaned, recalling the sight of Morning Star trussed up in the tribute traders' net, disappearing up the river.

'I should have known. As soon as I saw the ferryman was gone, I should have known.'

'Don't blame yourself.'

'Why not? I'm to blame. I put her in danger. Of course I blame myself.'

For a while the Wildman said no more. Then he groaned aloud again.

'I want blood!' he said. 'I want killing!'

'There are other ways,' said Seeker.

'What other ways?' The Wildman turned on Seeker with all the savage force of his frustration. 'Here's the only

302

ways I know. Eat alone. Sleep light. Strike first. Give no chances, because you'll get none. Watch men's hands, it's the hands that do the hurting. You know what I get my way? I'm still alive at the end of the day. Don't talk to me about *other ways*.'

Seeker said nothing in reply, aware that the anger was not for him. The Wildman was in the grip of an emotion he had never experienced before, which was guilt. He thrashed the air with his arms, as if trying to free himself once more from the entangling nets.

'I do what I do,' he growled. 'I live as I live. I'm ready to take what comes. But this other thing – ugh!'

He shook his entire body.

'How am I to do it for her?'

'That's when it gets difficult,' said Seeker. 'When you're not on your own any more. When you care about other people. When it's them that suffer, not you.'

'Ugh!' said the Wildman again, and he spat on to the ground. 'It's like a bad taste in my mouth that won't go away.'

'I don't think anything will ever take it away again.'

'Except blood! Except killing! Just let me alone with those traders for as long as it takes me to shake their hands – '

'Hush!'

There were others on the streets, and the Wildman had begun to raise his voice once more.

'We're on our way to find them now.'

He spoke to calm his friend down, and to turn his

thoughts away from rage and towards tactics.

'We start by the marketplace. My guess is they're still in the city. They'll stay until they've sold – until they've completed their sale.'

The Wildman groaned again.

'I'm going to kill them!'

'We have to find out where Morning Star is first. We want that more than we want to kill them. If they're dead, they can't tell us anything.'

They were making their way down the streets of the city proper, and, though neither of them admitted it, they were awed. Building after building on either side was larger and more magnificent than any house they had ever seen. Not only the roofs, but pillars and arches, window and door frames, were clad in gold. At every street corner there were water fountains for the people, and water troughs for the beasts. The paving stones on which they walked were kept clean. Here and there they saw men with shovels, scraping up the bullock droppings. The people on the streets talked and laughed as they went, swishing their expensive clothing and jingling their jewels. Fine carriages passed by, drawn by sleek-coated bullocks. Bright lamps burned in window after window. So many people, so many houses.

'I wonder where it is,' said Seeker softly.

'Where what is?'

'The weapon that will destroy Anacrea.'

The Wildman looked round at the windows glowing in the night.

'I want to slit necks!' he hissed. 'I need to slit necks!'

'Your time will come.'

They were stopped at a street corner by a street patrolman.

'Papers!'

They handed over their papers. He barely glanced at them.

'Just arrived?'

'Yes.'

'Find work tomorrow or get out.'

'Please,' said Seeker. 'Can you direct us to the market?'

'What do you want with the market? Everything's shut now.'

'We're meeting a friend there.'

'A friend, eh?' His bored gaze took in the Wildman, and lingered over his long golden hair. 'What are you, then? Dog or bitch?'

Seeker felt the Wildman shiver into stillness, his whole body tensing for a strike. He took back their papers, and pulled him away.

'We're late already.'

'Follow the street all the way. You'll find it.'

Seeker dragged the Wildman across the intersection. They could hear the patrolman laughing after them as they went.

'Let it go!' Seeker whispered. 'Just let it go.'

The Wildman jerked his arm out of Seeker's grip and rolled his shoulders, growling aloud as he walked.

'Soon,' he said. 'Let it be soon.'

As they walked on, the pavement rose up higher than the street, and became narrower. The building they were passing filled the entire street block, and was even more imposing than the rest. From behind its high doors came the sounds of voices and laughter, and through the imperfectly drawn curtains of its high windows they glimpsed long tables, where rows of very big men sat eating and drinking by candlelight. The sight made them hungry and cold, for the night was becoming chilly.

Ahead a bright little procession was approaching. A servant with a lantern was followed by a gold-robed priest, his train carried by a train-bearer, and a second servant with a second lantern came behind. The four of them were walking fast, keeping to the middle of the narrow pavement, unconcerned about who might be in their way. Seeker drew the Wildman into one of the doorways of the long building, to allow the procession to go past. As he did so, the door opened, and a massively big man came blundering out, smelling of wine.

'Out of my way, scum spikers!' he boomed, and barged Seeker over the edge of the high pavement to the street below. As Seeker fell, his flailing hand struck the lantern held by the servant bringing up the rear of the priest's procession, and it too fell, and smashed on to the cobbles.

Seeker landed hard. For a few moments he lay winded and bruised, his cheek to the ground. When he opened his eyes, half-stunned by the shock of his fall, he found he couldn't see clearly. Somewhere close by there was a glowing light. As his eyes slowly found focus, he saw that the smashed lantern lay a few inches from his face. Burning oil was trickling out from a crack in the lantern's reservoir, and running between the cobblestones in a little river of flame. Unable to move, he watched, helpless but fascinated, as the flame made its way towards him. Because his eyes were right on the cobbles themselves, the flame seemed as tall as he was, and to move with a terrible and deliberate purpose. Then, just as it must reach his face, the rivulet of burning oil took a turn between the cobbles, and passed him by. The flame passed close enough for him to feel its heat on his cheeks. His eyes tracked its passing, and a sensation came over him that this was no accident. This was a sign. As soon as this thought had entered his mind, he recalled the voice he had heard in the Nom, as clearly as if it was speaking to him again.

Surely you know that it's you who will save me.

All of this must have taken no more than a few seconds, because as he clambered back on to his feet he found that the big man was still on the pavement above, and the Wildman was attacking him.

'You great heap of pig-dung! Come and get me! See how I bite!'

The big man was staring at the Wildman as if he couldn't believe his eyes.

'You sick in the head, boy?' he said. 'I'm an axer! In

there' – he gestured at the open door – 'there's another fifty axers!'

The Wildman had no weapon, but he knew how to use his powerful hands. He threw a diversionary punch with his left fist, while his right hand struck hard at the axer's throat. The axer gave a gurgling grunt of pain, and started to choke. The Wildman struck again, this time with his right foot, a driving punch-kick up into the axer's groin. The axer staggered and sank to his knees.

'Who's sick in the head now?' crowed the Wildman.

Seeker reached up and pulled at him.

'Wildman! Run!'

He had seen other big men rising from the table in response to the sounds from the street.

'You can't fight them all! Run!'

Together they set off at a run down the street. Behind them they heard a roar of rage as the injured axer finally regained his voice. Ahead they saw yet another street patrol.

'Walk,' said Seeker. 'Walk.'

They slowed to a walk, and so passed the patrol without attracting undue attention. The Wildman was still charged up and hopping with aggression.

'If I had my spike that ox would be a dead man!'

'He was a monster!'

'And I'm the Wildman! I can take him down!'

He danced from foot to foot, shadow-boxing the night air.

'You can too,' said Seeker. 'You did take him down.'

For all the danger they were in, Seeker had been

impressed, and his voice showed it. The Wildman liked that.

'You didn't believe me before, did you? You thought I was all mouth and no teeth. But I know how to bite!'

The broad street they were following became narrower, and the houses became humbler, until it was little more than a rutted lane. On either side other even narrower lanes ran off into the night. The people they passed here made no noise, and avoided their eyes. The street lamps became further and further apart, so that at the halfway point between lamps they were making their way in darkness.

Then, just when they had begun to doubt the patrolman's directions, they found themselves in the market. It was a long open space, down which ran lines of wooden stalls, all of which were bare. The ground between the stalls was littered with refuse from the day's trading, and here and there dark crouching figures were at work scouring the droppings for anything that could be eaten or sold. A few lanterns hung from house-eaves round the market perimeter, but in the centre there was no light, and the scavengers were working by feel and smell.

'Now where?' said the Wildman.

'Now we ask.'

Seeker accosted one of the scavengers.

'Can you help us, sir?'

The scavenger rose and stared. He was a very old man, and his face was disfigured by a broad scar that ran down one side, pulling his mouth into a perpetual snarl.

'No, sir,' he said, and returned to his scavenging.

The Wildman seized him by the neck and jerked him back up.

'Yes, sir,' he said.

The scavenger whimpered and went limp.

'We're looking for tribute traders,' said Seeker.

At that, the scavenger grinned a knowing grin.

'Buying or selling?'

'Just looking.'

'Just looking!' The old man cackled. 'You keep on looking! You keep on looking!'

The Wildman shook him till he rattled. The scavenger squealed with terror.

'Help! Help! Murder!'

No one heard. No one came.

'Where should we look?'

'How would I know? Look where they go to spend their money. Tributes is a fine trade. Good money in tributes.'

'Where do they go to spend their money?'

'Anywhere there's wine and women. Not that you'd know about that, seeing as you're a boy.'

'You want your neck slit, chicken?'

'Let him go.'

The Wildman released his grip. The old man tottered but did not fall. He rubbed at his neck.

'Tribute traders have got a friend of ours,' said Seeker. 'We want to find her.'

'And if you do? You got money to buy her back?'

'No.'

'Then save your legs. Next time you see her she'll be playing birdies.'

He flapped his arms and nodded up at the distant crag.

'Money's not the only persuader,' said the Wildman, flexing his strong hands.

'You're new here, aren't you?'

'Yes,' said Seeker.

'Lay a hand on anyone here, and you're in the tanks. No one gets what they want by violence here. All the violence happens in the evening, up on the big rock. That's enough violence for everyone. You hear what I'm saying?'

'Come on,' said the Wildman to Seeker. 'This old fool's no use to us.'

'Wait,' said Seeker. 'He's telling us something.'

'Oh, you're a quick one.'

'Tell us where to look.'

'Well, now. If you were to follow that lane over there, in the corner, all the way to the canal, and if you were to find a hostel there by the name of the Ham Bone, why, you might well come upon the fellows you're looking for. And if you did, and if you had words, and if your friend here came over with the violence – well, that would be a surprise to all concerned. A tremendous surprise. Quite a novelty.'

Seeker looked closely at the old man.

'You'd like that, would you?'

'I'd like it well enough. You'll end up on the rock, of course. But me, I'd like to see some feathers plucked from them vultures. I'd like to hear them squawk.'

311

'The Ham Bone. By the canal.'

'You better have money. The Ham Bone likes money.'

With that, he returned to his scavenging. Seeker and the Wildman crossed the dark marketplace and set off down yet another narrow lane, in the direction he had indicated.

'You believe him?'

'We'll see soon enough.'

The lane did indeed run to a canal, and here on one side, through a narrow arch, there was a brightly lit court-yard, loud with the sound of company. Tables crowded the yard, and between the tables ran sweating barmen carrying trays of brimming glasses high over their heads. Almost every chair was taken, and every customer was shouting to be served.

Seeker and the Wildman entered the courtyard and found a bench in the corner where they could sit undisturbed and study the company. The drinkers were all men, and all were drinking brandy. Seeker's eyes ranged from face to face, hunting for the two who had attacked them on the ferry.

'Will you know them?'

'I'll know them,' said the Wildman. 'And then, they'll know me.'

'Remember. We want information, not revenge.'

'First information. Then revenge.'

Seeker checked every face. They weren't there. He was sure of it. He felt a chill form inside him. Where now?

'We might as well get something to eat. You still have money left?'

'As much as you want.'

They ordered wine and water, and bread, and cold beef. By the time it came they had both begun to realise how hungry they were. Then, as they started to eat, the two tribute traders came swaggering into the courtyard. Their appearance was greeted with a small cheer from one of the tables.

'Look who's back! The dogs return to their vomit!'

'Ho, barman! Brandy for this band of villains!'

'What was that? Did I hear Sol offer to pay for our refreshments? Pinch me! I must be asleep.'

'Found a buyer for your one-legged spiker, Sol?'

'Laugh all you want, friends. And drink your brandy on us. We're celebrating.'

'Celebrating what?'

'Call it a sweet little trade. Call it a satisfactory price.'

'Satisfactory? If Ease calls it satisfactory, it must be fat enough to choke a priest.'

'Don't you believe it. He strapped a wooden leg on the crippled spiker and passed him off in the dark for a hundred shillings.'

'If you say so,' smiled Ease, patting his money pouch. They all heard the sound of that pat.

'He's got over a thousand shillings in there.'

'A thousand shillings is well enough. But nobody comes swaggering in to the Ham Bone over a thousand shillings.

Look at the fellow smirking! You'd think he'd broken the record.'

'You'd think that, would you?' said Solace, smirking some more.

'By the Sun, he has! He's broken the record!'

'Have you? What did you get? Four thousand?'

Solace looked at Ease and Ease looked at Solace and they just raised their eyebrows and smirked.

'More? Impossible!'

'If you say it's impossible, then it must be impossible,' said Ease.

'Not – five thousand!'

'No figures, friends. No figures.'

'By the steaming Sun, they've got five thousand!'

Seeker and the Wildman ate and drank, and kept their heads down, and listened.

'It's them,' murmured Seeker.

'Oh, yes. It's them.'

The Wildman had hold of the knife that had come with the loaf of bread, and he was stabbing with it at the crust, chopping the bread into ever smaller pieces.

'Not yet,' said Seeker.

It was another hour before either of the two tribute traders rose from the table. Then it was the one called Solace who announced he must attend an urgent summons.

'If I don't piss now, I shall – I shall – I shall piss now!'

'Go! Go! Spare us!'

So Solace tottered out of the courtyard, heading for the

open lane, where it was the custom for the hostel's patrons to empty their bladders into the canal. Seeker and the Wildman watched him pass close by them, and then they rose and followed.

After the glare of the courtyard, the lane was blind dark. As far as they could tell, it was empty but for Solace. He stood by the canal railing, one hand taking his weight as he leaned forward, and with many a sigh of pleasure he proceeded to enjoy a long copious release.

'Let's do it!' hissed the Wildman.

'No. Wait.'

The Wildman wanted fear. Seeker wanted cooperation. For all the Wildman's superiority in age and strength, Seeker had become the one who made the decisions.

Now the tribute trader was done, and was hitching his clothing back into place.

'Go, Wildman!'

The Wildman loped across the dark lane, hissing with the intensity of his rage. The tribute trader heard his approach, and turned towards him.

'That you, Ease?'

He quickly discovered his mistake.

The Wildman seized him by the throat, half-throttling him with one hand, and with the other he drove three sharp blows into the trader's belly. Solace closed his eyes and folded like scythed corn. The Wildman jumped on to his prostrate body, seized his head by the hair, and banged it on the stones, in the splash of his own urine, until the trader opened his eyes again. Seeing that he had his attention, the Wildman whispered to him,

'I'm going to tear the flesh off your face with my own teeth! I'm going to hurt you so bad you're going to beg to die!'

The trader was so paralysed with terror that he couldn't even frame a reply. He just choked and moaned in the darkness. Seeker now moved in. He knelt down by the trader and spoke close to his ear.

'Listen very carefully. This morning you took a girl. She is our friend. We don't want your money. We don't want to hurt you any more. We just want to know where she is.'

Solace heard him and rolled his eyes and gurgled.

'Let go of his throat, Wildman.'

The Wildman released his grip.

'I want to rip his face off!'

'I know you do. But let's see if he's going to help us first.'

The trader was gulping air.

'Don't kill me!' he said. 'Don't let him kill me!'

'So where's the girl?'

'The oil merchant. We sold her to the oil merchant.'

'Where's his house?'

'I don't know.'

Seeker looked down at Solace with a sad gaze.

'We've already broken the law. We can be thrown off the high rock just for assaulting you. Then we're as good as dead. So we might as well kill you. The punishment doesn't get any worse.'

316

'No! Please! His house is in the street leading to the temple. There's a sun sign over the gates.'

'Let him go.'

'Why?' said the Wildman.

'He's done as we asked.'

'So? We don't need him any more. We kill him.'

'No. We made a deal.'

'I never made a deal. I don't do deals.'

'I made a deal. I honour my deals.'

Reluctantly, the Wildman released the shivering trader from his powerful grip. Solace stumbled to his feet.

'Remember,' said Seeker, 'you don't know who we are, but we know who you are. If you give us any trouble, we'll come looking for you, and I'll take your five thousand shillings, and my friend will tear your face off. But if you say nothing, we'll say nothing, and you keep your money, and what happens between us and the oil merchant is none of your business.'

The trader nodded. His eyes flicked nervously back to the lights and safety of the hostel.

'You can go now.'

Solace hurried away. The Wildman watched him go with burning eyes.

'I don't see why I couldn't kill him.'

'I'll explain later. Come on.'

They crossed the dark city, taking care not to run, and after some searching they found the street that led to the temple. In this street there was a house that was more substantial than the others, and over its arched gateway was set the sign of the sun. They stood in the street, in the greater darkness of a doorway facing the house, and studied it carefully. Its windows were small, high, and well shuttered. The tops of mature trees rising above the walls indicated that there was an inner courtyard. The only entrance was the arched gateway, and its gates were heavy, and studded with iron bolts. There was no hope of breaking into a house as well built as this.

They walked up and down the night street, examining the house from every angle. A narrow alley ran down one side, leading along the high house wall to the back. They found the wall was unbroken and impenetrable on every side.

'How do we know she's in there?'

'We don't.'

'So what do we do?'

'Come back in the daylight. Wait for the gates to open.'

'Then what?'

'Then we see what we see.'

Seeker had no plan. He was responding with nothing but instinct to each new development. But he sensed that the Wildman wanted to believe he had a plan. Already he was learning that all that is necessary to get others to follow you is to lead. There was something else too, which he was sure the Wildman sensed in him. He was no longer afraid. This was more than strange. He was in a place of great danger, and was about to risk greater danger still. He had never thought of himself as having natural courage, in the way that his brother Blaze had. And yet he was sustained by a powerful inner conviction that was like an act of trust. He believed – not that he was protected, nor that he would be spared pain or harm – but that his journey had only just begun. It would not, could not, end here. Therefore, however many terrors lay before him, he would survive them.

He had no external evidence for this belief; perhaps it was no more than the product of his imagination; but it made him strong.

CHAPTER TWENTY-SEVEN

SCHEMES AND DREAMS

SEEKER and the Wildman spent what was left of the night in the open, sleeping on the worn grass of a lakeside park. They were not alone. Many other migrant workers were to be found curled up here, some with blankets, but most uncovered. In the chill small hours, Seeker rolled towards the Wildman in his sleep, and they huddled close together to share warmth.

Sunrise woke them, its dazzling rays skating over the waters of the lake. All over the city they could hear the greeting calls with which the people of Radiance welcomed the return of their life-giving god.

'The Lord is come again! Light of light, glory of glories!'

Seeker was fully awake first. He stood and stretched, and shook the sleep-wrinkles out of his clothes. Then he went to the lakeside and splashed cold water over his face, and returned to his friend.

'Wake up, Wildman. We don't have much time.'

The Wildman groaned and turned his face away from the rising sun. A priest passed by on the shore road nearby, his train-bearer scuttling after him.

'Arise, good people! The Lord is come again!'

'Wake up, Wildman. We have to look for Morning Star.'

The beautiful youth rolled over, groaned again, and rose. His eyes were still shut. He stretched his entire body in a slow, rippling movement, at the end of which his eyes snapped open, and he was wide awake. Seeker, waiting for him, thought to himself: he wakes like a wild animal.

They walked back up the streets that they had followed in darkness, finding their way by making for the looming bulk of the temple. By daylight, the street of the oil merchant's house revealed itself to be grander than they had realised. The well-kept verges, the mature trees, the high walls and the imposing gateways all showed that this was the territory of the city's elite.

They reached the oil merchant's house just as the big gates were swinging open for the start of the day's business. Servants came and went in a slow bustle, leaving the house carrying big empty baskets, returning with fresh bread and milk and vegetables. Other servants swept the courtyard, throwing up little clouds of dust with their stiff brooms. A maid went by with a tray laden with breakfast, presumably for the owner of the house.

Seeker and the Wildman lingered in the shadow of a tree, watching while trying not to seem to be watching. The Wildman grew restless.

'If she's there, it's not likely they'll bring her out.'

'We'll see something.'

'What?'

'I don't know.'

But Seeker knew they didn't have much time. For their

321

papers to be in order they must do a full day's work, and the working day would soon be starting. He felt frustrated, and angry with himself, because he knew he had been counting on luck.

The temple bell rang the hour.

'We have to go.'

As he turned to go, he saw a man emerge into the courtyard bearing the breakfast tray that had been carried before by the maid. The tray was no longer so well stocked, but nor did it hold the remains of a completed breakfast. There was just enough there – half a small loaf, a glass of milk, some cherries – to feed one person. The man carrying the tray was middle-aged, and dressed in expensive materials. He could only be the master of the house: the oil merchant himself.

'Look!'

As they watched, the saw the man pass down a flight of steps on one side of the courtyard, and so disappear from sight.

'The cellar!'

'What cellar?'

There was no more time. They must hurry back to the lakeshore and the floating gardens. Seeker explained as they went.

'That was the master of the house, taking food to someone who's being kept in a cellar.'

'How do you know that?'

'I don't. But I'm sure of it. Morning Star's being kept in a cellar.'

322

When they reached the floating gardens they found a long line of migrant workers waiting to be assigned their tasks for the day. Seeker and the Wildman joined the line.

Ahead, stretching out into the lake, were wooden walkways, floating on sealed barrels; and on either side of the walkways, in shallow earth-filled tubs, the lush green foliage of the plants. Here were row upon row of tomato plants, carefully tied to long fences made of bamboo. The heavy red fruit dangled between the dark green leaves, while down at their feet, where the roots of the plants spread their filaments into the damp earth, the roped tubs gently jostled each other as people came and went, rocking the walkways. Beyond the tomatoes were the squashes and the marrows, and beyond them the twining tendrils of the bean plants. Everything was in constant movement, bobbing and swaying with the slow shifting of the water of the lake.

Seeker and the Wildman were set to tomato-picking, and so alongside the lines of other workers they moved up and down the walkways, bent over in the morning sun, their baskets on their arms, bobbing up and down with the plants. After an hour or so of this work, constant motion became the norm, and the distant mountains and the temple rock and the city of Radiance itself seemed to rise and fall with the undulations of the lake.

A short break was permitted for lunch, for which they were given bread and ripe sweet tomatoes. Seeker and the Wildman kept themselves to themselves, resting and eating quietly away from the main group. Even so, there were many curious glances thrown in their direction; most of all from a band of young male spikers, who seemed to want to attract their attention. When they got no response, they came on over.

'Hey, boys! Look who's here. The Wildman himself!'

The Wildman nodded an unsmiling greeting.

'Never!' said the boldest of the band, grinning broadly. 'The Wildman don't work for his pay! If he wants something, he just takes it.'

'So maybe that's not the Wildman.'

'No, that's him all right. I'd know him anywhere. Didn't he stop me on the road and take everything I had? Him and his friends.'

'He's not got much in the way of friends now.'

They moved closer, forming a loose circle round the Wildman and Seeker. Seeker spoke low.

'Say nothing. Don't react.'

The Wildman nodded and looked down, and went on eating his lunch.

'Hey, Wildman! Where's your brave friends?'

'Still got your golden hair.'

'You come to rob Radiance? That I'd like to see!'

'Then maybe a little rock climbing? And then some lake diving?'

They all laughed loudly at that. The Wildman did not reply or look up.

'No, this isn't the Wildman. This is the Girlman. The Girlman with the golden hair.'

The bell rang for the return to work. Laughing still, the band of spikers strolled away. Seeker reached out and clasped the Wildman's arm.

'I'm proud of you,' he said.

'I don't know how much of this I can take,' said the Wildman.

They returned to work, and laboured on to the end of the day. A half-hour before sunset the bell rang again, and the workers came to shore. They were paid for their day's work, and their papers were signed, and they were free to stay in the city for another night.

Most of the workers joined the movement of people then taking place all across the city towards the temple square. The time of the evening offering was near. The band of young spikers was especially eager to see the ritual.

'They fall into the lake. What's so bad about that?'

'From five hundred feet up, dummy!'

'So? It's only water.'

'And what's under the water? Rocks!'

So arguing and exclaiming, they followed the crowds towards the square. Seeker and the Wildman joined the flow of people for part of the way, and then peeled off and headed for the house of the oil merchant.

Loitering once more by the tree in the street, they saw the members of the household leave for the offering. First to go was a handsomely dressed lady with a wide-brimmed hat who was accompanied by a maid-servant. Then the master of the house himself, wearing his robes of office, followed by two plump boys who were clearly his sons. Finally the main body of the house servants, the last of whom closed and locked the big gates behind him.

Sunset was now approaching. The street was deserted. It seemed safe to explore. Seeker led the way down the alley that ran beside the house.

'Cellars have to have air,' he said. 'We're looking for an air hole.'

Almost at once they found an air hole. More than one. They found small grated openings all the way round the wall, at the base, where the wall met the ground. Seeker knelt down and put his mouth to the first grating, and whispered.

'Morning Star?'

There came no answer. He spoke more loudly.

'Morning Star!'

No answer. He moved on to the next grating, and the next. He tried each one, without any result.

'They may have taken her out,' said the Wildman.

'It's possible.'

'She may not be in a cellar at all.'

'It's possible.'

'She may not even be in this house.'

'So what do you suggest?'

'Me? Nothing.'

'Then shut up.'

Seeker went on kneeling and calling, slowly working his way round the building.

'This is so stupid,' said the Wildman. 'There has to be a better way.'

Seeker was getting tired, and he was getting dispirited.

'Maybe you're right. Maybe she isn't here.'

He sat down and leaned his back against the wall.

'So what do we do?'

'I don't know.'

The Wildman looked back at him reproachfully. In the course of the last two days he had got used to the idea that Seeker made the decisions. Now, seeing Seeker close his eyes and give up, if only for the moment, he felt a surge of determination that was all his own.

'At least let's finish what we started.'

He moved on along the wall, kneeling by the gratings, calling as Seeker had called.

'Morning Star!'

He too got no answer; but he pressed on.

'Morning Star! Hey, girly! You down there?'

He moved on once more. But this time, as he was moving on, there came a faint voice from underground.

'Wildman?'

The Wildman spun round to Seeker.

'You hear that? She's there!'

He threw himself back to the ground, and put his mouth to the grating, forgetting in his excitement to whisper.

'Morning Star! Is that you?'

'Of course it's me,' said the faint voice.

'Are you all right?'

'Of course I'm not all right.'

Seeker was by his side now. All his tiredness was gone.

'Morning Star!' he called to her. 'It's me, Seeker. Are they keeping you prisoner down there?'

'No,' came the reply. 'I'm just sitting here to keep cool.'

Seeker met the Wildman's eyes and they both grinned.

'Good to hear you, girly,' said the Wildman. 'We'll get you out of there.'

'That would be nice.'

'Is the door locked?'

'The door is locked. I'm chained to a wall. Apart from that, there's nothing to keep me here.'

'Oh.'

They sat down on the dirt and leaned against the wall, and their euphoria at finding their friend drained away. The small voice spoke again, from the cellar below.

'You still there?'

'Yes.'

'Are you going to help me?'

'Yes. But how?'

'Here's what you do. Get a big leaf. Can you get a big leaf?'

'Yes.'

'Get a knife, or a sharp stick. Scratch writing on the leaf. Write three words: Seek – your – daughter.'

'Why?'

'Just do it. Do exactly what I say. What are you to write on the leaf?'

'Seek your daughter.'

'Good. Roll the leaf up, and tie it with grass. Got that?'

'Yes.'

'Then come back tonight and leave the rolled up leaf in the iron ring on the gate.'

From the temple square came the sound of the people singing. Both Seeker and the Wildman looked up towards the temple rock, the top of which was visible from where they were sitting. They could just make out the priests standing on the rock's high lip, with the day's tribute held between them, his head hanging.

Seeker asked, 'How long do we have?'

'Three more days.'

'We'll get you out.'

'No, you won't. I'll do that myself. You just do exactly as I tell you. Leave the rolled-up leaf in the iron ring. Don't let anyone see you.'

'When shall we come back?'

'Same time tomorrow.'

'We'll be here.'

The singing stopped. They looked up. They saw the tribute fall. They heard his thin distant scream as he fell. Then there was silence.

The little voice emerged from the grating once more.

'Thanks for finding me.'

The next morning the servant who opened the gates of Cheerful Giver's house found a rolled-up leaf in the gate ring, and pulled apart the grass with which it was tied, half-expecting to find it contained something. Instead, he found a mysterious message. He took the leaf to the housekeeper. The housekeeper took it to the master. Cheerful Giver studied it while eating his breakfast, and then showed it to his wife. His wife studied the message on the leaf, and like everyone else, she could make nothing of it.

'Seek your daughter? Whose daughter?' She herself had only sons. She summoned the servant who had found the leaf.

'You say it was on our gate?'

'Yes, my lady. Rolled up.'

'Do any of the servants have daughters?'

'Yes, my lady.'

'Have any of them lost their daughters?'

'No, my lady.'

The puzzle of the leaf-message was still filling Blessing's mind when she paid her morning visit to her tribute. She had taken on herself the task of removing the breakfast tray.

'Such an odd thing has happened,' she said.

'I knew it!' exclaimed Morning Star. 'This is how I dreamed it would be!'

'Dreamed what?'

'A message has been sent to you. Oh, I can hardly breathe!'

She clutched at her throat and gasped.

'What is this, child? You must tell me.'

'A message has been sent to you. I'm sure of it!'

'Yes, in a manner of speaking. That is, a message has

330

arrived. For whom, we don't know.'

'Does it say – ' Again, Morning Star seemed overcome. She bowed her head, and struggled for breath. 'Does it say – Seek your daughter?'

Blessing went pale.

'Yes,' she said.

'Just as I dreamed,' murmured Morning Star. 'So it must be true.'

'What must be true?'

'How can I tell you, my lady? I am nothing. Why should you listen to me?'

'Please! I beg you! Tell me!'

'I knew it as soon as I saw you. I felt the connection. I felt the stream of love.'

'What – what – what are you saying?'

Blessing was flushing and stammering. She had begun to guess at an extraordinary possibility.

'Do you believe in other lives?' said Morning Star. 'Do you believe we have lived and died before?'

'Oh, my dear! I don't know – sometimes it does seem to me – but how can I tell?'

'Trust your loving heart!' cried Morning Star. 'I don't need to say the words. Perhaps you even dreamed the same dream.'

'Oh, child. I have such strange dreams.'

'Did you dream that in another life, a life now gone by, we were as close as two people can ever be? Did you dream that you were my – ?'

She never spoke the word. She just looked at Blessing, but all at once she smiled a sweet, shy smile. So it was Blessing who spoke the word, hardly daring to make a sound.

'Your mother?'

Morning Star bowed her head. Blessing felt a wave of ecstasy flow through her. She advanced on Morning Star and folded her in her stout arms.

'You were my baby girl!'

Morning Star was careful not to go too fast, too soon.

'Only a dream, my lady. Who is to say?'

'But the message!'

'These things are mysteries.'

'Why, from the moment I set eyes on you, I knew you were linked to me, in some special way.'

'I felt it too. I've been so happy, ever since I entered your house. Even with – '

She held up the wrist on which the manacle was fixed. For the first time, Blessing realised she faced a dilemma. She stared at Morning Star, stricken.

'I can't send you to be an offering! Not my own daughter!'

'Who better to die for you, my lady?' said Morning Star softly. 'You gave me life. It's yours to take away.'

'Oh, this is terrible!' Blessing wrung her hands and almost wailed with dismay. 'What can I do? My husband doesn't believe in dreams. He has his heart set on a willing tribute. And now – here you are – and oh! it's all going wrong!'

332

'Not wrong, my lady. Everything comes to pass as the Great Power wills.'

'But what am I to do?'

'Don't be afraid. If it's the will of the Great Power that your husband shall see the truth, then that too will come to pass. We shall see what messages the night brings.'

'Oh, I do hope so! There's so little time. The day after tomorrow, at sunset – oh! I can't bear to think of it!'

Seeker and the Wildman spent a second day picking tomatoes in the floating gardens. In the late afternoon, by ill luck, they found themselves working at a row of vines on the other side of which were the young men who had taunted them the previous day.

'Hey, boys! Watch your step! Here comes the Girlman!'

'Hey there, Girlman! Those tomatoes look kind of angry!'

'You take care, Girlman! A tomato can be real mean.'

They snickered softly as they picked.

'Hey,' said one of them, 'did you hear how Girlman picked a fight with a hoodie?'

'You stick with the tomatoes, Girlman. Hoodies are out of your league.'

Seeker could see how near his friend was to snapping under the strain. He decided to draw the taunts on to himself.

'Are you talking about the Nomana?' he said.

'What's it to you, babyface?'

'Only that I hate the Nomana.'

'You hate the Nomana! Oh, my! The Nomana must be pissing their pants!'

'The Nomana are rotten to the core,' said Seeker. 'The sooner they're smashed the better.'

Even the Wildman was surprised by this, until he recalled Seeker's plan to find the weapon. The workers on the other side of the vine hardly knew whether to laugh or be afraid.

'Smashed! Listen to the boy! So what did the Nomana do to you?'

'They ruined my brother's life. They disgraced him, for no reason. I hate them all.'

Seeker's outburst was so unusual in the controlled atmosphere of the working parties that word of it spread up and down the lines, and came to the attention of the supervisors. One of them strolled up the floating walkways to question Seeker more.

'Are you the one who hates the hoodies?'

'Yes,' said Seeker.

'Have you ever actually met a hoodie?'

'I was born on Anacrea. My brother was a Noma, until they cast him out.'

'Is that so! And what might your name be?'

'Seeker after Truth.'

'Now there's a name and a half. And do you seek after truth?'

'No. I seek revenge.'

'Is that so!'

The supervisor looked him up and down, and nodded, and strolled away.

When the working day ended, Seeker saw this same supervisor was standing on the shore by the pay desk with a priest, and that they were watching him.

'Wildman,' he whispered. 'I think they've taken the bait. If necessary, will you go to Morning Star alone?'

'Of course.'

Seeker was right. No sooner had he stepped off the bobbing walkway on to the lake shore than the supervisor came gliding forward and took him by the arm.

'Seeker after Truth,' he said. 'I have a holy man here who would like to meet you.'

The priest was bland-faced and middle-aged. He studied Seeker with a suspicious gaze.

'You come from Anacrea?'

'Yes.'

'But you have a grudge against the Nomana?'

'I'd kill them all, if you call that a grudge.'

'You're young to talk of killing.'

'Do only old men kill?'

The priest nodded at that.

'Perhaps you would like to meet some others who think as you do.'

The Wildman watched as Seeker was led away by the stranger. Seeker left without a word to him, or even a look, and was soon lost to sight. Everyone else was on the move, as the time of the offering approached. Alone now and full of unease, the Wildman crossed the city to the house where Morning Star was imprisoned.

As before, he waited for the household to empty. Then he found the grating through which he could talk to Morning Star.

'Heya!' he called. 'You still there?'

'Of course I'm still here,' came the familiar irritated voice. 'Where's Seeker?'

'He's gone off with some people who hate the hoodies.'

'Has he!'

There was a silence from the grating. The Wildman was about to say again, 'You still there?' but he stopped himself. Instead he said, 'You got a plan?'

'Did Seeker say where he'd meet you again?'

'No. He just went.'

'So there's only you.'

'Yes.'

'I suppose I'll just have to make the best of it.'

'You want your neck slit, girly?'

'Be quiet and listen.'

The Wildman became quiet and listened. After all, he told himself, it was because of him that she was locked in the cellar.

'The city is full of wild cats. Have you seen them?'

'Yes.'

'Do you think you could catch one of them?'

'Catch a cat? Sure I can.'

'Then catch a cat tonight. A yellow cat.'

'A yellow cat.'

'Take one of your own hairs. A long blonde hair.'

'My own hair?'

'Just one. Tie it round the cat's right front leg.'

'Why?'

'Just do it. Make sure it's tight. I don't want the cat pulling it off.'

'The cat'll hate it.'

'Feed the cat. Feed it all it can eat. That way it'll sleep.'

'Feed the cat.'

'And tie it to the gates of the house.'

'Like last night.'

'Except it's not a rolled-up leaf any more. It's a cat.'

'Yes, I know.'

'Just checking.'

'Do I come back same time tomorrow?'

'You or Seeker. Seeker would be better. But you'll do.'

'You want to get your – '

'Yes, I know. Let's hope I live long enough for you to slit my throat.'

The priest led Seeker to a section of the city which was mostly lodging houses. Because the people who lived here were not citizens of Radiance, and did not attend the evening offering, there was more life than elsewhere in the city. The bars were busy, and the lamps were lit in the windows. Seeker followed the priest to one of these bars, and here he was told to sit down and wait. The priest went back out into the street.

The bar was plain and bare, a drinking place for poor men, but it was clean, and well kept. The barman nodded at Seeker, and Seeker nodded back, and shortly he was brought the standard order of a slab of white bread and a small flagon of red wine. He was not asked to pay. He ate and drank in silence.

In a little while the priest reappeared, followed by a second man, a small balding man with staring eyes.

'Here he is,' said the priest. 'Born on Anacrea.'

'Born on Anacrea.' The small man studied Seeker with an almost hungry intensity. 'Young.'

'Too young?'

'No, no. It could work well for us. If he's got what we need.'

'Ask him.'

The small man had never taken his eyes off Seeker.

'So, young man,' he said. 'I am told you're called Seeker after Truth. But truth is not what you most desire.'

Seeker did not blink or look away.

'All I want,' he said, 'is for the Nomana to die.'

'The Nomana are powerful. What can you do against them?'

'I've heard there's a weapon that can destroy even the Nomana.'

'Have you now?'

'If I could find this weapon, I would use it.'

'If such a weapon exists, it must be something very

remarkable indeed. You're no more than a boy. Why should you be given the honour of using it?'

'The holy island is well guarded, but no one would suspect me. I've been to the heart of the Nom many times. I've looked through the silver screen at the Garden itself. I can go again.'

The balding man nodded slowly, as if to say he was satisfied so far.

'The question is this.' He spoke to the priest. 'Is the boy brave enough?'

'Try me,' said Seeker fiercely.

'Yes. Maybe we should do just that.' He rubbed his chin with one hand while he pondered. Then he turned to the priest. 'I have to be sure.'

'Perhaps,' said the priest, 'we should seek guidance from the Great Power above.'

'What did you have in mind?'

The priest took the little man aside and spoke to him in a low whisper. The little man nodded as he listened. Then he turned to Seeker.

'You will be brought back here tomorrow, at the same time. Then, when the good people of the city are in their beds, we will conduct a test, to discover whether you are the one destined to fulfil this historic mission.'

CHAPTER TWENTY-EIGHT

THE DARKNESS

SOREN Similin was wrong about the fine lady. All down the long hard road to Radiance, she kept pace with the men, and never asked to stop until they stopped. When her shoes began to split and flap, she kicked them off, and walked on barefoot.

For all of the first day she did not speak. Blaze looked at her from time to time, and Similin could see that he was haunted by the sadness he saw in her face.

On the second day, after walking through the cool of the morning, they stopped at noon to eat. After they had eaten, they rested. They lay down in the deep shade of a tree, and listened to the drone of insects, and the clop of passing bullock carts, and slipped into a short sleep.

When Blaze woke, he turned and saw that Similin was still asleep, but the lady had her eyes open. She was gazing up at the foliage above. There was a light wind stirring the branches, and as they moved, the pattern of leaves broke and re-formed, letting through brief dazzles of sunlight. The effect was both mesmerising and playful, as if the summer afternoon was engaged in its own shy dance of delight.

'I'm sorry you're sad,' whispered Blaze. 'But now is beautiful, isn't it?'

'Yes,' she said.

She turned her head on one side so that she could look at him.

'They've turned you into a child again, haven't they, Noma? I envy you.'

'Please don't be sad.'

'You'd be sad if you knew my story.'

'I'd like to know your story.'

'Would you? It doesn't have a happy ending.'

'Has it ended?'

He asked this so innocently, as if it might indeed have ended, that she smiled.

'No. I don't think my story has ended yet.'

'You could tell it as far as you've got.'

'Why would you want to hear my story?'

'I like stories. Stories help fit things together.'

'Don't things fit together for you, Noma?'

'No.' He shook his head, stating a simple fact. 'No.'

'Well, then. I'll tell you my story.'

She turned her head back again, to look up at the dancing light in the leaves above. For a while she said nothing, as she let her mind reach back over her life. Then she started to speak, in a soft and hesitant voice, as if she was rediscovering herself as she spoke.

'There was once a girl who lived in a village by the sea.'

Blaze said nothing. He listened like a child, with his thumb in his mouth.

'She was ordinary in every way, and had no reason to

341

think she was different from everyone else. But she was. From her earliest childhood she had dark days. They came without warning, and lasted for a day, or two days, sometimes even more. When the dark days came, she knew that she was a person of no worth at all. She knew that she was a burden to those who loved her, even a curse. She could do nothing to escape the darkness, except perhaps to throw herself in the sea, which she would think about longingly, day after day, wanting only to shut her eyes and stop her ears and silence her thoughts. Her parents told her about the Loving Mother, the Quiet Watcher who is always near, but she knew that on the dark days the Quiet Watcher had abandoned her. Then the darkness would pass, like a cloud shadow floating away over the hills, and she would be calm again.

'So she grew up, and was married, and had a baby. Her life was very simple, and she was happy, until the dark days returned. And they always did return, for longer and longer periods. When they were at their darkest she was afraid to leave the house, afraid she would run back to the sea, so she shut herself in her room, she imprisoned herself, to save herself. Not because she was worth saving, but for the sake of her baby.

'It was on a day when she was alone in her room like this, at the darkest time of the dark days, that she had a strange experience. The room filled with light. The light was so bright she had to shut her eyes and cover her face with her hands. A voice spoke to her, saying, "Come to me." She knew at once that it was the voice of the Quiet Watcher. And she knew that this was the only way she would ever escape the darkness.

'So she decided to go to the holy island, where the Quiet Watcher lives, and dedicate her life to the service of the one who is also the Clear Light. She believed if she did this the darkness would let her go. She knew it was a terrible thing to leave her child and her husband, but she believed she was called by the All and Only; and she knew that if she did not go, the darkness would overwhelm her.

'So she went to the holy island. She stood before the Community of the Nomana, and offered them the rest of her life. And they did not want her. They sent her away.'

'Ah,' said Blaze, sighing a long sigh.

'What could she do? As she left the holy island, rain was falling, and the dark days were returning. This time the darkness was so profound that she no longer knew where she went or why. All she wanted to do was die, and cause no more pain to those who loved her. So she never went home. She walked down the road in the rain, the road that led further away from home, so that the ones who loved her would not be cursed by her darkness. And somewhere down that road, near a roadside hostel, she met two small soaking children, who told her they were running away. So she said, Could she run away with them? They said yes she could, and hand in hand they ran away together. They ran back to the hostel, where it was dry, and where their father was waiting. He was grateful to her for returning his children to him, and seeing that she was only a poor peasant woman, he asked her if she was seeking employment. He was a widower. He needed a nursemaid for the children.

'She thought to herself, why not? If it made the children happy to play with her, why shouldn't she? So she became a nursemaid. Then, as they grew a little older, a governess. And then a wife. Why not? If it made their father happy to love her, why shouldn't she let him? There was nothing else before her, except the darkness.'

She turned again to rest her eyes on Blaze.

'Another governess came. My husband liked her, as he had once liked me. So you see, I was not required any more.'

'May I ask your name?'

'My name is Mercy. But I'm the one in need of Mercy. We live to see our names mock us. What do they call you, Noma?'

'I am Blaze of Justice.'

'And do you blaze with justice? Do you burn to make all things right?'

Blaze looked over towards Similin and saw that he was awake now, and listening.

'Yes,' he said.

It was time to be on the move again, so they said no more. They rose, and took to the road, and walked on all through the long hot afternoon, and were close to the city of Radiance by the early evening. Similin now confided in Blaze.

'I can get you into the city on my papers. But not her as well.'

'What will happen to her?'

'She has a husband. She can ask for him.'

'Her husband no longer wants her. We must look after her.'

'Don't concern yourselves about me,' said Mercy, seeing that they were speaking about her.

'Do you have any other friends in the city?'

'Perhaps. It doesn't matter.'

As they crossed the boundary into the city, they were accosted by the border police. The secretary showed his papers, which had the effect of making the officers respectful. He explained that Blaze was accompanying him on business for the king. The officers then issued Blaze with papers of his own.

'And this lady,' said Blaze, turning round to indicate Mercy – but she was no longer there. Nearby stood a grove of trees. He caught a flicker of white running between the trunks, in the twilight shadows. Then she was gone.

'Stupid,' said Similin.

'What lady?' said the policeman.

'It's of no importance,' said Similin. 'We've no time to waste. Thank you, officer. We're on the king's business.'

He strode firmly away down the road into the city, with Blaze at his side. Blaze spoke to him in an undertone.

'What about the beautiful lady?'

'She left us of her own free will.'

'Will she be happy? I want her to be happy.'

'I don't think she's a happy sort of person.'

'No. She's sad.'

Similin knew he must move Blaze's attention away from their runaway companion.

'We'll sleep in my quarters tonight. Tomorrow I'll show you the way to be the noblest warrior of them all.'

'Ah! I'm to be a Noble Warrior!'

He spoke with eagerness.

'You're still willing?'

'Oh, yes!'

'Even if it means you have to give your life?'

'Of course! What else do I have to give?'

Similin was satisfied. His plan was back on course. All he needed now was the final act of will. Once Blaze was in the chair, and the charging process had begun, there could be no turning back.

Silently to his mistress he said, 'Am I not deserving?'

CHAPTER TWENTY-NINE

SEEKER'S TEST

WHEN the servants opened the gates of Cheerful Giver's house the following morning, they found a wild cat tied to the iron ring. The cat was taken, yowling, to the housekeeper, and the housekeeper took it, still yowling, to the master of the house. Cheerful Giver eyed the noisy creature with displeasure.

'Tied to the gates?'

'Like the leaf, sir.'

'Like the leaf? So does the cat carry a message?'

'No, sir.'

'Send for the mistress.'

Cheerful Giver had already exchanged hard words with his wife, before bedtime the previous evening. His wife had got it into her head that the tribute he had bought was too special to be sacrificed. He had made short work of that. 'Five thousand shillings is too special to be sacrificed,' he had told her, and the subject was closed. Now there was this cat. He didn't know what his wife would make of the cat, except that it would cause him more trouble.

Blessing entered, and was shown the creature.

'There must be a message,' she said at once.

'No message,' said Cheerful Giver. 'Just a cat.'

'Then it's a sign. Our child will know what it means.'

'Oh, yes, I've no doubt. Our child will reveal it's a sign that she's to be set free. Well, let me assure you, I have signs of my own, and my signs say, Nobody fools me.'

'Nobody wants to fool you, dearest. You know you've always wanted a daughter.'

'A real daughter, maybe. This one's no more my daughter than she's a slice of pudding.'

'Even so, dearest. I shall ask her about the cat.'

'It's no use you dearest-ing me. That girl goes up the rock tomorrow evening, and if you can get her to go with a will, you'll be a good and loving wife, and I'll dearest you as much as you like.'

'Whatever you say, husband.'

Cheerful Giver rose from his chair, his face dark with suspicion.

'I'm coming with you,' he said. 'And you're not to say a word about any cats. I'll do the talking.'

The master and the mistress of the house took the breakfast tray down to their imprisoned tribute together. Morning Star was polite as always, and ate and drank gratefully. Blessing kept issuing small squeaks, which were escaped portions of the words she longed to utter, but her husband obliged her, with ferocious looks, to remain silent.

'So,' he said, when Morning Star had eaten. 'Do you have anything more to say to us?'

'Anything more about what, sir?'

'Perhaps you've had another dream. Perhaps you've

found out that in a past life you were my grandmother.'

'No, sir. But I have had another dream.'

'You see!' cried Blessing.

'Be quiet, wife! Another dream, eh?'

'In my dream there was a cat.'

'A cat!' shrieked Blessing.

'Silence!' thundered Cheerful Giver. 'Go on.'

'The cat spoke to me.'

'What did the cat say?'

'It was a golden cat. It spoke to me, here in your house, sir. It spoke about you.'

'About me. Very good. Go on.'

'It said, Tell the master of this house that if he heeds my command, he will stand on the right hand of the king.'

'If I heed this dream cat's command?'

'Yes, sir.'

'This useful cat's command,' said Cheerful Giver grimly, 'does it by any chance refer to you?'

'Yes, sir.'

'You see?' Cheerful Giver snorted at his wife. 'It's all no more than a trick to save her own neck.'

'There was nothing about saving my neck, sir. Only that I'm to pass on the command. Then you will stand on the right hand of the king.'

'Oh, husband!' exclaimed Blessing. 'The right hand of the king! That must mean you're to become High Priest!'

'Nonsense!'

But Morning Star was watching carefully, and she saw

his colours change from the browny-orange of his refusal to be fooled to the tawny-yellow of ambition.

'So what exactly are these commands that I'm to heed?'

'The golden cat gave me only one command, sir. It said, Guard the treasure that lives after you.'

'What treasure?'

'Oh, husband!' cried Blessing. 'That means our children! What other treasure lives after us? You must guard our children. Including our new child here.'

Cheerful Giver's colours darkened with renewed doubt.

'Naturally,' he said. 'What a surprise.'

Morning Star decided it was time to deliver the clincher.

'In my dream,' she said, 'as a sign that you would stand on the right hand of the king, the golden cat wore a golden bracelet, on its right foreleg.'

'Golden bracelet? That mangy animal has no golden bracelet.'

'In my dream, the golden bracelet was made of a single golden hair.'

'Fetch the cat!' cried Blessing.

The cat was brought down to the cellar. And there, after some searching, a single golden hair was found to be tied round its leg. Blessing didn't cry out this time. She just looked at her husband. Cheerful Giver stood there, shaking his head from side to side.

'You believe her now, don't you?' said his wife.

'Give me time. I need to think about this.'

'Not too much time, dearest. Your name day is tomorrow.'

*

Seeker and the Wildman spent a third day working in the floating gardens, knowing that time was running out for Morning Star. Seeker also believed he was getting close to the weapon they had originally set out to Radiance to find. They talked over the problem of what to do next, as they moved down the tomato vines.

'I think I should go to these people this evening,' said Seeker. 'If I can get them to trust me, maybe they'll help us free Morning Star.'

'What should I do?'

'Go back to the house this evening, as Morning Star said. Do whatever she tells you to do. She's working out some plan of her own.'

When the day ended, Seeker left with the same priest as on the day before. The Wildman was in no hurry, knowing that he couldn't speak to Morning Star until the streets emptied for the evening offering, so he lingered by the lake. Here the young spikers who had taunted him before found him.

'Hey, boys! Here's the Girlman!'

'You scare me so bad, Girlman! See my knees knocking!'

'He don't see your knees knocking at all. Maybe he wants a closer look.'

'Hey, Girlman! You want my knee in your face?'

They gathered round him, reaching out and flicking his long golden hair. Control did not come naturally to the Wildman, but he held his silence.

351

'The Girlman's a real beauty, isn't he, boys? Look at those gorgeous lips!'

'Heya, Girlman! Do you love me?' They began to imitate his old cry. 'Do you lo-o-ove me?'

The Wildman avoided their mocking eyes. He set off away from them up the street into the city. But his tormentors followed.

'Do you lo-o-ove me?'

Hands reached out to paw him, to stroke his hair, to rattle his bracelets.

'Gimme a cuddle, Girlman! You're a real beauty!'

Hands pulled at his arms, to twist him round. Laughing mouths swung close. He felt the brush of a mocking kiss. It was too much. The Wildman's rage boiled up and gushed from him in a howl of fury. His powerful right hand shot out and seized one of the spikers by the throat, and even as he choked him he slammed the spiker's head into another head. Too fast for them to land returning blows, he gripped wrists and twisted arms till the bones cracked. The spikers screamed in terror. Patrol officers came running. He struck out at them too, sending them flying back. But more came, and more, and by sheer weight of numbers they grappled him to the ground, and crushed him into submission.

'One more for the tanks,' they said.

Morning Star heard the household members leaving for the evening offering. She heard the big gates swing shut, and the heavy keys turn in the lock. Then she waited for Seeker or the Wildman to call to her down the vent that brought air into the dark cellar. But no call came.

In time she heard the sound of the key in the lock once more, and the tread of footsteps in the courtyard above. Then she knew her friends would not be coming that night. Something had gone wrong.

The Wildman was yelling at the top of his voice. He had no more need to control his anger. He beat at the overhead bars of the tank in which he had been thrown, and screamed at the guards.

'Chickens! I'll slit your throats! You come near me, I'll rip out your hearts!'

The guards paid him no attention. Other prisoners, lying on the stone floor of the tank trying to sleep, called to him irritably.

'Shut that noise. Save your breath. You're not going anywhere.'

Unable to attack the guards, the Wildman turned on his fellow prisoners.

'You got a problem, blubber-piss? You want your throat slit?'

'Go to sleep.'

The tanks had no benches, no bunks. The inmates lay mostly curled up on the stone floor. At one end of each tank was a stinking trench in which the prisoners were expected to excrete and urinate. At the other end was a stone trough, into which a kind of gruel was poured twice a day. This gruel, made of ground maize diluted with water, was both food and drink for the miserable inmates. They were given no implements with which to eat it. They were to push their faces into the trough and lap like cattle.

The Wildman had been dropped into the tank without explanations or threats. A wide hinged section of the grid had been unbolted and raised, and he had been pushed over the edge to fall on to the hard stone floor. The patrol officers who had brought him in, and the guards who now watched over the tanks, had no further interest in him. He had fallen into a living grave.

The roof overhead was pierced with roof-lights, and through these moonlight fell, past the criss-cross bars to the prisoners below. The Wildman, grown weary at last of shouting at men who didn't respond, sat himself down in this silver light and looked about him and considered what to do. The bars above his head were set deep in the stonework, and were as thick as pick-handles. No chance of escape there. The hinged section was also strongly made, and the bolts, once driven home, were held in place by iron hasps. Anyone on the outside could undo these bolts: but to the prisoners down in the tanks they were as unmovable as if they had been welded shut. The only way out, therefore, was to wait for the lid to be opened, and then to make a break for freedom. The Wildman counted the guards who were lounging round the tanks. Even now, when the prisoners were mostly asleep, there were ten men on duty. For any break-out to succeed, every prisoner would have to take part.

The Wildman scanned the other prisoners, looking to see how much will to resist he could detect among them. What he saw gave him very little hope. Even in sleep they seemed to cringe with fear. Those who were not asleep lay staring unseeingly up towards the moonlight. There was no conversation, no fellowship, no attempt to make the best of the situation. These were people who had given up hope, and were waiting like beasts in a slaughterhouse for their coming extinction.

Only one other prisoner met his gaze with any hint of human contact. She was a woman with a sad sweet face, and she looked at him as if she pitied him. She wore a white dress, of the kind that rich people wear, but she lacked the sullen, resentful look of a rich person in trouble. She looked, it struck him, as if she wasn't aware of herself at all. She was aware of him.

'Well?' he said to her, his voice sounding surly in the night silence. 'What do you want?'

'I was thinking how beautiful you are.'

'Much good may it do me.'

'It does me good.'

Her gaze was so direct, so unguarded, that the Wildman decided she was not mocking him, but saying in its simplest form what she felt. He relaxed a little.

'So why have they put you here?' he asked.

'No papers.'

'You know what they do to us?'

'Yes. I know.'

'They're not going to do it to me.'

'Oh?' She was curious, not unbelieving. 'Why not?'

'Because what I want, I get. And what I don't want, I don't get.'

She smiled at that. He could tell by her smile that she was glad for him that he could still believe such things.

'I think you're perfect,' she said.

Such a strange word to choose: *perfect*. And such a strange way to say it, the way you would speak of someone far away, or even of a god. But he liked her for it. He knew she wanted nothing from him. What she offered was simple admiration, as refreshing and as undemanding as sunlight.

'So what's your name?' he asked her.

'Mercy,' she said.

'I'm the Wildman.'

'Wild man?' Her voice parted the syllables. 'I can see that you're a wild man. But that wasn't the name your parents gave you.'

'I have no parents.'

'You must have had a mother.'

'Not that I ever knew.'

'So she abandoned you when you were still little. Do you hate her for leaving you?'

'I can't hate someone I don't know.'

'It was wrong of her. But perhaps she had no choice.'

'I don't care. I can look after myself.'

'Not so easy any more, Wildman.'

'Oh, I shall find a way. No one holds me down. No one keeps me in a cage. You wait and see.'

Seeker was obliged to sit alone at his hostel table for a long time. His evening meal was long eaten, and he was beginning to feel sleepy, before the small balding man appeared at last. He was accompanied this time by two priests, one of whom carried a coil of rope, and the other a covered lantern.

'Come along,' said the man, as if it was Seeker who had kept him waiting. 'We've no time to waste.'

They went out into the night streets.

'Last night you said, Try me. That is what we mean to do.'

He led Seeker across the city to the temple square. Here in inky shadow a flight of broad steps wound their way up the many levels of the temple, to the towering summit of the rock above.

'You'll need strong legs,' said the man, 'It's a long climb.'

Seeker looked up. The temple rock was outlined against the silver-grey of the moonlit sky.

'Do you mean to throw me from the rock?' he asked.

One of the priests answered him.

'The rock is a place of offering to the Radiant Power who made all things. We ask the Radiant Power to guide us. You will either be acceptable, or you will not.'

'How will you know if I'm acceptable?'

'The Radiant Power will give you back to us.'

Seeker didn't understand what this meant, but he feared the worst. The little bald man saw his apprehension.

'Don't be afraid,' he said. 'Trust us. This is a test of many things. Of the will of the Radiant Power. Of your courage. Of your trust.'

'Why should I trust you? I don't even know who you are.'

'That's easily settled. My name is Evor Ortus. I am a professor of science.'

'And if I pass your test – what then?'

'Then we will know that you are the one chosen to fulfil this historic mission. So – will you come, or will you not?'

Seeker came. The steps ran from level to level of the massive temple in a series of long, zigzagging flights. As they climbed, Seeker looked down from time to time, and saw the city laid out beneath him, glimmering and beautiful in the silver moonlight.

When they reached the topmost level he could see the moon itself, low in the northern sky, shining on to the still waters of the lake. He felt his legs trembling beneath him from the effort of the climb, and from fear of what was to come, and so he let himself sink down on to the terrace floor. Professor Ortus made no objection. He and the two priests were busy unfurling the coil of rope.

Seeker saw behind him the arches of the royal terrace, now shuttered for the night. Before him was the railed platform where the king stood for the offering. And no more than twenty paces away there was the projecting lip of rock from which the tributes fell – from

358

which Morning Star would fall, if he failed this test.

The thought of standing on that high edge made his insides melt with fear. All he wanted to do was press himself to the paved surface and never move again. This, however, was unlikely to be the plan for him. Somehow he must find the courage to face that fearful drop.

Ortus now set about knotting the rope to the iron railing. Seeker watched him pulling it tight, testing the strength of the knot, and guessed the way in which he was to be offered to the Radiant Power. In the same moment, he knew he did not have the courage to do it.

What would happen if he refused the test? It seemed unlikely that they would let him go. If against all odds he escaped, then he and the Wildman would concentrate all their efforts on rescuing Morning Star. If against all odds they were successful, they would make their escape from the city. What then? Was he to go back home? Was he to go back to school, and have everything go on as if Blaze had never been cast out? It was unthinkable.

He knew without doubt that he was close to the weapon designed to destroy Anacrea. These very people now preparing the rope for him were surely the servants of the enemies who were carrying out the will of the Assassin. How could he abandon the search now, when he might be on the point of achieving all they had set out to achieve? If he could win control of the secret weapon, it would give him the power to save both Morning Star and Anacrea; or so he hoped. And he had no other hope.

So he must not fail the test.

He closed his weary eyes and prayed.

Wise Father, give me the courage to do what they ask of me. Take away my fear. I can't do this alone. But with your help I know I can do all things.

'Up you get,' said Ortus. 'Raise your arms.'

Seeker did as he was told. The professor ran the rope twice round his waist and tied it with three strong knots. The rope lay in coils on the ground, its further end fixed to the railing.

'The rope will hold you,' Ortus said. 'The rest is in the hands of the Radiant Power above.'

Seeker felt his skin prickle with fear. He touched the rope between his fingers, and knew that it was strong enough to hold him. The knots were secure. He was in no danger of falling all the way down to the water and the rocks of the lake. But to fall at all! To jump of his own free will over that jutting edge, out into nothingness!

He trembled with raw fear. All that stood in his way was this fear. The fear took on the appearance to him of a closed door, a door that barred his way to all he wanted.

Where your way lies, the door is always open.

Of course! That was how to face his fear. He saw it, all in a blink of his mind's eye, as if it were laid out before him. He would look beyond this rock, and the dizzying drop to the ground below. He would look beyond the lake, and the mountains, and the moon above. He would even look beyond his own life and death. He would leap from the rock eagerly, as if out there, just within reach, was the door to the calm green home of the Lost Child he sought to protect, the Child who waited for him in the Garden. He would throw himself at the door, and it would burst open before him.

'I'm ready,' he said.

He closed his eyes for a last prayer.

Wise Father, let the door open to me, and I will come home. I will run into your loving arms. Catch me and hold me, for ever and ever.

He opened his eyes. He looked directly ahead, out over the shining surface of the great lake, to the rim of the mountain range on the horizon. He pictured to himself a closed door, and on the far side of the door a small child, not yet able to walk, crawling towards him across the sky, reaching out one chubby hand. He drew a deep breath, and ran, and jumped, hurling himself at the door – and it melted before him – and he passed through into nothingness – the rope uncoiling behind him – and for a few blissful moments he was flying, sailing over giant moonlit space – and then he was dropping, down, down, down, and the blood sang in his ears – and then there came a savage cracking pull on the rope that made him cry out, and knocked the breath from his lungs – and he was spinning, or the world was spinning, and swinging back in a long, sweeping curve beneath the jutting overhang of the immense rock.

His suspended body slammed against the face of the

rock, and for a short time he lost all sensation. He dangled there, stunned and oblivious. The priests on the top of the rock now hauled on the rope, and slowly they dragged him back to safety. They untied the rope, and felt his body all over, and satisfied themselves that nothing was broken. When he opened his eyes, there they all were, looking down at him.

'Did I pass the test?'

Professor Ortus was beaming.

'The Radiant Power has given you back to us!' he said. 'You are the chosen one.'

Seeker stumbled to his feet. He had survived. He felt a thrilling surge of pride, and with it a reawakening of his numbed body, and the onset of pain. All his bruises began to ache fiercely, but he didn't care. He had faced the fear, the door had opened before him, he had asked for courage and had been given it. He knew now he could dare anything, anywhere.

Professor Ortus led Seeker directly from the high rock to the tanks. They made their way along the iron walkway over the sleeping prisoners below, and Seeker passed within six feet of the Wildman, without either of them knowing it.

The laboratory was plunged in darkness. The scientist led Seeker to the far side, where there was a storeroom. Here he laid him on the truckle bed he had himself used, night after night, to snatch short hours of sleep during the most intense phase of the scientific enterprise. Seeker was aching and exhausted, all his energy drained by his ordeal. Tomorrow was the day on which Morning Star was to be thrown from the temple rock, but he was helpless. All he could think was that somehow, if he came to be in control of the terrible and mysterious weapon, he could use the threat of it to save her. For now, he could do nothing.

As soon as he lay down, he was asleep.

CHAPTER THIRTY

NAME DAY

CHEERFUL Giver's name day began in the traditional fashion, with all the household assembled in the courtyard to greet him as he emerged from his bedroom. He stood on the steps and assumed what he hoped was a suitable expression of dignified joy. The truth was that he felt terrible. He had hardly slept all night, and he still did not know what to do. So as his family and his servants sang to him the name day song, he nodded his head in time to the rhythm, and went on worrying.

'Hail the day of Cheerful Giver!

Cheerful Giver! Hail his day!'

When, he thought to himself, will this cursed business of the tribute ever end? How can I send the child up the rock? What if she truly is a messenger from the Great Power?

'Radiant God, you rise in glory!

Shine your light on him today!'

But if I don't offer the child, he worried, I have no tribute. Not only will I have thrown away a fortune, but today, on my name day, a common spiker will be sent up the rock. I've promised the king twice now that the tribute I offer on my name day will bring great honour to the Radiant Power. How can I not send the child?

'Praise the name of Cheerful Giver!

Proud his name and proud his day!'

After the song had been sung, somehow he had to go through all the usual little customs, sipping from the glass of wine brought him by his wife, nibbling at the little cakes brought him by his sons, and accepting a prayer mat embroidered by the servants. As usual, the pattern was hideous. It would join all the others he had received over the years, in a musty pile under the cellar stairs. But as usual, he made a gracious speech of thanks, and announced a small bonus in pay for all the servants, which they fully expected, and which was all they were interested in. Then he retired to the breakfast room with his wife to enjoy his name day in the sweet peace of a contented marriage.

'Get your own breakfast!' screamed his wife as soon as the door was closed. 'I shan't lift a finger! I hope you starve to death!'

The argument that had raged between them for most of the previous day had not been resolved.

'Thank you,' said Cheerful Giver bitterly as he sat down. 'What a grateful wife I have after all. Seventeen years of living like a queen, due entirely to my efforts, and she tells me on my name day she wants me dead. Thank you so much.'

'You know what I want.'

'And am I to shame myself and my family on my name day?'

'There'll be another soon enough.'

'Do you want me to lose my position? Do you want

Small Dream to be given the handling of the corona?'

'Do you want to stand on the right hand of the king?'

'Phoo! That's all nonsense! She's making it up to save her skin.'

'Like she made up the writing on the leaf? Like she made up the bracelet on the cat?'

'What does she know about the right hand of the king?'

'Why don't you ask her?'

'Very well. I will.'

This was in fact the conclusion Cheerful Giver had reached himself. He would question the child one more time, and then reach his final decision. So after a short and unsatisfactory breakfast he and his wife carried a tray of food down the cellar steps to their puzzling tribute.

Morning Star was ready for them. She had had as much time as Cheerful Giver to think about what she would do today, but she had thought to rather more purpose. She had no clever surprises to spring. She must rely on her instincts. But she did have a plan.

As soon as Blessing and Cheerful Giver entered the cellar she sensed the tension between them; and of course, she could see it. The wife's colours were a dusty yellow, made up both of pity and self-pity, with a rim of red, which showed she was angry. The husband's colours were mostly the angry red, but here and there were flickers of green, the colour of uncertainty. From the very first moment, Morning Star watched Cheerful Giver's colours with care, and adjusted her words accordingly.

'Any more dreams?' said Cheerful Giver roughly. 'Any more cats? Any more commands?'

'I've brought trouble into your life,' said Morning Star, bowing her head humbly. 'That was not my purpose. Please forgive me.'

'It's my name day, that's all.' Cheerful Giver's anger turned to petulance in the face of Morning Star's humility. The red aura softened into grey. 'I have a position to keep up. Certain things are expected of me. It's not easy.'

His wife too sensed that his stubborn refusal to change his mind was weakening.

'Husband, ask her. Perhaps she has had another dream.'

'Well?' he said, not very graciously. 'Have you?'

'I think my dreams make you angry, sir. Perhaps it would be best if I were to be returned to the source of all life and all power, as you had intended. Then the message I came to deliver can pass through another child, of another family.'

'What message? What other family?'

'I don't choose the family, sir. A greater power than me decides who is worthy of that honour. I was told only that this was a family which has given notable service to the people of Radiance, and to their king, and to their god.'

'And so I have! Why, my oil presses supply half the oil of the empire!'

Morning Star noted the change in his colours. His aura was now tinged with orange. He was becoming competitive.

'What is the message, child?' This was Blessing.

'The message is for the ears of the king only.'

'For the king!'

'At the time of the evening offering.'

Cheerful Giver's colours radiated a sudden muddy brown. He had become suspicious again. She added hastily,

'I have been sent, as your child, to bring you great honour in the eyes of the king.'

As he heard this his colours modulated again, turning to the brighter yellow of self-satisfaction. Morning Star could see him running the calculation of risk and advantage through his mind. Would the king think better of him for offering so fine a tribute on his name day, or for bringing this so-called child of his with this unknown message?

'Oh, husband!' cried Blessing, clasping her hands together and rolling up her eyes. 'What did I tell you? All things happen for a reason! I longed for a daughter, and now a daughter has been given to me who will bring honour to all the family!'

'What sort of message is this message?' said Cheerful Giver.

Morning Star saw that she was going to have to give him more proof of her divine mission. Since she had no pre-arranged surprise to reveal, her only option was to make some intelligent guesses. She had already picked up that there was competition at court for the favour of the king. Where there was competition, there was also suspicion.

'There are some who are close to the king,' she said, 'who are not his true friends.'

Cheerful Giver's yellow aura turned at once to pulsing orange. Morning Star had touched a nerve.

'Can you name them?'

'I know no names. But there is one who is very close to the king indeed.'

'She must mean the High Priest,' said Blessing. 'Who else is so close to the king?'

'Hush, wife!' said Cheerful Giver. But he couldn't help adding, 'I've always known that man was a snake.'

The priests, Morning Star knew, wore gold robes.

'He glows with a golden light. But his heart is dark.'

'It's him!' said Blessing. 'His golden robes!'

'What is it he plans to do, child?'

'My message is for the king alone. But you are to take me to him.'

Cheerful Giver's aura was still pulsing orange. Morning Star knew he was now hooked. She allowed herself a little game-playing, to lock him into his decision.

'But I do understand how much you had hoped to present the king and the High Priest with a willing tribute on your name day. I'm sure the High Priest will thank you for your offering.'

'I don't see why the High Priest should think I do it for him.'

'I think,' said Morning Star slowly, 'he is a very clever man. But he is – No, I can say no more.'

'Damn him!' Cheerful Giver's aura went a dark red. 'I won't have him standing there smirking as if it's all for his benefit! I've known for years that he's not to be trusted! I'd give a lot to wipe that smile off his face!'

Blessing took Morning Star in her arms.

'Child, he has seen the light. You'll come with us this evening, and speak to the king.'

Her aura, a soft prayerful blue shading into the green of stupidity, wrapped round Morning Star also. Morning Star let herself be petted, and watched the master of the house.

'Here's what I'll do,' he said, speaking more to himself than to either of the others. 'I'll go to the tanks and pick out the best of what they've got there. I'll have to pay a guard or two. And a priest or two as well, I've no doubt. But that way I'll have something for my name day.'

'How wise you are, husband! What an inspired solution!'

'As for the child.' He turned to look at her. She gazed back at him from within the embrace of his wife's arms, making her eyes as round and innocent as possible. His aura softened to a red that was almost affectionate. She knew then that she had won. 'As for the child. Wife, get her some clothes to suit her position as a member of my family. She will come with us to the king this evening. And we will see what we will see.'

As soon as the working day began, Evor Ortus called on the High Priest and told him that he had recruited a suitable volunteer. The High Priest already knew about the boy from Anacrea. He also knew, which the professor did not, that Soren Similin had returned to Radiance with a volunteer of his own.

'Already!' The scientist went pale. 'So we're too late!'

'Not at all. You still control the device, I take it?'

'Yes, of course.'

'Tell our ugly young friend that some small repair is needed. Tell him the device will be ready tomorrow.'

'Ready tomorrow?'

'And this evening, while our friend is at the offering, put the boy into the device. How long do you need?'

'A few hours.'

'Then later tonight – shall we say at midnight? – I'll have a boat waiting to take him to Anacrea.'

'To Anacrea!'

Their eyes met, and they both smiled.

Soren Similin kept Blaze alone and in hiding in his shuttered apartment all through the long hot day that followed their arrival in Radiance. He himself felt it necessary to report to the king that he was back, and that his mission had been successful. Blaze seemed unconcerned. He sat and stared at nothing, and showed no interest in his surroundings.

'I'll return as soon as I can,' said Similin. 'Will you be all right on your own while I'm out?'

'Yes,' said Blaze.

'What will you do?'

'Nothing.'

The boy has as much drive as a sack of bran, thought

371

Similin. Stop pushing him and he just sits there. Well, that has its uses.

'When I return, I'll show you something you've never seen before. Something that will amaze you. Something that will give you the power to strike the greatest blow ever struck for justice.'

'That will be nice,' said Blaze.

The secretary had to be content with that.

Shortly after noon, Cheerful Giver paid a visit to the public tanks. He paced up and down the iron walkway, peering down through the bars at the miserable prisoners below, accompanied by an officer of the guards and a priest.

The prisoners did their best not to attract attention. They knew that whoever was chosen would go up the rock that very day. Only the Wildman refused to be cowed. He yelled out insults and challenges, he banged on the bars, he taunted the other prisoners with their cowardice; he even reached his arms up through the grid to snatch at the ankles of the guards as they passed by.

'Come and kill me! Come on! What are you waiting for?'

Then he turned on the cowed spikers in the tank and shouted at them.

'You blobs of blubber-piss! You're going to die! We're all going to die! That's why we're here! So don't make it easy for them! Yell! Kick! Scream! What are they going to do? Kill you? Don't you get it? *They're not allowed to kill us!* They're not even allowed to hurt us! They have to keep us alive so the priests can take us up the rock!'

The other prisoners were impressed. They admired the Wildman's craziness, and his courage. And he was, in his way, a source of entertainment.

'Take him,' said the officer in charge, pointing to the Wildman. 'He's young and healthy. A fine offering.'

'Take me!' screamed the Wildman from the tank. 'Take me! I'll rip your heart out!'

'No,' said Cheerful Giver. 'I want a willing tribute.'

'Give me five minutes alone with him,' said the officer. 'I'll make him willing.'

'I'm sure you will, officer. But will he be able to walk afterwards?'

The priest pointed out an extremely fat lady huddled in one corner.

'There's one with some flesh on her,' he said. 'The crowd always cheers for a fat one.'

Cheerful Giver shook his head irritably.

'This is my name day offering. I want style.'

As he spoke, his scanning eyes fell on Mercy. She sat quietly, on her own, her hands folded on her lap, still wearing the white dress of a lady.

'You,' he said, pointing.

She looked up. Her eyes were calm and free from both the fear and the hatred he saw on every other face. She had dignity, and she was good-looking. Clean her up, put a new dress on her, and she'd do very well.

The priest had also had his eye on Mercy ever since

she'd been brought in. He had an arrangement with one of the tribute traders for those rare occasions when a good specimen showed up in the tanks. He slipped the specimen out to the trader, and they shared whatever price he got.

'She's not available, honoured sir.'

'You're a thieving rogue!' said Cheerful Giver.

'His Holiness himself has marked her out for the next Festival of Light.'

Cheerful Giver ground his teeth.

'I will of course make a donation to temple funds.'

'His Holiness was saying only this morning that a tribute such as this is a rare and precious jewel.'

Cheerful Giver scowled.

'A jewel of great price,' added the priest.

'Yes, yes, yes. I'm not entirely stupid.' He lowered his voice so that he could speak to the priest without the officer of the guard hearing. 'A hundred shillings.'

'Honoured sir!' The priest sounded shocked. 'I would not dare to tell his Holiness that I had let so precious a jewel go for so insignificant, so imperceptible, so invisible a sum!'

'Name your price.'

'A thousand.'

'Five hundred.'

The priest turned away with a shrug. The officer came up smiling, as if to help. He too was after his cut.

'Very well,' said Cheerful Giver to the priest. 'As you wish.' To the officer he said, 'Assist this godly gentleman. He is following my instructions.' He slipped five ten-shilling coins into the officer's waiting hand. And turning back to the priest, 'The temple will receive my donation after the evening offering.'

The priest inclined his head. Cheerful Giver added with a tight bright smile, 'Guide me with your wisdom. Protect me with your power.'

Then he turned and left, adding as he went another thousand to the immense sums he had already laid out in obtaining a suitable tribute for his name day.

'Chuck-chuck-chicken!' cried the Wildman after him. 'You want your neck slit? Heya, bravas! Do you love me? Do you lo-o-ove me?'

Mercy gazed back at him with a smile, unaware that her fate had now been decided. She loved to watch the beautiful golden-haired youth, and to hear his unbroken spirit crying out.

'Yes,' she said. 'I love you.'

At the end of the afternoon, Soren Similin too passed by the tanks, leading Blaze over the iron walkway to the secret laboratory. He found the blinds closed, and the big space in deep shadow. Professor Ortus came hurrying forward, a smile of welcome on his face. Similin was too bent on his own plans to stop to consider how uncharacteristic this was.

'Why aren't you charging the device?' he said.

'It is fully charged,' said the scientist, 'but we have had to interrupt the power while we work on a small repair. A fault in the flow-valves. Nothing serious, I assure you.

375

We'll have it fixed by tomorrow morning.'

'Tomorrow morning!' Similin frowned with vexation. 'I had hoped to proceed tonight. Can't you work faster?'

'Perhaps,' said the scientist, 'if we worked through the offering . . .' He closed his eyes and made calculations in his head. 'Perhaps we could be ready by midnight.'

'Midnight, then,' said the secretary. 'That way our new friend here doesn't have too long to wait.'

Ortus studied the young stranger by the secretary's side. He was not impressed. The fellow looked like a halfwit.

The king's secretary now made a speech to the assembled team.

'I'm proud to be able to tell you,' he said, 'that we are at last very close to the fulfilment of all our hard work. We will be proceeding with the final phase at midnight tonight.'

The team applauded.

'May I introduce to you a brave and selfless young man – one who fully understands and shares the nobility of our cause – and one who has the key to the island of Anacrea, and to the Nom itself, because he is – a Noma!'

A gasp went up from the team. Evor Ortus went white. He had never expected Similin to persuade one of the Nomana to join them. It was a brilliant coup.

'Blaze of Justice!'

Blaze bowed his head, blushing at the applause.

'Would you like to say a word or two to the team?'

Blaze looked back in silence for a moment. Then he said, 'Hello, team.'

A titter of laughter ran round the room: quickly suppressed.

'Our young hero,' Similin explained, 'has been cast out of the Community of the Nomana. As part of that process, he has been, as they call it, cleansed. He has lost much of his understanding. But he has not forgotten that he is a Noble Warrior.'

Blaze smiled and nodded, happy to hear words he recognised.

'And that his cause is justice for all.'

Blaze smiled and nodded again; and then rather spoiled the effect by putting his thumb in his mouth.

'What is more,' continued Similin, 'he has told me that he is willing – that he is eager – in the service of that cause, to give his life itself!'

The team applauded. Blaze took his thumb out of his mouth and clapped his hands too. Soren Similin accepted the applause as his due. He felt justifiably proud. A better volunteer could not have been found.

'Let us show our brave young friend the device.'

Ortus signed to his team, and the blinds were rolled back. The late afternoon sunlight streamed down from above, making a dazzling display of the banks of glass tubes.

Blaze stared at the vats and pipes, the grids and the dangling yoke, at the rubber tubes and the stout chair with its straps and pads. Then he asked, puzzled, 'Where is the weapon?'

'You will be the weapon.'

He frowned, still not understanding.

'I will be the weapon?'

'You will carry within you the power of the sun itself!'

'Will I?' said Blaze.

'No need to understand. All you need to know is that the most brilliant minds of a generation have combined to create the ultimate weapon. Here, in a city that worships the sun, we've found a way to harness the sun's mighty power. To harness it, and then – to set it free!'

'That must have been very difficult,' said Blaze.

'It is a complex device. We've been at work for many long days and many long nights. None more so than the professor here.' He bowed to Ortus. To Blaze he added, 'This good man is the chief scientist on the technical team. It is he who has built this remarkable device.'

The professor nodded and smiled, and Similin remained entirely unaware of the hatred that burned within him.

'That's a good strong chair,' said Blaze.

He went over to the wooden chair, and sat himself down in it. Ortus squealed with dismay.

'Not yet!' he cried. 'There are repairs to be made. We can't start yet!'

The secretary took Blaze by the arm and drew him out of the chair.

'Please don't distress yourself, professor,' he said. 'We have agreed that we will begin at midnight.'

'You propose a full charge?'

'A full charge.' Similin nodded gravely. 'From midnight to dawn.'

'To dawn!'

Everyone in the team knew what that meant. They were awed. The axer on whom they had carried out the test was far bigger than Blaze, and he had been charged for no more than twelve minutes.

'By dawn,' said Similin to Blaze, 'your body will hold the most massive accumulation of pure energy on the face of the earth.'

'That will be nice,' said Blaze.

'And then – one small cut. A little blood. All it takes is for your blood to be exposed to the air, and – '

He parted his hands, slowly and majestically, to convey what could not be conveyed: the devastating force of the blast that would then ensue. As he did so, Similin felt as if it was he himself who was bringing about this historic coup. He, the son of a poor weaver, the despised outlander, was about to change the world.

'My good friend the professor will find you a place to rest, and food and drink. It would be wise, I think, for you to remain here until midnight, out of sight of prying eyes. Perhaps in the storeroom.'

He moved to open the storeroom door. Ortus jumped into his way.

'Not there. There's so little air there. I'm sure our hero would be far more comfortable in our canteen. Especially if he's to eat and drink.'

'But that room is used all the time.'

'We would be proud to offer it to him for his sole use.'

The secretary beckoned the scientist aside, and spoke to him confidentially.

'Please help me here, professor. I'm sure this young man is entirely reliable. But I'd be happier if the door to the room in which he rests is locked while I'm away at the evening offering.'

Ortus had anticipated this. He held up a key.

'Of course.'

Similin was pleased. The scientist was showing more initiative than he'd given him credit for.

'Nothing must be allowed to go wrong, now that we're so close to the end.'

Closer than you think, said Evor Ortus to himself, as he smiled and bobbed his head.

CHAPTER THIRTY-ONE

SUNSET

THE time for the evening offering was getting close, and in the house of Cheerful Giver there was an air of mounting excitement. Blessing had had a new outfit made for the purpose, and her husband, who was in the habit of saying he didn't care what he wore, had put on a formal coat that was heavily embroidered with silver thread. The two boys were dressed in pure white, and ordered to sit still, so as not to dirty their clothes. And as for Morning Star, all day long a seamstress had been at work making her up a white dress, on which she was sewing delicate panels of contrasting white, so that all could see how highly Cheerful Giver valued his new daughter.

Morning Star had at last been released from her chain. Indeed, it was necessary if she were to be fitted for the new dress. She showed no inclination to escape.

'The king is very magnificent,' Blessing told her. 'I hope you won't be overawed by his presence.'

'I come with a message from a power even greater than the king,' said Morning Star quietly.

When Soren Similin arrived on the temple terrace for the evening offering, the High Priest greeted him with more warmth than usual.

'Ah, secretary. I hear you've been away from court. I trust you return refreshed.'

'Thank you, Holiness.'

From beyond the closed doors came the sounds of the king's hate session.

'Suffer and die! Suffer and die!'

Ba-ba-ba-bam! Ba-ba-ba-bam!

'Nomana die! Nomana die!

Ba-ba-ba-bam! Ba-ba-ba-bam!

The priest on duty for the evening offering entered.

'Am I to prepare the tribute, Holiness?'

'Yes. Go ahead.'

'We have a name day offering this evening, Holiness.'

'Oh? Whose name day?'

'The oil merchant Cheerful Giver.'

'That money-grubber! Hoping to buy himself more status, I suppose. What sort of tribute is he offering?'

'A female tribute. The word is she's willing.'

'I'll believe that when I see it.'

The secretary heard this exchange, but he had no interest in the details of the ceremony. As soon as it was over, he would return to the laboratory, and there he would set in train a sequence of events that would change everything.

The priest on duty proceeded to the tanks to collect the evening's tribute. The guards opened the grid door, and the priest pointed to Mercy.

'She's the one.'

Mercy rose and made her way up the steps without a moment's hesitation. The Wildman took in what was happening just a few seconds too late.

'No!' he cried. 'Not her! Don't take her!'

The grid door dropped down on to him, knocking him to the floor. The heavy bolts slammed home. He was up and hanging from the bars, rattling and screaming, before the priest and the tribute were out of the door.

'Not her!' he screamed. 'Not her!'

Mercy turned and looked back and gave him a sweet, sad smile. He saw in that look that she was ready, even willing, to die, but all the raging life force in him cried out against it. He turned and howled at the rest of the prisoners, who looked on, silent in the tank.

'Are you dead already? Why don't you shout? Why don't you scream? Don't let them do this! What are you? Chickens? We're going to die anyway! Don't die silent! Die noisy! Die yelling! Die loud!'

He followed this with a great wordless howl of fury.

'Aieee-ee-ee!'

Outside the bells were ringing, and the people of Radiance were streaming into the temple square. The sun was dropping towards the lake horizon, and market traders were calling out their wares. The chatter of the crowd filled the air.

Cheerful Giver and his family, which now included

Morning Star, reached the temple terrace just a little too early. The king had not yet emerged. The High Priest began at once to make the speech required of him by tradition, thanking Cheerful Giver for providing the evening's offering. This speech should have been made in the presence of the king. Cheerful Giver, smiling and bowing as if he was the happiest man in Radiance, understood very well that the High Priest meant to deprive him of his due honour. He consoled himself with the thought that the High Priest had a surprise coming.

In the secret laboratory, Professor Ortus had now pretended to repair the fault he had pretended to find. Therefore he called his team together and instructed them to attend the evening offering.

'We have a long night ahead of us,' he said. 'Pray to the Radiant Power for the strength to complete our great task. Return at midnight.'

He himself remained in the laboratory.

As soon as they were gone, he unlocked the storeroom, where Seeker was hidden, and, putting one finger to his lips, beckoned him to come out.

'We must make as little noise as possible,' he whispered. 'No one must know.'

He glanced at the locked canteen door, beyond which Blaze, the only other person now in the laboratory, was resting. No sound came from within. With luck, he was even asleep. So long as they kept their voices low, the scientist was confident that Blaze would not guess what was happening. And even if he did, Ortus had seen that blank, foolish face. He expected no trouble there.

Seeker was standing gazing in awe at the banks of solar tubes, now glowing pink in the light of the setting sun. He asked no questions. But as Blaze had done, he moved forward to the chair that stood bolted to the floor at the centre of the apparatus, and ran his fingers over its sturdy arms.

'This is the weapon that will destroy Anacrea?'

'This is it.'

'How does it work?'

'I'll show you. But first, I have to strap you in.'

Seeker looked round the looming towers of pipes and vessels, and up at the yoke that hung above him. He found it all extremely frightening. But he was also puzzled.

'Sit in the chair,' said Ortus, trying not to sound too eager.

Seeker hesitated for a moment longer. Then he sat in the chair.

A small cheer from the crowd greeted the appearance of the procession of three priests escorting the evening's tribute. Morning Star looked across the terrace, and saw the indistinct figure of a woman in white. She felt a sharp pang of guilt. This should have been her. All the time she had been plotting to free herself, she had somehow managed not to think that her survival was someone else's death. Distressed, she looked away.

385

The king emerged at last. He came hobbling on to the terrace, his face pink from shouting, and stood with his arms raised to be dressed in the ceremonial cape. At this point the High Priest should have presented Cheerful Giver and his family, but he made no move to do so. Cheerful Giver, smiling even more grimly, was obliged to present himself.

'Radiance, today is my name day, and I am proud to offer this day's tribute.'

'Proud? What's there to be proud about? Oh, yes. I see. Your name day.' The priest-king peered towards the tribute procession. 'Well done. That's the spirit. Though I don't suppose you won him in battle, eh?'

He laughed, and so Cheerful Giver laughed.

'No, Radiance. My tribute is a lady.'

'A lady! I say! Well done!'

'Aieee-ee-ee!' screamed the Wildman in the tanks. 'Die noisy! Die loud!'

Now the younger spikers caught his rebellious mood, and joined his cry.

'Yaa-aa-ee-eee!'

Now others were shouting too. They lived with so much fear, the screaming came as a release. As more and more joined in, the level of noise rose, until even the most fearful felt they had nothing to lose. The Wildman stood at their head, banging the hinged grid against its bolts, and the hundreds of prisoners bayed like demented animals.

386

On the temple terrace, Blessing stood at her husband's side, looking before her with a beatific gaze. She whispered to her husband.

'Present the child.'

The High Priest, his eyes on the tribute procession, determinedly paying no attention to Cheerful Giver's moment of glory, became aware that some sort of commotion was going on in the tanks. He beckoned to one of his priests.

'That noise. Put a stop to it.'

The priest departed. The High Priest turned to see Cheerful Giver presenting a girl in a white dress to the king.

'Radiance! May I introduce my adopted daughter, Morning Star.'

The king looked at Morning Star with mild surprise.

'I didn't know you had an adopted daughter.'

'She has a message for you, Radiance.'

Cheerful Giver saw that the keeper was holding up the corona, ready for him to place it on the king's shoulders. The ceremonial procedures could not wait. The sun was descending. So, with an encouraging nod to Morning Star, he went about his duties, pleasantly aware that his words had caused general surprise.

'Message?' said the king.

'Message?' said the High Priest.

In the adjacent laboratory, Evor Ortus too heard the shouts

from the tanks, but he paid no attention. His hands were shaking as he fastened the straps round Seeker's wrists. He couldn't help himself, he was nervous. So much was at stake.

'There we go,' he said. 'Nice and snug.'

'I don't understand what this is supposed to do,' said the boy.

He was shivering. It struck Ortus that the boy was frightened, and he should say something to reassure him.

'It's to make you strong,' he said. 'Stronger even than the Nomana. You'd like that, wouldn't you?'

'How will it make me strong?'

'This machine is going to fill you with power. Once I have you joined up, you'll feel the power flow into you. Then you'll be a conqueror! You'd like that, wouldn't you?'

The boy didn't answer. Ortus reached up for the dangling yoke, and drew it down, into position over the boy's shoulders.

'All you'll feel will be a tiny prick on the side of your neck.'

The Wildman screamed and banged at the overhead bars of the tank, and with him all the other prisoners screamed and banged. They were delirious with the sound of their own fear and anger: all wildmen now. The guards on duty struck the grid with sticks and shouted orders, but to no avail. When the High Priest's envoy entered, demanding that the prisoners be silenced, his instructions could barely be heard.

'Stop them!' he shrieked. 'Beat them! Crush them!'

388

The guards unbolted the door in the grid. Two of them lifted the heavy hinged lid so that the others could drop down into the tank and beat the rioters into silence.

This was a mistake.

Morning Star saw every face on the temple terrace staring at her. Cheerful Giver's brow was shining with nervous perspiration. The king was glowering at her with mounting impatience.

Blessing prompted her.

'Remember what you told us,' she whispered. 'There is one whose heart is dark.'

Morning Star knew she must speak.

'I am to bring you a warning, Radiance,' she said. 'The enemy is nearer than you think.'

They all heard her. An electric silence fell.

'The girl is a messenger,' said Blessing. 'From the Radiant Power.'

'Radiance,' said Morning Star, lowering her voice to a tiny whisper. 'My message is for you alone.'

The king's eyes opened wide, and he crouched down, to hear her more clearly.

'Come,' he said. 'Whisper it to me. But hurry. The sun is setting.'

Morning Star approached him. As she did so, she studied his colours, and there at last she found the clue she needed. There, almost hidden beneath the dominant deep yellows and browns, the arrogance and the indifference, was a shade of pale blue that merged as she looked into blue-green, the colour of unmet need. All men look to the king for praise. Where is the king to look?

'Radiance,' she whispered. 'The Great Power loves you, and calls you his son.'

'His son!' The king's eyes widened further.

'Radiance!' warned the High Priest. 'The sun is setting!'

The king stood up again, and saw that the priests and the tribute were now in place on the temple rock. He fixed his gaze on the red orb that was dropping towards the lake horizon.

'Father!' he murmured. 'I thank you!'

Turning to Morning Star he said, 'We will talk more later, child. You will tell me of this enemy.'

Morning Star drew a quiet breath of relief. She had survived; this far at least. She looked guiltily towards the tribute, the woman in white who was now about to die in her place. And as she looked, she had a strange sensation. It was as if she knew her.

Who are you?

The tribute turned and looked at her, exactly as if she had heard her silent question. For the first time, Morning Star saw her face: and as she did so, a flash of pure memory broke through into her trembling mind. She had seen that sweet head turn like this before. She had seen that sweet face look down on her before. She had felt before this simple overwhelming sensation that she was loved.

Mama?

The first guard swung himself down into the mass of howling prisoners in the tank, and struck out to left and right.

'Get the yellow-haired one!' shouted the second guard. 'He's the ringleader!'

The Wildman backed away before him, drawing him deeper into the tank, and the rest of the guards followed. Then with a howl of startling ferocity he sprang forward, seized the guard by the throat, and smashed him to the ground. At once, as if this alone had been the signal they had been waiting for, the other prisoners charged the guards, making up in sheer numbers what they lacked in weaponry.

'Die loud!' yelled the Wildman. 'Die fighting!'

'Radiance! We must proceed with the ceremony at once! The sun is setting!'

'Why is the tribute staring at us like that?'

The sun was nearing the surface of the water. The tribute stood motionless, looking back. The priests round her urged her forward, but she would not move.

'Why doesn't she move?' said Cheerful Giver. 'She must fall!'

Morning Star knew that it was her eyes and her will alone that held the tribute motionless. She held her gripped in her mind and in her heart. Soundlessly she called to her.

Mama!

Cheerful Giver was filled with a sudden dread. This was

his tribute. She was supposed to go willingly to her death. Even the ones who were not willing were made to look as if they accepted their fate, with the help of tranquillising drugs. There could never be an unseemly struggle on the rock. That stained the purity of the offering in the eyes of the Radiant Power above.

But the tribute would not move.

The High Priest, now thoroughly alarmed, looked from the staring tribute back to the group round the king, and saw the expression on the face of the girl in white.

'It's her!' he cried. 'She's doing it!'

The king now saw it too. He shouted to his bodyguard, a giant axer.

'Seize her! Kill her!'

Professor Ortus readied the second needle, which had to be inserted in a vein in Seeker's arm. The boy was very jumpy, and Ortus himself was nervous. He fumbled the insertion.

'Ow!' yelled Seeker. 'That hurt!'

'Sit still!'

For his second attempt he held Seeker's arm steady with one hand, while he inserted the needle with the other.

'There!' he said. 'All done! How are you feeling? Are you ready for the power?'

'What will it do to me?'

'Make you into a god!'

He crossed to the master controls. As he did so, he heard a stirring from within the canteen. The boy's shout of pain must have woken Blaze. Still, he thought, the door is locked.

'Here we go!' he said. He threw the main switch.

The people in the temple square were starting to panic.

'Fall! Fall!' they shouted.

The priests on the rock pleaded with the tribute.

'Come!' they said. 'It's time! Fall into the arms of the Radiant Power! Give us life!'

'Fall! Fall!' shouted the crowd as the sun sank unstoppably to the water.

On the temple terrace the giant axer seized Morning Star in both massive hands and raised her high in the air, breaking her eye contact with the tribute. The tribute gave a shudder, and turned to face the setting sun.

'Fall! Fall! Fall!' chanted the people of Radiance, in an agonised pulsing cry.

The doors from the tanks burst open: roaring, golden, beautiful, the Wildman sprang, his clasped hands out-reached in a flying double fist. The blow snapped back the axer's huge head, breaking his neck. He buckled and fell, and Morning Star fell with him. Spikers from the tanks came streaming on to the terrace, howling their crazed rage. Priests and officials, terrified, fled from them towards the broad stairway.

'Call out the axers!' cried the king. 'Call out the dogs!'

Seeker was in the grip of the machine. He was jerking in the chair, and his skin was prickling all over, and he could no longer control any of his muscles. He could hear himself uttering a shivery stammering crying sound. He knew he had gone too far, but he had no way now to escape his fate.

Professor Ortus heard the yells of the riot outside. He also heard movement behind the locked door of the canteen.

'Everything's all right!' he called, trying to sound calm.

A voice from within called out.

'What's happening?'

It was a voice Seeker had hardly expected to hear ever again. He was quite unable to reply.

'Stay where you are,' called the professor. 'Everything's all right.'

There came a rattle on the door. Then silence. Then the door shattered before his eyes, and out stepped Blaze, transformed. One glance was enough. He strode to Seeker's side and pulled the needles from his neck and arms. Ortus ran at him, frantic to stop him. Blaze turned, and his eyes locked on to the scientist's eyes. Gone was the blank expressionless look. Ortus stopped dead, frozen by the pure power in those eyes. Blaze raised one hand and extended two fingers towards him. Ortus felt a great weight descend on his shoulders and chest. He sank to his knees. The weight bore down on him, crushing the life from him.

'Please – ' he cried, choking, unable to breathe.

Blaze turned back to Seeker, and with rapid movements he snapped the straps that held Seeker to the chair, and caught him as he crumpled forward.

'Little brother! My little brother!'

He took him in his arms.

'I didn't know! What have you done? I didn't know!'

Seeker felt his brother's arms round him and tried to speak and couldn't. The terror of the machine, the shock of the minutes he'd been in its power, the astonishing appearance from nowhere of his beloved brother, all staggered his mind and scattered his thoughts. But then, looking up through the windows in the roof, he saw the red sky and he remembered.

'Sunset! They're going to throw her from the rock!'

Blaze lifted up his head and uttered a long high whistling cry.

'Fall! Fall! Fall!' chanted the people of Radiance as the sun sank into the water.

On the emptying terrace there was pandemonium. The court officials were scrambling to escape the revenge of the spikers, even as the great dogs came bounding up the crowded stairways. The tribute was facing the very edge of the rock, and seemed about to fall. The priests had left her side, afraid of the spikers. Fearful for their own lives, they were running for the safety of the stairs.

The sun was half-gone below the horizon.

'Fall! Fall! Fall!' shrieked the people.

The great dogs burst baying on to the terrace, rending the crazed spikers with their jaws. After them came the axers, swinging their chains. The Wildman stood over

Morning Star and prepared to fight. A dog crouched to spring. An axer closed in, his sweeping chain hissing by so close it rattled the bracelets on the Wildman's golden arm. The dog sprang –

A high whistling sound came lancing through the air. Out of nowhere dropped a tall hooded man in a grey tunic. The leaping dog folded in mid-spring. The axer's chain fell to the ground with a clatter of heavy iron links. A second hooded man appeared on the terrace, and a third. The shouts faded on the lips of the escaped spikers. As more and more hooded men threw off their disguises and revealed themselves, the terrified priests and officials scrambling down the stairways came to a stop. The panic in the temple square faded away. A sudden stillness came upon the people of Radiance.

The Nomana had taken control.

Now at last, in utter silence, the sun slipped away and was gone, and no tribute had been offered.

Night had come for the people and city of Radiance. The unthinkable had happened. The day had ended, and no offering had been made to the Radiant Power that gave life to all the world. Therefore the sun would not rise in the morning. The end of the world had begun.

As this realisation spread, a terrible lamentation rose up from the temple square. The people began to groan and keen like wounded animals. Halfway down the broad stairway the king dropped to his knees, and bowed his head. The High Priest staggered as if in pain, uttering low guttural cries. Blessing breathed rapidly, and felt hot, and tore off her head-dress, and felt hotter still, and tore at her gown. Only the king's secretary remained in control of himself. He looked round at this city of fools, and thought of the weapon he had caused to be built, and of Blaze, who was waiting for him, and he felt only a contemptuous pride. What did he care if their god had failed them? What did he care if a handful of Nomana destroyed their entire city? He possessed the ultimate power. His move was yet to come. When it came, it would be final.

Morning Star rose to her feet and made her way across the terrace towards the rock edge. The lady in white stood still, rimmed by the crimson afterglow in the sky, waiting for her. She was so beautiful, and so familiar, and so sad.

'Mama?'

Morning Star was timid in the face of what she had wanted for so long. If this was her mother, why didn't she reach out to her and hold her?

'Not Mama,' said Mercy. 'I lost the right to be your Mama long ago.'

But it was her mother's own sweet voice, long remembered, long forgotten.

'You'll always be my mother,' said Morning Star. And she knelt before her.

'My darling,' said Mercy. 'What use am I?'

'You're no use, Mama. You're just my mother.'

At that, Mercy too sank to her knees, and kissed her

child on one cheek, and then on the other, meaning by these kisses to ask her forgiveness, which Morning Star understood and gave. Then at last the mother took the child in her arms.

Seeker came limping and stumbling over the iron walkway above the now-empty tanks, and so out on to the temple terrace. Here he saw the aftermath of the chaos that had struck the city. The last of the escaped spikers were making their way off the terrace, down to the square below. Dogs lay whimpering in the shadows. The mountainous body of an axer half blocked the doorway.

And there stood the Wildman, silver bracelets glinting crimson in the dying light.

'Heya, Seeker!'

They fell into each other's arms.

'She's safe!' said the Wildman. 'She's good!'

Seeker then saw Morning Star, kneeling on the rock, holding the hands of a lady in white.

'So she found her.'

No one had told him. He had not needed to be told. As he looked, Morning Star rose to her feet and left her mother, and came towards them.

'My friends,' she said. She had tears in her eyes.

Seeker reached out his trembling arms. She came to him, and he held her, and the Wildman hugged them both, and for a few sweet moments they were close, and did not speak.

Then Morning Star said, 'The Wildman saved me.'

The Wildman said, 'The hoodies saved me.'

Seeker said, 'My brother saved me.'

They looked round. There were the Nomana; and standing with them, as one of them, was Blaze.

The Noble Warriors raised their arms high above their heads, each one reaching up his forefingers and touching them together, to make of his body an arrow pointing to the stars: the Nomana salute.

Blaze looked from the Wildman, to Morning Star, to Seeker.

'Be proud, little brother,' he said. 'The Nomana honour you.'

CHAPTER THIRTY-TWO

NIGHT

ALL that night the people of Radiance walked the streets, weeping and calling for mercy, gathering in open squares round improvised bonfires to share their terrors and hide from the dark they feared would never end. The king, the High Priest, all the higher court officials and the senior priests gathered in the main sanctuary of the temple, where they abased themselves on the marble floor before the golden hearth, in which burned the night fire that was the symbol of their god. Here they waited in dread for the dawn that they knew would not come.

Cheerful Giver called together his wife and his sons and his servants, and lit a ring of torches in the courtyard of his house, and there they passed the whole night in prayer. Blessing, who had always been the most devout member of the family, had almost lost her wits with fear and shock.

'I had a daughter,' she kept saying. 'Where have they taken my daughter? Why doesn't she come?'

Cheerful Giver understood very little of the disaster that had struck them all, but he was sure that he personally had been duped. Somehow the tribute he had purchased for so high a price had turned out to be in league with the Nomana. He was consumed by a bitter rage. Somehow, for reasons he could not fathom, everybody had conspired to cheat and humiliate him.

'She's gone,' he said savagely. 'She made a fool of us all. I knew it all along. But you would believe her.'

'Where is she?' cried poor bewildered Blessing. 'She's my own little girl.'

Soren Similin stood in the dark laboratory, and saw by the light of the moon the devastation that had overtaken all his hopes. The complex apparatus that had filled the high room was destroyed. Blaze, his perfect volunteer, was gone. All his planning, all his work, was lost. How had this happened? How had the secret laboratory been found, and entered?

Suddenly weary, he sat himself down and put his head in his hands. What had he done wrong? What clues had he missed? He had been as surprised as everyone else by the coming of the Nomana, but he had told himself it was not his war. He was no part of Radiance, or its god. Only now, before the shattered remains of his greatest creation, did he begin to guess that it was his war after all: that the Nomana had attacked not a false god – for why should they fear the superstitions of fools? – but a real weapon.

He heard a movement in the darkness.

'Who's there?'

Out of the shadows crept Evor Ortus.

'All gone,' he said. 'All gone.'

'Did you see what happened?'

401

'Oh, yes. I saw.'

'Was it the Nomana?'

'It was the one you brought here. The Noma you brought here. It's all because of you.' Ortus started to laugh, in a jerky hysterical fashion. 'He smashed it! He broke everything he could break! Smash! smash! smash! All because of you! You wanted all the credit. Well, take it! It's all yours! You brought him here! And because of you, he destroyed my life's work.'

'Nonsense! We can build it again.'

'How? The sun will never rise again. It's over. It's all over.'

Similin said no more. The man had lost his mind, he could see that. The little scientist shuffled away through the open door, babbling and cackling to himself, no longer of any use to anybody. Similin's calculations moved on.

So somehow Blaze had been using him all along. He must take responsibility for that. So be it. He would accept the consequences. Let there be punishment. Let there be disgrace. Once more he would turn the enmity of the world into his own peculiar source of strength. The more they mock me, the stronger I become, he said to himself. I am myself like the weapon I created, and will create again. All the hatred and contempt that is hurled at me flows into my blood, and makes me ever more dangerous. I have not been defeated. I have only been delayed.

But first, he knew, must come the punishment. He sank

to his knees and let his forehead fall until it was resting on the ground.

'I have not done well, mistress.'

You have not done well, came the reply.

'I must be punished.'

You must be punished.

So it came. Like sharp needles run deep into his flesh, the keen pain lanced him again and again, causing his limbs to spasm and then to thrash. But not one sound did he make. He writhed on the floor, and his eyes rolled back in their sockets, and the sweat streamed from his brow, but he never cried out. When he was deserving, there came the sweetness. When he failed, there came the punishment. Both were supreme gifts of love, and in return he loved his mistress with all his being, even as she made him suffer.

When the punishment was over he picked himself up from the floor and sat, drained of all strength, in the wooden chair built for the carrier. He looked up through the roof windows at the stars in the night sky above. In a few short hours it would be the dawn of a new day.

'A new day,' he said to himself.

An idea began then to grow in him.

'A new day.'

As the first light of the new day spread across the sky, the frightened people of the city looked up in confusion and disbelief. Were they to rejoice, because the world had not ended? Or to despair, because their god was shown to be indifferent to them? For all their lives the ritual and drama of the evening offering had demonstrated to them, like a test ever renewed and ever passed, that they were a chosen people. So long as the Radiant Power that gave light to the world required their daily tribute, their god was in some sense tied to them. Their god needed them. But if the daily tribute was not necessary after all – if the sun rose whether or not they showed themselves to be worthy – then who was to say that the Radiant Power looked on them with any more favour than on anyone else?

These were shocking thoughts. Too shocking for some. Cheerful Giver, still on his knees in the courtyard of his house, saw the pre-dawn light in the sky, and smelled another trick designed to fool him.

'Just because there's light over the mountains,' he said, 'doesn't mean it's dawn. It could be moonlight. Or firelight. Or a false light sent to test our faith.'

But even as he was speaking, the sun itself rose over the rim of mountains. From all over the city there went up shouts of wonder and consternation. The sun had risen after all.

Cheerful Giver no longer knew what to think. He clambered to his feet, and doused the torches. His wife and his two boys were fast asleep, as were many of his servants. His housekeeper was watching him with frightened eyes.

'What will happen now, sir?'

'How do I know? I'm just an oil seller. The High Priest will tell us.'

404

He spoke with a profound bitterness. He could see no advantage to himself, however this catastrophe developed. Either the priests would know what to do, in which case their prestige would be enhanced; or they would not, and the social order would collapse.

He heard a murmuring sound from the street outside, and went to the still-open gates to look. There, advancing from the lower city, was a great crowd. They weren't threatening, they were imploring.

'Guide us with your wisdom! Protect us with your power!'

They were converging on the temple square, chanting the familiar words, now charged with desperate meaning. They wanted to be told what to think of all that had happened, and to be reassured that somehow life would go on as before. But beneath the pleas, Cheerful Giver also heard a more ominous note. The people were coming to the temple to be saved. And if they were not saved –

He shuddered.

'Come,' he called to his household. 'We should hear this too.'

The crowd gathered in the temple square. The square was big, but even so it was not big enough for the great numbers that came pushing in from every side street. People climbed up on porches and railings, and filled the houses that looked on to the square, and even crowded on to the wide portico of the temple itself. They left a space before the great sanctuary doors, because it was here that the king and the priests would appear before them.

The pleading cries of the crowd rose up and echoed from the temple walls.

'Guide us with your wisdom! Protect us with your power!'

No answer came from within the temple. But the people did not go away. At first patiently, and then impatiently, they cried their cries and beat on the great closed doors.

At last there came the sound of bolts being drawn back. Word ran through the great crowd, and down all the packed streets leading to the square.

'The doors are opening!'

As the news spread, a silence fell, reaching ever further out, like ripples in a pond. By the time the great doors began to open, an expectant stillness lay over the whole multitude.

When the doors were fully open, the temple priests appeared. They were in two lines, and each priest had one hand on the shoulder of the priest in front. They came out uncertainly, weaving slightly from side to side as they came. The people watched, and held their breath.

Then the High Priest came into view. He walked with his hands reached out before him, and felt his way with careful probing footsteps. After him came the king, Radiant Vision himself. He too had his hands reached out before him. The watching people saw, and were bewildered. Why were their leaders acting as if they couldn't see where they were going?

Radiant Vision fumbled his way to the front of the steps, and his eyes gazed out over the sea of faces; but it was clear he saw none of them. The High Priest stood by his side, unseeing eyes also reaching out to nothing. The priests of the temple stood in their lines on either side, and though their eyes were open, they too were blind. It was no trick. These were the true believers. All their life they had known that if the tribute was not paid, the great light would not rise again; so for them it had not risen.

'My people!' said the king, his voice breaking with grief. 'My dear people! Darkness has come upon us! The night has begun that has no end! There is no hope for any of us! It is over!'

The people heard this in silence, thinking it must be the beginning of a longer speech. But then they saw the king turn and begin to hobble back into the temple. That was when their fury broke.

'Liar!' they screamed. 'Deceiver!'

'Sacrifice!' The cry rang out from high above. 'There must be sacrifice!'

A dazzle of gold flashed from the temple terrace, from the place where the king presented himself to the people each evening. A figure in a golden cloak stood catching the bright rays of the rising sun, his arms outreached on either side.

'Our god is angry!' the shining figure cried. 'The Radiant Power is angry! There must be a death!'

'Death!' cried the people. 'Death!'

They had no idea who it was who spoke to them, but his call sounded as the true voice of their fears, and gave them a way to save themselves from the horror into which they had been plunged.

'Death to the deceivers!' cried the shining figure above. 'Throw them from the rock!'

This was all it took. The crowd knew at once that this was right, that this was fitting, that this would return them to the favour of their all-powerful god. Without further hesitation, they surged up the temple steps and poured into the sanctuary, and hunted down their former masters. For all their lives they had trembled before them, but now the Radiant Power no longer favoured them, and the proof of it was that they had been struck blind.

The mob hunted them down, and dragged them up the stairway to the high rock, and from there they hurled them to their death. The king and the High Priest, the lesser priests and the court officials, in twos and threes and fours, fell screaming from the high rock to the bloody shallows of the lake far below.

The man in the golden cloak stood in the rays of the rising sun and his heart was filled with gladness. He saw clearly now. All that the little people asked in life was to be told how to save themselves. He would tell them. When they were unsure what their god wanted of them, he would guide them. All they required was clarity, and consistency.

Soren Similin had discovered the secret of power.

Now the little people would kneel before him and call him lord. Now he would deliver them to his masters, and they would be harvested.

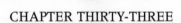

CHAPTER THIRTY-THREE

THE BEGINNING

THEY travelled together, Seeker and Blaze, the Wildman, Morning Star, and Mercy, her mother. The Nomana who had come to their rescue accompanied them too, on the long road south. Morning Star and Mercy spoke very little, still overcome by the immensity of all that had taken place. The Nomana spoke not at all. They walked quietly, their faces shaded by their badans, and seemed almost to be asleep.

'They have emptied themselves,' said Blaze. 'They need to rest.'

There was so much that Seeker didn't understand; and now, on the road home, his brother answered his questions as best as he could.

'From the moment I left Anacrea,' said Blaze, 'the Nomana have been watching over me. And over you too. Many a spiker you passed on your way was a member of our Community.'

'But you were cast out!'

'Forgive me, little brother. It was all a pretence. Forgive me for hurting you. But it had to look real, even to you.'

'You were cleansed! I saw you!'

'Only enough to teach me how to pretend. I had to make them believe me. I was the bait. We had to find the makers of the weapon, before it was used. So we decided to let them find us.'

'So you did nothing wrong. You're not a traitor.'

'No. I've done nothing wrong. Except to cause grief to those who love me, and to put you and your friends in danger.'

'I always knew it. I knew you were good and brave and strong.'

'Like you, little brother.'

'Oh, no. I could never be like you.'

'You found the weapon before I did. You let them put you in their machine. You knew it would kill you.'

'Yes,' said Seeker, remembering. 'I did think I was going to die.'

'And why were you willing to die?'

'Because – '

He wanted to tell Blaze about the voice. He wanted to tell him how the voice had said, *Surely you know that it's you who will save me.* But the words would not come.

Blaze put his arm round Seeker's shoulder, filled with loving pride.

'It doesn't matter why. I know why.' Then he added with a smile, as he had always done in the old days when they were at school together, 'Time to go home, little brother.'

Morning Star reached the little house in the hills as twilight was gathering. Amik heard her coming and loped out to meet her. After Amik, bouncing and squealing with excitement at seeing her again, came Lamb. Morning Star knelt down and nuzzled Amik's face, and took the puppy in her arms.

'Not forgotten me, then, little Lamb?'

The puppy wriggled in her grasp, as he tried to wag his tail and lick her face all at the same time.

'Come on. Let's go home.'

She went on through the open door, and there was her father sitting at the table, at work on his copying by the light of two candles. He looked up, and pretended not to be surprised, but she could see his colours and caught the quiet surge of joy.

'So you're back,' he said, and returned to the sentence he was copying.

'Yes, Papa. I'm back.'

'They didn't want you, then?'

'No. They didn't want me.'

He laid down his pen and pushed back his chair and gave her a long look.

'More fool them,' he said.

She put the puppy down and went to her father and he embraced her. His arms shook.

'I've brought someone with me, Papa.'

'You're enough, child,' he said. 'What do I want with someones?'

'I don't know, Papa. But you can always send her away.'

'Oh, it's a her, is it? I thought maybe you were bringing

412

me a young man of your own.'

'No, Papa. It's a her.'

She turned and called to the open doorway.

'Come on in.'

Nobody came.

'The her doesn't want to come in, child.'

'She thinks you'll be angry.'

'Why should I be angry?'

'Because she was here long ago, and she went away. And the people she went to didn't want her. And she was ashamed to come back.'

Her father said nothing after that. He just sat very still and gazed at the doorway. Outside the shadows were lengthening, but it was still brighter than in the candle-lit house.

'Will you be angry, Papa?'

'I might,' he growled. 'She always was a stupid woman.'

At that, Mercy showed herself in the doorway.

'And you always were an ungrateful man.'

'Oh, it's ungrateful now, is it?'

'Just look at you, ruining your eyes! Candlelight isn't good enough for book work.'

'They're my eyes, and I shall ruin them if I want to.'

'Well, don't ask me to lead you about on a string when you've gone blind.'

'I won't. You can be sure of that. I'll hold my own string.'

'Your own string! Listen to the man!'

By now she had come right into the room, and was

looking round. Little had changed in thirteen years. He watched her, and waited.

'You keep the place well,' she said.

'So I should. It's me that lives here.'

'You keep yourself well too.'

'I live quietly,' he said.

'I've no wish to disturb you.'

'I've no intention of letting you.'

Morning Star watched their colours change as they spoke, and she knew it would be all right between them. She saw Lamb creep forward to sniff at her mother's feet, and saw her mother bend down to take the puppy in her arms.

'We have only one life,' said Mercy.

'And you seem to have made a mess of yours.'

'So I have.'

'Ah, well. I don't know that I've done much better. If it suits you to stay a while, it suits me to have you here.'

Morning Star slipped out, unnoticed by either of them. She climbed up on to the familiar hills, where the flocks were grazing, and there she watched the last of the sunset. Tomorrow she would go once more to Anacrea. She had her father's quiet determination and her mother's broken dreams. Let the one mend the other, and why should her dreams not come true?

Seeker and Blaze went home together. Their mother wept for joy, and their father shook his head and said nothing, because he was so proud of his two sons, and so ashamed

414

of himself for having doubted Blaze, and so bewildered by the sudden change from grief to glory.

'We thought you were gone for ever,' said their mother, scolding and laughing. 'We thought we'd never see either of you again.'

'Forgive me for disobeying you, Father,' said Seeker.

'You're back,' said his father. 'Safe home. That's all that matters.' He cleared his throat and coughed. His voice wasn't as controlled as he liked it to be.

'And forgive me for a second act of disobedience, Father.'

'What now, my boy?'

'I mean to ask permission to join the Community.'

His father frowned. Blaze put one arm round his young brother's shoulders.

'I shall present him myself, Father. He was born to be a Noma.'

'I see. You think so? I see.' He fidgeted and coughed and showed his discomfort in every way, but as they both knew, his discomfort was with himself, not with them. 'I wanted only the best for you. For both of you. A father must do what he can to guide his children. To guide his children, you know.'

'And so you have, Father,' said Seeker. 'But I'm sixteen now. I'm of age. I ask your permission to find my own way.'

'I see. Yes. Well, you seem to have found it.'

The Wildman waited at the harbourside for his friends to return. He sat with his legs dangling over the dock wall, feeling the warmth of the sun on his face. His mind was empty: no fears, no demands; at least, not in this sun-filled moment. He felt safe and he felt trusting. A new path in life was about to unfold before him. There would be guides on this new path. For the first time in his life, he would not be meeting each new day alone. And as for where the path led –

'I'm to be a hoodie!' he told himself; and he smiled with delight at the thought. He had seen the hoodies in action in Radiance, and wanted more strongly than ever to possess that potent stillness.

Seeker would see to it all. This was Seeker's home, and his brother was a hoodie. The Wildman trusted Seeker more than he had ever trusted anyone in his life. More even than Snakey, who had protected him when he was little; because one day, without warning or explanation, Snakey had gone.

Seeker had clasped his hand and said, 'I stand with you from today to the end of the world.'

The Wildman believed him.

He looked up at the bright sun above and laughed aloud. He called out to nobody, to the gulls and the falcons on the cliff, to the fishermen mending their nets, to the blank windows of the castle-monastery high above.

'Heya! Do you lo-o-ove me?'

Blaze led his brother up the steps to the top, where the two lines of old pines grew. Here, instead of turning towards the high walls of the Nom, he pointed the other way, to the cliff end of the path. There, by the rails that guarded the cliff edge, Seeker saw a hunched figure in a wheelchair.

'He's waiting for you.'

'Won't you be coming with me?'

'No,' said Blaze. 'He wants to see you alone.'

So Seeker walked down the path alone, between the twisted pines, in and out of the shadows cast by their high fists of foliage. The shrunken old man in the wheelchair paid no attention to his coming, but went on gazing out over the sea. Seeker came to a stop, standing quietly by his side.

'So, Seeker after Truth.' The Elder turned his head at last to look at him. 'They tell me you have served us well, and now you want to join the Community.'

'Yes, Elder.'

'Is your heart still full of anger?'

'No, Elder. I know better now.'

'And yet there will come a day when you will hate the Nomana and all we stand for.'

'And after that, will I learn to know better again?'

The Elder smiled.

'You begin to understand.'

He turned his watery eyes back on the great ocean.

'Have you ever wondered what lies beyond the horizon?'

'Yes, Elder. Many times.'

'Other lands?'

'I like to think so, Elder.'

'And in those other lands, is the Always and

Everywhere there too? Does the Clear Light shine beyond the horizon?'

'I'm sure of it, Elder.'

'Our life is hard. You know that.'

'Yes, Elder.'

'Hard in ways you can't yet imagine.'

'I'm sixteen years old, Elder,' said Seeker. 'How can I know what lies ahead for me? I must do my best with the little knowledge I have.'

The Elder nodded.

'You rebuke me. You're right to do so.'

'No, Elder, I didn't mean – '

The old man waved one hand, to indicate that he wasn't angry.

'If you wish to join our Community, you shall do so. You have won that right for yourself.'

Seeker felt a great calmness flow into him. It wasn't a feeling of triumph at all. Just a sense of rightness: that this was how his life was meant to be.

Then he remembered his friends. He had wanted friends for so long, and now he had two friends who he knew would be with him for the rest of his life.

'And Morning Star? And the Wildman? They too will be joining the Community?'

'The girl, yes. But the other one – I think even you can see that he's not suited to our way of life.'

'No, Elder. I don't see.'

The Elder looked up in surprise.

'He's shown himself to be brave. That I grant. But he has no understanding of what we do, or why.'

'He'll learn, Elder.'

'But he has no faith.'

'He'll find it.'

Seeker didn't mean to be so stubborn in contradicting the Elder, but he found himself without any arguments other than his own conviction. He could see how unlikely a candidate the Wildman must seem; but he himself had no doubts. Also, the Wildman trusted him.

'Perhaps you allow your friendship to colour your judgement,' said the Elder gently.

'We made a compact to help each other. We stood by each other. I can't walk away from him now.'

The Nom bell began to toll, calling the Community to their daily gathering.

'Wheel me back, will you?'

Seeker took the handles of the wheelchair and swung it round to face back down the tree-lined path to the Nom.

'What if we were to take this wild young man into the Community,' said the Elder, 'and then find we'd made a mistake? Would you admit you had been wrong?'

'Yes.'

'And accept responsibility?'

'Yes.'

'He would have to leave us. And you, if you take on this responsibility, you would have to leave us also. Do you understand that?'

419

'Yes.'

'He would be stripped of his powers. And so would you.'

Seeker felt a chill over all his body. The Elder did not use the word, but Seeker knew well enough what he meant. He would be cleansed. How could he dare to take such a risk?

And yet, he knew the answer: risk or no risk, this was the way before him, and he had no choice but to take it.

Where your way lies, the door is always open.

The voice had not meant him to see his true way wherever there was an open door. He had learned that much on the high rock in Radiance. The voice had meant, Follow your true way, and the doors will open before you.

'Did I imagine the voice I heard in the Nom, Elder?'

'No. The voice was real.'

'Do you know where it came from?'

'Yes. I know. And you will know, when you're ready.'

'When will that be?'

'Patience. You wouldn't wish to be old before your time, I think.'

'No, Elder.'

The Elder said no more, and let himself be wheeled between the twisted pines towards the Nom. When they reached the Pilgrim Gate, Blaze was gone, and a meek was standing there, waiting to take the Elder on into the Nom itself.

Seeker dared to speak.

'What is your decision, Elder?'

'Have you understood what I have said to you?'

'Yes, Elder.'

'Then you will all be invited to join the Community. All three. But yours is the responsibility. Does that content you?'

'Yes, Elder.'

The Elder nodded, and held up one hand. Seeker took it, and, respectfully bowing his head, he kissed it. Then the Elder in his turn drew Seeker's hand down to his own dry lips, and he kissed it.

'We have been waiting for you, Seeker after Truth.'

They stood together in the shadow of the high walls of the Nom, beside the small door that had no handle. Each carried a simple night-bag that contained all they now possessed in the world. The Novice Master stood before them, ready to admit them, with one of the Nom meeks in attendance. Watching from the side were Seeker's mother and father, and Morning Star's mother and father.

In this humble manner, they made their vows.

'I swear to live my life simply and in the truth. To possess nothing, and to build no lasting home. To love no one person above all others. To use my powers to bring justice to the oppressed, and freedom to the enslaved. To love and protect the All and Only. And always and every-where to obey the Rule of the Nomana.'

Morning Star was watching Seeker as he made his vow, and she saw again in his aura the shimmer of gold she had noted before. This time, perhaps because of the solemnity

421

of the occasion, she caught the sense of the colour: it was a high reaching, a longing for the ideal, a hunger for what was lasting and true.

Oh, my friend, she thought as she gazed on the fine glow that trembled about him. *You and I and the Wildman will all become Noble Warriors. But your journey will take you further and deeper than either of us.*

Then she turned to embrace her father and mother, and Seeker did the same. Morning Star cried a little, as did the two mothers; but already the thoughts of the new novices were reaching beyond this time of parting, to the new life that was about to begin. For each of them, the speaking aloud of the vow had been the moment at which their old life had ended. This lingering self that accepted kisses and words of farewell was no more than a retreating shadow.

The door to the novitiate then opened: that narrow, iron-bound door that had no handle on its outer side. They passed through without looking back. Then came the clang of the door as it closed, and the scrape of the long bolts as they rang home; and they were gone.

The End of the First Book